GIRLS
OF
STORM
AND
SHADOW

Also by Natasha Ngan

Girls of Paper and Fire

GIRLS
OF
STORM
AND
SHADOW

NATASHA NGAN

HODDER &
STOUGHTON

First published in Great Britain in 2019 by Hodder & Stoughton
An Hachette UK company

1

A CIP catalogue record for this title is available from the British Library

Hardback ISBN 9781529342598
Trade Paperback ISBN 9781529342604

Printed and bound in Great Britain by Clays Ltd, Elcograf S.p.A.

Hodder & Stoughton policy is to use papers that are natural, renewable
and recyclable products and made from wood grown in sustainable
forests. The logging and manufacturing processes are expected to
conform to the environmental regulations of the country of origin.

Hodder & Stoughton Ltd
Carmelite House
50 Victoria Embankment
London EC4Y 0DZ

www.hodder.co.uk

To James,
Two Jimmys made these books happen.
You are one of them.
Love, always.

Please be aware that this book contains
scenes of violence and self-harm, and references to sexual
abuse and trauma recovery.

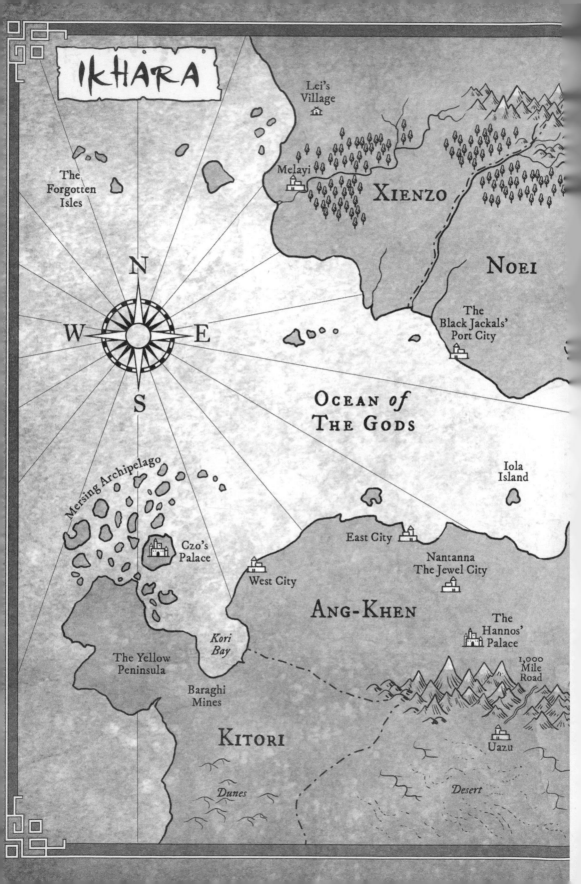

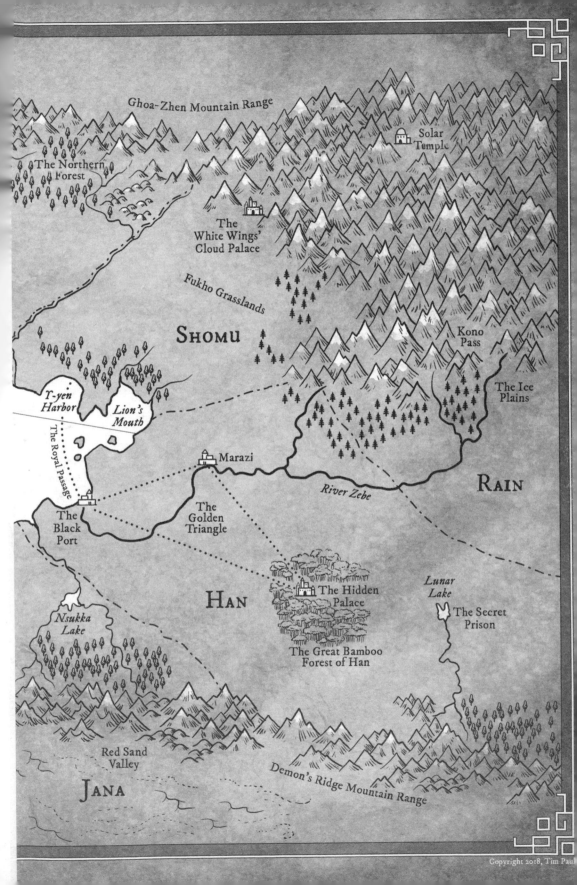

Ghoa-Zhen Mountain Range

Solar
Temple

The Northern
Forest

The
White Wings'
Cloud Palace

Fukho Grasslands

SHOMU

Kono
Pass

The Ice
Plains

T-yen
Harbor

Lion's
Mouth

The Royal Passage

Marazi

River Zebe

RAIN

The
Black
Port

The
Golden
Triangle

HAN

The Hidden
Palace

Lunar
Lake

The Secret
Prison

Nsukka
Lake

The Great Bamboo
Forest of Han

Red Sand
Valley

JANA

Demon's Ridge Mountain Range

CASTES

At night, the heavenly rulers dreamed of colors, and into the day those colors bled onto the earth, raining down onto the paper people and blessing them with the gifts of the gods. But in their fear, some of the paper people hid from the rain and so were left untouched. And some basked in the storm, and so were blessed above all others with the strength and wisdom of the heavens.

—The Ikharan Mae Scripts

Paper caste—*Fully human, unadorned with any animal-demon features, and incapable of demon abilities such as flight.*

Steel caste—*Humans endowed with partial animal-demon qualities, both in physicality and abilities.*

Moon caste—*Fully demon, with whole animal-demon features such as horns, wings, or fur on a humanoid form, and complete demon capabilities.*

—the Demon King's postwar Treaty on the Castes

GIRLS
OF
STORM
AND
SHADOW

DEEP IN THE DARK HEART OF the royal palace, the King was hiding.

He'd been there for weeks, eschewing all visitors save for the shamans who worked on his injuries and his two closest confidants to nurse wounds both of the body and of the ego. He would never have admitted this was what he was doing, of course. And if anyone were to dare even *suggest* he was struggling, he'd swiftly have them executed. None of it was painful. None of it was too much for the great Demon King of Ikhara to handle.

Yet like most lies people tell themselves, it came apart in the shadow and quiet of the night. The King, however much he expressed otherwise, *was* shaken. His wounds had penetrated deeper than flesh and bone. They had burrowed, insidiously, down each vein and cell and pore, until he could feel the fear echoing alongside every beat of his heart. And this fear took a shape. A name.

Lei-zhi.

He refused to speak it out loud, but his body betrayed him. It whispered her name to him in the rhythm of his pulse. Showed him her face when he was asleep: blood-splattered porcelain skin;

furled lips; wild eyes, those bright golden eyes honed with so much rage it pierced right to his soul, right down to places within him he thought he'd long since stamped out of life.

When it got too much—when her name and face would mock him so that he felt he couldn't breathe and the walls of his rooms were closing in—the King called for a girl.

None of *those* girls, of course. Those girls he had yet to properly deal with.

Though he would.

But another girl. A pretty Steel caste lynx-form from the Night Houses with softly furred hips perhaps, or a young Paper slave fresh from a raid. He didn't care. They would bring him a girl, and he would ruin her, just to prove he could. To feel once again that he was all-powerful. One human girl would not get the better of him— even if the constant sting and ache of his scars reminded him how close she had come.

Each day, royal shamans came to heal the injuries to the King's throat and face. Naja had done well. The shamans had arrived just in time after the girl's attack to save much of his vocal cords, though it hurt to speak and his voice was hoarser than before: rough, a guttural grunt. His right eye however was beyond repair. The socket had been a mess of severed nerves and pulpy flesh, too damaged even to fit a glass eye. In the weeks since the attack, it had grown a little less horrifying under the magic of the shamans. While it would be many months more until the rest of his face was back to normal, even shamans couldn't bring back life from the dead, and his missing right eye would forever be a reminder of that night.

The King recalled one of his generals, also a bull-form, who'd once come to him about using the royal shamans to remove an ugly slash across half his face. "Battle scars are a badge of honor, General

Yu," he'd told the soldier. "They are marks of power. To rid oneself of them would be to show weakness. Wear your scars with pride."

Wear your scars with pride.

What godsdamned crap. He always knew it, of course, but some part of him had believed in the sentiment once.

Not anymore. The King knew now exactly what scars were: reminders of your own failings. And so were those who dealt them.

The girl was still out there. But the King had faith. Naja had not failed him yet. She would find her, just as she promised she would, along with the traitor Ketai Hanno's daughter, and she would bring both of them back to the palace for him.

Because this was something else the King had learned about scars—they were a brilliant furnace of hate. And if rage like this could give a weak human girl the power to attack *him*...well. They would see what it could do to a Demon King with a ferocious hunger for revenge.

ONE

FROM THE NIGHT WE ESCAPE THE palace, what was at first a light scattering of flakes grows into a snowstorm.

It takes less than twenty-four hours for the first layer to settle. Just over a day until it builds into a thick blanket of glittering white. One more day and the snow has covered everything, a carpet of muffling powder that stings your eyes in the daylight and casts strange shapes at night from the shadows. After two weeks, it's as though we've lived in this frosted world forever.

I trudge through the deep drifts beyond the temple, my boots breaking the snowpack with heavy crunches. The cold has numbed my entire body. I flex my stiff fingertips in my gloves. Melting shucks of ice keep sluicing over the tops of my borrowed leather boots no matter how tightly I lace them. But at least my hands and feet have some sort of protection from the weather. My face battles directly with the elements—and this is a war it is losing.

Wind stings my exposed cheeks as I peer through the dancing flakes, trying to see where the leopard demons have gone. We've been trekking through the mountains for almost an hour now. The steep forested hills are packed with snow, each leaf-stripped tree encased in ice. The afternoon is eerily silent: just rustling snow crystals and boot-crunch and my own heavy breathing.

"How you doing back there, Little Princess?"

I sigh. Not *quite* so silent.

"My *name*," I shout back, "as I've told you a million times, Bo, is *Lei*."

No sooner are the words out of my mouth than they are whipped away by the wind. Ice flakes dance around my nose, land cold, wet kisses on my raw cheeks.

"Princess?"

Bo's voice sounds again, this time clearer. The siblings must be just a few yards ahead.

My breath billows around me as I hurry to catch up. Their tall forms materialize through the snow-blurred wind, as long-limbed and willowy as the trunks of the trees around them, and almost human in appearance. As I get closer, their demon details reveal themselves: snubbed leopard ears, athletic haunches, long tails flicking from side to side, sheathed in the same beige-black spotted fur that covers the rest of their bodies. Green eyes glint from dark-rimmed lids. Their round faces are so similar it's hard to tell them apart at a glance.

One of the two sets of eyes is soft and kind. Nitta.

The other pair—her brother Bo's—dances with amusement.

Nitta rushes to me with a relieved cry, brushing the wet straggles of hair back from my brow. "Thank Samsi! We were scared for a moment we'd lost you. Sorry, Lei, we're moving too fast. We were trying to go slowly, but—"

"Any slower, and we'd be traveling back in time," Bo quips. "You Papers," he adds with an impatient cluck, scratching the underside of his chin as he regards me down the length of his flat, feline nose.

Nitta shoots him a frown. "Bo."

"What? Anybody born without built-in weather protection is missing out, I say."

"Maybe we should turn back." Snowflakes dust Nitta's spotted fur, and she brushes a hand over her brow absentmindedly, looking worried. "We haven't found anything yet, and Lei looks frozen half to death. Merrin was right. This was a bad idea."

Bo rests a hand on his bony hip. "You're going to trust Feathers now? Come on, Sis, what does that bird-brain know?"

"*You'll* defy Merrin's orders just to annoy him," Nitta retorts.

"Why else do you think I agreed to let Lei come along on our little hunting trip?" The leopard-boy grins. "No offense, little one," he tells me, "but it wasn't exactly for your expert tracking skills."

"A lot of good *your* tracking skills are doing us," I point out. "Found anything yet, hmm?"

While Bo cocks his head in amusement, I straighten, squaring my shoulders. I'm still barely half the height of the leopard siblings, but it makes me feel stronger all the same. "I asked you to let me come today because I'm sick of hiding away in that temple. It's been more than two weeks now. If I have to spend another day listening to Hiro's endless chanting and the rest of you sparring or talking war tactics while refusing to let me do *anything*, my brain will burst." I reshuffle my scarf, bunch my gloved hands into fists. "Now, can we please go catch something good to eat? I'm sick of roasted taro for every meal."

Nitta hesitates, but Bo tosses up his hands. "You know what? Princess is right. If I have to eat one more piece of taro I'm going to *become* a taro." With a dramatic huff, he throws himself onto his back. Snowflakes rain down around him. "Look," he croaks in mock-horror, blinking up at us from a distinctly Bo-shaped hole in the snow. "It's already starting. I am one with the taro. And it feels...taro-ble." He flounces back up, coat covered in ice, and beams his wide, snaggle-toothed smile. "Get it? *Taro*-ble?"

"Oh, Little Bro," Nitta sighs. "Your jokes are just so *taro-iffic*."

All three of us laugh at this, the sound breaking the eerie quiet of the snow-draped forest, until a loud *crack* to our left cuts us off. We whip around, my heart lurching into my throat, only to see a pack of snow that had been balanced on a banyan's branches crash to the floor with a heavy *flumpf*.

Nitta and Bo straighten from the defensive stances they'd instinctively adopted.

Bo snorts, releasing hold of the knife at his belt. "Scared of snow, Big Sis? Afraid it'll turn your pretty hair wet and scraggly?"

Nitta's eyes slice his way. "Don't think I didn't see *your* reaction." But there's a touch of something cautious as she turns around, lifting her nose to test the air. Her ears twitch, listening. Then she starts forward. "Come on," she says. "Something's definitely out there. And, Lei, stay close this time."

We continue into the swirling white. It's all I can do to keep up with the siblings, their lithe Moon caste bodies slinking easily between columns of ice-wreathed trees. While Nitta and Bo carve the layers of snow cleanly with each neat lift of their lean leopard haunches, I slog clumsily through the thick drifts. The snowpack is as deep as my knees. Hidden tree roots tangle with my boots. Every drag of frigid air cuts my throat, but despite the chill, sweat beads inside my coat and under the fur scarf wrapped around my neck.

The demons don't let up their pace. We stop only to take swigs of the water flask at Nitta's waist or to check for signs of the animal she and Bo are tracking, the siblings dipping their heads together to discuss its markings in low voices.

After one hour of focused trekking, Bo breaks the silence. "We're closing in," he announces, half-hidden by the sheets of driving white where he's walking a couple of feet ahead.

Nitta cants her nose higher. "You're right. I've got something, too. Sharp, musky…what do you think it could be?"

"Your delightful natural scent?" her brother suggests.

Nitta rolls her eyes. "See these?" she asks, pointing to a nearby tree.

Bo and I move closer. Two deep grooves are etched into its bark, just below my head height. They look freshly made: only a light dusting of snow covers them.

Bo traces the marks. "Could be a large mountain goat."

"Wait," I say, backing up to take in the tree's low, twisting branches. "This is a mango tree. A *mango* tree," I repeat, awed. "Does it usually snow here? We can't be that high up in the mountains if there are banyans and fruit trees."

Neither of them shares my surprise.

"The Sickness has caused all sorts of weird climate changes," Nitta says with a shrug, then turns back to her brother, forehead wrinkled. "That would be one big goat. I'm thinking more along the lines of yak."

"Ugh, I hope not. Yak meat is gross."

"Do you want taro for dinner again?"

"Better than yak butt."

Nitta peers ahead into the glittering drifts, her rounded ears twitching. Like her brother's, her ears are peppered with studs and hoops in a variety of tarnished silvers and golds, and dim wintry light winks off them as she looks left and right. "This way," she says, already moving.

Bo winks at me. "Ready to play your part in the hunt, Princess?"

"What part is that?"

"Bait," he replies with a grin.

I glower as he stalks off. It takes a few moments for a retort to come to me. I stomp through the snow, ready to deliver it—when a movement to my left snags my attention.

I freeze. My heart beats loud in the hush of the ice-limned forest. The still, empty forest.

Under my scarf, gooseflesh plucks at my skin. "Are you—are you sure there's only *one* animal around?" I call ahead.

Nitta and Bo both spin around, silencing me with identical green-eyed glares.

"We need to be quiet—" Nitta starts.

There's the sound of snow crunching. She whips back around, lowering into a defensive stance. Bo points into the swirls. Smoothly, he loosens his knife while Nitta swings her bow from her shoulder. She holds it out in front of her with her left hand, her right plucking an arrow from the quiver strapped to her back. In one swift movement, she fits the feather-tailed arrow in place and draws her right arm back to extend the bowstring, resting the tip of the arrow on her left knuckles. Lean muscles flex under her cotton shirt as she aims into the iced air, but Nitta doesn't loose her arrow.

Not yet.

Ears pricked, face focused, she slinks on between the trees. Bo crouches slightly as he moves after her, fingers clamped around his throwing knife.

I fumble at my waist for my own knife with clumsy glove-clad hands. It's a short, plain blade—one of the others' spares. Gripping it tightly, I follow the siblings, doing my best to keep to the path they create with their precise steps. My skin prickles with unease. A few times I think I catch movement—not ahead where Nitta and Bo are advancing up the wintry slope, but at the corners of my vision. The shadowy shape of something large and...not human. But when I look, there's nothing there. Only thick swirls of glittering flakes. Wind-chill and billowing breaths and deep, blizzard-muffled silence.

Nitta and Bo move faster now. Though I do my best to follow them, the gap between us begins to widen. Ahead, Nitta turns abruptly, leading us up a steep incline, the glimmer of a frozen waterfall to our right. My breath comes out in thick clouds as I try to keep up—and then my toes catch on a rocky outcrop beneath the drifts.

With a yelp, I fall face-first into the snow. Clumps of ice latch to my skin, melt trickles down the sides of my scarf. Grimacing, I push myself to my knees, shaking the snow from my face and hair, when I sense movement behind me.

A voice—light as a feather, yet deep, deep as gods' bones and earthshakes—uncurls on the wind.

I've found you.

Something cold trickles down my spine that has nothing to do with the snow. In an instant, *his* face comes to my mind.

Grooved horns, etched with gold, tips as sharp as knife-points.

A slim, handsome face, bovine features melded immaculately with human form.

A smug, satisfied smile.

And those eyes—irises such a clean, clear arctic blue I can recall the feel of them piercing me even now. More than two weeks on from that night, the very moment I drove a blade deep into his throat and cut the life free from him.

The King.

I've found you.

Crouched in the snow, I swirl around with my knife brandished in trembling fingers, heart thumping against my ribcage. But the forest is empty. The trees stand tall, silent sentinels armored in frost.

Blood rushes in my ears. I look once more in all directions, shivers still rippling up my arms and the back of my neck. The voice had seemed so real. So *close.*

When I get to my feet to carry on after Nitta and Bo, there's no sign of them. I'm alone.

Then my breath hitches.

Because maybe I'm not. Though I couldn't have heard the King's words, the feeling that someone's watching us could be because we *are* being followed. Not by the ghost of the dead King, but by one of his soldiers or elite guards.

That's why Wren and the others haven't let me out of the temple all this time. We know it's only a matter of time until they find us, if they haven't done so already. It's been more than two weeks since the attack on the palace the night of the Moon Ball. Plenty of time for them to have tracked us down, even to our remote location here in the northern mountains. Plenty of time to wait outside the temple, where we've hidden ourselves with protective magic. To wait until we leave for our next location, or until *I* get stupid and reckless enough to disobey my orders to stay hidden.

Exactly as I've done today.

An alarm screeches to life in my head, at the same moment more movement—real, this time, paired with panting breaths and the crunch of breaking snow—comes from ahead, higher up the slope.

"Lei!" Nitta's yell cuts through the blizzard, pitched in panic. "Run!"

Just as a hulking shape leaps across my path and loosens a bone-shattering roar.

TWO

TIME SEEMS TO STRETCH AS THE beast reveals itself in two long, loping bounds, springing from the columns of trees and emerging through the driving sheets of ice as if in slow motion, its large front paws—and claws—outstretched.

Black markings on sandy-white fur dusted with snow.

Heavy haunches.

Powerful, muscled shoulders.

A snarling face, lips drawn back to flash curving incisors.

And eyes: crystal blue, bright as the King's.

The animal lands a few paces in front of me, rearing down, a tail as robust as an arm flicking from side to side. Its feline ears press back. Teeth bared, it lets out a snarl that rips all the way to my core. And for a moment, I'm trapped in place, weighed down not by fear but by memories. Memories of the demon who had eyes just like this. Who snarled, too, before using his teeth and power not to tear apart my skin—but my clothes.

My soul.

I've found you.

In a way, the King *has* found me—because he's never *left* me. Not even death could take away the scars he left upon me, imprinted deep, the way history carves its marks into the very bedrock of a kingdom, forever to shape and influence its future.

Then the animal hisses, its eyes swiveling as it surveys the three of us with feral curiosity. And I realize three things all at once.

This isn't the King; this isn't even a demon. It is an animal.

The snow leopard's wet, pink-black nose twitches. Ice-cold eyes home in on me. My heart clenches; the familiar color draws me in. Without thinking, I raise my knife and crash forward with a yell— at the same instant the leopard pounces.

An arrow whirs past, burying itself into the snowpack between us. The creature growls, swerving at the last minute, and into the space that opens up, Nitta leaps.

She tosses aside the arrow she was wielding and knocks her bow from her shoulder to brandish it lengthwise like a staff. Less than a second later, the leopard barrels into her. She thrusts the bow into its spit-flecked muzzle. The creature's jaws clamp around it. There's the crack of wood, but the weapon holds. The leopard shakes its head, throat rumbling. Nitta doesn't let go, and though her hands are too close for comfort to the animal's massive pointed teeth, she holds firm. She's only a few years older than me, but she seems suddenly decades more mature now, taller and stronger and rippling with a warrior's confidence.

I lurch forward, dagger lifting once more, when Bo barrels into me.

We crash into the snow. "Are you crazy?" I cry. I kick at him, but he doesn't let go, wrestling to keep me down as icy powder flies everywhere.

Less than five feet away, the leopard growls. Deeper, louder. It pushes forward with its strong legs.

Her muscles rippling, Nitta digs her heels in, chin jutted—and growls right back.

The animal blinks. Pauses. Its ears swivel to the front, its snarling mouth softening.

Nitta growls again. No words, just a guttural sound from the pit of her belly that ripples up her chest and out of her throat with the same feral quality. It's only an echo of the wild animal's own snarl. Even so, the creature seems to recognize it.

It lowers the paw that was hovering mid-step. Their noses inches from each other, the two leopards face off in silence. Bo and I are still half-hidden in the snow where he tackled me, but from my low vantage point I have a full view of the snow leopard. Towering over us, it is majestic and fierce, beautiful and terrifying, its round, wide-snouted face and turquoise eyes shimmering with intelligence. Snowflakes nestle in the thick tufts of its fur coat. It pants, jaw still clamped around Nitta's bow, heat billowing from its whiskered maw.

The creature doesn't take its eyes off the demon girl. Could it be that it's noticing the same resemblances between them that I am? How even though Nitta is standing on her hind legs, there is a feral power to her stance that mimics the leopard's own? How though her limbs are willowy and long with their human influence—Moon castes are the perfect midpoint between human and animal—they share the shape of the leopard's haunches? How her features carry the same feline cast as that of the animal whose eyes she is staring into?

Despite their differences, it seems as though the leopard recognizes all this—that Nitta is somehow kin. Because after a few more tense seconds, it opens its jaw and releases her bow. With a lick of its muzzle, the creature backs away slowly, its keen blue gaze still focused on her. Then, kicking up a flurry of snow, it turns and bounds back up the mountainside, disappearing as quickly as it arrived.

Nitta drops her bow. "Are you two all right?" she asks, rushing to help Bo off me. She's breathless, a tremble running through her as she lifts me to my feet. She brushes clumps of ice from my coat. "Lei, are you hurt?"

"I'm—I'm fine," I pant, doubling over to gulp lungfuls of cold air.

With a distracted nod, Nitta turns to Bo. "Did you see...?"

"I know—"

"The way it looked at us—"

"I *know*—"

"Do you think it knew—"

"I mean why else would it have—"

"Those *eyes!*"

"*Incredible!*"

"Why did you do that?" My shrill shout cuts through their excited voices. I brace my palms against my knees, glaring up at the two of them accusingly, still catching my breath. "You had a clean shot, Nitta. *I* had a clean shot. It was so close. It could have killed us!"

The siblings stare back, their pale green eyes wide.

"Princess—" Bo starts.

"Lei!" I growl through gritted teeth.

"Lei." Bending down to hold my shoulders, he brings his round face close to mine, snowflakes nestled in his spotted fur and clinging to the hoops looping his ears. "Do you know who that was?"

"Who...you mean the snow leopard?"

Bo and Nitta swap an exasperated look, though their excitement is still alive, lighting their faces with a feverish glow.

"I forgot you humans don't have spirit animals," Bo says. "If you were a demon, no matter what caste or form, you'd understand how amazing that meeting just then was. For some of us, it's incredibly rare to come across our spirit animals. You have demons who see their animal kin all the time—"

"Dog-forms, bull-forms, bird-forms," Nitta lists.

"But for those of us with rarer ling-ye," Bo continues, "we can go our entire lives hoping for such a meeting, and never having such luck."

"That's what we call them," Nitta explains. "Ling-ye. Wild souls. And for any demon, the thought of killing your own..."

They both shudder.

"But you eat meat," I say. "From each other's ling-ye."

"And thank Samsi," Bo replies. "Can you imagine a life without roasted lamb? Or ox cheeks in tamarind sauce? Or—"

"Kind of getting off topic here, Little Bro," Nitta murmurs.

He blinks. "Oh. Right. The point is no demon would ever eat the meat of their own form. To us Moons especially, ling-ye are as revered as gods. That's why we couldn't let you harm the snow leopard." He pats me on the head. "Sorry about tackling you like that. Instincts, and all that." Then, loosening a long exhale, he turns to his sister. Their eyes are lit with the same luminous intensity. Without a word, they clasp hands and dip their foreheads together, eyes fluttering shut.

Something jealous darts through me as I watch their silent embrace. All of a sudden, I want to be back at the temple.

Back with *her*.

Wren had been asleep when I stole out of the temple this afternoon, twisted in the furs we'd been wrapped in during our post-lunch—and post-*love*—nap, her dark hair fanned across her cheek.

She'd looked too peaceful to disturb, and I'd slipped out from the blankets, careful not to wake her. Now, I'm craving the sight of her beautiful face. I want to hold her close to me, see her sweet, dimple-cheeked smile.

I shift guiltily. She won't be smiling when she finds out I snuck out to hunt with Nitta and Bo.

As if reading my mind, the siblings release each other. Their faces are still radiant with a secret spark, though they seem calmer now.

"We should head back," Bo says. "The others will be getting worried."

"And who knows," Nitta adds, bending to pick up her bow. "We might still run into a yak on the way."

Bo beams. "Awesome! Lei's first time eating yak butt."

"Lucky me," I mutter with a grimace.

Wren is waiting on the steps under the eaves when we arrive back at the temple an hour later. Though my heart can't help but lift at the sight of her, the way she's glowering at us as we emerge through the trees into the clearing, the snowstorm still swirling all around, makes my steps falter.

Bo lets out a low whistle. "Check out that *glare*. It's enough to shrivel any demon's privates."

"Luckily Lei isn't a demon, then." Nitta nudges my shoulder. "Don't worry," she says kindly. "She'll just be glad you're safe."

"And we brought food." Bo waggles the bodies of the two mountain goats we caught on our way back. "No one can be too mad with you if you bring them food." He puffs out his chest, looking self-satisfied. "Just a little something I've learned from my many romances."

Nitta arches a brow. "Oh? Which ones are those? I must have missed them somehow in *all the years I've known you.*"

The siblings continue to bicker as we approach the temple. Its stone walls are dark against the snow-cloaked trees. Muffled light glitters off the frozen surface of the lake sweeping to its right. A steep cliff face rears behind the temple, and it's from this rock that half of the building itself is carved, giving the impression of a great stone monster with jaws splayed wide, ready to swallow us whole.

Wren stands at the top of the steps in the temple's open entrance-way. She's wrapped in a heavy wool overcoat, her dark hair tumbling over the deep purple fabric. Her arched lips are pink from the cold. An iciness emanates from her that has nothing to do with the snowstorm.

"Good luck," Bo whispers, only half hiding the gleeful tone in his voice.

The siblings hang back at the bottom of the steps. Wren watches as I make my way up to her, my calves aching after hours of trekking through the mountains. She stands so stiffly it's as though she were hewn from the same dark stone of the temple, her arms crossed, chin tilted slightly up, the dance of her wind-teased hair around her high cheekbones the only movement. She's so beautiful, even in her anger, and I resist the urge to throw my arms around her and bury her in kisses. *That* will come later.

Instead, I pull down the ice-crusted scarf where it was covering my mouth and give her a bright smile. "Good afternoon, my love!" I sing. "Did you have a good nap?"

Bo's mock-whisper—"Bold opening"—carries from the bottom of the stairs, along with Nitta's snicker.

Wren's eyes flick behind me, silencing them in a flash. "Don't joke about this." Her husky voice is clipped, her eyes narrowed and dangerous as she rounds on me. "Can you imagine my panic when I woke up to find you gone? How scared I was?"

My expression sobers. "Wren—"

"This was the only thing Merrin and I asked of you. Lei, you *know* why you can't go wandering off into the forest. Let alone the fact you're still recovering from what happened at the Moon Ball. What if you'd run into royal soldiers? Or anti-Paper groups who'd murder you just for fun? It's not safe out there—"

"When is it ever?" I cut in, my lips pursing. "When has Ikhara *ever* been safe for girls like us?"

Something melts in her features.

"I couldn't stand to be useless anymore," I mumble, dropping my gaze to the floor. I scuff the tips of my boots against the wet slabs. "We've been waiting for your father for more than two weeks now. The rest of you have had stuff to do, while I've just sat around doing nothing."

Wren takes my gloved fingers with her bare hands. "Lei, you are *far* from useless."

"So let me help! We're not in the palace anymore, Wren. You don't have to keep protecting me. I know what I've gotten myself into. I *want* to help."

Her liquid brown eyes soften. "If you were hurt…"

I step in close, turning my cheek against her chest. "You can't keep me safe from the rest of the world forever," I whisper.

Her breath warms the top of my head. "Watch me try." Then she circles her arms around my back, squeezing me close.

I smile into the fabric of her coat. Behind us, Nitta and Bo burst into applause.

"Awww!" Nitta croons. "You two are the cutest!"

"Kiss! Kiss! Kiss!" Bo whoops.

Wren laughs, a sound that brings warmth to my cheeks despite the still-bitter air. I lean back, lifting my mouth to hers. But just as our lips meet, footsteps sound from within the temple.

Wren pushes away from me in an instant, her face tightening into the closed mask she usually reserves for others.

"What's wrong?" I ask.

Before she can answer, the steps ring louder. They are smart and assured, neither the click of Merrin's talons nor the light, almost silent movements of Hiro, the shaman boy who makes up the last member of our group. Moments later, a tall Paper caste man strides out from the temple's entranceway.

His smile is the first thing I notice—wide and dazzling, lighting up the rest of his handsome face. A midnight-blue traveling coat sweeps across the wet stones behind him, and underneath it he is broad-shouldered and lean. Wavy hair threaded with gray falls in a shock over his forehead; more white peppers the stubble across his jaw. Like his smile, his eyes are bright and shining. Deep-set and tapered, they are black as coal, gleaming with the same keen intensity I saw in Nitta and Bo earlier after our encounter with the snow leopard.

I know who he is in an instant. Ketai Hanno, leader of the most powerful Paper clan in Ikhara. And, as of recently, the King's number one enemy.

Well, perhaps number two now... behind *me*.

Wren bows her head respectfully. "Father."

But he moves past her, spreading his arms wide as he comes instead to me. His sparkling grin seems to stretch across half his face. "Finally," he says. Taking my hands in his, he bends at his hips in a half-bow and brings my knuckles to his forehead. Then he straightens, grasping my shoulders with a clap. "I've been waiting so long to meet you, Moonchosen."

My forehead furrows. "M-moonchosen?"

"Haven't you heard? That's what they're calling you. You're celebrated among us Papers, Lei-zhi. Even some of our demon clan allies are using it. We owe so much to your bravery."

Lei-zhi.

It hits me like a slap to the face. The last time I heard my old title was from the King's lips as he pressed me to the ground in the gardens of the Floating Hall, seconds before Zelle came to save me, embedding her knife in his eye.

The last time I heard it, I thought I was about to die.

"We don't use that title anymore, Father," Wren says sharply.

Ketai's eyes glitter. "Of course not. Forgive me, Lei. I'm so accustomed to courtly pomp and ritual. I forget that much of the time, titles can be as cutting as weapons—and employed as such."

There's a cough behind us.

His eyes slide over my head. "Nitta, Bo. Good to see the two of you again."

"Missed you, too, Lord K," Bo says with a grin. Then he lifts his arms, showing off our catch with a flourish. "Impeccable timing as always. How do you fancy goat butt for dinner?"

THREE

ETAI HANNO'S DARK EYES GLIMMER AS we walk down the
temple's tall corridors, our footsteps echoing off the stone.
His arm is clamped around my shoulders. His smile doesn't
falter as he looks down the length of his slim nose at me, observing
me with the keen, almost knowing look of someone who can see
right through your skin and flesh to the murky core of you where
your darkest secrets and desires hide. "My second-in-command and
I just arrived," he tells me. "It's ferocious out there, is it not? The
snow came earlier this year. We're lucky we made it before nightfall.
You've been out there for hours, you must be freezing. Let's get you
warmed up and fed. I brought plenty of treats from my palace. Are
you a fan of salted fish, Lei? In Ang-Khen, we serve it with fresh dipping honey. Dear gods, it's so delicious it'll bring tears to your eyes."

He talks easily, smiling all the while. I nod noncommittally, aware
of the murmur of Wren and the siblings behind us—Wren, who
pushed me away the instant she realized her father was coming. I'd
thought maybe she'd told him about us when she was back with her
family before the Moon Ball. Evidently not. Moreover, she doesn't
seem keen to tell him.

My stomach squirms. I hope it's only meeting-the-parents nerves, and not anything more…complicated.

"Tell me, Lei," Ketai Hanno asks, switching subjects with ease, "how are your wounds from the night of the Moon Ball faring? Hiro is excellent with healing daos, isn't he? I trust you're making a speedy recovery."

"I'm doing well, Lord Hanno." Then I press eagerly, "Please, do you have news of my father and Tien? Wren promised me your clan would be looking after them, but—"

"Don't worry, Lei." He squeezes my shoulders, his smile warm. "They are both well and safe. We are looking after them in my palace in Ang-Khen."

It's news I've been waiting to hear for a long time. I sag, tears rushing to my eyes. "Thank you," I gasp. "Thank you."

Ketai tosses his head to dislodge the long sweeps of hair grazing his eyes. He lifts a hand to my cheek. "You know, I can see your father in you. You have his quiet strength. The same guarded look in your eyes. And that charming lynx-aunt of yours! She's a feisty one, isn't she? Already has half my kitchen staff cowering. She was rather unimpressed by our food, so I let her take on some work there."

I let out a happy sob. "Sounds like Tien."

"Both of them are being protected at all hours by some of my finest guards," the Clan Lord continues. "And while I hope to reunite the three of you soon, I'm afraid it could be a while. There is much work we have to do first. Important work. I hope to have your support."

Before I can ask more, we turn the corner into the large hall we've used as our living quarters since arriving. Late-afternoon light gleams in from the far side of the room, which opens to look out over the frozen lake. The fire we were eating lunch around earlier is still going, and by its flames sit Merrin and Hiro, along with another tall Paper man I've never seen.

Ketai leads me forward as the man gets to his feet. "Lei, meet Master Caen. Or Shifu Caen, if you will. I take it Wren told you about him?"

The man's slate-gray wool cloak is as plain and threadbare as Ketai's is fine. A few years younger than Ketai Hanno, he's built like an ox, the lines of his body and face strong and rugged like weathered stone. Muscles bulge beneath his robes. His long hair is tied back into a ponytail. A plaited beard streaked with white winds down to his chest.

I bow. "Shifu Caen."

He sweeps his cloak over his shoulder and returns my bow. "It's an honor to meet you, Lei." His voice rings out smooth and deep and clear, like water beneath the frozen surface of a lake. "What you did at the Moon Ball was truly impressive. You really have had no formal martial arts training?"

"I...had a lot of help." A jab twists my gut as Zelle's beautiful face comes to mind; the whip-crack sound of her neck snapping. Swallowing, I add, "And I had a few last-minute lessons."

Shifu Caen glances to where Wren is standing off to the side, his gaze affectionate. "Your teacher must have been very good."

"Oh, very."

He smiles. "Then *her* teacher must be excellent."

Ketai claps me on the back. "Take a seat by the fire, Lei. Merrin—put another pot of tea on to boil. It's time to get to business."

There's noise and activity as everyone settles around the fire. Hiro sits cross-legged next to Shifu Caen, the two of them seemingly comfortable with each other's presence. Wren told me Hiro was rescued a few years ago by Ketai Hanno from a raid on his clan, and has worked for the Hannos since. Other than that, I still don't know much about the young shaman boy. Most of the time he keeps to himself, his gray eyes almost always trained on the floor, and throughout the sessions he worked on my injuries the only words he said were the ones required to weave magic. I'm more acquainted with the shining top of his bald head than his face.

Settling beside them, I shuck off my coat and bundle my wet hair up in a tie I made from a scrap of the gold slip I was wearing the night we escaped the palace. Wren brings me a blanket. She smiles, draping it over my shoulders—then suddenly stiffens. When she sits down next to me, she leaves a markedly wider space between us than usual. She shoots her father a quick look, but he's already deep in conversation with Nitta.

Across the fire, Bo rolls up the hem of his trousers and leans back on his elbows, lifting a bare pawed foot up to the flames. "Ahh," he sighs. "That feels good."

Merrin's feathers ruffle irritably. "Yes, though it doesn't *smell* so good."

The owl-form demon is almost twice Bo's size. Though we've shared close quarters since he helped Wren and me escape the palace the eve of the New Year, I haven't gotten used to his appearance quite yet. Out of all demons, bird-forms are the strangest, with their long, humanoid arms wrapped in feathers, taloned fingers and feet, and sharp, beaked jaws. Though not quite as intimidating as the eagle-form of my palace guardian Madam Himura, Merrin is the biggest bird demon I've ever seen, tall and roped in lean muscle. A pale blue hanfu that he keeps meticulously wrinkle-free offsets the gray-white of his feathers, the exact color of a cloudy winter sky.

Bo wiggles his furred toes. "You know you love it, Feathers. Tell you what would feel even better—why not give my paws a little massage, eh? I was out in the snow for hours catching you dinner. It's the least you could do."

"I think you'll find *this* is the least I can do, darling," Merrin retorts, and with a huff, turns away to pour the tea.

Masking a snort, I hold my fingers out to the flames, glad for the first bit of heat after hours fighting the blizzard. More warmth shimmers down my veins at the thought of what Ketai told me earlier: Baba and Tien are safe.

As if reading my mind, Wren leans in. "Did my father tell you...?"

I nod, unable to hold down a grin. "Tien's apparently already got the whole kitchen whipped. They'll be sorry they ever rescued her."

"No, they won't. Everyone is so grateful to you, Lei. They'll be treating anyone associated with the Moonchosen like royalty."

There's a beat. My lips twist. "So, stabbed to death by their concubine?"

Her face falls. "I didn't mean—"

"I know. I'm sorry." I puff out a breath. "Anyway, I'm pretty sure neither Tien nor Baba have concubines. That's probably something I'd have noticed growing up, right?"

Wren gives me a small smile. But her eyes are still worried, and I avoid her questioning gaze as Merrin passes around steaming mugs of honeyed tea.

With a clap of his hands, Ketai gets to his feet and the group's chatter immediately drops. The Clan Lord cuts a commanding figure with his elegant clothes and straight-backed posture. "Let me start by saying what a delight it is to finally all be together like this. After all these months of planning"—he glances at Wren and Caen—"years, even, for some of us, it gives me great pleasure to finally

speak to you as a group. It truly is an honor to be in the presence
of each one of you." He runs a hand through his flop of raven hair.
His voice carries loud and clear through the cavernous room, seeming even to still the snowstorm outside, where it rages beyond the
temple eaves, blustering ice-flecked gusts of wind to our backs.

"No doubt you have many questions——" Ketai continues.

"Oh, just a few," Nitta murmurs.

"And you can bring them to me afterward. For now, here are the
essentials." He pauses, and his glittering eyes land on me. "The
King is dead."

Bo leaps up with a gasp. "Wait, what?!"

Nitta and Merrin snort. Despite myself, the corners of my mouth
tuck up. Ketai shoots Bo a withering look that makes him sink back
down.

"The royal court is in turmoil," Ketai goes on. "According to our
spies in the Hidden Palace, they have yet to decide what to do. With
no heir to claim the throne, they have been left without a ruler.
Such a situation is unprecedented. Some advisers are supporting the
idea of taking a young bull demon from some remote Moon family
to pass as the King's offspring…"

Nitta lets out a shocked hiss at this. I sense Wren stiffen.

Ketai opens his hands. "Thankfully, however, most of the court are
in opposition to this. A rift has formed between those who believe
they should announce the King's death—again, an unprecedented
event, given the original Bull King's decree that the births and
deaths of all subsequent Demon Kings remain hidden—and those
who believe the situation should be resolved in secrecy, privy only
to those within the court. The latter faction is claiming that to
reveal the King's death at such a time of weakness, what with the
Sickness still worsening and the increase in rebel activity, would

be tantamount to inviting war to the palace. As we ourselves know only too well, there are many clans in Ikhara who would be willing to seize such an opportunity to make a claim for the throne."

He pauses, his piercing stare tracking slowly over the group. "This is a problem for us. Our original plan was for Wren to quietly assassinate the King, therefore keeping our involvement a secret and allowing us to have Kenzo lead our revolution from within. But after the events of the Moon Ball, the court knows we have been plotting against the King. Our allies and I have been exiled from the Hidden Palace, with bounties placed on our heads for treason—with any who support us to be condemned to the same sentence."

A hush has settled over the room. The only sounds are fire-crackle and the low song of the wind.

"The fate of the palace hangs in a vulnerable position," Ketai summarizes, "either to be open to attack once the rest of Ikhara becomes aware of the King's death or for the royal line to be continued under false pretenses, damaging all that we have worked for."

"Has an interim leader been appointed?" Merrin asks, worry in his croaky voice. Wind flutters the tips of his feathers as he watches the Clan Lord intently, his taloned hands folded neatly in his lap.

There is a grim set to Ketai's mouth. "It appears the King left instructions for who would rule in his absence. He chose General Naja. The fox demon is one of his personal guards and closest confidants."

At the mention of Naja's name, my heart gives a dull kick. I swap a dark look with Wren. I know she's remembering the same scene I am: the white fox, her pointed vulpine jaw pink with spit and blood, relentless in her fury, setting first upon Zelle, then me, then Wren, then—

"What about Kenzo?" I blurt out. "Do we know whether he's…"

"Alive?" Ketai responds calmly. "He was seriously injured after the Moon Ball. But yes, our Wolf lives. My spies tell me he is being kept imprisoned at Lunar Lake, where the court sends all of its political prisoners."

I loose a long exhale, slumping back with relief.

"I told you she couldn't beat him," Wren whispers. She brushes my arm with her fingers, just for a moment, and I respond with a wobbly smile, tears stinging my eyes.

"I met her once."

All of us are visibly startled at the sound of Hiro's soft voice. He's looking away, staring out over the lake. Firelight glides across the smooth curve of his scalp.

"When the King's army came for my shaman clan," he continues, muted, "she was leading the raid. She took joy in killing those who resisted."

Ketai's face is somber. "General Naja being in command is certainly unfortunate for us. She is one of the most aggressively anti-Paper demons in the court and is fully committed to continuing the Demon King's legacy of oppression. We can be sure that under her guidance, the court will not make decisions that are favorable for us. Especially now." His lips pinch, and he pauses a moment before continuing, a flinty edge to his voice now, "My final piece of news is a personal one. As you all know, the day before the New Year, my wife—Wren's adoptive mother—was murdered."

My eyes cut sideways to Wren. She's watching her father, her mouth a tight line, her stare hard and unblinking. I shift a fraction closer, pressing the side of my thigh to hers. Her mother's death is a topic Wren has refused to talk about with me. Just like me with so much of what happened at the palace, she's been holding it somewhere inside her, too deep for me to reach.

Sadness flickers in my chest. Before, we could talk about every-thing. Before, it seemed as though the only thing between our hap-piness was the King and the palace itself.

That once we left, we would be free.

"I wasn't in our bedroom that night," Ketai continues into the quiet. "Perhaps if I had been, things would have been different. Instead, I fell asleep in the early hours of the morning in one of my council rooms, having spent the whole night going over our plans for the next day one final time." He glances at Shifu Caen. "You remember how it was, my friend. Though we knew myriad things could go wrong, somehow we were so certain it would work. That all of our plans and dedication these past years—past *decades*—were about to pay off. I slept soundly that morning for the first time in weeks, drunk on confidence and anticipation. We were so certain," he repeats hollowly.

His Adam's apple bobs as he swallows. "I was woken by my guards a few minutes past seven. My wife's maids had gone to fetch her for her morning bath. They found her lying in bed, seemingly unharmed, apart from the fact that her blood was cold and her heart lifeless in her ribs. The only sign that she had been attacked was a black mark on her chest. The Demon King's insignia."

Wren's eyes drop to her lap.

Bo sucks in a breath, sharing a dark look with his sister.

"Ketai," Merrin says slowly, "you didn't tell us this."

"I needed to be sure of it first. I had my most-trusted medical and spiritual advisers analyze Bhali's body. The process took longer than I thought, as we had to be discreet. And the magic that was used was so refined and powerful it was unlike anything any of us had come across. That's why I was late coming here. My apologies for not sending word. I couldn't risk it."

"So it was the King," I mutter. My voice catches.

"It would seem so. But we cannot be certain. The attack could also have been issued by someone trying to make us believe it was him. Someone who knew of our plans and wanted Wren out of the palace."

The group's attention is rapt, all of us considering the impact of his words.

"Possibly they wanted to stop the assassination from happening," Ketai suggests. "Maybe they hoped the mark would scare us into rethinking our plans against the King. Or it could be possible they wanted to force us to declare war against him. They *wanted* to bring the fight into the light. If this is indeed the case, then that means someone besides the court is plotting against us."

The others shift uneasily.

"How fantastic," Merrin murmurs. "More enemies. Just the thing we need."

I angle my face away, taking a deep draw of the fresh, wintry air blowing in from outside. The ice-locked lake glitters under the winter sun. Meltwater drips steadily from the eaves of the temple, a ticking sound that matches the quick patter of my heart. Because there's something else I haven't told anyone about that last night in the palace. Another memory I've been suppressing, forged in blood and agony and desperate breath.

"You can kill me," I hiss, forcing each word past his tightening grip, "but it won't stop them. They are coming for you."

It's fleeting, but I see it spark across his eyes then—fear. And I comprehend now that it's not a new emotion to him. It's just been in hiding. All it needed was something to call it forth, to trip his mind into panic.

He stills. "You know." A pause, then his voice rises. "Who? Tell me! Tell me who dares plot against me!"

Blood trickles down my forehead. I blink it away. "Go ahead. Kill me. I'll never tell you."

He didn't know. Unless he was acting, the King didn't know the Hannos were about to betray him—which means it's highly unlikely he ordered the murder of Ketai's wife.

Ketai is right. Someone out there other than the King is plotting against us.

Turning back to the group, I prepare to tell the Clan Lord exactly this. But the second our eyes meet, the words disappear, burying themselves deep in my chest where I can't call them forth.

Ketai watches me for another long moment, something unreadable moving behind his coal-black irises. Then he breaks contact, turning slowly to look at each of us in turn. "This is where we currently stand. There is a bounty on my head. The King's court, though broken, still clings on. From the news my spies have been bringing me of the palace, we have about two months, three at most, until the fractures are resolved. But whatever the court decides, we can be sure it will not be in our favor." He spreads his arms wide, fingers clamping into fists. "So we must act before then. We must strike while they are uncoordinated. Since we cannot avoid a war, we are going to bring one to them. And this group here, each of you, are key to making certain it is a war we will win."

My skin prickles. I shrug deeper into the fur blanket around my shoulders, shifting my eyes from Ketai's intense gaze.

Bo lifts a hand. "Um, a *few* questions, Lord K."

"How many times have I told you not to call me that?" Ketai sighs.

"I understand why I'm here, of course," Bo goes on, "what with my incredible fighting skills and superior intellect."

Merrin scoffs at this.

"And I suppose Nitta is pretty great, too."

"Thanks, Little Bro," his sister says with an eye-roll.

"But what about everyone else? No offense, but this is one odd assortment of demons and humans."

Ketai's arms relax. "If we are to amass an army strong enough to definitively take control back of Ikhara, we need to secure alliances in strategic locations with powerful clans—and fast. Before the court can win them over. Caen and I had planned for this in case of our original plan's failure, which is how we were able to get word to you all so quickly after my wife's death. You must travel across Ikhara to Shomu, Kitori, and Jana to gain the alliance of the White Wing, the Czo, and, of course, the Amala clans."

"It would appear *that's* why you two are here," Merrin says, leaning in toward Bo, his orange eyes glinting. "To lead us to the secret camp of your old clan, and not because of your...how did you put it? 'Incredible fighting skills and superior intellect'?"

He laughs huskily at Bo's affronted look.

Ketai holds out a hand. "Now, Merrin. I know you birds and felines have a complicated history."

"Understatement of the century," Nitta mutters.

"But in order for the mission to go smoothly, this group must act as a united whole. You are to look out for and protect each other, at all times. All of you." Ketai stares down Bo, Nitta, and Merrin. "Is that understood?"

"Yes, Ketai," Nitta murmurs, while both Bo and Merrin give curt nods.

"The journey will not be easy," Ketai continues, "which is why Wren and Hiro are here to provide any magical protection you might need. Caen will act as leader in my absence. Merrin is our navigator and eyes from the sky. Then, of course, we have our good luck charm, though she is far more than that." Shimmering, his eyes rest on me. "As Moonchosen, Lei, you will hold favor with some of the clans. I have no doubt at least one of the negotiations will come down to your alliance with us."

I swallow. "No pressure, then."

"I have no doubt you are more than capable of handling it," he replies warmly. He claps his hands. "Tomorrow, we will go over the details of the plan so you are ready to set off the morning after. But tonight…" Ketai smiles once more, a beam that cuts through the murky darkness of the temple. "Tonight, we celebrate! Our kingdom is poised on the precipice of change, and we are the ones who will see to it that it is for the better." He throws his hands up. "To a new era of peace and unity!"

"A new era of peace and unity!"

Though I cheer along with the rest of the group, the words feel clumsy on my lips, and I can't help but be reminded of another ruler who once spoke some very similar words, not too long before I drove a knife into his throat.

FOUR

THE ATMOSPHERE OF THE TEMPLE THIS evening is completely transformed. The usual hush has been replaced with rowdy chatter and laughter. Dark stone walls dance with the light of the crackling flames. Human and demon eyes shine with liquor and the promise of glory, of honor, of shared purpose, the group buoyed by Ketai's infectious confidence, keen to drown out the parts of us still whispering doubts like poison into the corners of our hearts—or at least, in mine.

Wren and Hiro go outside to recast the magical incantations that keep our camp hidden from spies or accidental passers-by, as they have done every morning and night since we arrived, while Nitta and Merrin prepare the two mountain goats we caught earlier, skinning them before roasting them over the fire. The smell of cooking meat fills the lakeside room. Even plain, it would have been enough to satisfy us; the last time we ate meat was more than a week ago. But the goats are stuffed with fresh herbs Ketai produced from his bags like the best kind of magic, and the aromatic flesh is so delicious it brings tears to my eyes.

"What else have you got in that magical sack of yours, Lord K?" Bo asks between bites. He groans with pleasure, sinking his feline teeth back into the piece of leg he's eating. Juices drip down his furred wrist. "Who knew the Heavenly Kingdom could be accessed through roasted goat thigh?"

Across the fire, Merrin gives him a cool, haughty look. "Ah, naïve young one. You will come to discover there are far more pleasurable ways to access the Heavenly Kingdom."

Bo's mouth curves. "Watch it, Feathers. At your age, you should be careful with any... *strenuous* activity. Might pop a hip."

Merrin's face turns thunderous the same instant Nitta guffaws.

I can't help but laugh, too—until I catch Ketai watching me with a strange, knowing look, unnervingly similar to the ones Wren used to give me back at the palace when she was thinking about me. But while I soon came to know exactly what these thoughts of hers contained, I can't quite work out what it is her father wants of me. My smile dropping, I toss the bone I've been licking clean into the fire and take a sip of one of the bottles of plum wine we've been passing around. Another one of Ketai's treats. The sweet alcohol scours my throat, but I force it down, and as I stare into the dancing flames my vision swims with them. Moving images appear in the flickers. A horned silhouette looming over me. The kind amber eyes of a wolf demon who once carried my broken body in his muscled arms with the carefulness of a newborn. The spray of blood as I wrench the knife from the King's ruined eye socket.

I turn away from the flames, a quiver rippling down my arms. Almost every night, the same memories haunt me, so real it's as though I'm living them over and over again.

I'm about to take another swig of wine when Ketai sits next to me. "I brought you something," he says, drawing two bundles from his pockets as I hurriedly set the bottle down. "Actually, two things. Nothing I could ever give you could reflect the thanks you deserve for what you have done for us, Lei." He hands them to me. "But please consider them a small token of my gratitude."

One of the items is heavy, wrapped in a swathe of luxurious velvet fabric. The other is soft and light, bound in lotus leaf. I open the lotus leaf package first. My stomach does a strange loop as I see the four small diamond shapes of emerald-green kuih nestled within.

"Wren told me they're your favorite," Ketai says.

I lift the delicate rice cakes to my nose, inhaling their syrupy coconut scent. Tears prick my eyes as I remember the last time a Hanno brought me these as a present; what they meant to me then.

To *us*.

"I had them imported from Malayi," Ketai tells me. "My council assures me these are the best in the kingdom."

"Thank you, Lord Hanno." I fold them back up. I have never been to my own province's capital, but I can't believe anyone anywhere could make these better than Tien does—even in the Heavenly Kingdom. When I was young, I once ate so many of her kuih that I made myself sick.

It was absolutely worth it.

Ketai blinks. For a moment, he seems disappointed. Then his smile reasserts itself. "The other gift comes from my palace. I had it made especially for you. Our Moonchosen."

I unwrap the cloth to find an expensive-looking dagger as long as my forearm, its end tapered. A dark leather scabbard embossed with delicate winding patterns covers the blade. Because I know it's what Ketai wants, I grasp the ivory hilt and draw the blade free. The instant I do, a hot rush of magic shoots up my arm, leaving my skin prickling. Copper light bursts across the room as the metal catches the glow of the fire. I turn the dagger, examining it. The blade is bronze, almost the same hue as my eyes, and the magic-imbued metal glows with an unearthly light that reflects my face back at me.

I wince at what I see.

It's the first time I've seen myself since we escaped the palace. That night, preparing for the Ball, my maid, Lill, lifted a mirror to my face to show me the marvel she and the other maids had created: pale skin smooth and glowing; hair twined with beads and delicate flowers; eyes adorned with kohl and shimmer to bring out the gold of my irises.

The face that stares back at me now can't possibly be the same girl. She has flushed, ruddy cheeks. Frayed hair falls in frizzy tangles around her shoulders. Her eyes are sunken and rimmed in shadows, not by makeup but from fatigue, the dark patches under them like two bruises, violet-tinted and deep, the physical imprint of the nightmares that chase her each night.

I slide the dagger back into its sheath, my fingers still tingling from the magic. "Thank you," I say flatly. "I'm...honored."

Ketai leans in, running a finger along the scabbard's delicate patterns. "I consulted with my fortune-tellers to have this created specially for you. It should bring you good luck—not that you need any more." Gently, he lifts my chin with his thumb and finger. "Incredible," he breathes. "Moonchosen, indeed."

I'm used to people reacting this way about my golden eyes. But the way Ketai is staring at me now—his excitement almost feral, something predatory in his expression—sends a shiver down my arms.

I shift out of his grip. "I'm flattered by the title, Lord Hanno. But really, I'm just a normal girl. I did what needed to be done."

Ketai nods, softening. "You know, Lei, I am not only thankful for all you've done to aid our cause. I'm also grateful for all you've done to aid my *daughter*. I know how much your friendship helped her during those months in the palace. Kenzo told me what a support you were to Wren, how close the two of you are. You were there when she needed a friend the most, and I will be eternally grateful to you for that."

Friend. The word is far too small, too simple to encapsulate what Wren and I share. Of course we're friends. The closest of them. But we are also so much more. The love and care we have for each other can't fit into that single word, one syllable, so easily passed around. Wren is family, as important to me as my father and Tien. As important to me as the sun is to the sky, the moon to the stars; Suna, Goddess of Beginnings, to Lo, Goddess of Endings.

She is my air. My shelter.

The birth-blessing pendant resting between my collarbones seems to glow with warmth. I think of the word it holds within: *flight*.

Wren is my wings.

"We were there for each other when we needed it the most," I tell Ketai carefully. "And we will continue to be."

His eyes sparkle. "Indeed." He motions to the knife. "As you might have sensed, the blade has been layered with daos. The magic reacts to your touch alone, and will ensure each strike lands true and strong. Hiro and Wren have orders to keep the enchantments active." He reaches into the pocket of his coat, pulling out a bound roll of paper. "A final gift. Perhaps the most precious of all."

I frown at the scroll. Then my heart leaps, almost jolting me, as comprehension sweeps through me.

I snatch the roll from Ketai with a gasp. He lets out a booming laugh, starting to his feet. "I'll let you two get reacquainted alone."

After months of waiting for this moment, I don't have the patience to take it slowly. I open the letter in such a rush, I almost tear it.

My dear, dear, Lei,

It has taken me more than twenty attempts and two hours to write this letter. You can imagine how frustrated this has made Tien. I've had to lock her out of my room to complete my task in peace. I feel sorry for whoever she's gone off to complain about me to.

I think the true reason this letter has been so hard to write is that I simply don't know how to put into words all the ways I am proud of you. My brave, brave daughter. The things you have done. The incredible feats you have accomplished.

I will not lie to you. It wasn't easy listening to the stories from Lord Ketai and others who knew what you endured at the palace. But Tien and I made sure to listen. I asked them to tell us everything so I could know what it is you have suffered and what it is that changed you, that turned you into this strong, selfless girl they call the Moonchosen.

Do you know they call you this? Mama and I always knew you were special. But for us, it was nothing to do with the gods, or luck, or your eyes. It was your soul, my love. I knew from the first moment I held you in my arms. From the first moment your little hand wrapped around the tip of my nose as I held you to my face for a kiss. I could feel your soul then, and it was light, and pure, and burned with such a brightness I have not been able to see clearly since. You blinded me in the best way, my darling — with love. I feel so much hope and pride for you, Lei, I could burst.

Lord Ketai has explained to us what his plans are. What it is you and the others are setting out to do. Again, I can't say it was easy to hear. But I won't tell you that you shouldn't do it. I won't tell you to protect yourself rather than putting yourself in harm's way like this, no matter how much I wish I could. I won't tell you any of this, because I know it is not what you want — and not what you deserve to hear after all you have fought for.

I also know that you would just go ahead and do it any-way. You are as stubborn as your mother, my dear. And, just like her, you are also brave, and strong, and caring, and full of fire. I trust you to know your own heart. If this is what you must do, then do it, and do it well. Do not doubt yourself for one second. You may come from humble beginnings, but you have proven to everyone what a young girl from a tiny village in Xienzo can do. Take that fire of yours and don't let anyone put it out. Know that I am championing you from here. Tien, too. Anything we can do to support your cause — our cause — we will do it.

Lord Ketai promises me that you will be returning to the palace within two months or so, once your mission is over. I am already counting the days. Until then, burn bright, my brave daughter.

Love, now and always,
Your Baba

Laughter erupts around the fire, but I feel worlds away. I read the letter again, but soon my eyes are too wet, my shaking fingers making the paper tremble, the words a blurred mess, so instead I clutch it to my heart. Tears spill down my cheeks. I breathe slow and deep, feeling strength coursing through me from Baba's words, an overwhelming rush of hope and sadness, of happiness and love.

"Now and always," I whisper thickly, the words a promise.

The last time I saw my father was at the Moon Ball. Tien and Baba and I had clung to one another and cried, before the guards pried us apart. The briefest of reunions, after dreaming about that very moment for months.

More roars of laughter jolt me back to reality. I fold the letter up carefully, placing the small square into the breast pocket of my wrap shirt. Then, sniffing, I scrub my eyes, trying to compose myself as Nitta hands me a bottle of plum wine with a kind smile. The liquid burns as it goes down. It merges with the warmth that filled me at Baba's words, and in the pit of my belly, something hot and fierce stirs.

Burn bright, my brave daughter.

My eyes pass over the group. Bo's right. We're a strange mix. But Ketai Hanno seems so confident we're the *right* group, and two times now in my life I've made families out of people others might never have put together—once with my father and Tien, then at the King's Hidden Palace with my fellow Paper Girls. I know that sometimes the combination least expected can forge the strongest bonds.

Just then, Wren and Hiro return from outside. Wren comes straight to me, shrugging off her coat and shaking out her long hair, flakes of snow caught in the wet tangles. "Please say there's food left," she sighs tiredly, rubbing her hands together in front of the flames. "The whole time we were setting the dao I was worrying the siblings would have eaten everything by now."

"Bo tried," I reply. "But Nitta was kind enough to save you and Hiro some. Here."

I hand her a banana leaf piled with roasted goat flesh, still deliciously fragrant. Wren takes it gratefully. After a glance over to where her father is deep in conversation with Caen, the two of them half-turned from the fire, their heads tilted together, she dips in quick to press a wind-frozen kiss to my lips. "I love you, Lei," she whispers, her brown eyes sparkling and beautiful, despite the deep circles beneath. "I know my father can be...I know what he can come across like. But he wants to bring down the King's court just as much as we do. So I trust him when he says this is the plan that will do it." Checking over her shoulder once more, she grabs my fingers, squeezing hard. "I need to know that you believe so, too."

My own father's letter seems to glow with heat where I hid it. And again, in the depths of my gut: heat. Burning embers. Not just from the alcohol, but from the thought of the King. Of what he did to us, and what *we* did to *him*—and what we are going to do to the rest of his legacy, to all remnants of his rule.

"I do," I tell Wren, and I mean it.

Wren and I might not be Paper Girls anymore, but we are still capable of creating fire.

And now we have a whole *world* to set ablaze.

FIVE

NAJA

IN THE HIDDEN PALACE, THE WHITE fox was dreaming.

She stirred, restless, her furred face scrunched while the storm rolled outside her private quarters in the Inner Courts, beyond the embroidered rugs and the meticulously cataloged collection of butterflies on the wood-paneled walls, which hung also with delicate batik paintings by a famous artist who came from the faraway province she was dreaming about.

Xienzo.

She never spoke of it—never even let herself think of it—during the daytime. But her past found her when she closed her eyes, as if it had been crouched there all along, waiting for her nightly returns.

It was distorted in its dreamscape, bizarre details twisting it out of its original shape, but the general features were present. The tiered stretch of their farm, either dark and glossy from the monsoon rains or faded under the unforgiving burn of the summer sun. The rubbery feel of the tea leaves between her fingers. The ache of her back after hours working the fields or bent over shaking the plucked leaves in bamboo trays to speed up the oxidation process, the pain

so deep and fierce she can still recall the quality of it: like fire on the
surface of raw bones. Biri, Reikka, Chaol, Poh, and Min, her meek,
brainless siblings, so different from her. And, of course, her parents,
rice-wine-addled and gods-blinded, obsessively reading her fortune
in everything they could, from the shape of clouds to the scattered
patterns of petals in the wind; from the type of birds that landed in
their daughter's path to the voices that whispered to them as they
oversaw their children's work, never without a drink in hand. Voices
they claimed belonged to the gods themselves.

As if the gods would waste their precious breath on the likes of
them.

Tonight, Naja was back in her family's cottage. In real life, it had
reeked of mangy fur and old tea and alcohol fumes. In her dreaming mind, it was clean. The air smelled of dust and endings. She
moved through the bare space as voices eddied around her.

born under the three archer stars
with her tail curled, remember what the diviner said that meant
destined for glory
a Lolata Clan Queen, imagine it
she will bring us honor and fortune
build us a palace
but remember, she can't be spoiled
we must keep her working
prove our dedication to the gods
earn her fate with blood and sweat
whip her if she cries
whip her
whip her

Even though she was alone in the room, Naja clutched her arms
around herself. The voices themselves felt like lashes, raw and

searing across her skin. But she didn't let herself cry, as she had done when she was young. Instead she shouted back, growled at the bare walls where the ghosts of her parents' obsessive plans for her still lived.

"I am General Naja!

"I am the King's closest confidant!

"I am more than enough!

"I am glad I left you all to rot—"

She woke up in a flash. Someone was shaking her. The light of a lantern blinded her for a moment, and she hissed, knocking it aside—along with whatever fool dared touch her.

"G-General Naja," came the voice of one of her maids. It was Kiroku, a lizard-form girl just a few years past her teens. She picked herself up from where she had fallen to the floor and bowed low, her russet-scaled hands splayed. "I'm so sorry to wake you this way, General. I tried shouting but you seemed in a deep sleep—"

"What is it, girl?" Naja snarled, sitting up. She shrugged off the dream the way she always did: in one smooth motion, discarding it from her body like a lover stepping out of her nightdress.

"There is a—a man demanding to see you."

"Good gods, girl. If this is all you've woken me for—"

"He told me you were expecting him," Kiroku cut in, head still down. "That you asked him to come if he caught a"—she recited it carefully—"a red, double-tailed Kitorian sand scorpion."

Naja threw aside her heavy blankets and was on her feet before the girl had even finished the sentence. "Dress me," she commanded. "Then take me to him."

The man looked as though he'd ridden for hours through the storm. His cheeks were wind-lashed, his sage-green traveling cloak soaked through. Fat drops of water splashed from his clothes onto the newly laid bamboo matting of Naja's reception room, and from the doorway she eyed the mud he'd tracked across the floor with disdain, battling the urge to reach for one of the ceremonial swords mounted to the wall.

The man sprang to his feet as she strode in, not waiting for Kiroku to announce her. Another maid, impeccably dressed despite the late hour, was already waiting by the low table in the center of the room. A copper kettle sat on the stove, steam billowing from its spout, filling the air with the delicate scent of silver needle leaves—tea far finer than that her parents' farm had produced. The maid went to pour some, but Naja waved her away.

"Leave us."

Both girls lowered their heads, shuffling from the room at once.

"G-General Naja," the Paper caste man stuttered, bowing deeply. Black hair flopped over his head in wet straggles. "It is an honor to meet you again."

She gave a tiny jerk of her chin as she knelt opposite him. "Councilor Shiu."

Even without the cushion she knelt on, Naja would have come to just under twice his height. Shiu was short even for a human. He kept his head half bowed, his eyes flicking up every so often from his lap to meet her steel-eyed glare then promptly dropping, as though the sight of her hurt his sensitive human eyes. The pink tip of his tongue poked out to wet his cracked lips.

Naja's nose twitched, her own lips furling. The pungent mixture of his sweat and the tang of horsehide wasn't pleasant, to say the least. This was one of the rare instances where she thought it might be better to be without her enhanced demon senses.

"I—I've been riding with barely a break for two days," Shiu

stammered into the quiet. "I rode my horse to death, and had to walk the last four miles."

He said it as if it were something to be proud of. Naja waited, glaring, her distaste deepening.

He gestured hopefully at the tea and the plate of flower-shaped almond cookies set out on the table. "May I?"

"If you must." She watched him shovel the biscuits into his face, washing them down with big gulps of tea—three added spoons of sugar, no less. The second he was finished she asked curtly, "You bring news of Ketai Hanno's whereabouts?"

Shiu swiped a sleeve across his crumb-speckled face. "It certainly wasn't easy. Accessing the palace to get information from inside was out of the question. Lord Hanno has the place on lockdown. The gates are only opened once a day for essential supplies and preapproved visitors, and his guards have orders to kill on sight if they spot anything suspicious. And it is widely known that Lord Hanno is skilled in qi manipulation. It would be near impossible to track his departure from the palace the traditional ways."

"I am well aware of all the facts," Naja snapped. "Do you not think we have spies of our own within his walls?"

"Forgive me, General." Shiu bowed. But he wasn't dipping his head quite so low anymore, and a touch of the stammer had dropped from his voice. "I simply mean to explain that while others have been sending spies to watch or break into the palace, I knew it would be more prudent to use shamans to track the use of magic *around* the palace. Lord Hanno would undoubtedly use some sort of dao to hide his movements, at least at first while he was close to his palace and sure that spies would follow him. That sort of magic is powerful. It would leave a trace."

Though she didn't show it, Naja's focus tightened.

"Four nights ago," the Councilor went on, "my shamans detected the presence of qi work in the perimeter of the palace. Its immediate movements were too quick for them to follow on foot—no doubt the Lord was on horseback—but they managed to track him the next few days through the echoes of his enchantments to a location northeast of the Hidden Palace, almost equidistant between Marazi and the River Zebe. He was traveling with another man who I'd be willing to bet is his closest adviser, Master Caen. The two are known to be almost inseparable. From this point out, no doubt believing they had made their exit without being spotted, the two of them dropped their magical guard and continued north, into the mountains bordering Han and Rain."

"And then?"

Shiu hesitated. Spreading his fingers on the table, he took an inhale before admitting, "The blizzard and mountain terrain made it difficult for my spies. They lost track of Lord Hanno and Master Caen in the mountains." He licked his lips, and crumbs tumbled from his chin as he continued eagerly, "But it disproves the popular theory that Lord Hanno would travel south to meet with the Cat Clan—his most likely alliance, as we are all aware. The northern mountains are restrictive. There are not many places they could be traveling to. My guess would be either they are heading to Rain to meet with the Noon Clan or to the White Wings' palace in Shomu. If you wish, General, I could send my scouts—"

Naja lifted a hand. "Thank you, Councilor. That won't be necessary. We can take it from here."

"Of course. Now, uh…" His smile twitched; he leaned in closer. "I don't mean to assume, General, but you did mention a reward for information such as this."

Naja's fur bristled. The cheek of this man. Papers were always like this; assuming they deserved things. Demanding more.

"Don't worry, Councilor," she replied smoothly. "You shall be rewarded. What would you prefer? Something of monetary value, or a decree for a full royal pardon should you ever need it?"

Shiu's eyes glittered. "A royal pardon is truly generous...."

With a nod, Naja started to her feet. It was the answer she had been expecting.

"And yet."

She stopped. On her feet, the white fox towered over the Councilor, but despite the intense look she gave him he didn't seem to cower. He met her eyes and smiled, something dark behind his flash of crooked teeth.

"I think I'll take the monetary reward."

Naja knew immediately what Councilor Shiu was declaring with his choice: that he didn't believe in the power of the court anymore. That he thought them weak. Even without proper knowledge of what had happened to the King.

After the Moon Ball, the court had tried to keep the news of what had happened from spreading. While they couldn't hide the fact that the palace had come under attack—there were too many witnesses at the Ball, too many Clan Lords and guests who had to flee for their lives when the Floating Hall went up in flames—Naja had done her best to limit the rumors. She'd made sure no one outside of the court's inner circle knew that the King had been seriously injured.

Still, she knew the news couldn't be contained forever. Rumors had leaked from the palace walls like blood through cracks in stone and were spreading across Ikhara in whispers and shocked utterances: the King had been killed. Or, he lived, but had been seriously injured.

The rumors were, like gossip always was, muddled. Some of it had even been directed for their own purposes, such as those they fed to Ketai Hanno's spies to keep him unaware that his plans to assassinate the King had failed. It was a tactic to delay Hanno's clans and their allies' ability to react when they discovered he had survived. All of that gave the court some time. But if they didn't come together to decide what to do soon, the truth would escape. And, just as truth always did, it would cleave a sword through the very fabric of the world.

It would change everything.

Naja stared down at Councilor Shiu, her silvery eyes gleaming. "A monetary reward it is, then." She motioned for him to follow her.

He practically skipped to her side. "Thank you, General! I knew you would appreciate my information and the hard work I did to gather it. I am sure it will be of much use to the King. Ever since you put the request out, I had the gods-blessed feeling that I would be the one to deliver it to you."

Letting his inane babbling wash over her, Naja strode across to the wall where her display swords were mounted. Lantern light cast her fur in a golden tint. She ran her gaze across the swords, her look as loving as a caress.

It took a moment for Shiu to catch on. Then he gasped. "You— you know, General, I have always appreciated beautiful weaponry. Particularly those with honorable histories."

"Miraculously, something we have in common, Councilor. Does one in particular catch your eye?"

Naja waited as he looked over her collection. When his arm shot out, indicating his choice, she wasn't the least bit surprised. Though he certainly could pass for one, she knew Shiu was not as much of a fool as he appeared. Like any educated Ikharan, he was well versed in the kingdom's history.

With care, she lifted the sword he had chosen from the wall. It was a straight-blade saber, quite a common style of dao, though slightly longer and slimmer than average. The scabbard that protected it was garnet red and inlaid with rubies and pearls. As Naja drew the sword free to reveal its infamous black blade, she thought of the times it had been drawn. The impressive opponents it had felled.

"The famous Black Blade of Lady Uh-rih," Shiu breathed. His beady eyes glimmered. "May I?" he said, even as he was already reaching out.

"With pleasure."

Naja moved so quickly the Councilor was still smiling when the blade pierced his skin. Her forward thrust was powerful, her aim exacting. All it took was one clean sweep of her arm to bury the sword between his ribs and into his heart.

Councilor Shiu's eyes popped. Blood welled up at its edges as his hands wrapped weakly around the blade where it protruded from his chest, his mouth flopping.

Naja held the sword with two hands, steady, her face expressionless. As the man fell to his knees, she slid it free, pondering how the famous weapon's latest opponent was no doubt the least impressive of all. What a shame to add his name to its inventory.

"Thank you again, Councilor," she said, wiping the blade on her robes. Blood soaked darkly into the expensive silk. No matter. She had many more hanging in her wardrobes. "You were right to come to me. The King will be extremely pleased with the information you have provided us. But I couldn't let you live, of course. Your shaman spies shall have to be disposed of, too, though they should be easy enough to find. We would much prefer to find Ketai Hanno and deal with him ourselves. It is a political matter, but a private one, too. You understand."

She didn't add that she couldn't risk others discovering the Clan Lord before her. If, as she believed, the two human girls would be found with him, then the truth about what happened to the King would be known. She would find them, and silence them before they could speak.

And she didn't need the help of some Paper nobody to do it.

Slumped at her feet, the councilor's lips moved, a wordless croak escaping him. But Naja was already turning away. There was a metallic *shing* as she returned the sword to its sheath. Carefully, she set it back into its place on the wall then strode to the door.

Before she left, she looked over her shoulder. Shiu had finally fallen still, collapsed in an embarrassing position on the floor, face down, hips high. A pool of red circled him, blood already leaching into the bamboo matting.

Naja clicked her tongue. Hopefully the maids wouldn't take too long to clear it up. Bodies were easy to dispose of. But bloodstains on fur and furnishings?

Noticing a speck of scarlet on her wrist as she slid the door open, the color stark against her snow-white coat, the fox demon sighed.

Always a nightmare.

SIX

KETAI HANNO'S VISIT PASSES SO QUICKLY that in what feels like
no time at all it's time for us to set off on our mission. We
go over the plans once more over breakfast of congee laced
with mountain ginger before ferrying our supplies outside. Wren
and I perform a final sweep of the temple to make sure we haven't
missed anything. The others are waiting out front as we walk down
the wide stone stairs for the last time. Morning sunlight sparkles
on the forest's snowy carpeting. The once perfectly laid drifts have
been mussed by our movements, but beyond the temple the grounds
stretch still and crystalline. High overhead, the sky is a lid of cerulean. The blizzard calmed sometime yesterday afternoon, and coming out of the temple's shadow into the sunshine gives me the sense
of being cleansed, of being washed by light.

I take a full breath. The air tastes fresh and sweet. Hopeful.

Two snow-made pecalang sit at the bottom of the temple steps.
Bo and I made them yesterday while taking a break from preparations. One has slumped out of shape, now resembling a drunken
man more than the snow leopards we created out of respect for
the creature we met in the forest three days ago. A hastily covered

patch of vomit sits behind the other one, a reminder of Bo's hang-over from a second night of plum wine overindulgence. As we reach the bottom of the steps, I give the pecalang closest to me a pat.

"Wish us luck," I whisper—only for it to promptly collapse into a heap of glittering ice.

Wren arches a brow. "That can't be a good sign," she says, though there's amusement in her voice.

I snatch my hand back guiltily. "Maybe it represents the royal court crumbling to nothing under our might? Or the dissolution of corruption and oppression across Ikhara?"

"Or our total abandonment by the gods," Bo suggests as he and his sister come over. "How all our lives will amount to is a pile of crushed hopes and dreams. You know, *something* like that."

"Of course," Nitta says, "it could also just mean that Lei here is as clumsy as ever." She swings a big leather pack into my arms. "Tell me if this is too heavy. I know you're not used to this sort of thing."

Though I've already doubled over from the bag's weight, I grit my teeth and heft it onto my back. Wren helps me adjust the straps. "What?" I say. "Questing? Conducting secret war missions? All in a day's work for me." I try to shrug, but my shoulders don't move.

Bo raises an unimpressed brow that instantly disappears when Nitta hands him a pack. "This one's yours."

"Sweet baby Samsi!" he curses. "What's *in* this thing? Your secret stash of plum wine? Anti-fungal creams? Fanmail from my many admirers you've been hiding all this time?"

Nitta rolls her eyes. "If only it *were* your fanmail. Then the bag would be empty and you wouldn't be complaining."

Before the siblings' squabbling can gain momentum, Ketai's voice rings out through the clearing. "Ready, everyone?"

Wren lifts her own bag with ease. Sunlight gilds her head, a shimmering crown atop her wild raven hair. She gives me a look blazing with determination so fierce it ignites hope in my belly like a match being struck, and we join the others around Ketai.

"Well," Ketai says simply. "This is it." He looks every inch the assured Clan Lord, standing with his hands on his hips, head slightly cocked. Wind musses his shock of gray-peppered hair and ruffles his fine robes, the sunlight picking out strands of silver in the navy. His features are alive with that same feverish kind of excitement I saw the first night he arrived. Confidence rolls off him, a wave that catches all of us in its pull.

"We've been over it enough times the past two days, so I'll keep it brief. Travel to the three clans, persuade them to ally with us against the court, and return home safely. I have the utmost faith in all of you. The next few weeks will not be easy, but I know you seven can cope with whatever comes your way. You are fine warriors, and even finer people."

Merrin shoots a look in Bo's direction. "Are you sure about that, Ketai? We do have two thieves in our midst."

Nitta sniffs. "I prefer the term 'procurer of discrete items'. *Thief* is so provincial."

Bo bats his lashes at Merrin. "What's wrong, Feathers? Something to hide? Some delicious secret you're worried we might tease from that pretty head of yours?"

"Hey." Nitta nudges her brother. "Bet I can get his secret before you can."

Bo's mouth curls. "You're on."

I snort, but the others give them exasperated looks.

"We're about to visit three of the most powerful clans in all Ikhara," Caen says. "Could you two at least try and act as grown-ups?"

Bo pouts. "But we're *not* grown-ups. Unless you're saying twenty-three is old, in which case you're *ancient*, Shifu—"

"Enough!" Ketai interrupts. "Remember you are representing me and my clan, as well as your own. Not to mention, these are some of the most long-standing demon families in existence. They are as prideful as powerful. You must be extremely cautious with everything you say around them, or you don't just endanger your own lives but our entire cause."

"You're welcome to join us, Ketai," Merrin says with a lift of his wing. "Help ease some of the"—his eyes skim over the leopard siblings—"cat-sitting duties."

"You know very well I'm needed back home, Merrin. The fissure in the royal court could be mended at any time, and after that it won't be long till their army descends upon us. I have guards waiting south of the mountains to escort me back to Ang-Khen."

My stomach kicks dully. Even though Lord Hanno promised to keep Baba and Tien safe, the thought of them being in a place that might so soon be under attack isn't comforting.

Bo claps. "And on that happy note, are we done here? Because this pack already feels like a hippopotamus is hitching a ride on my back, and according to Feathers, we have six hours of traveling ahead of us."

"Eight, actually," Merrin corrects, which makes Bo glower at him.

We say our good-byes to Ketai. When it's only Caen, Wren, and me left, I hang slightly back, feeling as though I'm intruding on something private. From what Wren has told me, her father and Caen trained her in secret for all her life to be the Xia warrior that is her blood right, and the three of them surely formed strong bonds during all that time together. I'm anticipating a big, heartfelt good-bye scene. Maybe not so far as to involve crying—though Ketai might well employ it for dramatic flair.

In the end, Ketai only grasps Wren's shoulders. His dark eyes gleam. Then he nods, lips pressed, before turning to Shifu Caen.

He wraps his fingers around the warrior's broad upper arms. "In a few weeks, my friend." There's a tightness to his voice I haven't seen before; something shadowed in his expression.

Caen's face remains impassive. "A few weeks," he echoes.

"Remember what I told you last night." They break apart. Ketai looks to Wren. "The both of you."

Even just from the back of her head, I can tell Wren stiffens at this. When she turns, the two of them heading over to join me, her eyes are low, an uncharacteristic slope to her shoulders. Whatever it was Ketai told her, she's uncomfortable about it.

A trickle of unease runs down my spine. Then Ketai's eyes flick up to where I'm hanging back. He lifts a hand. "Bring us luck, Moonchosen!"

Wren, Shifu Caen, and I make our way to the border of the clearing. The snowdrifts sparkle under the rising sun, which casts amber glitter through gaps in the leaves like coins at the bottom of a well. A trail of broken snow leads to where the rest of the group have already disappeared into the forest. The leopard siblings' throaty laughter floats back to us.

Caen adjusts his pack as we start down the path. "They could at least try to be a little more discreet," he complains.

"Merrin is probably cursing the day he agreed to this mission," Wren says wryly. "We should catch up with them and relieve him of—what did he call it? Cat-sitting duty."

"Hiro's with them, too."

"Yes, but *he* has the ability to block sound out through meditation."

"A trick I must get him to teach me on this trip," Caen muses.

As their conversation flows, I look behind us. Nothing stirs in the forest. The only movement comes from the steady drip of snowmelt from the trees. Still, my focus is drawn beyond the trees to where the temple clearing is hidden. Ketai Hanno will be setting off back south to meet his guards and return to his palace. He might even have left already. But for some strange reason I get the notion he's standing right where we left him, staring ahead, his dark eyes piercing a line through the bare branches and frigid air, tracking our movements like a predator surveys their prey.

Bring us luck, Moonchosen.

A shiver licks my neck. Because it isn't the first time I've been viewed as a good luck symbol by powerful men—and the last time resulted in me losing everything I knew, and almost my life with it.

We march for hours through the icy drifts. The high spirits we set off with have long since dwindled away to sullen silence, the only sounds our labored breaths and the crunch of our boots in the snow. As navigator, Merrin is responsible for our route, while Caen is in charge of the group in general, so between the two of them they keep us moving, allowing only toilet stops and a brief break for lunch, which consists of now-stale paratha from Ketai's palace and winter berries foraged along our path, so acidic they numb my tongue. Nitta and Bo keep an eye out for anything we can hunt for dinner, but the mountains are eerily still.

That night we make camp in a grove of maples. Moonlight filters through their naked branches, casting intricate patterns across the snowy floor. Even though we've been walking almost nonstop for eight hours, there are so many chores to make a safe, comfortable camp for the night that another hour passes before we can finally rest.

We collapse around the fire Bo and I built into a deep pit. The grove is lit with its leaping flames, painting our silhouettes bronze and gold. Something sweet is roasting.

"Water chestnuts," Nitta says, turning their leaf-wrapped shells over the fire with a stick. "I found them on the banks of the river nearby. It's a bit tricky to access, but it isn't iced over. We can wash there in the morning and refill our flasks."

Merrin nods. "We're not far from the Ice Plains. It must be one of the tributaries of the Zebe."

Hiro looks up from the mug of tea cupped in his palms, feathers of steam rising past his face. "The sources of the Zebe are extremely spiritual places," he says in his soft, monotone voice. "It would be a great honor to be blessed by their waters, but to bathe there without proper ceremony would be sacrilege."

"I didn't know," Nitta says, looking apologetic.

Bo winks at Hiro. "Lucky we have a resident shaman, then." The leopard-boy stretches forward, curving his cheeks toward the flames. "I for one can't wait to have a proper wash."

"I think we *all* can't wait for that," Merrin murmurs.

"I thought bird-forms have a terrible sense of smell," Bo shoots back.

"Then perhaps you understand how dire the situation is."

The two of them continue to snipe at each other as we pass the cracked husks of the roasted water chestnuts around, along with more stale paratha. The air fills with chewing and our tired sighs of satisfaction. After a day of hiking, I don't have the patience to eat slowly, and I'm soon finished, following the food with generous swigs of plum wine straight from the bottle.

It used to be difficult for me to stomach alcohol. Though Ketai's wine is far sweeter than the sake I had to drink with the King, the strong tang of liquor is still present, reminding me in the way it stings in my throat of my last private meeting with the King. How he'd forced my head back and poured the liquid straight into my mouth. How it had made me choke and cry. After that, alcohol brought a new taste with it: shame.

But since that first bottle of the Hannos' plum wine a few nights ago, I've begun to enjoy the warm, wobbly feeling it flushes through my body. How it blurs my vision.

Blurs my memory.

"Careful," Caen warns as I take another long gulp before Wren takes it from me. She takes a sip before passing it to Merrin. "We need that bottle to last. It'll help keep us warm."

Nitta flutters her thick lashes at him. "Cuddles can do that, too, Shifu."

Caen blinks primly. "People of Han do not…cuddle."

"What about fondling?" she asks.

"Nuzzling?" her brother suggests.

"Spooning?" Nitta's tongue toys with the word. She curves in a feline slink to reach for the wine. "There's no one in the whole world who doesn't like spooning."

Despite his deadpan expression, the tiniest hint of color touches Caen's cheeks. He adjusts his long wool overcoat, pulling it closer together at his collarbones, the tip of his plaited beard tickling his fingers. "I don't know what that is exactly," he replies, "but it doesn't sound comfortable."

The leopard siblings burst into raucous laughter, Merrin's croaky snorts joining them. Wren and I hide our grins, pretending suddenly to be very interested in the hems of our traveling cloaks as Caen gives us all a death stare so strong it would make even the hard-as-nails Blue, one of the other Paper Girls, wither.

As soon as dinner is over, tiredness overtakes us with a fresh fierceness. With theatrical yawns, Nitta and Bo are the first to crawl to
bed—or rather, the pile of blankets Merrin and Caen placed inside
the small tent, having dug away most of the snow in an attempt to
create a somewhat cozy spot to sleep. Hiro heads off next, having
done a check of the magical protection he and Wren weaved around
our small campsite. The light vibration of magic is just about detect-
able in the air, masked almost by Bo's snores.

Across the campfire, Caen and Merrin are deep in conversation,
discussing tomorrow's route. Wren has been quiet for most of the
meal. I cuddle closer. "What are you thinking about?" I ask softly,
dropping my head to her shoulder and slipping my gloved hands
into her lap.

She squeezes them. "My childhood," she answers after a beat.
"Our palace in Ang-Khen."

"Do you miss it?"

She doesn't reply straightaway. "It's strange. I've spent almost my
entire life there, but it doesn't feel like home. It's just…a place I
know."

I wait for her to go on, the two of us leaning together, watching
the crackling fire.

"Because of my training, my father kept me away from other
children. And though I was constantly surrounded by maids and
servants, I felt so lonely. I was always just *waiting*. Waiting for the
time when I could do what I was born to do. Waiting to fulfill my
destiny." She releases a long breath, clouds curling around us. "No,
Lei, I don't miss it. I don't have to wait anymore. I'm finally doing
something important, something I believe in." Wren leans back, a
soft shimmer in her eyes as I tip my face up to hers. "And now I'm
not alone." She smiles, revealing those dimples that break my heart

a tiny bit every time I see them, two short dashes in her cheeks, like symmetrical twins of the character for "one."

Then she asks, "Do *you* miss it?"

"The herb shop?"

"The Hidden Palace."

I jolt back, tugging my hands from hers as though stung. "You're really asking if I miss that place?"

Wren glances across the fire to where Caen and Merrin are still deep in conversation. "I don't mean—you know I don't mean..." With a jerk of her head, she turns away. Her jaw ticks. "I was there, too, Lei. We went through the same thing. I know exactly what kind of torture it was to be there. To have to spend time with him."

Instantly, my hard manner melts. I grab her hands. "Wren, I'm so sorry. Of course you did. It's just sometimes I forget that it hurts you, too, because you seem so strong."

"I told you before, that's how I was made to act. I'm not always as brave as I want to be. Not like you."

"Don't say that. You *are* brave, Wren. Incredibly so."

She looks back at the fire, its flames dancing in her dark eyes. "Do you remember last night, just after we ate dinner? My father wanted to speak to me alone, so we went out by the lake?" She pauses. "He told me I've disappointed him."

I gape at her. *"What?"*

"You have to understand, Lei, he trained me for one purpose. *One.* Even before that, when he came to Rain to find me because of the fortune-teller's prophecy. My whole life was about assassinating the King. It shaped everything I did, every aspect of me. So when I didn't do it..." She forms the words delicately here, and I understand what she's skirting around: that *I* did instead. "It changed something in the way he looks at me, I think."

"But it wasn't your fault!" I say, almost shouting. I huff out air, drop my voice. "Wren, your mother was *killed*. You were forced to leave the palace. And then you came back to save me. So that even though everything had gone wrong and nothing was turning out the way you'd planned, you could be there to follow it through."

She still doesn't meet my eyes. "That's the thing. My father didn't support my decision to go to the Moon Ball. But we had already been exposed. It wasn't like I was giving anything away by going. And I couldn't let you go through that alone. I know how it feels." Her lashes are low. "They don't tell you about that—how taking a life takes something from *you*, too."

Silence spins out. The letter from my father seems to throb where it sits nestled in the shirt pocket over my heart. Having finally met Wren's own father, I think I understand better now why she is the way she is.

"I don't know what Ketai's problem is," I say, drawing her closer, "but he's got it wrong. There's nothing to be disappointed about when it comes to you." The words of Baba's letter flash into my mind. *You are brave, and strong, and caring, and full of fire.* I squeeze her hands as she presses her lips together, looking unconvinced. "What does it matter who did it anyway? The King is dead. He's out of our lives once and for all, and we need to start letting ourselves feel good about that. This is our time, Wren. Let's show everyone what two human girls can do."

I plant a kiss on her lips. But she doesn't smile.

"We'd better get to bed," she says, and gets to her feet, her hands slipping from mine. "Tomorrow will be another long day."

SEVEN

*T*HE PALACE BURNS.

Orange and gold, flickering tongues in an indigo sky.

The smell of ash and blood.

The King lies dead, one eye mutilated, his throat ripped open where you stabbed him—you, yes you—where you jerked the blade again and again, tearing flesh and ligament and scraping bone.

You did this.

Don't turn away—look at your hands.

I SAID LOOK—

"Get up, Lei."

The low voice carves my nightmare in two, waking me so cleanly that I sit up with a gasp. The shadowy figure crouching over me moves back to give me space.

I rub the heels of my hands into my eyes. "Sh-shifu Caen?"

"Come with me. Bring your weapon." Then he strides out of the tent without another word.

I hunch over for a moment in the dark, trying to disperse the horrible images still racing through my mind. Beside me, Wren stirs. She turns over sleepily and releases a contented sigh, her breath shifting the curls of hair that have spilled across her cheek. I resist the urge to curl myself around her, fold into her warmth. Careful not to disturb her, I peel the blankets off and scoot to my feet. The rest of the group minus Caen are lumpy shapes in the dark. Bo's rumbling snores fill the tent. In their sleep, he and Merrin have turned toward each other, Bo curled like a fetus into the space Merrin's body opens. With a wry smile—the two of them are going to be very grumpy about this when they wake—I root around in my things, grabbing my coat and gloves and the dagger Ketai gave me before slipping outside.

Shifu Caen stands by the remains of last night's fire. He's tying his long hair back into a knot on the top of his head. The chilled air is still, nothing stirring the crystalline trees and snowy floor of the forest, nor Caen's long traveling robe, which hangs from his big frame almost to the ground.

I stifle a yawn as I rush to put on my coat and gloves. "What's going on?" I look around the grove. Weak morning light tints everything in a pale silver-blue. The back of my neck prickles as I imagine dark shapes hiding behind the trees, the nightmare still with me. "Are we in danger?"

"Not immediately. But we will be, many times on this mission. Which is why Ketai asked me to train you." Caen's eyes narrow as I fail to hold back another yawn. "Are you ready for your first lesson?"

Despite the ache in my muscles from a full day hiking, and the fact that all I want to do right now is dive right back into bed with Wren where it's warm, a rush of eagerness thrums through me. *This* is what I've been waiting for.

"Yes!" I answer keenly.

Caen turns, already striding away. "Then let's get started."

My boots crunch as I hurry after him. I squint against the ice-cold air and flex my fingers on the hilt of the knife in my pocket, remembering the last time I held a blade like this in my hands. What I did with it.

It wasn't long ago that I was a girl with fire in her veins. A girl who brought flames and destruction to the royal palace. A girl who took the kindling that the King's cruelty and her lover's empowerment created for her and lit up her whole world in a single stroke.

Not long ago, I was a girl of paper and fire. And I'll be damned if I'm going to let a little bit of snow smother those flames.

The memory of my nightmare rushes back to me: the heat, the burning, the look on *his* face, the King's face, as he realized for the first time in his life that this was a battle he had lost.

Holding back a shudder, I set my face into a steely expression and tuck the dagger into the folds of my coat. Despite what some of the others might think, I am *still* that girl of paper and fire—and I'm going to prove it to them.

I grit my teeth. I'm going to prove it to *myself*.

Our boots sink into the snow as we leave the camp behind. "Aren't we going to break Hiro and Wren's protection?" I ask. "The dao will only keep us hidden as long as we don't break it ourselves, right?"

"It's already wearing off," Shifu Caen replies. "Besides, the others will be getting up soon. Hiro rises each morning at sunrise to pray." His voice softens. "It's a difficult life, that of a shaman."

I peer up at him. Despite how broad and muscled he is, there's a delicacy, an elegant purposefulness, to the way he moves. It reminds me of Wren. How every movement she makes seems full of intention. How she moves through the world as though she knows its secrets—and it hers.

"You knew Hiro before this?" I ask.

He nods. "Ketai brought him to the palace three years ago after the raid on his clan."

"What was the raid for? I thought the King respects shaman clans."

Caen's voice turns stony. "A few years ago, the Hidden Palace released a royal edict. All shamans in Ikhara, no matter what province or clan they come from, have to offer their services to the court if the King calls for them. Those who refuse will be taken by force."

My heart beats darkly. "Sounds familiar," I mutter.

"Hiro was half-dead when Ketai found him. The poor boy lost his entire clan. His whole family."

I cut him another sideways glance. "That *also* sounds familiar."

If he senses the note of derision in my voice, he ignores it. "Ketai tries to pay him for his work, but Hiro refuses. Says he wants for nothing more than a place to sleep and food to eat, and to fulfill his teachings and continue his clan's work."

We walk on, our boot-fall crisp in the morning snow. Trees garlanded in frost tower around us.

"Is magic something shamans are born with?" I ask him after a while. "Like with Wren—I know she had to learn how to use her magical abilities, but she has the talent already, being a Xia. Is it like that for everyone who performs magic?"

"Not at all. It helps that shamans are taught from a young age. They're brought up understanding the techniques and intricacies of qi manipulation, and the language of daos is one handed down between generations. Shaman clans are extremely secretive with it. But as long as you have access to this language and know how to properly draw qi from the world, anyone can wield magic. Though it's not something many of us would willingly choose. As you know, it is not a process without its sacrifices."

My brow furrows. "As I know?"

Caen hesitates. "My mistake," he says. "I assumed Wren would have shared that with you."

"Shared *what* with me?"

But he stays quiet, and I fall silent, pouting as I glare ahead at the shadowy, softly glimmering forest. So. Even now—more secrets.

After a few more minutes, the sound of flowing water meets my ears. As we draw closer it rises to a strong, steady rush. We emerge from the bony trees onto the steep riverbank, a jutting cliff puckered with rocks. Water rushes over the bed below, its surface flashing silver like the scaled backs of fish. It looks deep; the water is dark, almost purple.

Caen gestures ahead to a dip in the bank where animals have carved out a path to the pebbled bank of the inner curve of river. "Go ahead," he says simply.

I goggle at him. "You want me to go in *there*?"

He waits, impassive. "The first thing a warrior faces in battle is fear. The second is the unexpected. You must be prepared at all times for these two elements. Not to overcome them—none of us ever truly do that, I think, no matter how calm or certain we may appear. But we must always be ready for them. To know how to face them, and win." He folds his arms. "Your task this morning is to submerge yourself fully in the river and then return to me here. That is all."

I hold up my knife, looking at it grumpily. "What was the point of bringing this, then?"

"A warrior should also always be armed. From now on you should carry your weapon at your belt at all times. But perhaps leave it with me for this task." He holds out his hand. "Just in case."

Hesitantly, I pass him the dagger. Then I look down at the river.

I'm already shivering in all my layers just standing here; the last thing I want to do is get wet. The water moves fast, with all the ferocity of a wild animal, and my heart trips. But I think of the promise I made myself earlier. With a loud huff, I start toward the cliff top.

"Careful," Caen adds as I crunch through the snow. "The current is strong."

I scowl. "Thanks for the reminder."

Down below, the water glistens, clear as glass. I shrug off my long, fur-lined traveling coat first. Just this one loss makes me suck in a breath; the morning air is bracingly cold, and my cotton wrap shirt and trousers do little to protect me. My bare soles scream on the frozen ground as I kick off my boots. Clamping my arms across my chest, I pick my way down the steep slope. The river rushes inches from my toes. I'd been planning on making my way in slowly, holding on to the jutting roots dangling from the scraggly rock face, but it's so cold that immersion seems like the best strategy. So, flexing my already numb fingers, I puff out a big breath, bend my knees—and throw myself in.

The water clamps around me, so strong and fierce and gods-shocking cold it's as though some giant ice creature has seized me in its huge paw. It's so much worse than I'd anticipated. I'm immediately pulled downstream without even a second to react, to move back toward the bank. Bubbles burst from my lips as I scream, tumbling with the current. Under the surface, the water is a dark, deep indigo. I kick and flail, searching for something to grab hold of.

But the river is too strong. It moves with the force and determination of a stampede of wild bison. I'm spun around so much I don't know which way is up. Screaming for breath turns to choking turns to lungs filling with water. My vision starts to swim.

Then an image rears ahead in the darkness.

It swells, expands, until it's the height and width of the river itself, so real it sends fear thundering down my veins to replace the frozen cold: the Demon King's leering face.

Crazed, arctic-blue eyes glitter out of the shadowy vortex.

His mouth yawns open in a roar.

The whole river seems to scream at me, fill my ears with the same words I heard in the forest when hunting with Nitta and Bo; the words of the fears and shame that haunt me in my nightmares.

I'VE FOUND YOU.

And then the current drags me through the King's gaping maw, and the vision disappears around me in a swirl of bubbles. As I'm realizing that's all it was—a vision, not real, it can't be real—I feel the water flowing around a corner. I'm tossed against the riverbank. My forehead smacks against a protruding rock. Spots burst across my vision. But the pain wakes me, fires my instincts. Flinging my arms wide, I scrabble at the bank, catching a submerged tree root that juts from the cliff face.

Heart pounding, muscles screaming, I cling on. The current is strong. I grit my teeth, pulling one hand over the other to bring myself toward the bank.

Bubbles burst around me. A hulking creature looms over me, clasping me in a vise-like grip before I can get away. It drags me up through the froth. My head breaks the surface of the water, and I'm struggling, terror screaming through me, because—the King. It *is* him.

He came back for me.

I squirm, coughing and spluttering, whacking at the arm clamped around me.

The King doesn't let go. He lifts me higher as he scales the steep cliff of the riverbank. It's only when we get to the top, the two of us collapsing on the snow-packed ground, that I realize the arm flung across me is pale and fur-less.

I wriggle out from under it, panting hard. Shifu Caen has stripped to his trousers. The boulder-like muscles of his dense, water-slicked torso ripple as he pushes to his knees and reaches for me.

"Get away!" I scream, kicking at his hands.

"Lei!" he shouts. "You are going to die of exposure if you don't let me warm you!"

My teeth chatter. "I j-just n-need my coat!" I try to pick myself up, but my muscles are clenched, my joints locked from the cold. With a frustrated growl, I force myself to my knees, only to drop back down a second later when my knees buckle.

"Let me help," Caen insists. Droplets of water trace his face, clinging to his hair and beard. "You're bleeding."

Ignoring him, I push myself up once more, and despite how wobbly my legs feel, I manage to stay upright. I trudge past him back along the rocky ledge to where I'd left my things. Tremors rack my body, but another shiver entirely separate from the cold shudders through me as I think of what I saw under the water.

"I k-killed you," I snarl under my breath. "Just leave me alone!"

Never.

The voice is a whisper, a nightmarish slither on the air.

I spin, eyes wild, panting hard.

Caen holds my gaze, the skin of his torso covered in gooseflesh. Around us, the forest is still.

Feeling something drip into my eyes, I swipe my hand across my brow. It comes back red. Forcing back recollections of last night's nightmare—*every* night's nightmare—I dart over to where my things lie discarded on the cliff edge and drag my coat and boots on. Shifu Caen waits until I'm fully dressed to approach me. He's put his shirt and cloak back on. He sweeps his hand over his wet hair, still pulled back into a knot at the top of his head. My own is plastered to my skin in straggly patterns. Silently, he reaches for my face, and though I flinch, I let him touch me. He cradles the back of my head in one hand, lifting the other to press carefully around the cut on my forehead.

"It's not as deep as I feared," he says, using his sleeve to clean the blood. "But we should still get Hiro to heal it. We don't want it to get infected." When he draws back, the light catches on the amethyst flakes in his dark eyes. "What *was* that back there? Did you not realize it was me?"

I clamp my arms across my chest. "You surprised me. That's all."

It seems as though he wants to press me more. But he only sighs. "If you say so."

We walk back to the campsite in silence, the forest slowly waking around us. Light—a warmer, rosier golden-blue—slants in through the canopy. Birdsong breaks the morning hush. When we reach the maple grove, we find Merrin and Nitta busy preparing breakfast. They've lit the fire, Merrin crouched over the stove suspended above its flames, prodding at whatever is inside, while Nitta cuts up a slab of dried meat. The others must still be sleeping.

Hearing our footsteps, Merrin glances up, his feathered face friendly. "Good morning, lovelies. How did it—oh." His orange owl-eyes slide to my cut.

With a cry, Nitta drops what she's doing and bounds to me.

"Just a minor snow-related slip," Caen says, as the leopard-girl squeezes me tight. "Training is difficult enough without ice for a floor. Nothing Hiro can't help with."

"He's doing his morning meditation," Nitta says, pointing. She brushes the wet hair from my face. "Oh, Lei." She shoots Caen an angry look. "You shouldn't push her so much."

I shrug her off me with a smile. "I'm fine. You know what's *really* life-threatening, though?"

"What?"

"My hunger."

Though she still looks concerned, the corners of Nitta's eyes crinkle. She gives me a salute. "One breakfast coming right up, General."

I find Hiro just beyond camp in a denser part of the grove, the morning light creating latticed patterns on the icy ground. He's kneeling on a patch of cleared snow, hands on his lap, eyes closed. His lips move, but they make no sound; gods don't need us to speak in order to hear our prayers.

I notice a small lacquered case sitting on a folded piece of fabric beside him. Something peeks out of its top. I'm leaning closer to see what it is when the shaman boy's eyes open.

I move back, looking guilty. "Sorry to disturb you, Hiro." I gesture at my face. "I, uh, had a little accident at training this morning."

Hiro motions for me to sit. I push away some of the snow and kneel opposite him.

"Here we are again," I say, winking. "We've got to stop meeting like this."

"You should stop getting yourself injured," he replies, then closes his eyes in a way that tells me I should also stop with the jokes.

Keeping his eyes closed, Hiro lifts a hand to my brow with a careful but firm pressure. Nothing happens at first. Then: *there.* The change is invisible but unmistakable. A ripple rolls from Hiro's body, pricking the hairs on the back of my neck. The forest stills, as if it, too, senses his focus. Unlike when I've seen Wren work magic, Hiro always does it with his eyes closed. He mumbles under his breath in that strange, twisted Ikharan that I've come to recognize as the language of magic, the secret code for manipulating qi that, as Shifu Caen explained to me earlier, shaman clans pass down through generations.

Heat prickles my forehead. Under his hand, my skin feels overly tight. There's barely any pain—nothing like the hours of discomfort it took to heal my wounds from the Moon Ball. Not to mention the itch after. Some days I rolled around on the floor just to get some relief. Wren found me like this one time and laughed in that loud, boisterous way of hers when she's forgotten to be self-conscious before I'd grabbed her and pulled her down, smothering her laugh with my mouth, and I was rolling again, though this time for an altogether different—and far more pleasant—reason.

After a few minutes, Hiro removes his hand. "Better?"

"Perfect," I say, skating my fingertips over the perfectly smooth skin there. They tingle with the last traces of his magic. "Thank you."

I wait for him to get up. Usually he leaves as soon as he's done, and it seems almost a point of politeness for me to let him be the first one to move. But he stays seated, a tiny furrow in his brow.

"Hiro? What's wrong?"

He shakes his head. "Excuse me." He gets to his feet. "Just a little tired."

As he smooths down his robes, one of the hems of his sleeves snags, and I spot marks there. Neat lines of puckered pink flesh.

Though I avert my eyes, he notices me looking. Spots of color come to his cheeks as he swiftly pulls his sleeve down.

"You know," I say as I stand, "you don't always have to help me with things like this, Hiro. It would have easily healed on its own. I hope you know you're always free to say no."

He gives a tiny shrug. "It's why I'm here, to protect the rest of you. Besides, I'm lucky Ketai makes me use my magic for protective and healing purposes. Not like—" Hiro cuts off, his eyes sparking with worry, as though he's already said too much. Stiffly, he picks up the little case that was on the ground next to him and hides it within the folds of his robes. "I'll be better after breakfast," he mutters.

"That's if there's anything left after Bo gets to it." Keen to lighten the mood, I add, "We're lucky *he's* not a shaman. All he'd use his magic for is filling his belly with food and his house with gold."

Though I laugh, Hiro's face remains serious. "There are far worse things to use it for," he says quietly, and turns his gray eyes back to the floor as we head back to camp.

EIGHT

OUR DAYS TREKKING THROUGH THE NORTHERN mountains fall into a familiar sequence. Shifu Caen wakes me up before sunrise to train, though all we've done so far is meditation and simple defensive work, him teaching me the dance of fighting, how to duck and dodge, how to anticipate your opponents' movements and use their attacking style against them. "You're small," he tells me. "Your reactions are fast and you have the element of surprise. Use those things to your advantage." After training we eat breakfast with the rest of the group before packing up camp and setting off for another full day's hiking. Just before sunset, we find a new camp spot and have dinner by the fire before collapsing into bed for a fitful few hours' sleep before it begins all over again.

"Let's play a game," Bo announces late one morning after hours of marching in silence.

It's the ninth day of our journey. Everyone is half asleep on their feet, lulled by the monotonous tramp through the snow and the muzzy light of the overcast day. For the past day and a half, we've been hiking at a rising incline, heading higher into the mountains toward the midsection of the Goa-Zhen range. Up this high, the forest is cloaked in clouds. The trees have thinned out, and the granite face of the mountain pokes out from under trappings of snow. Huge rock formations loom out of the mist like half-hidden monsters, and it sets my nerves on edge. What more could the clouds be hiding from us?

Every now and then, a shadowy shape on the outskirts of my vision catches my attention. Yet when I turn, there's nothing there.

"Oh, come on," Bo whines when none of us answer him. "We need a bit of livening up. You guys have about as much energy as a Hungry Ghost procession."

"If I'm unfortunate enough to be trapped here as a ghost after I die," Merrin mutters from where he's leading the group, "it won't be difficult for me to decide who to haunt."

Bo snorts. "I'm quivering in my boots, Feathers. Why don't you go first, then? Fact or Fiction. All you have to do is give us two statements, one true, the other made up. We guess which one is true."

"How will we know whether we're right?" I ask. A few flecks of new snow have begun to fall, and I lick their freshness from my lips.

"The person making the statements will tell us," Bo answers.

I lift a brow. "So…talking, then."

"Exactly! But with added fun."

"How about you go first, Bo?" Wren suggests wearily.

She's walking a few paces behind me, close to where Hiro trails at the back of the group. Out of all of us, he seems the most exhausted by our journey. Dark half-moons shade his eyes, and his breath comes slightly wheezy. Wren's kept close to his side for most of the trip, and I don't miss the concerned looks she gives him when she thinks he's not looking.

"Thank you for your enthusiasm, Wren!" Bo replies cheerily. "I'd be delighted to! All right. Fact one: I once found out a secret about a Clan Lord that was *so* secret they themselves didn't know it. Two: I have a beautiful singing voice."

Nitta snorts. "Easy. Fact one. You sing like a shrine-maiden with a head cold."

"Annoying older sisters aren't allowed to participate in the game when it's their brother's turn," Bo retorts, holding up a palm. "Any other guesses?"

"Fact one is true," I say. "I trust Nitta."

"You do realize she's a thief, Princess?"

I nod. "A thief of secrets. And I can bet she's stolen all of yours."

"A long time ago," Nitta confirms with a smirk.

Her brother pouts. "If you're all just going to mock me, someone else can play."

When no one volunteers, Merrin groans. "Oh, fine. If it'll get you to stop asking." He takes a moment to consider. "Fact one: when I was young, my baby feathers took so long to shed that my parents almost disowned me. Fact two: I've eaten leopard meat, and it's delicious."

"Fact one," Nitta answers confidently. She narrows her eyes at him. "And I have it on good authority that leopard meat is chewy and bland, so don't even think about trying."

"Unless, of course," Bo adds slyly, "you mean to taste it while it's still alive."

Nitta and I burst out laughing at the look on Merrin's face. The owl demon sighs heavily, marching on up the uneven cliff top. "Unbelievable," he mutters.

Bo beams. "A word often used to describe me—"

He cuts off with a yell.

"Bo!" Nitta screams, running to where he's disappeared from view. Bo had been walking at the far left of the group, close to the edge of the cliff—the cliff he's just toppled over. One second he was swaggering along with a grin as broad as his face, the next he's been swallowed up by the clouds.

As the rest of us lurch forward, Merrin pushes off his strong legs. In one leap, he's airborne, the feathers curled around his arms ruffling open to create wings. He dives over the side of the mountain with astonishing speed.

Nitta drops to her knees. She stares down into the swirls of gray, her face ashen. Wren wraps an arm around me. We wait, huddled at the cliff top, the seconds stretching out agonizingly so that they feel more like minutes, hours even, none of us daring to breathe until we hear the rising flap of wings. Slowly, Merrin emerges from the mist, Bo dangling upside-down from his talons. The leopard-boy's eyes are wide. He gulps like a fish to draw in air he must have thought for at least a few moments he would never get to taste again.

Caen leans forward, reaching out an arm to help, only to loosen a cluster of rocks under his own weight. He jerks back as they scatter noisily down the sheer cliff face.

"Everyone back!" he orders.

We shift to a safe distance as Merrin comes in to land. Nitta and Wren grab Bo to help him down, while I press my hands to Merrin's scratchy pewter-white feathers as his talons meet the snow, feeling the uneven rise and fall of his chest. He nods at me, smoothing down his robes as he catches his breath. For the first time I notice how his robes are slit along the bottom of the sleeves so that he can fly at a moment's notice—and luckily so.

"Stupid Cat!" Merrin scolds, glowering. "That's it. No more games." He turns to Caen. "I managed to get a look at our location while fetching Bo, and I recognize these peaks. We're almost at the Cloud Palace."

"Wait," Bo says, still panting where he's sprawled on the ground,

"Bird-forms have the keenest eyesight of all demons," Hiro adds, his soft voice almost whipped away by the wind.

Without a word, Wren unbuckles her pack. She swings it off, bending to root through it.

"You want to stop for lunch now?" Bo sniffs. "Here?"

Nitta points back down the mountainside. "We should get some shelter. There's a copse of snow pine back there—"

She cuts off as Wren draws out her swords.

"We should be prepared," Wren says, strapping them across her back.

It takes me a few moments to understand. While the others immediately begin to swing their bags off and arm themselves, I look around, squinting against the wind, the back of my neck prickling. Then I check the knife at my belt. Though I still haven't drawn it once in my lessons with Shifu Caen, its presence has begun to feel comforting, a familiar weight at my hip. As my fingers brush the bone hilt, the magic imbued within thrums, sending warm tingles up my arms.

I shift closer to Wren's side. Everyone's armed: Bo with his throwing knives and staff, his sister with her bow and arrow, Shifu Caen with a long sword almost his height. Though Hiro's hands are empty, as a shaman they are weapons of their own.

"What's the plan?" Bo asks, blurred by the sheets of dancing flakes. "Or are we just going to stand around like we're at some warriors' impromptu mountaintop tea party?"

"There's no point moving on without Merrin," Caen says. "We should make camp and wait out the day. If he still hasn't returned by tomorrow, we'll know for certain something has happened to him. Perhaps the weather will clear a bit. If the clouds shift, even for a few moments, we should be able to see the palace and plan our route."

"And what, then we just wander right up to it?" Nitta replies incredulously. "White Wing guards are allowed to kill on sight.

We all know how bird demons are. One look at us and they'll be sending a small army down to dispatch us. Merrin was supposed to be our way in. If they've captured *him*…"

"Maybe," I suggest, "Hiro and Wren could hide us with their magic?"

All of us look at the two of them.

Hiro's watery eyes are hooded in dark circles, his frame as thin as the scraggly branches of the mountain pines clinging to the cliff. But he straightens, squares his shoulders. "I can do it," he says.

Wren puts a hand on his shoulder. "Me, too."

Caen's eyes flash. "Out of the question! This isn't some sake house we're talking about, where one can order enchantments on tap. You do not demand magic with a click of your fingers. Protection daos consume a lot of qi to create, especially when it's to hide a group as big as ours. We had multiple shamans working for more than a week on the spells that hid Ketai and me when we left the palace in Ang-Khen. Hiro and Wren need rest."

"Then let me go on my own," Wren contests, shifting her weight so the long swords on her back thud against each other. "It'll take far less magic *and* it'll look less suspicious. Besides, I've met Lady Dunya. She'll speak to me."

"Then I'm coming with you," I say. "None of us should go anywhere on our own right now."

Before Wren can argue, Caen holds up a hand. "Whatever we decide can wait until morning." He recites the old saying. *"A day to plan saves a week of pain."*

None of us look convinced.

"If Merrin has been captured," Nitta points out, "he might have told the White Wing about us. They could come for us in the night."

"They won't find us with Hiro and Wren's protection," Caen replies.

Bo juts a bony hip. "Who's demanding magical services now, huh, Shifu?"

"Even so," Wren says, "we can't rely solely on the protection enchantment."

I squint at her through the icy wind. "What do you mean? As long as we don't break the enchantment ourselves, we're safe."

"Yes, but—"

Bo flings out an arm. *"But?"*

"We should tell them, Wren."

Everyone looks around at Hiro's voice. Its gentleness carries power in the rising tension, and for a moment no one speaks. The snow swirls harder, pelting us with glittering shards of ice.

"Tell us *what*?" I press Wren.

There's something apologetic in her eyes. "Our magic is weakening," she admits. "Or at least it takes more to call it forth. We think it's due to the Sickness."

Nitta and Bo goggle at her. I stare, my heart thudding harder. Memories click through me: the shadows under Wren and Hiro's eyes growing deeper, Hiro's tiredness after healing my wound from my first day of training, the scars on his forearm. When Shifu Caen told me about the difficult life of a shaman, is this what he meant?

But from Caen's expression, Wren's announcement is clearly news to him, too. "Ketai connected the problems with qi-draining long ago, but neither of you told us it was giving you any problems. I didn't realize it was that bad."

"My clan had been noting the changes for years," Hiro adds. "Whatever dark magic is causing the qi-draining, it's powerful."

Bo flicks his head to shake off the collecting snow, his face murderous. "Brilliant. Godsdamned *excellent*. The one thing we need more than anything on this trip, and it's already failing."

"It's not as bad as it sounds," Wren says.

Bo laughs harshly, one corner of his lip curled to reveal a crooked incisor. "Yes it is, and you know it." His tail flicks, agitated. "What are you, anyway, without your enchantments? Ketai told us about your Xia heritage. He made you sound like some undefeatable warrior. But without magic you're just some Paper Girl with a sword—"

I slam into him. He lets out a grunt as I tackle him to the ground, pinning him against the snow-dusted rock. "Don't you dare talk like that to her!" I yell.

Hands seize my shoulders. "Lei!"

I wrestle Wren off me. Breathing hard, I get to my feet. "Apologize," I snarl at Bo.

He brushes off his clothes as he straightens. "Are you joking? Your girlfriend's the one who should be apologizing. All this time, she's been keeping secret something that could cost us our lives."

"Bo," Nitta warns, landing a hand on his arm. "We're all exhausted and worried about Merrin. Take a few moments. Cool down."

Bo shrugs her away. "Great idea, Sis." He spins on his heels, already stomping away. "I'm going to find myself something to eat. That should take the edge off a little."

Nitta's round amber eyes flit over us, apologetic, before she follows her brother.

"We should stay together," Hiro reminds them. But they've already been swallowed up by the storm.

Caen sighs. "I'll talk to them. Hiro—come with me. Lei, Wren—perhaps it's best if you two wait here."

Then they, too, disappear into the thick swirls, leaving me alone with Wren.

I cross my arms and direct a cold stare her way. "I thought we were done keeping secrets."

Her breath furls around her, mixing with the snowflakes pattering thickly down. "I didn't want to worry you."

"Don't you get it yet?" My voice is harsh, but I grab her hands, clutching them to my chest. "Wren, I'm here to *share* your worries. To try and make them lighter. Remember what you told me the other day—you're not alone anymore. So stop acting like it." Her eyes soften, and I go on, gentler now, "The other day, I saw...marks on Hiro's arm. Do you know anything about them?"

Like most everyone I know, I understand little of how magic works beyond a few basics. Pain has long been used as a tithe for magic, though usually through the form of tattoos; the skin of most shamans is woven with their dark patterns. Since they are essentially gifts to the earth, qi offerings are meant to have beauty in them. Hiro's raw, still-pink scars, however, seem to suggest something else.

Something darker.

When Wren doesn't answer, I draw her closer. "If this is a shaman thing, something to do with magic—something *you* do, too—then you have to tell me, Wren. Please."

She looks away for a moment, then her gaze snaps to me: hardened, resigned. Right when she opens her mouth to reply, there's a skirr of movement over our heads.

Two large shapes loom out of the sky. I only have a few seconds to recognize them as bird demons before they bear down on us through the swirls of clouds and mist. Viselike talons lock into our shoulders. Then, in a flurry of feathers, they rise back up, and my jagged screams are whipped away by the wind as Wren and I are wrenched apart and lifted high into the ice-studded air.

NINE

THE BIRD DEMON THAT HAS GRABBED me moves with incredible speed, rising up into the cloud-wreathed sky with great beats of her wings so powerful they rattle my teeth. I dangle from her talons, legs kicking empty air. We fly fast. I can't tell what type of bird-form she is, but she moves far less smoothly than Merrin did the night of the Moon Ball. She swoops and dips and cants from side to side, making my stomach lurch. At one point she banks so abruptly that for one sickening second I'm sure we're falling. I cling to her talons, my heart thundering. All it would take for her to kill me is to let go.

The old wounds of Naja's attack at the Moon Ball reawaken in my shoulders under the demon's fierce grip. But though my eyes water, it's not pain but *panic* that makes me scream.

"Wren!" I yell blindly. "Wren!"

She doesn't answer. The dense clouds make it seem as though she's miles away, even though the bird demon that captured her can't be far if we're being taken to the same place. Beneath my boots, billowing white hides the mountain range, but every now and then a dark spur of rock looms out of the clouds like black teeth in some great earth god's maw.

I don't see the White Wings' palace until we're almost upon it. One second, we're enveloped in mist, shards of ice stinging my cheeks. The next, the clouds open to reveal a vast skyline of serrated shards and snow-covered mountainside. In its center, an elaborate structure clings to the tallest peak.

The Cloud Palace. Even in my panicked state, it is glorious.

It's just as I imagined from Merrin's stories. White spires. Marbled alabaster walls. Gilded balconies ringing tall, twirling towers. Delicate bridges run from turret to turret, and glittering staircases wind around the outside of the palace, texturing the otherwise polished rock the entire building is carved from. The palace itself is an extravagant construction, tiered like some enormous rice cake, glowing against the smudged granite peaks that surround it.

Spotting our approach, an armored owl-form guard launches off one of the jutting minarets. "Commander!" he calls, flying toward us on wings the color of the clouds around us. "Did you find all of the prisoner's accomplices?"

"Yes, Ruhr." The bird-woman carrying me answers in a smooth, deep voice, punctuated by clicks of her beaked jaw. "Send a message to Lady Dunya that we will be bringing them to the Audience Hall immediately."

"Yes, Commander Teoh." The guard tucks his head in what I guess constitutes a midair bow. "Open wings."

"Open sky," the Commander returns.

The guard flies away, casting his wings to swoop toward a veranda at one of the palace's middle levels.

Now we're nearing the palace, other bird demons appear at our sides. My heart clenches as I spot Wren hanging from the talons of a wiry kestrel demon, whose dark-umber feathers have been painted white. From the other guards dangle the rest of our group: Hiro, Nitta, Bo, and Shifu Caen.

Commander Teoh aims for the base of the palace. White marble walls hug the mountainside. In some places where the rock falls away in sheer cliffs, the building is even suspended from the stone, hanging from its underside with shaded terraces in place of a ground floor. The Commander cups her winged arms to slow us as we approach one of these terraces. She throws me up with an easy kick of her feet before catching me in one arm. Her other sweeps out as we skid across the marbled floor. For a moment, I'm bundled in her scratchy, white-painted feathers, her heartbeat thumping against my back. Then her feathers puff down, laying flat against her body. Behind us, there are the thuds of the rest of the bird demons landing. I hear Nitta and Bo's shouts.

The moment we stop sliding, the Commander tucks me easily under her arm and strides to a weapon rack set against the far wall. Among the pikes and swords and bows and arrows, silver chains hang from the nails.

Realizing what she's about to do, I wriggle my hand to the dagger at my belt. My fingers touch the cold ivory hilt. Magic quivers up my arms as I pull it free. Straining against the bird-woman's grip, I twist my wrist around as far as I can and stab the blade back.

Hammered metal sinks into soft flesh. Commander Teoh lets out a surprised squawk. By sheer luck I've found a gap in her armor where her underarm meets her side. Warm blood sluices over my hand.

She drops me. I get a glimpse of glassy black hawk eyes rimmed with long lashes. The strange jaw of bird demons: half human chin, half hook-tipped yellow beak. Then in one swift movement, the Commander flips me onto my stomach, pinning me against the cold marble. She wrenches my arms back. My dagger clatters to the floor.

"Don't you dare try that again, human!" she croaks, blood dripping at her talon-tipped feet.

"*Lei!*" Wren's shout comes from behind us. "Let her go! You don't have to treat us like this. We're not here to harm you!"

"Would you say the same to a stranger who attacked *you* with their sword?" the Commander returns.

"You attacked us first!" I growl.

"And we had every right. You were trespassing in our territory. Not to mention, your accomplice has been trying to trick us with lies for the last few hours. Do not pretend you're here for honorable reasons."

Wren's voice rings out. "I am Wren Hanno, daughter of Ketai Hanno. I come with an offer of cooperation from my clan."

"So we've heard." Commander Teoh drags me roughly to my feet, keeping one arm twisted behind my back. "You've come to ask for our help in supporting your civil war. That with you travels the girl they're calling the Moonchosen. The girl who killed the King."

"Yes—" Wren begins, but the Commander interrupts her.

"Well, we had another visitor today who's said otherwise."

It takes a moment for her words to sink in. Then a cold shiver trails down my spine. "What visitor?" I ask. "What—what did they say?"

Commander Teoh doesn't reply. With a gesture to the rest of the bird demon guard, each one holding one member of our group, she heads to a staircase that leads from the terrace up into the palace. She pushes me along, pain flaring in my shoulder as her talons pinch tighter.

"We will refrain from shackling you, out of respect for your clan's status," the Commander says. "But if you try and attack us again in any way, we have the right to kill you. You have been warned."

"In *any* way?" Bo speaks up from the back of the group. "What about tickling? Does that count?"

"Bo, be quiet!" Caen shouts.

"Hey, I'm just trying to be clear on the rules."

"Don't pretend to care for rules, Cat," Commander Teoh retorts. "We know what your kind are like."

Nitta lets out a low hiss at this while her brother shoots back, "Like we know all about yours. Guess I shouldn't expect anything less from uppity, jumped-up *chickens* like you—"

There's a heavy thump.

"Bo!" Nitta cries, and I hear her struggling to get free.

"Don't worry." Bo's guard hefts his body onto her back. "He's only knocked out. But if he continues to speak this way, it's only a matter of time before one of us knocks him out for good."

Though I sense the agitated alertness in the group, we stay quiet from then on as the demons lead us through the White Wings' elegant palace. We climb up spiral staircases that wind from floor to floor and cross vaulted corridors of gleaming marble so polished it reflects my own face back at me, pale and nervous. The Cloud Palace is decorated just as ornately as the King's, but in an entirely different style. Instead of vibrant colors and deep obsidians and reds, the White Wings' style is more minimal. Touches of silver accent the pearly hue of the walls. Chiffon curtains drape across the arched entrances of halls and rooms, fluttering in the breeze from the tall, narrow recesses carved into the exterior walls to let in light and air.

Despite it being daytime, the palace is quiet. Servants move around near silently, feathered heads low. Whispered conversations cut off as we pass.

"Does anyone laugh in this place?" Nitta mutters behind me.

Commander Teoh's voice is clipped. "Unlike *your* kind, we birds know how to appreciate silence."

"Well, if everyone is as much of a joy to talk with as you, that's not surprising."

This might have earned Nitta a knocking-out, were it not for the gasp I let out, distracting the guards.

We've reached the end of a hallway, arriving at a huge cylindrical space carved out of the center of the palace. A wide stairway runs from the bottom level to the top, circling an open atrium and crowned by a wrought-silver glass dome, beyond which gray clouds billow. On a sunny day I can imagine it would be even more stunning, crisscrossed with beams of golden sunlight bouncing off the polished walls. Bird demons of all kinds move up and down the steps, some holding hushed conversations by the balconies, while others fly swiftly across the central chasm. Like the guards, all the demons are dressed in white hanfu, their feathers either naturally pale or dyed to match.

While many of the demons are Moon caste, there are Steels, too. They stand out with their human forms, the only markers of their demon status light scatterings of feathers or beaked noses, or long legs that taper to claw-tipped talons. As with the Moons, any visible human skin is also stained white.

I crane my neck, looking over the staircase balcony to take in the magnificent atrium as we ascend two flights before heading down a corridor leading to an immense archway. Ivory chiffon hangs across the opening, its ends whispering across the marble floor.

"Commander Teoh reporting for Lady Dunya," the bird demon announces.

"Open wings," comes a voice within the archway.

"Open sky," the Commander finishes.

The servant draws aside the gossamer sheets with a hook.

The White Wings' Audience Hall is just as impressive as the palace's central staircase. Long and wide, it stretches from the heart of the palace all the way to the outer edge. Gray light pours in through the towering latticed window set in the far wall. Pillars of white stone—so smoothly connected from floor to ceiling they could have grown from the rock itself—line the room like porcelain trees. Between each two stands a guard, a silver pike clasped at his or her side.

We start across the hall, our steps echoing off the vaulted ceiling, and the most impressive part of the room reveals itself beneath my feet.

It takes my eyes a moment to adjust to what I'm seeing. At first I think it's a painting, then for one nauseating moment that the floor simply isn't here at all. This part of the palace is perched over a chasm in the mountain. Down the center of the hall, a glass rectangle stretches across the drop, revealing the jagged rock of the mountain below. My hands grow clammy as we cross the glass. Clouds swirl below, a murky seascape it feels as though I could plummet into at any second.

Commander Teoh and her guards march us briskly to the end of the hall. Lined in front of the tall window are six thrones wrought in silver. The middle two thrones are largest, as are their occupants: a pair of Moon swan demons, alabaster-feathered and willowy, their long hybrid wing-arms folded in their laps. Silk robes glisten under the light bathing them through the window. They must be Lord Hidei and Lady Dunya, the leaders of the White Wing Clan.

To either side, sitting as still and stately as their parents, are their four daughters. Two look very young, hardly more than toddlers, while the other two are older, both somewhere around sixteen judging by their fresh faces. With a jolt, I recognize one of the teenage daughters from my initial journey to the Hidden Palace many months ago. General Yu pointed out the White Wings' carriage to me as it passed our own on the road from the Black Port. The girl watches us as we approach with open distaste, her beaked mouth puckered.

We line up in front of the family. Commander Teoh and I are in the center, Nitta and Wren flanking me. Wren leans over to catch my eye. I force a shaky smile, even though my shoulders are searing from the Commander's taloned grip and I feel exposed by the unblinking stares of the bird demons all around.

"Lady Dunya, Lord Hidei, honored daughters," Commander Teoh greets, bending to one knee. "Open wings."

"Sweet Samsi, not this again," Nitta murmurs under her breath.

"Open sky."

The family responds in unison, creating a strange echoing sound that pulls the hairs on my arms on end.

"These are the owl demon's accomplices?"

It's Lady Dunya. Her eyes are the same midnight-black as those of her husband and daughters, small and hard, like pitted olives. She's tall, sitting shoulders above Lord Hidei to her right. While her luxurious hanfu robes are simple in design, a complicated crown of delicate twining strands of silver studded with opals and diamonds sits upon her feathered head; more gems wind around her slim fingers and wrists, adorn her long neck. They look heavy, but she sits rod-straight, as cool and unyielding as the marble beneath her feet.

"Yes, my Lady," Commander Teoh answers. "We found them less than two miles from the palace—"

"Lady Dunya." Wren's voice rings out through the hall. "We've met once before at a ball at the Hidden Palace two years ago. I am Wren Hanno, daughter of Ketai Hanno."

The swan-woman's body doesn't move, but her head swivels, black eyes locking on Wren. Her soft down glitters, powdered with a silver dust I recognize from when I saw her daughter in the carriage on the road from the Black Port. Even her beaked mouth is painted white, a smooth, perfect shell.

"I remember." Like all bird demons, the click of her beak punctuates her speech, yet with Lady Dunya it's as though she orchestrates them to the beat of her words. Her voice is pure and lyrical as music. "We discussed the recent uprising in Kitori and the state of the mining economy. I had hoped to meet you again, though certainly not under such circumstances as these."

"Which are *what*, exactly?" Nitta asks brashly.

From my far left, Caen cautions, low, "Nitta."

But it seems the leopard-girl is determined to continue her brother's rebellious nature in his absence. "*You're* the ones who brought us here without our permission. We were minding our own business, having a nice little chat on the mountaintop—shame about the view, by the way, far too many clouds, totally not worth the hike—when your guards came along and plucked us up like rabbits for their dinner."

One of the toddler daughters, her face a haughty mask, says in a high-pitched voice, "Don't compare yourself to something we'd actually eat, feline."

I can feel the shock rolling off Nitta to be addressed in this way by someone hardly older than a baby.

"Now, Tish," Lord Hidei reprimands his daughter flatly, "remember your manners in front of guests."

The swan-girl pouts. My eyes shift from her to her beautiful teenage sister, whom I saw on the road to the palace. Her imperious glare bores into me.

Lady Dunya lifts a hand, and the room falls silent at once. "Lady Wren, I have to say I'm tired of your accomplices lying to us. It is not a good way to establish a respectful relationship."

"How exactly have we lied to you, Lady Dunya?" Wren asks.

"Your feline friend here tells us you were simply minding your own business on the mountaintop, which we all know is far from the truth. No one comes this far into the northern mountains unless they have something to hide. When we captured your owl demon companion earlier today, he told us that one of you—a human girl, no less—had killed the Demon King, and now Ketai Hanno seeks our help in securing the throne."

"Yes, that's the reason we came—"

"But tell me, Lady Wren," Lady Dunya interrupts coolly. "How can you have killed the King when we just this morning received a message from the palace, written by the King himself?"

An electric pulse ripples through the hall.

For a moment, I'm sure I've misheard.

"E-excuse me?" Wren replies.

"That…can't be true," Caen utters.

Lady Dunya's gaze sweeps over us all, as ice-cold as the air blowing in from the tall window. "An official notice was brought to us today from the Hidden Palace. Our experts checked the seal and the handwriting. It has been verified as the King's own. As such, it is impossible for him to be dead. Unless he passed away in the last few hours, of course."

"No!" Nitta exclaims.

The same word rises within me, but it gets lodged in my throat, swelling and cutting off air. Memories fly at me, vivid with color and fear, each one a stab in the heart.

The King's mangled, bloody eye.

The snap and tear of cartilage beneath my blade.

Zelle's awful scream: "Finish it!"

I *killed* him. I saw his body. He was dead.

But a tiny, serpentine voice in the corner of my mind whispers, *Was he?*

Shivers pluck my skin as the words sink in. Naja tore me away while I was still attacking him. When Wren and I were escaping the grove, Kenzo keeping her occupied in battle, I had seen the King's body on the ground, blood splattered and immobile. I'd thought—I mean, it had *looked* like he was dead. But what if he wasn't? What if it was just that that I saw? His body, bloodied and immobile, but still conscious, still living. I was too far away to see if his chest still rose and fell with staggered breaths. If his eyelids fluttered, one eye still able to move behind them, chasing dreams.

The King's dreams. *My* nightmares.

Horror wells up inside me. Because if he lived, if there was even a scrap of life left in him, no matter how shredded...

Shamans can't do anything to save someone who's already dead. Every Ikharan knows the moment of death untethers the soul from the body. There is no point to fixing an empty mortal shell. Yet even grievously injured, shamans are able to mend and mold, to fuse ripped flesh back together again.

While we were trapped in the temple, it took Hiro two weeks to reweave the torn skin of my shoulders and fuse my broken rib, each session a few hours long. That was one shaman. The King has hundreds.

Thousands.

And as Caen told me the other day, he is even capturing more. He has as much magic as he desires, and a heart gluttonous for power.

The ground shifts beneath my boots, as though the glass is melting and any second now I'll plunge through the clouds toward the hungry teeth of the mountains. Because if the King didn't die—if *I* failed—then it was all for nothing. The Hannos exposed themselves as traitors. The court didn't collapse. The King could still possibly father an heir. And now getting to him will be a million times harder, because the palace will be on high alert for the rest of his reign. They might even stop his access to Paper Girls, in case one of them would finish what her sister—what *I*—started.

How many times I wished for an end to the Paper Girl tradition. How many nights I've dreamed of a future where girls like me would be free.

Never would I have believed the thought of it actually happening could bring me fear.

Wren and I angle toward each other at the same time, as though pulled by cords. Though her expression is blank, her eyes blaze with so much confusion and horror and deep, unutterable sadness that it sparks a flaming coal of anger in the pit of my stomach.

After all we've been through. How *dare* the King have the audacity to live. How *dare* he take this from us.

Her face still wrested into a composed mask, Wren turns back to the White Wing. "Lady Dunya," she starts into our shocked silence, her voice echoing with bottled emotion, "I don't know what exactly this letter says, but I urge you to listen to what we have to propose. The King's rule has led to a wider gap between castes, and the Sickness has grown worse with every passing year, showing no signs of abating. Even all the way out here, Merrin—the owl demon you captured earlier—has noted the worsening of the air currents. What happens when you cannot even fly anymore in your own lands?"

Commander Teoh's feathers ruffle. Some of the guards clack their beaks, looking as though Wren is mad to suggest that they might not have total control over their skies. But Lady Dunya remains still.

"My father is not seeking glory or dictatorship," Wren continues, gaining strength now. "He simply wants to redistribute power back to the clans. He fights for freedom. Equality. For the restoration of Ikhara to its prior greatness. The longer we do nothing, the faster our earth dies, and the more fractured our people become." She makes a fist. "We *must* act now."

Silence stretches through the hall.

Then Lady Dunya's commanding voice rings out. "Take them to the cells."

Nitta lets out a hiss. Caen bursts into speech, spurting praise of Ketai and the Hannos' cause and why we need the bird demons' help, arguments the White Wing court lets fall over them like half-melted snowflakes.

I stare with uncomprehending eyes. Lady Dunya looks so unaffected; I want to grab her, rattle her, just to see if there's anything inside. How can she remain so detached? Does she not care if the rest of the kingdom falls, as long as her walls remain standing?

To my left, I can see how hard Wren is battling to restrain herself. Ketai told us not to fight unless it was absolutely necessary. We need to win the clans over, not give them further reason to be suspicious of us. She throws me a fierce look, eyes flaring with regret and desperation and love, before our connection breaks as Commander Teoh twists both arms behind my back.

Pain shoots into my shoulders. I struggle, but her taloned grip is unflinching. She snatches a pair of iron cuffs from the belt slung across her chest. Snaps them over my wrists. The cold metal bites into my skin, reminding me of another time I was restrained like this, and it's this that wakes me.

They're locking us away—while the King still lives. He'll send an army to the Hannos' palace for revenge any day now, and my father is there, and Tien, and so many Papers.

It will be a bloodbath.

"Lady Dunya!"

My cry rings off the polished marbled walls.

Commander Teoh starts to twist me around. I know I can't overcome her strength, so instead I fall suddenly limp, throwing her off balance. Taking advantage of her momentary lax grip, I move back. Aim my bundled fists for the place where I stabbed her earlier.

The metal chain bites into her open wound. She hisses, her hold loosening just enough for me to shake her off and dash forward.

I drop to my knees in front of the White Wings' imperious Clan Lady. "Lady Dunya," I beg. "I know you don't know who I am, and my life doesn't mean anything to you. But please, just listen to what I have to say—as one woman to another. As someone else who lived their life in an isolated part of the kingdom, believing the King's reach would never touch them. Who believed they were safe."

The swan demon regards me down the length of her long, beaked nose. Behind me comes the click of Commander Teoh's talons. Lady Dunya flicks her eyes up, and the steps stop.

"Speak," she commands me.

"Th-there are many differences between us," I begin, splaying my fingers across the floor to hide their shaking. The chains around my wrists clink. "I'm not a demon. Not even Steel. But, like you, I am female, and in this kingdom that's a caste of its own. One often lower even than Paper." I blow out an unsteady breath. "I was about your youngest daughter's age when the King's soldiers first came to my village and took my mother. I was your eldest daughter's age when they came back for *me*. They killed my dog. They threatened to kill my family if I tried to resist. That was...just the beginning. Over the next few months, I learned there were many more ways to break a person. Especially a woman."

Lady Dunya's dark eyes glitter.

"I've only had a glimpse of the society you've made here," I say, lifting my chin higher now. "Even so, I can see that what you've created is something special. I understand why you've kept away from the turbulent politics of Ikhara. It's not only because of the terrible casualties of bird demons during the Night War. You've got something more to protect than your lives—your *values*. Your way of life. But you can't keep them safe forever by ignoring what's around you. As the Sickness worsens, the King will only grow more desperate. And when the King is desperate, he becomes fearful. When he's fearful, he thinks only of reasserting his power. Soon, it won't be enough to oppress Papers. He'll turn to Steels, other demon clans. Anywhere he feels dissent toward his rule or weakness to exploit."

"She's right, Mama." The teenage daughter I recognized speaks up. Like her little sister, her voice is high and smooth, coiled with aristocratic intonations. But it's fuller, richer, filled with a passion that takes me by surprise. Her taloned hands are clasped into fists; she grinds them into the arms of her throne. "At weapons practice yesterday, Shifu Pru told me that one of the wolf clans in the mountains was attacked last week. Demons who have only ever shown loyalty to the King."

"I heard that, too, my Lady," comes the voice of the guard holding

Hiro. "The King's soldiers claimed it was in response to an act of treason by a wolf demon soldier whose ancestors belonged to one of the clan families, but they wouldn't give any more details."

"They slaughtered the entire clan!" the daughter declares in a disgusted tone.

Kenzo.

I want to turn around, see from Wren's expression if she's thinking the same as me. But I force myself to remain kneeled. "Please, Lady Dunya. All we ask is that you listen to us. If you don't like what we have to say, we'll leave without a scene."

The hall is as quiet as a tomb, my pulse deafening in my ears.

Finally, Lady Dunya gives a tiny nod. "I will listen to what you have to say."

I shudder with relief. I lower my forehead to the cold glass floor as shocked murmurs fill the room. "Thank you, Lady Dunya," I say breathlessly.

She holds up a hand. "You will attend dinner with us tonight. You can explain your plan then. Be warned—there will be guards watching your every movement. If you threaten any of my clan in any way, they have my permission to attack."

I keep my head bowed as I get to my feet.

"Remove their shackles," she orders. "Take them to guest rooms on the nineteenth level. Give them a maid each, and fresh clothes."

"A little pre-dinner snack would be much appreciated, too," Nitta pipes up. "And perhaps you have a masseuse or two going spare? My feet are aching from all that hiking."

Lady Dunya acts as if she doesn't hear her. As Commander Teoh unlocks my cuffs, the Clan Lady watches me, her piercing eyes sparkling. "What is your name, girl?"

Something within me stills at the word.

Girl. Such a simple title. One I've been labeled all my life. But nowhere was I called it more than at the Hidden Palace: spat from the beaked mouth of Madam Himura, hissed with contempt by Naja, thrown with derision by General Yu. But in the Cloud Palace, with the magnificent Lady Dunya before me and her bold, fierce daughters, I feel for one of the first times the hidden power contained within its single modest syllable.

Because this is what I am. Not a Paper Girl anymore, just "girl." Almost, as I told Lady Dunya, a caste of its own. An oppressed caste, yes, but one braver and bolder and capable of more brilliance than any other in this world.

The faces of all the incredible girls I have known come to my mind: Zelle, Aoki, Lill, Chenna, Zhen and Zhin, Mariko. Even Blue, who, despite everything, was just doing what she could to survive, was simply acting how she knew best within the constraints the world had placed upon her. And of course, I think of *my* girl. Wren.

"My name is Lei," I tell Lady Dunya, before Commander Teoh turns me with a sweep of her feathered arm.

Wren comes to my side as we march back across the glass-floored hall. "You saved us," she says. But like mine, her relief is tainted. She slips her hand into mine, and all resentments from our earlier argument fall away as realization settles over us, cold and final. We face it down in silence, needing the grasp of the other's hand to stop us from dropping to the floor from the unbearable weight of it, the awful truth.

The King is still alive.

You saved us.

My gut curdles at how wrong Wren's words are. Because if the King lives, then it's the very opposite: I have failed. I've condemned us to a harder, darker journey. Everything—everyone—we lost at the palace that night was for nothing. And it means that all this time I felt something following me, I was right. And it wasn't just scary dreams, or the shadow cast by bad memories.

You can't be haunted by the ghost of someone who isn't dead.

TEN

OUR GROUP IS BROUGHT TO A set of rooms in the mid-levels of the palace. Wren asks if the two of us can share one, and guards lead us to a beautiful suite of interlinking chambers, all high ceilings and polished marble floors. Light from the setting sun falls in through the carved windows, striping the floor in rosy bronze. Chiffon curtains hang between each chamber. They flutter as we move through them, two maids accompanying us to light the lanterns mounted to the walls. The rooms are peaceful, but the silence clings to me, thick and sickly. The horror of what we just learned courses through my veins; my blood is suffused with it.

"Wren," I croak. "We should talk."

"Not yet." She avoids my eyes as we arrive at the bedchamber, the room dominated by a grand sunken bed draped with cream sheets. "We need to rest before tonight. It can wait a few hours."

"But the *King*—"

She drops my hand as though burned. "I *know*, Lei," she hisses, and amid the hardness in her voice is a buzz of panic. She presses her lips together, then tilts her head over her shoulder at the maids lighting incense nearby. "Thank you. Could you come back in an hour to take us to bathe?"

They bow. "Of course, Lady Wren."

Once we're alone, Wren stands awkwardly by the curtained archway. I perch on the end of the bed, pulling my tangled hair from my ragged gold band and shaking it out. Wind blows in from the windows, stirring the curtains and the fingers of incense smoke rising from burners in the corners of the room. Wren stands straight, shoulders rolled back. If you didn't know her the way I do, you'd think she was her calm, confident self. But I see the tightness in the line of her lips, the way her chest rises and falls a fraction faster than usual.

I want to throw my arms around her, tell her that it'll be all right. But I know she'll come to me when she's ready. Besides, if I tell her I know everything will turn out fine, it would be a lie.

The King is alive.

My heart clamps around the words. They're as sharp as a sword edge.

Eventually, Wren cants her head toward at me. "You're getting the sheets dirty," she says.

I look in mock horror. "I am? I had no idea! Better not do *this*, then." With a wicked grin, I flop fully back onto the bed, muddy boots and all.

She snorts. "I can't take you anywhere."

"But you know you want to." Understanding it's what she needs from me right now, I play it up, spreading my limbs across the sheets with a sigh. After weeks of sleeping on the frozen forest floor, the pillowy mattress is a welcome change. "Come here," I groan. "You've never felt something this soft."

Ignoring me, Wren crosses to the arch to the right of the bed that leads to a dressing room. "These remind me of the Paper tradition in Ang-Khen for newlyweds," she mutters.

I roll onto my side to look. She's running her fingers down the curtain hanging across the archway. "What tradition?"

"They hang a sheet up in the entrance to the couple's house on their wedding day for them to walk through. It's a sign of purifying themselves for their new married life, which they enter into hand in hand."

"Does it work for two women?"

"Why shouldn't it?"

My lips lift. "How about we try it, then?"

Wren gives me a strange look. "Not now."

I nod, eyes fluttering shut. Suddenly, despite everything, I sense sleep stealing in at the edges of my consciousness. I haven't slept properly since leaving the Hidden Palace, and Caen and I have woken early every morning since we started our journey to train. I stuff my cheek into the silk pillow. "No problem," I mumble. "I'm too tired to get up anyway."

There's the rustle of clothes. The mattress shifts as Wren lies down beside me, curling around my spine. She laces an arm across me. Her fingers slip between mine. "Not because of that," she says, quiet, sad, just as exhaustion overtakes me and I tip into unconsciousness, only half registering her words. "Because it's bad luck to mock a ritual you one day hope to partake in."

After a short but deep sleep, which even the nightmare that's haunted me for the past few weeks doesn't disrupt—my subconscious perhaps knowing I've now got a scarier one to face in real life—Wren and I are woken by our maids. Night has fallen. Lanterns light the hallways as we are taken to a bathing suite, the palace even more hushed than earlier. In the antechamber, the maids strip us of our dirty clothes before leading us through to a large room dominated by a sunken bath. Hot perfumed air hits my nose. I throw my head back to admire the domed ceiling arching overhead, glittering with iridescent gems that mimic the spill of stars outside.

"Just a few more minutes, I beg of you."

"Lord Bo, it's not healthy to be here so long."

"It's not healthy to be at war, but here we are."

Bo's lanky form appears through the steam. A young Steel bird demon crouches beside him, her knees near his head where he's relaxed against the side of the sunken bathing pit, head tipped back over its rim.

Over the weeks of living and traveling together, I've grown used to being in intimate quarters with the others. Still, we've not really been fully naked in front of each other. I snap my hands across my body, even though the steam clouds are doing enough to hide me.

"Lord Bo, *please*—"

"Wren!" Bo beams, spotting us. "Lei!"

As our maids offer us their feathered arms, helping us down into the water, I can't help but think Bo's got it right. The water is a perfect temperature, warm and fragranced with bergamot and something pine-like, a touch of freshness from the forested mountains that surround the palace. Mist lifts off its surface, shifting as Wren and I settle onto the seat ringing the sunken bath, the water covering us up to our collarbones.

The leopard-boy's eyes glint. "I was wondering when you two would get here. Too busy enjoying having a private bedroom again, were you?"

There's a beat of awkward silence.

"Where are the others?" Wren asks stiffly, ignoring the question.

"Oh, they left ages ago. *Amateurs.*"

"Merrin was here?" I ask.

Bo flaps his hand dismissively. "Yes. And don't worry, Feathers isn't hurt. Though I'm amazed he didn't have a heart attack at the sight of *this* masterpiece." The water ripples as he spreads his arms wide to indicate himself, flashing his snaggle-toothed grin. Seeing the concern on our faces, he adds, "The White Wing locked him up in a room somewhere and asked him questions. No torture or anything. They basically just had a chat."

"We don't torture our prisoners," the maid kneeling by Bo's head says crisply.

He flicks her an annoyed look. "You're still here?"

She gets to her feet with a huff. "Fine. I shall leave you here to wrinkle and stew, my Lord, since it seems to be your desire. I'll be waiting in the antechamber when you are ready to leave. Please remember dinner is in one hour's time."

"Ah," Bo says happily. "So I have one hour left to soak."

The feathers dappling the Steel girl's arms rustle. "I thought felines were meant to hate water," she grumbles as she stalks off into the steam.

The other maids bow. "We shall wait for you there, too," they say before following her.

Bo sighs, sinking deeper. "Peace at last. I love being waited on hand and paw just as much as the next demon, but sometimes a cat just wants his own space."

Not just cats, I think, as under the cover of the water I shift closer to Wren. My left arm slinks across her waist. It's been so long since we've been like this, skin to skin, and it calms something deep in my soul. I lay my head into the crook of her neck. She angles her own face to kiss my hair, her breath warm and sweet.

Bo coughs. "Ahem. Would you two like some privacy?"

"Yes, thanks," I say. "That'd be great."

The leopard-boy climbs lazily to his feet. My cheeks redden at his naked form, and I shift my eyes to focus somewhere to the right of him.

"I get it." He shakes his head, water droplets spraying from his fur. "Traveling with your lover while being constantly stuck around the rest of us can't be easy. Take it as a mark of how much I care about the health of your relationship that I'm leaving paradise early for the two of you. Just be sure to remember this if I'm ever in need of the same treatment." He pokes a finger into his ear and tips out a few drops of water. "I may find myself a cutie on this journey yet."

I lift a brow. "Might have even found one already, hmm?"

Bo blinks. For the briefest moment, he looks almost embarrassed. Then he waves a wrist. "If you mean Feathers, he and I are just teasing each other. Nothing would ever happen." The tip of his tail twitches with a shudder. "A bird and a cat, together? The Heavenly Kingdom would collapse from the weight of all the gods and goddesses fainting."

"They've been witness to many worse pairings over the years," Wren says darkly.

The mood sobers instantly. All at once, it feels like the King is right there in the room with us, hidden in a corner, a horn-tipped silhouette with keen eyes glinting from the steam.

I've found you.

"Well," Bo says, breaking the tension, "I'm off to irritate that poor maid some more. May as well annoy as many bird demons as possible while I'm here." He winks. "Don't do anything I wouldn't. And if you find what that is—be sure to tell me later." His lanky silhouette slinks off into the steam.

I shift back to face Wren, my forehead pinched with worry. I lift a hand to smooth the damp tangles of hair from her brow. "I think it's time to talk about it, Wren," I say carefully.

"He's still alive," she replies sharply. "What is there to talk about? We go on with the mission as planned."

"I meant what happened at the palace. What he did to us."

The words—and the memories they bring—twist and writhe in my gut. But I force myself to confront them with calmness. It's easier to be strong when you're doing it for someone else's sake. Perfumed steam drifts around us, a protective veil. Under the water, I reach for Wren's hands, finding them curled into fists. I pry them open and she clamps them back around mine, almost painfully.

When she breaks the quiet, her voice is constricted, a half-echo of its usual assured, husky lilt. "How do you even *talk* about something like this?" She releases a puff of air. Her jaw clicks as she works it, trying to find the words. "I think that was another reason I built up walls around me back at the palace. The hardness kept me from feeling. I was so focused on my goal. I wrapped it around myself like a shield. And now it's gone."

I squeeze her hands. "We have a new goal now, Wren. One we can share the burden of together."

For a moment, she's silent. Then her eyes flash up, and like so many times before, I'm caught by her gaze. Back at the palace, our eyes would meet like this across a room or dining table, and she'd pin me in place with her look. It can be so fierce it'd strike me with the force of a lightning bolt. But this time, I'm frozen not because of its power, but by the *lack* of it.

Tears fill Wren's beautiful brown eyes. They shimmer for a second before they start to fall, cascading down her cheeks. Her face crumples. She lets out a racking gasp that sounds as though it's been torn right from the pit of her belly.

"Oh, my love," I breathe, and bundle her into my arms.

I hold Wren for what feels like hours, letting her release the tight hold she has on herself for perhaps the first time since we've met. I hold her and say nothing, even though it makes me sick to hear her raw, baby-like bawls. Though it wrenches my heart to feel the violent tremors of her body shaking against mine. Even though I know what it is each teardrop of hers means, what her sobs are declaring to the world.

This is a language I understand. A language of pain and horror that I, too, have learned.

That too many girls have had to learn.

When Wren finally falls still, we don't move, still clinging to each other in the water, wrapped in velvet steam.

"He's alive," she whispers.

And it's not like the previous times she spoke those words today. This time, they are full of everything that simple sentence means. The horror and realness of what we've been through. The fact that we'll most likely have to face the demon who did it to us again. Her words are haunted ones, and I feel them in my bones.

A sickening cocktail of hate and terror and shame shoots down my veins. For a moment I'm once again that frightened girl in his bedchambers, trying to drag my soul out of my body so I can pretend the hurt isn't real. That what's happening is happening to someone else, in another lifetime, another world. Not here, not now, not this, not *me*.

But it *was* me.

It was me, and it was Wren, and it was the other girls, my friends, and so many more before us, and no doubt more to come.

"He's still alive," Wren repeats, sounding so hollow and lost it breaks my heart.

I wrap my arms tighter around her. Something dark unspools in the pit of my belly. "It just means we have a second chance," I tell her, my voice cold.

"For what?"

I whisper the word into her ear. "Revenge."

ELEVEN

LIKE ALL OF THE CLOUD PALACE, the Dining Hall is a marvel. From the top of the grand central staircase, we cross a delicate bridge made entirely of glass, the nighttime clouds swirling against the panes, before arriving at a circular tower room, majestic in design. Marble walls stretch so high they could pierce the belly of the Heavenly Kingdom itself. Trees and flowers carved from metal and white stone create the effect of a glittering frozen forest, interspersed between tables of elegantly dressed bird demons.

A Steel servant draped in cream robes leads me and Wren toward a table at the center of the room, raised on a circular silver dais. Overhead, the branches of the metal and stone trees tower high, glistening with opals and pearls and filigree lights, dangling like jeweled fruit. The sound of hushed conversations and rustling feathers fill the room.

Living at the palace accustomed me to being around demons. But having spent the past few weeks with just our group for company, I've forgotten how unsettling it can be to walk into an entire room full of them. I lock my back, eyes fixed firmly ahead. I resist the urge to fiddle with my white hanfu. The skirt is too long, threatening to trip me with each step, and after being bundled in heavy, utilitarian fabrics for so long, the smooth glide of silks against my skin feels strange. It makes me recall nights back in the palace, dressed up for the King and the court in flimsy dresses and robes. Nights I thought I had left behind.

Only an hour has passed since Wren was sobbing in my arms in the bathing chamber, yet from the way she carries herself, no one would ever know. The maids dressed her in a similar hanfu to mine, but with her tall, athletic frame, it makes her look regal, a long-lost ice princess returning to reclaim her palace. She strides confidently beside me. Thick hair tumbles in lustrous waves to the small of her back. While I refused the paints and glosses the maids offered me, Wren instructed them to apply them the way she likes. Light from the hanging lanterns glaze her skin, catching the shimmering powder that dusts her brow and cheekbones and the deep plum-colored gloss on her lips.

"What?" she asks at my staring.

"You look like you own this place," I reply.

"Good. The way we arrived here earlier wasn't how I was hoping to make my first impression on the White Wing. I want to make sure that at least tonight I look like a proper Clan Lord's daughter."

"To intimidate Lady Dunya?"

"Not to intimidate. To impress. Appearance is important for the White Wing."

I arch a brow, looking around the exquisite tower room. "Who'd have guessed?"

Still serious, Wren adds in a low voice, "Appearances are also important for war."

"Lady Wren and Lady Lei," the bird demon announces us with a bow in Lady Dunya's direction. "Open wings."

Lady Dunya inclines her head. "Open sky."

She cuts a striking figure at the head of the table in opalescent silver-white robes spun through with tiny diamonds. The rest of the clan's family are spaced out along the table, each between one of our group. A beam splits my face when I spot Merrin.

As Wren and I pass him, he cocks his feathered head. "Miss me, darlings?"

"Not as much as Bo did," I reply with a wink, and though he rolls his eyes, he seems pleased.

The servant ushers us on to our seats, Nitta and Bo giving us boisterous whistles that make Caen glower as though he's wondering how to murder them from his seat.

Wren is directed to Lady Dunya's side. I'm placed a couple of chairs along, between the Lord and Lady's two teenage daughters. The one to my right gives me a bored look. "Papers in the palace," she drawls. "Has Mama really stooped so low?" She returns her attention to the poorly hidden set of scrolls in her lap. I catch a few lines—something about an eagle demon built like a mountain gathering a princess into his arms, their feathered bodies pressing against each other as they start to kiss.

"Eolah's always reading those."

The swan-girl to my left is unsmiling, her voice high and cool. She's the one I recognized, who spoke up earlier in the Audience Hall about the King's attack on the wolf clan. It's mostly thanks to her that we're sitting here freely, instead of chained in the belly of the White Wings' prison. Still, the way she's glaring at me makes it clear that any declaration of my gratitude will be returned with nothing but scorn.

"Do you like them, too?" I ask, just for something to say.

Her lovely face puckers in disgust. "I have no time for romance or reading," she scoffs. "Old-fashioned pastimes designed to keep women placid. Especially Clan Ladies' daughters."

From my own experience, I know both romance and reading to

do the very opposite. They can light a fire in you, ignite your soul with want and awareness and strength. Instead, I only say, "Your mother doesn't seem like the sort to want to keep you placid."

"Oh, this?" She waves a slender hand tipped with talons, perfume wafting off her powdered feathers. "*This* is all part of it. We can do whatever we like here, rule however we want. But only here. The Cloud Palace and these mountains are all we know. At the end of the day it's still living with your wings clipped. My mother's disinterest in involving us in Ikharan politics seeps into everything we do. It breeds passivity. And I hate passivity. You know," she adds abruptly, with a jut of her chin, "I'm being trained to take over from Commander Teoh when she retires."

I offer her a smile. "Congratulations."

"Oh, keep up," she huffs. "It's great if you like to be in charge of a tiny army that never sees any action. If you enjoy being nothing more than a pumped-up bodyguard. But what's the point of having wings if we're not allowed to fly?" Her voice softens for the first time. "I mean, really, properly, *fly*?"

Her words remind me of the character in my Birth-blessing pendant. How trapped I felt in the palace, having to hide my love for Wren and my desire to fight against the injustices of the King and his rule. Even without the King, that place would have felt like a tomb.

"I know what you mean," I answer, muted.

The swan-girl's dark eyes flash. "I thought you might." She jerks her chin. "I'm Qanna."

"Lei."

She picks up the crystal glass in front of her and tilts it toward me. "Open wings."

I lift my own glass. "Open sky."

Her round, heavy-lashed eyes don't leave mine as we take a draw of the crystalline sake.

"So," Qanna says as servers begin to weave through the hall, platters of delicious-smelling foods balanced in their palms, "You're
the one who tried to kill the Demon King."

A tight feeling crawls up my throat. I'm not used to someone cutting straight to the point in this way. The clan daughter's directness
reminds me of Blue—not to mention the haughty way she keeps
looking at me.

"Yes," I answer.

The second it's out, Qanna leans over, shooting her sister a smirk.
"See, Eo? Told you. That's three days of civic assistance duty you
owe me."

Eolah doesn't look up. "Whatever. I like civic assistance duty."

Qanna rolls her eyes at me. "See what I have to deal with?"

A server sets down the last of the various dishes now laid out
across the table: steamed angel fish swimming in soy sauce, turnip
cake fashioned into the shape of flowers, the curled ears of pork
dumplings floating in a clear broth. Qanna snatches the silverware,
moodily spooning large portions onto both of our plates.

"I made a bet with my sister that you were the one who attacked
the King," she explains. "Everyone thought it must be Ketai Hanno's
daughter, but I knew it was you from the moment you spoke up. And
there's your eyes, of course. They're really something, do you know
that? You might be human but you have the spirit of a demon." Hardly
pausing for breath, she adds curtly, "Well? Are you going to try again?"

It takes me a second to realize what she means. My gut twists as
I picture Wren earlier, shaking in my arms. I pick up my chopsticks
and clamp them around a stewed shiitake mushroom. "Yes," I answer,
popping it into my mouth and biting hard. "And this time, I won't fail."

"Good." Qanna's eyes search my face. "Men like that don't
deserve to live."

The dark intensity in her tone sends shivers down my spine.

"The world would be a far better place if us women had control of it, don't you agree? And we—our clan—have the power to make it so. With the court as weak as it is right now, it would be even easier. Many of us think so. Commander Teoh, Shifu Pru, half of the guards I've spoken to. It's only *Mama* who won't let us." Her voice reeks with derision.

"She's trying to protect you," I say, but Qanna only scowls.

"When there is danger, you stand up to face it. Not hide away in the mountains to pretend what you can't see doesn't exist."

We both look to where Wren and Lady Dunya are sitting. From the speed at which their lips move, I can tell their conversation is intense. The hall whirls with noise and energy, but Wren and Lady Dunya look separate from it all, completely focused on their own exchange.

"Do you think your mother will agree to join us?" I ask Qanna.

"Yes. Unfortunately."

"Unfortunately?"

The swan-girl stabs a marinated cube of tofu with more aggression than it probably deserved. "Out of all the alliances to make, we're going to put our faith in a human man?"

I bristle at this, though more because of the human part than anything. Out of a sense to defend Wren and her father, I say, "Do you even know anything about Ketai Hanno?"

Qanna shrugs. "What do I need to know? He's a Paper, and a man. *You* managed to impress me. You might be human, but you're a woman, and that gives you far more strength than he'll ever be capable of. Not to mention perspective. Only women truly understand the cruelties of the world. The depths of people's greed and desire, what dark things they can motivate someone to do." She glowers, and throws her mother another contemptuous look. "Does Hanno think all the clans are just going to calmly piece out Ikhara once the war is over? That we're going to be all, 'oh, here you go, here's your share of the kingdom back, now please play nice and leave everyone else's alone?' Please. We all know how this is going to turn out."

She spears a piece of still-wriggling eel-tail with her chopsticks and catches it in her painted beak. A line of blood trickles down her chin. "It'll be another Night War," she finishes, wiping it with a napkin, her face sour. "Another pointless, ruinous war. And at the end of it, Ikhara will be even more fractured and dying than before, and we'll have a new dictator lording it over everyone—only this time, a Paper one."

At that moment, I sense someone watching me. My eyes swipe up, meeting Wren's across the table. Her face is shining. She wears a small, triumphant smile. The lights overhead limn her in pale gold, casting streaks of starlight through her hair, and her radiance makes some deep part of me ache. She looks far more like Ketai's Moonchosen than I ever could be.

Wren is mouthing something to me when Lady Dunya speaks, and she shifts her attention back to the Clan Lady. But I don't need to hear her words. Her look has already told me everything.

Lady Dunya has agreed to ally with us.

I turn back to my plate, Qanna's words ringing in my ears. And instead of the elation I thought I would feel at this news, something uneasy slithers to life in my belly. I set my chopsticks on the table, swallowing down a lurch of nausea, and drain the rest of my sake.

TWELVE

AFTER DINNER, LADY DUNYA INVITES US to a private terrace not far from the Dining Hall, where she and Wren announce their alliance to the group. The others receive the information far better than I did, though Nitta and Bo only just manage to display a somewhat grudging acceptance as we lift our glasses to our new feathered comrades. Still, only Qanna looks openly disgusted with the news.

"All hail the Paper King," she mutters to me under her breath.

Ketai requested the clans send at least a third of their armies to the Hannos' palace within the first week of agreeing to ally with us as a gesture of allegiance. Lady Dunya begins negotiations with Wren and Caen, and the rest of us disperse across the terrace. Merrin falls into conversation with Lord Hidei. Hiro wanders over to the balcony edge, his slim fingers wrapping around the filigreed iron patterns of the railing he's barely tall enough to look over. As Qanna and I cross the terrace to a cushioned seating area, I curse the bird clan's love of glass-bottomed floors. My head is already woozy from the sake at dinner. It doesn't help when the sky whirls inches below your boots, the dark clouds occasionally parting to reveal a stomach-churning drop.

I breathe a sigh of relief as we flop onto the cushions. Eolah curls up behind us, still glued to her story. Beyond the railing, the night sky is an impenetrable misty expanse.

"See how easy it is to forget that there's a whole world out there?" Qanna says, gazing out.

Horribly out-of-tune yowling makes us look around. Nitta and Bo sway toward us, arms slung around each other's shoulders. I'm not sure what song it is they're singing—or if the noise they're making can even be considered singing. So much for Bo's true or false game earlier.

"So many princesses," he slurs, knocking into us as he and his sister slump on the cushions. "It's hard to keep track."

Qanna jolts to her feet. "Watch where you're sitting, *Cat*. And I'm not a princess."

Bo squints. "You sure look like one."

"Don't felines have terrible eyesight?" the swan-girl retorts.

"Still better than birds' smell," Nitta points out with a giggle.

In a perfect echo of Merrin's joke in the temple, Qanna lifts her head imperiously and shoots back, "Then you two really must reek if *I* can smell you."

Nitta and Bo let out indignant—and frankly, *impressed*—gasps as Qanna stalks off. Sprawling across the cushions, they turn their attention to a very disgruntled Eolah.

I get to my feet, wobbly. Hiro is still alone at the railing. The filigreed iron has been woven prettily with fresh flowers—all white, of course. As I walk over, he inspects one blossom, cupping it with gentle fingers. Then, quickly, he breaks it off and tucks it away into his robes.

"A souvenir?" I ask, joining him.

He avoids my eyes. "I...like flowers."

"Me, too. I used to work in an herb shop." He glances up at me with surprise, and I go on, leaning against the balcony, "One of my favorite times of year was the spring flower harvest. I'd spend hours in the meadows around our village picking the freshest young buds of camellia and primrose." I sigh. "The colors. The *smells*."

"Sounds like a nice life," Hiro says softly.

"It was. I hope to get it back someday."

The shaman boy stares out. Though his expression remains blank, I can sense the shifting emotions beneath it, and I feel suddenly guilty talking like this. Because while my life back in Xienzo is one I could rebuild after the war, Hiro lost his entire family. His entire clan.

"Are you happy with the Hannos?" I ask.

He shifts, straightens, seems to shake off some of his melancholy as he replies briskly, "It is not a shaman's business to pursue happiness."

"I'm sorry," I start, but he's already walking away.

Shifu Caen appears at my side. He glances over his shoulder at Hiro's retreating back. "Everything all right over here?" When I don't reply, he sighs, propping his elbows on the railing and rubbing his beard absentmindedly. "Not everyone seems pleased with tonight's turn of events."

"Qanna?" I shrug. "She's not that keen on her clan supporting a Paper man she doesn't know."

"I meant you, Lei."

Caen's dark, amethyst-flecked eyes watch me knowingly. I rub my hands over my arms. The night is cold, the winter chill breaking through the burners and lanterns dotting the terrace for warmth. All the others have wrapped heavy shawls or cloaks around their shoulders, but my own fell off back by the cushions.

Noticing me trembling, Caen unclips his cloak and drapes it around me.

I huddle into it gratefully. "It's just...I don't know Ketai like the rest of you. And I've seen what power does to people. I don't want—"

"Ketai to end up like the King?" Caen's face is kind. "You are right, Lei. You don't know Ketai like the rest of us. So you'll have to trust us when we tell you that *we* trust him. That he's a brilliant, compassionate, dedicated man, who wants to make things right in Ikhara again."

"But *can* things be made right? Sometimes things will remain forever changed by what's happened to them. You can try and make amends. Rebuild. Relearn. But there are some scars that won't heal. No matter how much someone wants them to."

There's a long pause. Then Shifu Caen asks gently, "Are we still talking about Ketai Hanno?"

I turn away. "We'll be on the road again soon, right?" I say, switching subjects. "Tomorrow?"

"Lady Dunya suggested the day after, so we can have another day to discuss our plans." Caen looks across to where Nitta and Bo are trying to teach Lord Hidei a traditional Janese dance, Merrin watching smugly until Bo snatches his hand and makes him join them. "And something tells me some of us won't be able to get out of *bed* tomorrow, let alone off a mountain." His lips lift, but my own twist.

"Oh, no," I say.

"What's wrong?"

"I'm going to be sick."

In one fell swoop, Caen lifts me up and holds me over the balcony. I vomit noisily. Tears leak from my eyes, my tongue turning sour as I retch until nothing comes up but acrid air. Carefully, Caen sets me back down. Thanks to the noise of the wind and no one else being nearby, the others haven't noticed. Still, my cheeks burn.

"I'm so sorry," I mumble, swiping my hand across my mouth.

He rubs my back. "Don't think anything of it. But you should get to bed. Shall I fetch Wren?"

I shake my head. Doing so makes the whole world spin again, and I stop, holding my head between my palms. "She's talking with Lady Dunya."

"If you're sure."

Taking utmost care not to look down at the glass floor, I shuffle across the terrace. A guard leads me back to my suite and I stumble through the rooms, wafting aside the gauzy curtains of lace until I reach the bedchamber. Then I tug my robes loose, letting them fall where I stand until I'm just in my small silk underslip. The second I plant face-first onto the mattress, I spin into darkness.

Movement wakes me, along with the muzzy warmth of Wren's body. Her ocean scent fills my lungs. I stir, half-delirious, my dreams sticking to me as I curl into her and sleepily return her soft, sweet kisses. She pulls me to her chest with a sigh.

"One down, Lei," she whispers. Her voice shivers with excitement. "Can you believe it? And possibly the most important allegiance at that. Bird demons are fierce warriors, but they also bring a huge tactical advantage. According to my father, the Oshai Clan and the Janese Flame Feathers already pledged their loyalty to the King, but the White Wing are more than three times their numbers combined. We needed this, Lei." I feel relief ripple through her body in the way she relaxes, plants more kisses in my hair. "We're doing it. We're building the army that will take down the King's court once and for all."

I stiffen. "And what court will it be after that?" I mutter. "Your father's? Our new Paper King?"

Wren draws back, her tone sharpening to match mine. "What do you mean?"

"You know what I mean."

My vision is blurry in my post-sleep, still half-drunk state. I rub a hand over my face, trying to focus, as she shifts back farther, propping herself on one elbow.

"No," she says, "I don't."

"I'm worried, Wren. About your father, his intentions. Lady Dunya's daughter told me—"

"Lady Dunya's daughter?"

"You know, the eldest one." I fumble my words. "She told me we shouldn't put our faith in Ketai. That he was the wrong person to be leading this war."

"The girl said that?"

I push back a lock of hair from my face. "In a less polite way. She's against the alliance between the White Wing and the Hannos. You should be careful. If she has enough sway with her mother she might even make the whole thing fall through—" I cut off to hiccup.

"You're drunk."

The words hit me like a smack, even though Wren delivers them without bitterness or derision. It's their truth that stings. Though she hasn't moved, something within her seems to have shrunk back, as though withering from me, withdrawing from my presence.

"Maybe I am," I say, pushing myself up clumsily. I try to wet my lips, but my mouth is dry. "But I know what I'm saying. I've been worried about it ever since I met your father. He reminds me of—"

"Don't say it." Wren's beautiful face hardens into ice. In one sleek motion, she slides off the bed, her shadowy figure in the dark of the room looming like the ghost of a lover at the edge of the bed. "I know you don't mean it. I know it's just the alcohol talking. But I don't want you to say it, because if you do, I'm not sure I can forgive you, and I don't want to do that to us." She rubs a hand at her throat. "I love you, Lei."

I jolt forward, immediately sorry. "I love you, too—"

But Wren steps back. "Not right now." She pivots, heading for the door to the other rooms of the suite.

"Where are you going?" I ask.

"The terrace. I need some air." She pauses for a moment, then cocks her head in a strange way. In the night-cloaked room, her eyes are gleaming crescents of white. "You have to remember what we're fighting for, Lei. Who we're fighting against. So my father isn't perfect. I can admit that. But he's a whole lot better than the demon he's trying to take down."

The lace curtain flutters as she steps out of the room before I have a chance to reply.

The rest of the night, my dreams are dark and twisted. I envision bird demons flying over the mountains bordering the White Wings' castle, carrying the broken bodies of my friends from the Hidden Palace. I see Wren creeping under the sheets beside me, blood on her face and hands, the metallic smell almost unbearable. I dream of Baba, Tien, and Ketai Hanno, dressed in armor on the backs of battle-horses, riding through a burning landscape littered with corpses and laughing, laughing, laughing.

When I wake the next morning, the sunlight startles me. I pull the sheets over my head with a groan. Everything is blurry, the previous night an incoherent mess. Moments slip from my mind's fingers when I try to grasp them. The one thing I do remember for certain is my argument with Wren.

I feel her stir on the other side of the bed where she's been sleeping. She shifts closer, tentatively at first. When I don't move away, she pulls me against her and I grab her back in a rush, twisting around and pushing my face into the scoop of her neck.

"I'm so sorry," I murmur.

Her fingers tangle in my hair. "*I'm* sorry. If you have worries, we should talk about them. If you're not sure about my father—or anything, for that matter—just ask me. I'll do my best to—"

The rest of her sentence is drowned by a clattering alarm.

We untangle, both of us scrambling up. The sound is almost like ceremonial bells: high and pealing. But there's a shrillness to them that makes it clear they're a warning.

Wren pulls on a robe. I shove the hair back from my face, my heart ticking a frantic beat, as I fit my arms through the sleeves of my own far less smoothly than Wren did. As we run into the entrance room of our suite, the door flies open.

Commander Teoh storms inside, her face vivid with anger.

"Commander!" Wren shouts over the clashing alarm. "What's going on?"

The hawk-woman is backed by two more of her guard. They stride forward, crowding us, as the Commander fixes us with her dark, piercing stare. Morning light catches on her painted feathers, the silver tip of the spear at her back.

"Lady Eolah was found dead by her maids," she informs us, her clipped voice at odds with the grief and rage playing across her features. "Lady Dunya requires your presence in the Audience Hall immediately."

My stomach plummets. I turn to swap a horrified look with Wren, but her stare is fixed ahead, her mouth clamped.

"I'm sorry to hear that," she starts slowly.

Commander Teoh barks over her. "Save your apologies!"

My mouth falls open. "You—you can't think we had anything to do with it!"

But the bird-woman turns her back on us, motioning for the guards to follow, and the three of them march us out of the room to the awful ringing of the palace alarm.

THIRTEEN

THE GLASS FLOOR IS CLEAR BENEATH our feet as we cross the Audience Hall in terse silence, only a light mist wreathing the spikes of the mountain crevasses below. The rest of our group is ahead, lined up before the clan family's thrones. They're on their knees, a bird-form guard behind each of them pressing a spear to the back of their necks. My heart clenches—it looks so much like an execution. Voices carry across the light-washed room: Bo and Nitta's frantic assurances, Caen and Merrin's steady pleas. Only Hiro is quiet, his bald head bowed.

Save for Lady Dunya's, the thrones are empty. My eyes pause on Eolah's. It seems bigger than the others somehow, glowing almost with her absence. I picture her reading last night. Did she manage to finish the story before she was killed? It's a ridiculous thought, but it strikes me as important.

The guards thrust Wren and me directly in front of Lady Dunya. She sits imperiously, statuesque, and yet grief and anger flood off her in waves, so forceful they're physically tangible. Her pearl-white feathers sparkle in the sunlight, but her eyes are a deep, pitiless black as she glares down at us.

"L-Lady Dunya," I begin, ignoring the warning look Wren cuts me. "You've got to believe us. We had *nothing* to do with Eolah's death—"

"*Stop.*"

The command is low, barely more than a whisper. Yet at once all noise in the hall ceases.

Lady Dunya gets to her feet. She moves slowly. Deliberately. The air around her seems to vibrate with the incredible power of her contained energy, the shriek of emotions she's holding back. She towers over us as she steps forward, the snap of her talons ricocheting off the marble floor as loud as whip-cracks, as sharp as the breaking of some god's great spine.

"My daughter is dead." The Clan Lady's voice is void of emotion; she could be talking about the weather. But like Eolah's throne, its absence makes it even more keenly felt. "She did not die naturally, nor peacefully. Her maids found her cold in her bed, her mouth open in a scream, her eyes wide. A mark was branded into her chest."

A mark? A ripple goes through our group at this.

"Her heart was frozen in her body," Lady Dunya continues. "There were no other physical signs of what might have killed her. Because of the mark—which doesn't appear to be dyed or printed on her feathers in any way—we can assume that my daughter was killed by magic."

A few of the demons around us make signs, mutter prayers under their breath.

Lady Dunya studies us, her dark eyes dangerous. "The practice of shamanism is prohibited in our clan, and we only employ from a select few as and when our needs arise. But no matter. I trust our people. None of them would hurt Lady Eolah. So I have to wonder, with the first guests to stay with us in more than a year, and at least one of them capable of shamanism, could it be merely coincidence that last night one of my innocent daughters was murdered by magical means? Wren Hanno," she finishes coolly, and the lack of a title is noticeable, "you may answer."

I skim my eyes to Wren. Even with a weapon drawn upon her, she sits confidently, chin lifted, chest forward. Her dark waves tumble down her back, stray strands picked up by the wind coming in through the grand window behind the thrones. Looking at her, I know with absolute certainty she'll be able to convince Lady Dunya we had nothing to do with Eolah's death.

Then she says, "You're right. It's no coincidence."

The hall erupts. Nitta, Bo, and Merrin surge against their restraints, letting out cries of disbelief. Caen whips his head around, barking Wren's name. Even Hiro turns, his pale gray eyes wide and alert. The guards wrestle them back into place, but the noise doesn't lessen, with everyone arguing.

Wren seems oblivious to the commotion she's made, still staring at Lady Dunya with absolute focus.

"Explain yourself," the swan-woman commands over the chaos.

"Think about it, Lady Dunya," Wren says, calm and cool. "We came to your palace to seek your support in a war against the Demon King's court. The very night we secure your allegiance, one of your daughters is killed. How self-sabotaging—and not to mention, completely illogical—would it be for us to have done that? We'd just gotten what we came here for. Why would we immediately ruin your trust in us?"

Lady Dunya's expression doesn't change, but some of the other bird demons fall quiet.

"I am so sorry for your daughter's death," Wren continues. "I am especially sorry, because my mother was killed in the same way, just before the turn of the New Year."

"I...heard of Lady Bhali's death," Lady Dunya acknowledges after a long pause.

Wren nods. "My father has kept the details of how she died quiet. But I share that secret with you now. Like your daughter, my mother was found in the morning by her maids in her bed, untouched except for a mark on her chest."

The hall is utterly still now.

"How do I know you're not making this up to throw suspicion off of your group?" Lady Dunya asks.

"Lady Eolah's bedroom. No one has been allowed inside it since she was found?"

"Only our doctors, a priestess, and our family."

"They're still with her?"

"Yes."

"And the maids who found her?"

"We have kept them for questioning."

"Then no one in the palace apart from you knows what the mark on her chest looks like."

"No."

"So," Wren goes on, her voice steady, "how would I know that the mark is the Bull King's insignia?"

Again, angry shouts bound off the marble walls.

"You would know if you were the killer!" Commander Teoh exclaims, pushing her spear harder against Wren's neck.

"Stop."

This time, Lady Dunya's command is not leveled at us, but at the Commander.

The clamor in the room dies. Hesitantly, Commander Teoh lowers her weapon. "My Lady?"

Lady Dunya looks back at Wren. "I believe her. The Hannos have no tactical advantage to gain from murdering one of my daughters. Especially not the same night we agreed to ally with them. We also had guards stationed outside their rooms all night, and none of them reported any of them leaving. Lower your weapons," she orders.

Relief floods me as the pinch of the blade releases. I slump with a gasp, while the others relax, rubbing their necks or, in the case of Nitta and Bo, turning to glare at the bird-guards behind them. But none of us say anything. Our victory feels too delicate just yet.

Lady Dunya and Wren continue to watch each other. Though she could, Wren doesn't get up, and I understand the message she's communicating: I am submitting to you. I am not the one in power here, and I understand that. I respect that.

"I presume you also trust none of your comrades to have a hidden agenda that would benefit from my daughter's death?" Lady Dunya asks.

"I trust them all completely," Wren answers, with a pride that swells my heart.

"Then you think it was the King."

Wren's mouth is set in a grim line. "Not just because of the mark. You were right to be suspicious, Lady Dunya. I agree that someone could have made it look as though the King sent the killer, to turn you against him. But it seems too much of a coincidence this happened the night we arrived. Someone must be tracking us."

A shiver licks up my spine, remembering all those times I felt eyes on me in the forest.

"The King's people are aware of what we're doing," Wren continues. "Even if they don't know our exact plans, they know my father will be campaigning for powerful clans like yours to join our side."

"So the King wanted us to suspect you so we'd break our alliance?"

"That's one possibility."

"The other?"

"The King *wanted* you to know the murderer came from him."

There are a few gasps at this. Lady Dunya's eyes flash darkly.

"He knows a war is coming," Wren explains. "He, too, will be campaigning now to secure as many clans as possible to fight for his side."

"Killing our children is not the best way to get Clan Lords to ally with you," Lady Dunya replies, and for the first time there's a tremor in the bird-woman's voice. Her shoulders stiffen. She angles away for a moment, features glazed by the morning sun. When she turns back, her face is composed once more.

"Most people would think that," Wren agrees somberly. "But the King is not most people. He rules Ikhara by power and force. Through fear and cruelty. We've all seen this. Some of us have felt it, too." She startles me by reaching for my hand. "As Paper Girls, Lei and I know more than anyone how the King gets what he wants. It is not through kindness, or clever politics, or fairness. The King *takes* what he wants, and he doesn't ask first. This is the message he is sending you with Lady Eolah's death—that he can ruin everything you love if you don't bow down to his wishes." Her words drop as hard as stones. "This is what we're fighting against. This is why we need you to join us. Why we cannot let him win."

Silence rings out. Wren grips my fingers so tightly I don't know whether she's trying to assure herself or me. Sunlight gleams off the glass floor and polished walls, but when Lady Dunya eventually speaks, her words are more radiant even than the light streaming in through the windows; they send golden light sparking down my veins.

"We will not let him win, Lady Wren. We will fight alongside you and the Hannos. And we will burn everything the King has built to the ground."

As Lady Dunya rises, there's the rustling of feathers as the rest of the bird demons in the room kneel. The ones with weapons take their spears and spikes from their backs and hold them upright in front of them in what must be a clan gesture of loyalty. But when Lady Dunya herself bends, holding out a hand, it is not to brandish a weapon but to help Wren to stand.

Wren blinks at the Clan Lady's beautifully manicured talons. Then she grasps her hand, rising to her feet. Lady Dunya brings both hands to her forehead and makes a small bow, which Wren returns.

Then the swan-woman turns to me. Her hand is warmer than I expected. "Thank you, Lady Lei. For convincing me to hear Lady Wren out." Looking between Wren and me, the coldness in her face finally breaks. A muscle in her cheek spasms as tears spring to her eyes, her shoulders sinking. "You are welcome to remain in the palace until tomorrow morning to prepare for your departure. However, I think it best you remain in your rooms. I hope you understand. We will make sure you have all you need, and I can offer you carriages to bring you to your next destination. As discussed, we will send a message to Ketai Hanno once you are a safe distance away that he can expect to receive our soldiers within a week. Is that everything?"

"More than enough," Wren answers. "Thank you for your generosity, Lady Dunya."

She nods distractedly. "Now I must go to be with my family." A crack runs through her words, but she keeps her chin high, the tears within her dark eyes refusing to break. "It is time for me to do the worst thing a parent could ever imagine."

She doesn't have to finish her sentence. Though I'm not a mother, I understand—even if I can't fully comprehend—the agony of grieving your child.

FOURTEEN

AOKI

Aoki's breath misted in the chilled air as she crossed the bathing courtyard. Half buried under snow, its wooden tubs sat empty and unused, looking like the discarded shells of strange ocean creatures. A light patter of flakes and her quick steps were the only sounds to break the stillness, the courtyard—just like the rest of Paper House—eerily quiet for this late in the morning. There was no wind to rustle the bamboo stalks. No birds wheeling noisily overhead. No laughter or chatter amid splashing water and wet footsteps across the floorboards, the morning soundtrack she'd grown so fond of.

At first, the quietness had unnerved her. She'd jumped at every little noise, stuck close to the others at all times, scared to be alone. But as with most of the changes after the Moon Ball, she'd gotten used to it over the weeks since. Now, her eyes only briefly flitted over the tubs. A familiar stab of loss pierced her before she pushed it away with a shiver and a sniff. Not bothering to stamp the snow from her shoes, she readjusted her grip on the cloth-wrapped bundle in her arms and stepped into the house.

It was dim inside, the narrow corridors lit only from weak winter light filtering in through the slatted windows. The silence was even thicker here, the building devoid of its usual activity. But when she turned into the hallway that housed their bedrooms, voices sounded from the far end—Chenna's room. She crossed the hallway. Only one door was open. As she passed, she did her best to ignore it and the empty room that lay beyond, even though it throbbed at her consciousness like a bad tooth.

This was an absence she had failed to get used to.

Aoki plastered a big smile across her face before sliding open Chenna's door. "Delivery for room one!" she sang, bursting in with the package proudly lifted.

Two of the girls inside laughed, while the third grimaced. "You have to stop doing that, Aoki! You'll give me a heart attack."

Aoki gave her an apologetic look. "Sorry, Chenna."

Still, the dark-skinned girl's face was warm as she got up along with the other two to see what Aoki had brought.

"Please say there's fresh fruit," Zhen muttered as Aoki knelt and began unwrapping the cloth. "I'd take a rotting banana at this point, it's been so long since we've had any." She looked to the girl beside her, who shared almost exactly the same face, their petite features set with doll-like symmetry: small, straight noses; rosy lips with pinched Cupid's bows; alabaster skin so delicate it was almost transparent. Their long dark hair was tied back. "I've been dreaming about Mama's jambu tree again, Zhin. Remember how we used to avoid the courtyard it was in because brother told us its fruits were actually the shrunken heads of children who displeased their parents?"

Her twin sister laughed. "We didn't eat jambu again until we were fifteen."

Zhen sighed. "I'd happily eat the whole tree now."

"Even if they *are* shrunken children's heads," Zhin agreed.

Chenna was frowning at them. "You two are strange."

Aoki, glad to be the bearer of good news, held up a green, spike-shelled fruit, which Zhin promptly grabbed. "Jackfruit!" she announced happily. "Kami said that nice lion demon in the teahouse next door gave it to her. And she found some mangosteen thrown out on the street. They're overripe, but—"

"Careful!" Chenna chided.

Zhen had found the purple fruit in the bag and was already crushing one open between her hands, the juice—notorious for leaving the most stubborn of stains—dripping down her wrist. She wiped it on her robes and kept on eating. "What does it matter?" she said between bites. "It's not like anybody is around to notice."

In an instant, the mood sobered.

"Mistress Eira and Madam Himura could come back any time," Chenna said after a pause, her thick brows knitted.

The girls glanced instinctively at the door. But there was no tall shadow behind its rice paper panel, no click of taloned feet on teak. The hallway was still. Blue's room was silent as usual, and the only other people who were still in Paper House were their maids, whose quarters were a few corridors away and whose numbers had diminished to three. The others had run back to their families the night of the Moon Ball, including Aoki's maid. Lei's maid, Lill, had been taken away by the guards that same night.

No one knew what had happened to her. Aoki hoped she was safe.

She hoped *all* of those who'd disappeared that night were safe.

"That's what we said the first few days," Zhin reminded them. "How many weeks has it been now?"

Aoki pushed down the rising flush of panic that accompanied any talk about their situation. "They could still come back," she murmured, tears pricking her eyes. Then she sniffed, and shot a defiant glare at the twins. "Chenna's maid didn't risk her life to steal those fruits just for you two, you know."

Looking guilty, Zhen and Zhin handed Aoki and Chenna what was left of the fruits.

They parceled out the rest of the things Aoki had fetched from the kitchens: pickled vegetables, salted dried meats, cold chrysanthemum tea brewed before the staff left. The fresh food was long gone, and only Chenna and her maid Kami knew how to cook, so most lunches and dinners they ate plates of rice together in one of the abandoned sitting rooms.

As they ate, the mood lifted. Their conversation was careful not to stray toward any dangerous topics. It was *almost* normal. But their smiles disappeared a second too soon, their laughter a little too shrill.

When they finished, Aoki picked up the portion of food she'd set aside and got to her feet.

Zhen gave her a sideways look. "I don't know why you still bother with her. It's not like she ever thanks you, or the maids."

Aoki worried her bottom lip. "Someone has to help her."

"You know she'd leave us to starve if it was up to her," Zhin said.

"Luckily it's not, then," Chenna replied, the curtness in her voice making the twins fall silent. She got up, sliding something into Aoki's free hand. "Tell her to use it sparingly. It's the last batch."

"Kami told me she was going to check the rest of the gardens, too," Aoki said, hopeful. "Just in case the wind transferred the seeds…"

Chenna shook her head. "I helped her look yesterday. We didn't find anything. Of course, neither of us are exactly experts on the subject. Not like—" She cut off, worry crossing her features as she realized what she was saying; whose name she had almost mentioned.

Aoki felt her heart squeeze. But she nodded, forcing her breath to remain even. "It's all right. I know L-Lei"—she pushed it out— "only taught her a few things with herbs."

Looking relieved, Chenna smiled. "She's going to ask the women who have been helping us. I bet one of them will be able to source some more." She touched Aoki's arm. "Don't worry. Blue will be back to normal soon."

"From the amount of scowling she does," Zhin grumbled, "you'd think she already was."

Aoki left Chenna's room and crossed to the opposite door. She knocked on the doorframe. After a few beats, she knocked again.

"I'm not hungry," came a curt voice from within.

It was as good as any welcome she was likely to get. "Good morning to you, too!" she trilled, sliding the door open.

A pale girl scowled at her from across the room where she was sitting on the floor under the window, her bony knees drawn to her chest, a fur coat draped over her as a blanket. The long azure-black hair Aoki used to envy so much had grown tangled and dull.

"Gods," Blue complained with an eye-roll. "Why won't you lot let me wither away peacefully?"

Aoki couldn't help but laugh. "Don't be so dramatic." She set the food down and held out the medicine Chenna and Kami had made. "We've used all the herbs, so take your time with this batch." Her voice was earnest. "We're going to do what we can to get you more, though. I promise."

Blue took the package. Aoki didn't miss how even this small

movement seemed to pain her, the wince as she moved her leg a little too much. The girl sat back carefully, dark eyes glinting from shadow-rimmed sockets.

"Still bad?" Aoki asked tentatively.

"I'm fine. It's just a cut."

"A cut you got four weeks ago from a *sword*."

Blue's scowl deepened. "How nice of you to remind me."

Aoki hovered over her. "Do you need...I can help you clean it, maybe—"

"I said I'm *fine!*" Blue snapped, harder now. Her eyes were dangerously narrow.

Aoki knew that look. She'd been on the receiving end of it many times in her life at the palace, both before and after the New Year. Before, it usually accompanied a scathing comment of some sort, most likely about what Aoki was wearing or a mistake she'd made at a dinner with court officials. Now, though, it was almost as if Blue were lost without her usual modes of attack. She still sneered and snapped and scowled her way through every interaction, but her edges were jagged, her demeanor less controlled. There was something broken about her, as though any moment she would either collapse into screams or tears, or both.

When guards had brought all the Paper Girls—well, almost all of them—back to Women's Court during the attack on the Floating Hall, they ordered them to stay inside until further notice. Aoki, Chenna, Zhen, and Zhin had been too distressed to notice Blue had been wounded in the fight. She'd squirreled herself away in her room for the next two nights as the girls waited and waited for news that would never come. Only after their panic had cleaved, giving way to the simmering sort of resigned dread that could be worked around, did Aoki and the girls finally check on her. Immediately,

Aoki felt guilty for leaving her alone for so long. The floorboards of her bedroom were dark with dried blood, and Blue was sickly and quivering, a deep wound in her left calf oozing pus.

Now, Aoki's eyes swept over the floorboards. They'd done their best to clean up, but the stains were visible, grayish patches against the brown. Guilt nicked at her again.

"Please, Blue," she said. "Let us know if you need anything. We're all in this together, you know—"

Running footsteps in the corridor outside cut her off.

"Mistresses!" a panicked voice called. "Mistresses, hurry!"

Across the hall, Chenna and the twins rushed out. After blinking a few times at Blue, Aoki stumbled into the corridor to find Kami.

The Steel girl was panting, snowflakes dusted in her hair and her curling ram's horns.

"What is it, Kami?" Chenna asked, the only one of them who looked calm.

The girl caught her breath. "General Ndeze is here with a message from the King," she announced.

It was as though she'd been pulled deep underwater in a fraction of a second. Aoki's ears were muffled with a throbbing hum, and everything seemed to sway in a slow, ocean flow. She heard Kami's voice as though it came from far away, even though the girl was just in front of her.

Just in front of her—and *looking straight at her*.

"The King wants to see *you*, Mistress Aoki."

There was a pulse of silence. Aoki sensed, rather than saw, the other girls turning to her. Her vision had narrowed to a wobbly point somewhere over Kami's head.

She felt a hand on her shoulder. "Aoki." Chenna's voice was sharp. "Do you want to go?"

It was a pointless question. As if any of them could ever ignore the King's summons.

They'd seen what would happen to those who tried.

Aoki ran a tongue over her lips. She opened her mouth, but no words came out. And she realized that, for the first time in a long time since she'd made her home here in the Hidden Palace, she genuinely didn't know what the answer to that question was.

The King wanted to see her. *Her.*

Before, this would have been good news. The *best* news. Even now, her heart beat with both terror and a guilty, shining joy.

A month had passed since the Moon Ball, and in that time the King hadn't called for any of his Paper Girls. He hadn't even sent any news or indication he was alive. The little information they did have came from the maids, who had been given updates on the state of the palace and the kingdom by the kind demons of Women's Court who smuggled them food and other necessities, or the occasional sympathetic guard. They'd learned that the King was alive but badly injured. That Lei and Wren, along with General Ryu, had planned the attack. That the King was soon to go to war with the Hannos. But they had no way of knowing if any of this information was even true.

Aoki was about to find out.

"General Ndeze is waiting," Kami urged her. "We have to go!"

Aoki nodded, still in a daze. She felt Chenna's steady touch, the tight embrace of the twins, heard their encouraging words. But it was as though a lid had locked around her, blocking these things from fully reaching her. As she started after Kami down the hall, Aoki looked back to the room she'd just left.

Blue was still sitting under the window. Her position was the same as before, legs pulled up, arms clamped around them. Yet instead of the scowl she'd been wearing just minutes ago, her expression had been swapped for one Aoki had never seen on her, though she'd seen it on others enough—had worn it *herself* enough—that she recognized it straightaway.

Fear.

General Ndeze and a group of guards led Aoki to Royal Court in silence. Like at Paper House, Aoki was struck by how quiet the rest of the palace was. The streets were almost empty, only the occasional scurrying maids or court official passing swiftly, heads down, as guards marched by in precise formations. In the King's fortress, their steps rang off the dark stone floor. The building had always had a cold, imposing feeling, but without its usual activity, the unwelcoming atmosphere was oppressive.

Her heart thudded in time to the heavy fall of General Ndeze's claw-tipped feet as they made their way down the echoing corridors. Her unease grew every second. Doors that led to beautiful courtyard gardens and glittering ballrooms were pulled shut. Whispers traveled around corners, only for the servants who'd been gossiping to scatter at the sound of their approach.

They were halfway up the long marble staircase leading to the King's private quarters when a door on the lower floor flew open. Two demon guards emerged, carrying a struggling lion-form man between them.

"Please!" he shouted, voice bounding off the stone walls. The guards dragged him so roughly he fell to his knees. His canary yellow robes were twisted, the beads in his braided mane falling free and bouncing off the floor in his struggle. "Bring me to whoever it is that accuses me of these crimes. I want to know who it is that would harm me with such false allegations!"

"The King has authorized your arrest," one of the guards growled.

The lion-man looked aghast. "But...but this is madness! At the very least I have the right to a fair trial! I can assure you, I have no affiliations with the Amala whatsoever!"

The second guard, a burly ape-form demon, thrust his knee into the lion-man's side. "Then perhaps avoid wearing their colors in the future," he sneered, and grinned nastily. "Not that you'll have one."

"My robes? They don't mean anything! Yellow is my husband's favorite color, that's the only reason I'm wearing this. Please, you have to believe me!" His panicked eyes wide, the lion-man looked up, spotting the General where he stood with Aoki on the stairs. "General Ndeze! Thank the gods. Please put a stop to this nonsense. You and I have worked together for many years. You know my loyalty is with the King. You have to say something! He cannot take me away like this with no proof. I am a Moon court adviser, for gods' sake, not some common Paper slave!"

General Ndeze's face remained impassive. He rested his olive-pit crocodile eyes on the lion-man for a moment more before turning. "*I* have to do nothing, Adviser Chun. And the Heavenly Master can do as he sees fit." With a twist of his wrist, he motioned Aoki and the guards to continue up the stairs.

Her hands trembled as they climbed the last few steps. The lion-man's desperate shouts didn't stop, only fading when they'd moved out of hearing range.

"What was that about?" Aoki asked in a shocked whisper, craning her head to look up at General Ndeze.

The crocodile-man stared ahead. "The court has been rooting out those disloyal to the King," he answered flatly. "Following the incident on New Year's Eve, the King issued an edict allowing those accused to be arrested and charged without trial."

"But the man said there was no evidence against him. And the penalty for treason is..." Aoki trailed off, her belly turning.

The General didn't answer. They had reached the King's rooms.

Aoki stared up at the high archway and the heavy wooden doors set deep into their recesses. Over the months she'd been a Paper Girl, the dark timber of these doors had come to mean many things to her. At first, they'd signified fear, the immense pressure and anxiety that came with meeting the King in private. But this pressure had warped, slowly morphing into something more serpentine and slippery, mixed now with a desire to please the demon who sat beyond those tall doors, and new hope that he was anticipating her arrival as much as she was.

The last time she'd been here, the sight of the doors had made her heart *shine*. Now, that old terror was back. But the joy and hope and desire were all still there, and they turned uneasily in her stomach, uncomfortable bedfellows.

General Ndeze motioned to the door with a claw-tipped finger. "Aoki-zhi," he prompted.

It had been weeks since anyone had called her that. She blinked, startled, and stumbled forward. The doors swung open with a groan.

The tunnel was pitch-black. Aoki winced at the sound of the doors closing behind her, but she pushed out a shaky breath and kept walking. Her light steps barely broke the silence. Ruby light glowed ahead, the sweet, sugary scent of the candles that filled the King's chambers unfurling on the warm air. The fragrance had always felt welcoming to her, a girl who loved desserts almost as much as she loved the King. But today the scent was overpowering, making it difficult to breathe.

He loves you, she reminded herself. *He told you he loves you. That he's thinking of making you his Queen. He won't hurt you. Won't blame you for what I—*

For what they did.

As always, another question promptly followed.

Do you blame him *for what they did?*

Then the King's voice sounded from amid the flickering red, and all else was pushed from her mind.

"Aoki-zhi."

The voice was all wrong, coarse and jagged and guttural. But it was his.

Something flared to life in her soul.

"My…my King," she gasped, tears prickling her eyes now, and she moved faster, out of the tunnel and into the candle-filled chamber, where the King sat on his golden throne.

He smiled when he saw her. "My sweetheart. I've missed you so much."

Aoki dropped to the floor in a low bow, pulse skittering. She pressed her fingers into the cold stone while she wrestled the shock off her face. But there was nothing she could do about the tears that were streaming down her cheeks, finally loosened at the sight of him.

His *face*. His beautiful *face*.

Kami and the other maids had been told of the King's injuries, and in turn shared this gossip with the Paper Girls. But that's all it had been: gossip. Someone said the King had lost both his legs at the knees. Another, an arm. Another, his eyes. One woman even said his heart had been torn out, and a shaman's transplanted in its place, its beat kept by other shamans working their magic around the clock.

"Any more lost parts and he'll just be a floating elbow," one of the twins had quipped, which had caused Aoki to burst into tears and run from the room.

Chenna had come after her and drawn her into her arms. "Shh, he's all right, I'm sure he's all right," she'd said, stroking her hair, though her voice had a tough edge to it, as if the words were tough to get out.

Aoki was sobbing, hysterical. "Then why doesn't he want to see me?"

She knew now why.

She straightened from her bow. This time when she lifted her eyes to the King's face, she was smiling, even though tears still tracked her cheeks. "M-me, too," she told him, her breath hitching. "I've missed you every day, my King. Every second. I wish you'd have let me see you sooner."

His arctic-blue stare was piercing. "Well, now you see me." His broken voice was low, a rough graze across her skin. "Tell me, my sweet Aoki. Do you still like what you see?"

Though it hurt, she made herself look at him. She blinked away tears as her gaze traced lovingly over the taut, raw-looking skin that stretched over the jagged indent of his empty right eye socket, the puckered ridges across his throat, where something sharp must have dug. The absence of his right eye was a presence all its own, and she had to force herself to look into his remaining eye as she addressed him.

"Yes," she whispered. "I'd love your face however it appeared, because it belongs to you."

His smile stretched, flashing teeth. He opened his arms. "Come here."

She ran to him, and melted into his embrace.

An hour later, Aoki was still in the King's arms, though now they lay in his grand bed, the sheets twisted around them. Sweat beaded her bare skin. Her heart thrummed happily, tiny hummingbird wings in her chest. The King held her as he always did when they were alone like this, one arm wrapped around her back where she curled into him, chin tucked, cheek to his chest. She was smiling.

"I've missed this," he murmured. His fingers pinched where they were splayed across her shoulder.

His broken voice was still grating, and it made her want to whimper when she thought of the agony he'd been through, the pain he still might be in. He'd told her of the daily shaman visits. The long, uncomfortable sessions as his skin and bones and tissue were knitted back together as best they could. Neither of them had mentioned who'd done this damage to him. There had been rumors about this, too, of course, and unlike the other rumors, Aoki had some information to base her own suspicions on. But she was too afraid to voice the question.

If it *had* been her—Lei—then that meant her best friend had tried to kill the man she loved.

If it *hadn't* been her, then she couldn't bear to think what had happened to Lei. Why wouldn't she have been brought back to Paper House with the rest of them if she'd had nothing to do with Wren and the Hannos' betrayal?

Her fingers played with the short brown hair that covered the King's body, the candlelight picking out their golden tones. "Can I see you again soon?" she asked breathily. "Please?"

He clicked his tongue. "I'm busy, Aoki. Busier even than before."

"Of—of course. I didn't mean to suggest you weren't. I just… I can't bear to be away from you for so long. And it's hard, back in Paper House. We're there alone, and Blue is hurt, she needs medicine—"

"Is that what this is?" The King drew away from her so quickly the air felt cold against her skin. He was glaring now, the scar tissue around his right eye puckered. "You've come to complain about how difficult *you girls* have it?"

Aoki pushed up onto her hands. "No!" she cried, reaching for him. "My King, I—"

He knocked her arm away. "I gave you girls everything. And how did you repay me?" His voice grew into a boom that bounded around the mirrored room. "One of you slept with one of my soldiers! Two of you slept with *each other*. And those same two—"

The King broke off into a hacking cough. Pain spasmed across his face. His hand flew to his neck, clutching it as his lungs racked.

Aoki wanted to throw her arms around him. To kiss his hurt away. But she could tell he wouldn't be receptive to it in this moment, so she waited, drawing a sheet to her chest, watching him through teary eyes.

When his coughs eased, his voice was even more jagged than before. "I have been betrayed by too many of you girls. I thought you were different, Aoki."

Her heart leaped. "I am!"

His one eye watched her, gleaming darkly. Moments later, the anger seeped from his face. He relaxed back down onto the pillows, scooping a hand out to tuck her back into the crook of his arm. He squeezed her to him, a fraction too tight. But she didn't mind. She closed her eyes and clung to him, dizzy with relief.

"I'm sorry," she whispered.

"No," he said, a familiar purr to his voice showing through the cracked, coarse edges. "You were right. You *are* different, my sweet Aoki. You always have been. In fact, I should be thanking you."

"Thanking me?"

"Yes. You were the one to tell me about the two girls being lovers, after all. If you hadn't, I wouldn't have been prepared for their second betrayal. Perhaps I would have ended up being even *more* hurt." His arm really was squeezing tightly now. "You helped me, my sweetheart. Thank you."

Aoki's body had gone numb. She tried to look up but the King's hand had moved to the back of her head, holding her down against his chest so she could only see his torso and legs, the flashes of their naked bodies entwined in the assortment of mirror pieces encasing the room like the broken shell of some giant beetle.

Silence pulsed.

She pulled in a shaky breath. "I—I didn't know anything about them," she lied.

The King tutted. "My sweet Aoki, there's no need to be ashamed. I know she was your friend. Maybe you loved her, even. But I know you love me more." He spoke as soothingly, as sweetly as his damaged voice allowed. "You remember. It was one of the nights we shared a couple of weeks before the Moon Ball. I asked you how the other girls were doing. You told me you were worried about—" He choked off. The hand on the back of her head twitched. "About your friend," he went on after a few seconds, though Lei's name was clear to both of them even in its absence. "That she'd been looking tired lately, and seemed distant. You said you missed talking to her, and when I asked you why you'd not talked as much recently, you went quiet and your cheeks turned pink. The same shade as when I kiss you—or when you have said something you shouldn't have."

Waves of ice were sloshing over Aoki now. She tried to lift her head again, and this time the King helped her, twisting her neck around almost painfully and bringing her head in close to his. He was smiling, but his one eye was cold. He smoothed a rough thumb over her cheek ever so tenderly.

Tears welled in her eyes. "I didn't mean anything by it—"

"Do you remember what you told me next? When I pressed you as to who else she was friends with, you told me Wren-zhi's name. And again, that lovely blush." He slid his hand to cup her cheek, fingers tangling in her hair. "It was other things, too, of course. Little things you'd said to me, and things I'd noticed myself, or heard from others. But that was when I truly understood what was going on. The very next day, I sent soldiers to Xienzo to bring her family to the Moon Ball."

Aoki felt sick. Her heart beating wildly, tears streaming down her cheeks, she stared at the King she loved so much. Like his voice, his face had been damaged by what had happened the night of the New Year. Yet more than that, *he* seemed damaged. She could see that now. Something was different about him. Darkness she hadn't seen before had come loose within him, as though a shaman had cursed a dark spirit upon his soul.

Guilt speared her even as she thought it. But she couldn't deny it.

"I'm s-sorry," she said thickly. "I didn't want to hurt you."

"Shh." The King drew her to him, wiping her tears away with his fingertips. "I know, sweetheart. You were trying to protect me. That's how much you love me. And that's what I'm doing for you, because I love you, too. You know that, don't you?"

"I do," she murmured, clinging to him with trembling fingers.

"That's why I have to keep you girls in Paper House. There are cruel people out there. Those who would hurt you to get to me. I couldn't bear it if that happened. You won't let that happen, will you, my sweet Aoki? You'll stay with the rest of the girls in the house, so I can keep you safe?"

"Of—of course," she gasped. "I'm so sorry, I'm so sorry—"

"Shh," he cooed again. "My sweet, sweet Aoki. All of this will be over soon. I have a plan. Those who turned against me will be punished, and those like you who have been loyal will be rewarded. So you have nothing to worry about, do you? You have always been loyal to me."

Tears streamed down her cheeks, wetting the King's fur. "Y-yes," she stammered.

Though it wasn't a lie, it wasn't quite the truth, either.

Because her tears weren't just for herself or the King. Aoki was thinking of Lei, too. Her beautiful, brave friend who had made her feel safe and loved in the palace even before the King had, with her kindness and laughter and care. Who had trusted her with her secrets, only for Aoki to betray the most powerful one of them all to the King.

Again, she wondered what had happened to her friend—and again, the fear kept her from asking. Not only because of how awful the answer might be, but because of the knowledge that she had, however unwittingly, played a part in making it happen.

FIFTEEN

NONE OF THE WHITE WING COME to see us off the next
morning. Not that I expected them to. The palace was
eerily silent after Eolah's death, and we spent subdued
hours hiding away from the mourning clan, Caen and Merrin going
over the logistics of our next move while Nitta and Bo did their best
to entertain us with nonsensical chatter and games and Hiro kept to
himself as usual. Claiming to be tired, Wren spent most of the day
sleeping—or at least, trying to. Most of the times I went to check on
her in our bedroom she was awake, staring at the ceiling with dull
eyes, the circles beneath them a fraction darker than before.

It felt wrong, being in the palace while its clan members were
mourning. The air itself tasted off. Soured. The polished marble
walls that had once given the palace gravitas and elegance now gave
it the cold, empty feel of a mausoleum.

After breakfast in our rooms, Commander Teoh and five of her
guards escort us through the palace. "We keep a set of carriages in a
guardhouse at the base of the mountains," she explains as she leads
us to the lower levels. "We'll fly you down."

None of us look keen to be taking to the air again.

"Isn't there a staircase?" Nitta asks hopefully. "Some sort of pulley system?"

"A slide, maybe?" Bo suggests.

"There are stairs," Commander Teoh replies coolly. "Feel free to take them—all fifteen thousand of them."

For a moment, the leopards look as if they're actually considering it.

Icy air hits me as we head out onto one of the verandas at the base of the palace. It's similar to the one we arrived at, a wide stone platform open to the front and sides, pillars suspending it from the floor above. A bunch of maids huddle together, hunched against the wind tearing in from the open sides.

"Our packs," Wren says, looking surprised as the maids hand them to us. "You collected them from the mountaintop?"

"We went back to retrieve them as soon as Lady Dunya invited you to stay," the Commander confirms.

I struggle to heave my pack over my shoulders. It seems even heavier now, digging into the small of my back. Caen, Merrin, and Hiro take their bags on without complaint while Bo mimes toppling over dramatically, his sister stifling her laughter.

"We refilled your flasks with fresh water from our central spring," Commander Teoh says, shooting the siblings disapproving looks. "And you have enough food for a week."

Each of us, except Merrin, is paired with one of the guards. I'm surprised when Commander Teoh comes to me, and even more surprised when she holds out my dagger: the one I stabbed her with two days ago.

I take it sheepishly and tuck it into my belt. "Sorry about that."

She shrugs. "You were attacked, and responded in kind. Any warrior would have done the same."

She walks me to the end of the terrace, then crouches low for me to climb onto her back. It's only a fraction less intimidating than the idea of dangling from her talons again. Her feathers are prickly, and she's shorter and slimmer than Merrin, so I feel her body more keenly beneath me, the shift and flex of her muscles as she prepares to take off.

The rest of the group mount the other guards. Only Merrin stands alone. Catching his eye, I shoot him a smile. He returns it before turning away, and I make a mental note to ask how he's feeling when we camp tonight. The White Wing may not be his clan, but being bird demons, they *are* his kin. Eolah's death might have affected him, too.

The canyon sweeps in front of us, open sky just inches from where we perch at the edge of the veranda. Cold wind teases strands of hair from my ponytail. I flick them away with a shake of my head.

"Open wings!" Commander Teoh shouts. I jerk as she pitches forward.

"Open sky!" the other guards return.

With a kick of her powerful legs, we launch into the air. A flurry of frigid wind hits me, taking my breath away. Even though I'm swaddled in my fur coat and thick traveling robes, the cold is so fierce it's like being lashed by demon claws. The sky stretches all around, a stunning crystalline turquoise tinted with ivory and gold. I cling firmly on as we soar out over the mountainscape.

Getting a strange urge to see the palace for one last time, I twist my head to look back. The Cloud Palace is magnificent. Rearing up from the mountain peaks like a godly finger breaking through the rock, its polished white walls are lit up, incandescent in the morning sun. I notice a figure on one of the upper balconies.

Qanna. Though we're too far for me to make out her expression, it feels as though she's staring right at us, and her sharp, lovely face comes to my mind: piercing black avian eyes, as round as eclipsed moons, and full of fury.

Then Commander Teoh banks steeply and I whip back around, flattening against her feathers. The other guards follow as she takes a sudden left, angling downward. I cling to her feathers and grip her sides with my thighs, teeth gritted with exertion. The pack on my back shifts my balance point. It's all I can do to stay on. We drop in tightening spirals, down through the clouds, then past the menacing spikes of mountaintops, snow-covered and speckled with gnarly trees.

We tilt right, then level out, flying low among the mountains. The Commander's muscles shift under my body as she cants her wings back to slow us. We descend steeply between two peaks, the dark mountain face whirring past in a blur. The valley floor rears up, higher and higher, until with a great jolt, she brings us down. I slip, only just managing to stop myself from sliding off over her head.

I climb from her back, easing out my tensed fingers. There are thuds and groans as the rest of the group lands. Readjusting my bag, I turn to see Wren dismounting her guard and looking as though she was born for this, every inch the composed, noble warrior, her hair tousled around pink-whipped cheeks. She goes to help Hiro dismount while Bo, in clear contrast to Wren, tumbles off his guard in an inelegant sprawl.

He picks himself up. "Never. Again," he grumbles through gritted teeth.

The demon fluffs her feathers. "The feeling is mutual."

We've landed in a deep valley dusted with snow. Towering cliff faces rear up to either side, and though they shield us from the winter wind, it's still bitterly cold. I clap my hands to spark some warmth, and as my eyes adjust to the low light, I make out wooden posts and fittings for reinforcement in a cave to our left—a guardhouse.

A croaky voice rings out from the shadows. "Open wings."

"Open sky," Commander Teoh answers, striding forward.

A short kestrel demon moves out from under the guardhouse eaves. "I've prepared two of the medium-sized carriages, as per your request, Commander," he says with a bow.

"Thank you, Jie." She turns to us. "Do any of you know how to look after carriage horses?"

"My father taught me," Wren says. "How fast can they run?"

"Our horses are some of the fastest in the kingdom. They're used to long distances. While you're in Shomu, the carriages will provide you safe travel. Everyone will recognize them as ours. Lady Dunya informed me you'll be traveling straight to the sea? We have emissaries all along the coast, they'll bring the horses and carriages back." She gives us a small bow. "Well, then. The next time we meet, we may be fighting side by side in a war. It will be an honor to battle alongside you."

Bo loops an arm around his sister's shoulders. "Even us?"

Commander Teoh's glossy black eyes flick over them. "Even you, felines. We have a common enemy now." She shoots the kestrel demon a few final instructions before she crouches, spreading her wing-arms wide, her white-painted feathers unfurling. "Open wings," she recites.

"Open sky," the other guards finish, and as one, they lift into the air.

Nitta sighs, her coat flapping in the wake of their wing-beats. "Thank Samsi we're done with all that. If I had to hear that *one more time*..."

The demon from the guardhouse brings us to the carriages and helps us set up. Merrin wants us to reach the Fukho Grasslands before sunset so we'll have time to eat and set up camp while it's still light out. We're not to stop unless there's an emergency. It's decided that Wren will ride with Merrin and Caen, while the siblings, Hiro, and I will follow in the second carriage. I'd prefer not to be split from Wren, but she tells me she feels safer if there is someone in each carriage who can cast magic.

"Besides," she adds quietly, "I'd like you to keep an eye on Hiro. Make sure he tries to get some sleep. This journey has been hard on him."

With a kiss, she gets into the other carriage where Merrin sits out front in the driver's seat behind a large white horse the kestrel demon told us is called Arrow. I give our horse, Luna, a pat on her soft nose. Like Arrow, Luna has a beautiful mane, long and thick. A diamond of gray marks her snout. She nickers, nuzzling my palm.

At the head of the other carriage, Arrow stamps the ground impatiently. "Get some rest, lovely," Merrin says. "We have a long journey ahead."

I arch a brow. "I'm sharing a carriage with the leopards. How likely do you think that is?"

He snorts, clicking his neck as he lifts Arrow's reins. With a final stroke of Luna's nose, I climb into the carriage, settling onto the front bench opposite the leopard siblings. Next to me, Hiro is pressed up against the wall, nose to the window. He pulls one of the silk blankets draped across the bench over his lap.

"Hiro?" I say gently. "How are you feeling?" My eyes travel over his drawn face and sunken eyes. Wren's right. He looks even worse than when we arrived at the Cloud Palace.

"I'm fine," he replies.

Bo waves at me. "*I'm* also fine, thank you for asking." With a sigh, he stretches, narrowly missing cuffing Nitta on the head with an elbow. "Finally free from that prissy birdcage of a palace. It was like no one had ever made a joke in those walls. Or even knew what one was."

"I'll miss the food, though," his sister admits. "You have to admit, their chefs are excellent."

"I could have stayed in that bathing room forever," Bo agrees fondly.

"That was probably their plan," I point out. "Boiled leopard demon for dinner."

Pebbles crunch under the wheels as we start moving, Luna pulling the carriage slowly forward. Bo slouches back, easing a hand behind his head and kicking his feet up on the windowsill.

His boots are just a few inches from my face. I glare at them. "Excuse me?"

Nitta shoves her shoulder into her brother. I give her a grateful smile as his feet hit the floor.

"Hey!" he complains.

Her lips curve. "Time to see who won our game, Little Bro. Or did you forget?"

Bo's face brightens. "Of course not!"

"Wait," I say slowly. "What *game*?"

"For every fancy clan palace we visit," Bo explains, beaming at me, "we have to steal the most expensive item we can find. Whoever steals the item that is worth the most, wins."

My mouth drops. "You didn't."

Nitta and Bo only grin.

I stare at them, aghast. "Caen will kill you. *Wren* will kill you."

Ignoring me, they grab their packs and start digging excitedly.

"When did you even get a chance to do this?" I ask, flapping a hand. "You didn't even have your packs until, what, half an hour ago? And we spent all our time either with the White Wing or confined to our rooms!"

"Still plenty of opportunity for thievery!" Bo's voice is muffled,

his head within his pack. "And I had my loot stashed in my undergarments. Alongside a few other precious things."

I groan.

Nitta surfaces a second later, something clasped in her fist. "I got
mine the first night, directly from under Lady Dunya's nose."

I gape at her. "Oh, my gods."

"You know," Bo says, sitting up, one arm still buried in his pack,
"*some*one sounds jealous. You can play with us next time, if you like.
The Czo are renowned for collecting fancy things. It's going to be
a lot of fun."

"Um...no thanks."

"I get it. Scared to go up against two of Ikhara's most skilled
thieves. That's understandable."

Nitta bumps Bo's shoulder. "Go on. Youngest first."

With a wicked grin, the leopard boy draws a small rectangular
box from his pack. Despite its size, it looks heavy, crafted from
iridescent agate and moonstones and inlaid in its center with pearls,
shaped in the form of the White Wing crest: a wing spread in flight.
Looking smug, he clicks the lid open.

"What's that?" Nitta asks, peering closer at the fine umber-
colored powder inside.

"Ground bison penis. The kingdom's finest."

She jerks back, scrubbing her nose.

I grimace. "Ground bison *what*?" Shaking my head, I say, "Forget
it. And please don't tell us what it's used for—"

"Erectile dysfunction," Bo declares proudly.

I sigh. "Never mind." I turn to swap a tired look with Hiro
and find him still staring out the window, resolutely ignoring our
conversation.

"It's Lord Hidei's, I take it?" Nitta sways with the rock of the

carriage as she inspects the box more closely, though also more
carefully this time. We've started to pick up pace. Pebbles strike
the sides of the carriage, kicked up by its spinning wheels and
the pounding hooves of the horses. After traveling in the muffled
silence of the mountains for so long, and then the somber quiet of
the White Wings' palace, it's a relief to have noise all around again.

"Took it right from one of his maid's robes at drinks the first
night," Bo replies.

"His maid's robes?"

"Well, he can't carry it around himself. What if someone found
it on him?"

Nitta smirks. "What if."

"So," Bo says, gloating. "Really think you can top this, Big Sis?"

The tips of her canines peek out from her lips as her mouth
sharpens. "Ah, Little Bro. You have no idea." She holds out her
palm with a flourish. "Feast your eyes on this beauty."

Even in the glum light of the carriage, the object is brilliant. A
sparkling, heart-shaped diamond pendant glitters against her tan
fur. The sleek coils of its chain lie in loops around it, like a silvered
serpent.

Bo ogles the necklace. "That's . . . you mean—"

"I told you I stole it directly from under Lady Dunya's nose."

"I didn't realize you meant it *literally*!"

Nitta clips the necklace around her neck, looking smug. "It suits
me better anyway."

"Don't you think Lady Dunya will notice something like that
going missing?" I say, a little coldly.

She waves a hand, smoothing down the caramel fur of her body
to better admire the necklace. "Oh, she had far more expensive jew-
elry on besides this. I bet she won't even notice it's gone."

"Nitta. The woman's daughter just *died*."

Her face softens. "Then she really won't notice," she replies sadly. The next instant, her eyes become sharp and playful again. "Come on, then." She nudges Bo. "Offer it up."

Her brother hands her Lord Hidei's box with a face as sour as old milk. Nitta nestles it in her lap, then digs a little metal pot out of her pack, the kind to keep spices in. Luna must be riding at full speed now. The rocky mountain pass is uneven, all of us thrown half out of our seats any time we hit a boulder or hole. Steadying herself, Nitta empties the pot's contents out the window before carefully replacing it with the contents of Lord Hidei's box.

"I'm not sure this'll be of much use to me," she says, handing the pot to Bo, "but it might come in handy to you at some point. Why don't you keep it?"

I can't help it—laughter bursts out of me as Nitta falls back, guffawing, Bo's cheeks flaming red.

Hiro finally looks around at this. He eyes us all with quiet distaste. "Erectile dysfunction is a serious problem," he says gravely. "Many men come to shamans for a cure."

This only makes Nitta and me roar harder.

"I'll remember this," Bo grumbles darkly, glaring at the two of us as though he'd like nothing more than to push us out of the carriage. He holds the offending pot at arm's length, perhaps considering it for the same fate. In the end, he tucks it deep within his pack. "To sell!" he practically screams when Nitta and I burst into further peals of laughter.

Nitta claps her brother on the back, tears leaking from her eyes. "Sure, Little Bro," she chokes out. "Whatever you say."

SIXTEEN

LUNA AND ARROW RIDE TIRELESSLY INTO the day. For the first two hours, we clatter noisily down the mountain pass, the horses navigating the narrow trail with practiced speed. The following hours are smoother as we reach the lower slopes of the mountain range, the snowcapped ridges smoother and less barren, hardy shrubs and leaf-stripped trees clinging to the cliff face. Still, Luna's hooves skid a few times on the scree, causing a couple of dangerous swerves. By the time we bring out some food for lunch, we've reached the flatlands that spread across most of northern Shomu. The day is cloudless and sunny. Fresh air rushes in through the windows as Luna gallops down the packed-earth road.

Outside, farmlands and paddy fields roll by. Though it's still winter, there's no more fresh snow here, the land a burgeoning brown-green just starting to break from the cold. I'm staring out, drawing in the scent of earth and new grass, so fresh after what feels like months of only ice for company, and feeling homesick—the terrain here is so similar to Xienzo—when the carriage begins to slow.

At the other end of the bench, Hiro sits a little straighter. We swap a nervous look. We weren't meant to stop unless there was an emergency.

Opposite, Nitta and Bo are slumped together on their bench, mouths hanging open in a post-lunch nap. Bo's snores fill the carriage. My pulse flits faster as Hiro and I wait to see if Luna picks up speed again. Instead, she falls from a canter to a trot.

Nitta's head rolls off Bo's shoulder at the drop in pace. "We're here?" she asks sleepily, rubbing her eyes.

"I don't think so," I reply. "It's still the afternoon."

Her brow furrows. Then alertness flashes to life in her eyes; her nose twitches. "Is that smoke?"

A pulse of dread ripples through my body. I can't smell it yet myself, but I trust Nitta's demon instincts. I twist to look out the window in the direction we're traveling. Paddy fields stretch to the flat horizon where cerulean meets faded emerald, as neat as a fold in a sheet of origami. I crane my neck further and see a plume of smoke lifting in the distance.

There's a yawn. "Why are we stopping?" Bo mumbles.

None of us answer him. The terse silence thickens over the next few minutes as we draw steadily closer. Billowing clouds of smoke darken the sky, and I can taste the ash now, bitter on the wind. Beneath them lie the collapsed husks of wooden houses. If the style of rice paddy huts here in Shomu is the same as the ones I've seen in Xienzo, then before the fire they would have perched above the muddy waterline on stilts.

Now they're nothing more than smoking wrecks.

"A raid," Nitta breathes.

I swallow down a rush of nausea, my stomach pitching. Because if she's right, then this is *my* fault. If I'd managed to kill the King, and Kenzo had lived to steer the court in the right direction, the raids would have stopped. Instead my attack only fueled the King's anger. Maybe he's ordered even *more* raids.

The thought cleaves me. I was trying to protect my people. But my actions might have put them in even more danger.

Before the carriage has come to a proper stop, I throw open the door and jump out. My boots hit the earth with a thud. Luna nickers as I run past her. There are shouts, more thuds as the others follow me.

Merrin leans down from his seat atop the other carriage to grab me as I pass. "Lei," he warns. "Don't."

"Then why did you stop?" I say roughly.

"Caen asked me to."

"That's right."

I wheel around at Shifu Caen's voice. He stands with Wren, the others behind them. Wren comes forward, Merrin releasing me so she can take my hand. But I pull away. To have comfort, to have love, meters away from the burned-out houses and what they might contain inside, what *I* might have helped put there…

Wren opens her mouth to speak, but Caen gets there first. "Ketai asked me to stop at any places that look as though they've suffered a raid to check for survivors," he explains. His voice is flat, resigned. "But this doesn't look hopeful." He nods to the carriages. "The rest of you should wait inside."

I let out an ugly laugh. "You can't be serious." Then I break into a run before any of them can stop me.

My footsteps are loud in the eerie hush of the abandoned paddy. Ash drifts through the air, an ugly mimicry of snowfall, its warm flakes brushing against my skin as I near the houses. What appears to have been three or four buildings are now nothing more than small square shacks. Stumps poke up through the scorched earth and piles of blackened wood. I approach the first house and step carefully into the mess of debris. Dimly, I'm aware of my hands still curled into fists, nails digging into my palms.

This was someone's home. People lived here.

Lived.

"Hello?" I call.

Only silence answers. Heat rises from the scorched remains, beading sweat across my brow and under my arms. I scrub the back of my hand across my forehead.

There are footsteps behind me.

"Lei," Wren says gently, "I don't think anyone is here."

Tears wet my eyes. "They could be trapped," I shoot back, venom in my voice that isn't directed at her. "They—they might need our help." I grab the nearest bit of wood: a cylindrical pole, possibly one of the stilts that had propped the house up. It's still hot. The skin of my hands shrieks with pain, but I grit my teeth and force myself to keep hold of it, lifting it and chucking it aside. Numbly, I register the blisters popping up across my palms. Ignoring them, I bend down to brush away lumps of ash.

Wren places a hand to the nape of my neck. Then, without a word, she crouches down next to me and starts to help clear the debris.

We work in silence. The others move carefully through the rest of the remains, following suit. Afternoon sunlight beats down on our backs, burning away the winter chill, and the heat from the still-smoking ruins sears my skin. But I let my sweat drip down, let my hands blister.

"I've found them."

It takes me a moment to register Hiro's words. His soft voice has hardened; he doesn't sound like himself. I look up just in time to see him take a few steps back and then double over, retching.

Nitta leaps over a fallen lump of wood to get to him. "It's all right," she says. She rubs his back. "Get it all up."

We make our way over to them. Wren peels away from my side to put an arm around Hiro. "Let's get you some water." She gives me a strange, sharp look before leading him back toward the carriages.

The others are all watching me. I jut my chin and step forward.

"Lei," Caen starts, "you shouldn't—"

I move past him.

The bodies are in a lump, as though they died huddled in one another's arms. It's impossible to make out their individual forms. The heat has melded them together, charred them beyond recognition. Through the smoldering black, patches of pink flesh peek out, so raw-looking it hurts my eyes.

I stare down, my heart wild. Silence ticks the seconds by. It takes me a while to realize that I'm shaking. A while more to realize I haven't breathed since seeing the bodies. With a gasp, I draw in a ragged breath, only to have the smell of burnt flesh assault me. I gag, eyes watering. I make the sky gods salute with shaking hands.

"Lei. It's time to go."

At Nitta's gentle voice, I pitch around, my teeth bared. She shrinks back.

"Some of them might have tried to run," I say. My voice cracks and I cough, forcing out my words louder. "We need to check the whole area!"

Veering from the path, I stamp down into the mud-packed trenches of the paddy. I stumble, falling onto the hard earth. With a snarl, tears coursing freely down my cheeks now, I pick myself up. Bits of earth and broken rice stalks have stuck to my palms, and I wipe my hands on my coat, then let out a ragged hiss as it makes the burns sear.

"Lei."

This time the voice is Merrin's, and comes from above. His flying form casts me in shadow. He hovers overhead, pumping his winged arms to keep himself still.

"I'm not leaving," I growl.

"I know. I came to help."

I sniff. "Good."

"Check around the houses," he suggests. "I'll look farther afield."

With a shift of his wings, he cants to the side, rising high. I squint as the winter sunlight pours back over me. Then I swipe a hand over my sweat-slicked brow and trudge grimly on.

After two hours, I return to the ruins, exhausted, wind-chilled— and alone. The others are waiting for me. I can tell from the look on Merrin's face that he didn't find any survivors, either.

The only thing left to do is tend to the bodies. In the northern provinces, most castes cremate their dead to release their souls to the sky. For the same reason, southern Ikharans bury their dead, feeding the souls back to the earth, their qi reclaimed by the land that lent it to them. Since these bodies have already been burned, we can only clean the space around them to give their remains a little more dignity. Nitta and Bo have the idea to lay fresh leaves over their bodies. Hiro offers a prayer, a touch of magic woven into his words that makes the air glimmer, the smoke shifting to allow a shaft of golden sunlight through to bathe the ruined house in light.

It's not until we're leaving that I notice the flag erected behind the ruins, snapping in the wind. A black bull's skull stamped on scarlet silk.

It's no surprise. I knew from the minute Nitta said she smelled smoke, as soon as I saw the dark plumes rising in the distance. Yet anger lands anyway, a solid *thunk* in the pit of my gut as I think of all the lives the King has ruined, the reckless rampage of his cruel rule.

It's not until we're back in the carriage—Wren insisting on me riding with her this time, sending Caen to ride with Nitta and Bo so we can be alone while she heals the blisters on my palms—that I make another connection.

Rice paddy. Northern Shomu.

Her name bursts into my mind with such force I gasp, doubling over.

Aoki.

Aoki's family are rice paddy farmers. Aoki's family lives in northern Shomu. Aoki, my friend, my sweet, beautiful friend—whom I left back at the palace with a King who knew *her* friend betrayed him.

"Wait!" I scream, banging on the carriage wall behind me.

Arrow jolts to a stop.

"Lei?" Wren asks. "What's wrong?"

I launch out of the carriage without answering. I come around to the front, where Arrow is snorting, tossing his mane impatiently. Looking confused, Merrin sits on the rider's bench, reins in his taloned hands.

"When you were flying," I demand, "when you were in the sky, did you see a lake to the east of here? Shaped like a heart?"

He nods. "Why?"

A howl rips through me. At least, that's what it feels like: as though the noise has come directly from the core of me and wrestled its way out, erupting from my lips with all the hurt and horror his answer brings.

I drop to my knees.

Back in the palace, during one of the precious nights where we would chat in our bedrooms, snacking on sweets Lill stole for us from the kitchens, Aoki told me about her rice-paddy home. How in summer she and her three sisters would go skinny-dipping in the heart-shaped lake to the east of their fields, believing it would bring them luck in love. Unless there is another rice paddy exactly like this one, then *this* is her home.

Her ruined home.

Her ruined *family*.

My gasping breaths scour my throat. There's movement around me: the slam of carriage doors, the concerned murmurs of the others. Someone crouches beside me. I tense as Wren lays a hand to my back.

It takes me a few minutes before the tears slow. Before I'm able to uncurl and catch my breath.

Tentatively, Wren leans in. "What is it, Lei?" she asks, quiet.

"A-Aoki," I choke out.

Her eyes widen. She jerks to look back at the smoking ruins.

"Not here!" I say, realizing what she must have thought. "But... this is her home. This—this is where she's from."

Wren's eyes flash. Then they melt, those warm brown irises seeming to spool past their borders as they grow. "I'm so, so sorry," she whispers.

I seize her hands. She squeezes them, clinging to me, a fierce heat building in my chest as I say, very carefully, "We will make him pay for this, Wren. For Aoki."

Her look hardens. She looks away, a spasm of something painful passing across her face.

Slowly, she helps me to my feet. None of the others question what has just happened or probe for further details. We move back to the carriages in silence. As I'm following Wren inside, I hear Bo whisper to Nitta, "Who's Aoki?"

Anger shoots down my veins. Who *is* she? The whole *world* should know who she is. My brave, beautiful friend, who got me through the darkest times of my life with her kindness and brightness. Who shined like a torch in the night.

I look at Bo, the ash-choked wind swirling my hair around my cheeks. "Aoki is my best friend," I tell him. "She is one of the kindest, most big-hearted, bravest girls I know." My eyes flick to Wren, and I add fiercely, "And I know many."

The sun is setting by the time we arrive at the Fukho Grasslands. Golden light washes over the undulating plains. It's no wonder this region is nicknamed the Amber Sea, with the winds blowing the grass, filling the air with a rushing sound like running water, and the soft dips and lifts of the hillocks mimicking the roll of waves, all tinted in gold. But my eyes are hollow as I stare out the window, my memories replacing the beautiful landscape with one of ash and destruction. The taste of fresh grass with smoke and burnt flesh.

We stop to make camp half an hour later. The sun is almost below the horizon now, its diffuse light gilding our darkening silhouettes as we get out of the carriages. The group gets to work quietly. Merrin sets up the tent with Bo while Caen heads off on a patrol walk, making sure the perimeter is clear before Hiro and Wren work their magic. Hiro helps Nitta with the fire. The comforting crackle of flames adds to the whistling rush of the wind through the meadows.

"Help me take care of the horses?" Wren asks, taking my hand.

I nod distractedly and she leads me to where we've tethered Arrow and Luna. Their heads are down, nuzzling the grass and making their sweet horse sounds, little snorts and nickers. She hands me a fistful of hard, coin-sized cakes. When she holds out her own to Arrow, he immediately snuffles them.

"The White Wing at the guardhouse gave them to me," she

explains. "Dates and roasted peanuts, and some vitamin powder to help them recover after all that riding."

I offer my hand up to Luna. She devours the treats in a few snuffles of her warm muzzle. Letting out a wet puff of air, she lifts her nose to my face as though I might have hidden more from her there. I give her a small smile as I swipe my sleeve across my face. "Thanks for that, Luna."

"Lei, I'm sorry," Wren says suddenly, making me look up.

"What for?"

Her shoulders are tight. "This. All of this. I just want you to know I'm sorry. All I want is for you to be happy, and instead you're…seeing things like that." She moves abruptly in the dark, cool hands finding mine, her face so close I can smell her ocean scent, that fragrance I've grown to know so well that I can draw it from memory, like a color or some childhood dream, pulling it around me like a favorite blanket. "I love you so much, Lei," she whispers, "and after all of this, I promise I'm going to spend the rest of our life together trying to fill it with reasons to make you happy. Every single day."

My eyes smart. "Those days feel like a long way away."

Wren squeezes my fingers, a hardness re-entering her voice. "We're one clan down. Two more, and then we'll have the power we need to overthrow the court. It's all going to be over soon."

I think of Aoki. Of her family.

Of *my* family.

"Some things can never be over," I say.

And without a word—because she understands there is no word to fix this, because she understands that what I'm saying is true, that some wounds cut far too deep to ever heal and you just have to live with them, love *around* them, acknowledging their pain when you shift against their edges and then simply *keeping on*—Wren pulls me to her. Her arms are warm and strong. I turn my cheek and she rests her head on mine, lips to my hair.

We stay like this until night has fully fallen and Nitta's voice rings out. "Dinner's ready!"

We join the rest of the group around the fire. Merrin passes out mugs of black tea laced with honey, and I stare into the flames, bronze light flickering over my face as the tea warms my hands. Though winter has broken its fierce grasp on the land this far south in Shomu, the air still carries the memory of ice, and it nips at my skin through the edges of my coat.

Shifu Caen is the last to arrive. "All clear on the patrol," he announces, gratefully accepting the hot mug Merrin hands him. "Just need to do the daos, and we're all set." Hiro starts to his feet at this, but Caen waves him down. "It can wait, Hiro. There are no settlements for miles. Get some food in you first."

"And more tea." Nitta grabs the kettle from where it's hanging over the fire and leans over to refill Hiro's cup. "Sugar is good for you."

"I'm... not sure that's true," Caen says.

Bo lifts a finger. "You're thinking of healthy, Shifu. Two different things. Most of the time, when something is good for you it's not healthy. And who cares about healthy, anyway? We're going into war. Healthy isn't going to help us much in the face of teeth and swords."

Nitta smiles sweetly. "Exactly. So—more tea?"

With a defeated sigh, Caen lifts his cup.

Merrin's face darkens. "Oh, no," he says.

Bo gives him a tired look. "What's wrong now, Feathers?"

"I think..." Merrin shudders. "I think I actually *agree* with you two on this."

The leopard siblings burst into laughter. Bo slaps Merrin's arm. "Feels good, doesn't it? Finally giving in to the feline way of things?"

The owl demon shakes his head back, smoothing down his feathers. "I wouldn't go *that* far, Cat," he huffs. But he uses the nickname with affection, and when Bo turns his attention to what we're having for dinner, I notice the way Merrin's eyes linger on him, something hot and curious in their gaze.

After we've finished eating, Bo brings out a bottle of sake he stole from the White Wings' palace. We pass it around as the night grows deeper, the darkness rich with the crackle of the fire and the song of crickets in the grasses. It's our first night back in the wild, and though the others relax in the warmth of the campfire, I can't help but jump at every distant animal sound. Even the wind's voice seems to take a shape. I didn't realize how much I'd relaxed in the safety of the Cloud Palace. Without any walls, I can sense the vast openness around us. My mind whirs with all the demons—literal or otherwise—that could be hiding in the shadows. While the rest of the group discusses tomorrow's plans, I hug my knees to my chest, playing nervously with the hair tie at my wrist.

I've found you.

The words are whispered right into the whorl of my ear.

I spin around, heart thumping. The grasslands stretch out, shifting blades illuminated by the flames deepening to a thick, impenetrable black.

He's not here, I tell myself. Then—

But he could be. He is alive.

"Everything all right?" Wren slides an arm around my waist, tugging me closer. "Lei, you're shivering. Do you want to go inside?"

"I'm fine. I just need a drink." I lean across her lap, reaching for the bottle clasped loosely in Bo's hand.

"Hey!" he complains.

I take a long draw. It feels good, the heat of the alcohol rinsing my insides, a woozy glow starting to dull the edges of my alertness. I drink more, even as my eyes water and my throat burns.

Bo's expression changes. I notice the shift from annoyance to concern. Then I let out a cry as the bottle is suddenly knocked from my hand.

Shifu Caen glowers at me, his hand half-raised.

The others have fallen silent.

It's my turn to look indignant. "I was drinking that!" I protest.

Caen's jaw ticks. "I saw. Don't you think you've had enough?"

Before I can argue, Wren stands up. "I think it's time for us all to get some rest. We're tired, and still reacting to what happened earlier." She looks over at Hiro. "We should cast the daos now, so everyone can get to bed." She holds out a hand to help me up. "I'll come join you as soon as I'm done."

For a moment, I consider refusing. Then the whispered *I've found you* slinks back into my mind, making the back of my neck prickle. With a final scowl in Caen's direction, I stumble off to the tent. I undress in the dark, keeping most of my clothes on but removing my boots and coat. Within a minute of snuggling under the blankets my eyes flutter shut. Whether it's the alcohol or the weight of the day's events, sleep pulls me under so swiftly and wholly that it feels like only seconds have passed when I open my eyes again.

I startle into alertness with a gasp.

I'm on my back, my mouth dry. The tent is dark. Bo's snoring fills the air. Wren's face is close to mine, her breathing heavy. The tail end of my dream lingers, and at first I think it's this that woke me, some scream or panic in my nightmare reaching through to my consciousness.

Then I realize I just need to pee. Careful not to disturb Wren, I get up, pulling on my boots and coat.

Outside, the night is thick and deep. Stars spill across the sky. Feathery rustling from the wind-teased grasses fills my ears, splinters of moonlight catching on their swaying blades, like the glinting of tiny animal eyes. I shiver. It's much colder without the fire's warmth. I find a spot a safe distance from the tent, and, crouching, I maneuver my coat and trousers aside. When I'm finished, I straighten, unable to stifle a huge yawn. I'm still yawning as I pull my trousers back up—as the darkness shifts beside me.

My yawn cuts off abruptly as a sword flashes from the shadows. Its cold edge presses to my throat.

"This," a familiar voice whispers into my ear, "is for the King."

SEVENTEEN

NAJA'S VOICE IS EXACTLY AS I remembered: cold, high-pitched, scoured with derision. As if in answer, the old wounds in my shoulders flare with pain. Fear darts down my veins. Yet something else answers from inside me, too—fury. Fury, because of everything the fox demon did and said to me at the palace. Because of the last time I saw her, her claws wet with blood. Because of Zelle. Because of Kenzo. And more than anything, because of what I saw today in the paddy fields.

Whether she commanded it or not, Naja is a part of the system that allows families like mine and Aoki's to be torn apart with hardly a second thought.

Naja's hatred for my kind has always been a mirror to my own fear of hers. But over the last few months, I've learned how to transform that fear into anger—into *action*—and now my new instincts spring forth, bright and burning.

Fire in, fear out.

"Get *off* me," I snarl, and hurl myself backward against her.

She stumbles. Not much, but enough to give me time to grab her arm and wrench it around. She drops the blade with a hiss. I lean down to snatch it, but my fingers have only just brushed the hilt when Naja slams into me

We roll on the cold earth, grappling messily, hands clasping coat lapels and tugging hair. Though she's more muscled than the leopard siblings, and her fox form is more threatening-looking than Merrin's owl features, I've been around demons long enough now that Naja's appearance doesn't intimidate me as much as it used to.

She hisses—and I hiss right back at her.

"You've been following us," I say, panting. "In the mountains. It *was* you I saw."

She forces me onto my back, straddling me, one hand jammed against my throat. Her eyes are ghostly mirrors in the dark, flashes of silver like fish turning in a lake. "I was meant to get to you before you reached the White Wing," she hisses, "but them finding you first threw my plans off. No matter. I have you now."

With a growl, she digs her hand harder into the underside of my chin, jutting my jaw up.

Lights pop in my vision. I scrabble at her grip, my breath coming wheezily. I choke the words out. "I . . . *will* . . . finish it."

Finish it. Her eyes blaze with understanding.

"You failed, girl," she snarls, dipping her wet fox's nose closer to mine. "You don't scare me, nor the King. In fact, we should be thanking you. Because of you, we have rooted out more traitors to the throne. Now all that's left to do is bring each and every one of them to their knees." Her incisors glint as her lips pull back. "We are coming for them, Lei-zhi. Don't think we don't know where your father and aunt are hiding. The King's army is growing in strength each day, and soon we will come for them. The Hannos will stand no chance against the full might of the royal forces." Her sneer widens, and she delivers the next words in a low purr. "But I have put in a special request to keep your father and aunt alive. The King and I would like to deal with them ourselves."

Horror sluices down my skin. "You—you won't get to them!" I try to kick her off, but she holds me down with ease.

"How will you know? You'll die here tonight. Along with your precious lover, and the rest of your group."

"You don't stand a chance against them!" I growl.

"It's not a fair fight, I agree. But I have something to help even the odds."

Up until now, my vision has been narrowed to the white fox and me, the small patch of grass behind my back and the whisper of starlit sky beyond Naja's face where she looms over me. But at her words, the world opens back up in a roar.

I smell it first. For the second time today, the acrid bite of smoke. Then I wrench my head to the side and see the flames.

They lick across the field to the right of the tent, vivid orange in the darkness. Naja must have set the fire right before attacking me. It can have hardly been more than two minutes, but the fire has caught easily in the dry grasses, and even as I watch it doubles in span, growing from a distant crackle to a throaty burr that sets the horses whimpering and tugging on their ties. Plumes of smoke rise to blot the sky.

Figures emerge from the tent. I start to yell—

Naja slaps me.

Pain ricochets from my cheekbone as it cracks against the ground. Then a new pain flares to life as Naja wraps both hands around my neck.

I splutter. Cough. Try to buck my hips to shift her as she takes her sword from the grass and sets it against my exposed throat.

Her silvery eyes are wild. "For the King," she repeats.

At the very moment I drive my own blade into her side.

Surprise registers first. Just as Caen taught me, being small and seemingly weak has its advantages. The magic of the dagger thrums in my fingers, and I sense it holding my hand steady, guiding me to push itself deep and sure into her taut flesh.

A grunt escapes her. With shaking, bloody fingers, I twist the blade between Naja's ribs, pulling a lower, rougher sound from her throat. Then I yank the blade out, heave my body to the side, and knock her off me.

She throws out a hand. Catches herself with a hiss. She's back on her feet in less than a second, but I've already scrambled to mine. I'm just beyond her reach when she swipes a claw-tipped hand at my back.

I lurch toward the fire. A wall of flames burns between the tent and me, scouring everything in deep coppers and reds. "Wren!" I cry. "Merrin! Nitta!"

A shadow speeds overhead. Merrin's outline is lit from beneath by the fire, and I register a flash of gray-white feathers and wide wings spread against a darkened sky before he swoops down toward us, a qiang clutched in his taloned hands. The silver of the spear flashes through the night. Merrin aims toward Naja—

Then pulls out of the dive at the last second.

We're too close. That's why he can't attack her from this angle. A split-second later my guess proves right as the fox demon barrels into me from behind.

I crash face-first. Gasping for breath, I find choking smoke instead. We're almost at the fire now; heat rolls off it in waves. Perspiration stings my eyes. I shake and squirm as Naja pins me down.

She lets out a ripping snarl. There's a flash of flame-lit silver.

I jerk, twisting my head and shoulders around at the last minute as her sword comes inches from my cheek and buries deep into the earth.

"Stay…still!" she pants.

She butts the back of my head with the heel of her hand. My chin smacks into the ground. I yelp, tasting blood. I spit it out with a scowl. As Naja shifts her weight to wrench her blade free, I maneuver my own sword-hand around and jab backward.

Metal meets muscle. Naja lets out a shriek that is half desperation, half disbelief, wholly animal and raw. I wrench my dagger free from her thigh. Groaning, Naja clutches her spurting leg while I use the shift of her weight to scramble out from under her.

The white fox struggles to her feet, lopsided and wincing. Stormy firelight shows splashes of red on her fur. Spit drips from her lips. She swipes a bloody hand across her jaw, smearing crimson so it makes her look as though she's been eating pounds of raw meat, and lifts her long sword.

A swooping shadow—

A flurry of feathers—

Merrin moves so quickly I don't have time to recoil. One second I'm standing there, facing Naja, her blade flashing silver as it carves through the air toward me. The next, her sword thuds to the ground as the pointed tip of Merrin's qiang, and then its shaft, passes cleanly through Naja's right arm.

The spear embeds itself into the ground inches from my boots. Its long handle quivers.

Naja's scream is unlike anything I've ever heard. She doubles over, cradling her blood-drenched arm.

"The horses!" Merrin yells at me from above. He gestures back at where they're tied, neighing and bucking as the flames devour the grasses in an advancing wall of glowing scarlet and gold.

I hesitate. Naja is within my reach, injured and distracted. My dagger vibrates, its magic eager for more. Blood gushes from the fox demon's wounds, making me remember again everyone she hurt. If our roles were reversed, she would step forward and slice her blade across my neck without a moment's hesitation. Half of me wants to run and do just that. To run screaming at her, plunge my blade into her flesh.

The other half pins me in place.

Then Merrin cries again, "Lei! The horses!"

With one last conflicted look at Naja, I shove my dagger back in its sheath and run.

Merrin lands at the same time I reach Arrow and Luna. Straight-away, he's working at Arrow's tether. My fingers shake as I pick the bulky knots keeping Luna in place. The blood makes it difficult to get a good grip, and she's straining, pulling the rope, rendering it tighter. I pry harder, almost there, almost—

The second the knot releases, Luna breaks into a run.

Merrin seizes her rope, dragging her back while holding on to Arrow with his other hand. His feathers are unfurled, his wing-arms beating to counter the horses' strength.

"The carriages," I gasp.

He shakes his head. "Burned. Take Luna and get the others."

"Wren—"

"Working on the fire with Hiro. I'll get them once the others are safe. Go!"

He pulls on the rope to keep Luna in submission so I can haul myself onto her back. She shoots off immediately, Merrin tossing me the rope just in time.

I cling on as Luna charges into the darkness. For a few horrible moments the thunder of hooves is so loud and all-consuming, and

mixed with the roar of fire at my back, I'm thrust back into my childhood, right back into my ten-year-old self, when my life collapsed
to the song of flame-crackle and the drumbeat of hoof-fall. The
way the King's soldiers had stormed my village, ruining and taking
as they pleased, leaving behind a mess of broken bodies and hearts.

Then I remember where I am. Who is counting on me.

I grab Luna's mane. I've never ridden a horse before, but I've
watched riders out in the plains beyond our village. I kick her right
flank with the heel of my boot. She stutters, kicking up grass as she
slows, scuffling in a loose, aimless circle.

"Please, Luna!" I sob.

She whinnies loudly, heading off away from the flames. But a second later she turns, and we speed back to our ruined camp.

I lay low over her body. The smoke-thick air lashes my hair,
embers dancing free to fizzle against my skin. In seconds we're facing down the wall of flames. I lead Luna to the left, and she follows
her own instincts to evade the fire, tossing her head from side to
side as we hunt for a way in.

The entire camp is alight. I can't see anything, just burning earth
and charred air.

"Lei!"

I jerk around at the sound of Bo's yell. Spotting a gap in the fire,
I urge Luna on.

The sound of more hooves. Arrow storms toward us with Merrin
on his back. "You take Nitta and Bo!" Merrin yells as he draws
level with us. "I'll get the others!"

Caen, Nitta, and Bo are in a close huddle, Wren and Hiro in front
of them, facing the flames. I yank Luna's mane, and we slow. The
leopard siblings are jumping up before Luna is even still, scrambling up behind me onto her back.

Nitta wraps her arms around me. "Go!" she cries.

Luna wheels around, just as the wall of flames closes around us. She lets out a trumpeting whinny of panic. She kicks back, then begins to circle, searching for a way through the fire. I rub her neck, shushing her even as my own panic flares.

The flames draw closer. To our left, Merrin launches himself off Arrow's back. Caen swings on in his place, deftly taking charge of the horse to steer him to Hiro and Wren where they face the fire, arms outstretched. Wren's hair blazes around her in an ethereal wind. Under the crackle and burr of the flames, it's just possible to make out their chanting. They keep weaving their dao right up until the last second, until the fire has almost reached us and we are huddled in a tight circle, our horses jostling each other. When the flames are licking just inches from their face, they move in unison, making a sudden thrusting movement with their arms.

A rushing veil of spinning golden characters shoots out. It breaks a passage right through the heart of the fire.

From overhead, Merrin shouts, "Now!"

Without hesitation, Caen drives Arrow toward the opening. He snatches up Wren and Hiro in one muscled arm, hurling them behind him as Arrow thunders down the shrinking pathway.

I slap Luna's side and we charge after them, making it out with barely a second to spare.

I sag over Luna's neck, gulping in deep breaths of blissful, smoke-free air, as we race across the plains. The roar of the fire dies down. Soon, we are enveloped once more in the thick hush of the moonlit night. When I dare look around, the flames are just a quiver of red on the horizon.

Merrin flies in low beside us. "Can you keep going?" he shouts over the clomping of hooves.

I'm still catching my breath. "Y-yes!" I force out.

"The fire will have drawn attention to us, and for all we know Naja has already sent word to the surrounding soldier outposts that we're here. We need to make as much ground as we can while it's still dark!"

"What if she didn't escape?" I notice my hands where they grip Luna's mane. They're black with Naja's blood. She was badly injured after all, and the fire spread fast.

"Maybe she didn't!" he yells back. "But we have to be careful, just in case. I'll keep watch!"

With great pumps of his winged arms, Merrin soars up, until he's a distant cutout against the wide eye of the moon. Ahead, Arrow, laden with Caen, Wren, and Hiro, leads the way across the starlit nightscape. I cling on, trying to rock in time with Luna's rhythm as she gallops, her powerful horse legs firing. Nitta clings to my waist, Bo behind her.

We ride on for hours. But despite the distance, I can't outrun Naja's words to me back at the burning campsite.

Because of you, we have rooted out more traitors to the throne. Now all that's left to do is bring each and every one of them to their knees.

We are coming for them, Lei-zhi.

Guilt racks my body. Just as we suspected, the King is preparing to attack the Hannos' palace. Where Wren's father is, where *my* father is, and Tien, and the rest of our allies; where Lady Dunya is readying to send her soldiers to right this moment.

And it's all my fault.

EIGHTEEN

NIGHT GIVES WAY TO DAY AS the horses charge tirelessly across the plains. I doze off at some point, lulled by the monotony of the grasslands and the rhythm of Luna's body beneath me. What feels like only moments later, I startle awake. I blink blearily against the morning light. The sun looms ahead, a muzzy ball veiled by cloud cover. Its belly hugs the horizon; it's not long past sunrise. Running a tongue over my dry lips, I straighten from my slump to see Nitta's arms reaching past my sides. Luna's white mane is wrapped around her fingers. I must have fallen back against her while I slept and her arms have been keeping me in place.

I crick my neck to look back at her. "Thanks, Nitta."

She's sandwiched in between Bo and me. His own arms encircle his sister from behind. He's sleeping, his head frequently lolling off her shoulder to jerk him awake, only for him to prop it back in the crook of her neck for the same thing to happen a second later.

Nitta's concerned green eyes flick over me. "How are you doing?" she asks.

"Oh, you know. As to be expected after an attempted murder. You?"

"As to be expected after almost dying from smoke inhalation." She lets out a throaty laugh before breaking into a cough.

A bird caw sounds overhead. We look up to see Merrin banking to loop over us, his shadow long on the ground. "Time to stop!" he shouts down. "We're almost at the coast."

Nitta nods, pulling Luna's mane to slow her. Merrin flies ahead to the others, and soon both horses come to a stop.

Bo slides off Luna's back with a groan. "Sweet Samsi." He stretches his arms overhead, twisting from side to side. "That was almost as bad as flying."

Merrin lands at his side. "Bird demons aren't so bad now, are we, darling?" he teases, as his feathers unruffle to lie closer to his body, his arms appearing to reduce to half the size.

"I suppose you have your benefits," the leopard-boy admits grudgingly.

"That's two times now I've saved your life, Cat. I'd be a little more enthusiastic."

Bo's mouth quirks. "Oh, I can show you enthusiastic."

"All right, boys," Nitta sighs, patting Luna's flank. "Settle down."

I let out a yelp when I dismount, my thigh and back muscles screaming as they're wrenched out of the position they've been stuck in for hours. I double over, rubbing my sacrum.

"Lei!" Wren hops from Arrow and runs over. "Merrin told us about your fight with Naja—are you hurt?" Her face is pale, the shadows beneath her eyes deeper than I've ever seen. Her hands run over me, checking for wounds, and instead of her usual steady touch I notice that she's trembling.

I draw her into a hug. "Don't worry," I say quietly. "I'm fine." Naja's words hover in my ears, and I mentally swipe them away. "She's the one who's not."

Wren stiffens. "You killed her?"

"No. But she's lost a lot of blood, and with the fire…"

Wren loosens a long breath, drawing back to address the group. "Naja must have followed us to the Cloud Palace and waited for us to leave."

"But how did she keep up with the carriages without us noticing?" Nitta asks, still petting Luna.

"And you and Hiro made the protection daos," Bo adds. "How did she break them?"

Realization strikes me in a flash. "She was hiding in one of the carriages already. Before we left."

"I think you're right," Wren agrees grimly. "For whatever reason, she didn't have the opportunity to attack us before we reached the Cloud Palace, so she lay in waiting. She must have been to the palace before on royal business and knew we'd leave via the guardhouse. She could have hidden underneath the carriages, or inside, in one of the benches maybe."

"So she would have already been within the protection of the dao last night," Shifu Caen says. "All she had to do was wait until we were asleep—"

"Before leaving her hiding place to kill us," I finish.

Wren and I share an anxious look.

"But why would she wait to attack us in secret?" Nitta asks. "She could have walked right into the Cloud Palace and arrested us all for treason right there and then. Why hide? Why wait?"

"She wants revenge," I answer coldly. "Naja's the kind of person to deal with things personally. If she arrested us, we'd have to be judged by the court. She's only interim leader. The King will return to power soon enough and then he'll be able to deal with us how he wants. Naja *wanted* to face us alone."

Caen crosses his arms. "Plus, the royal court is suspicious of everyone right now. I doubt General Naja is completely certain of the White Wings' allegiance. She probably didn't want to risk entering their palace only to be arrested herself."

"Speaking of being arrested," Merrin adds with a tilt of his head, "I spotted soldiers heading this way from both the north and the southeast. Either Naja managed to alert the nearby outposts or we have horrible timing."

Bo swears.

Wren swaps a dark look with Caen. "If there are any soldiers or royal representatives at the fishing village," she reminds him, "then they might already know we're coming."

"We'll just have to make our way through the village without anyone noticing."

Nitta's brows are drawn. "So we're sticking to the original plan? Caen, we lost all our equipment in the fire—maps, food, medicine. Thank Samsi we took our weapons before the tent burned down. It might be a good idea to forage some supplies from the village."

Caen shakes his head. "Too dangerous. We can worry about supplies later. For now, we just need to focus on evading capture." He shifts, the sword on his back clinking. "Everyone, stay alert. Lei, Hiro, walk the horses with us. They'll be looked after at the village until the White Wing can reclaim them."

As I go rub Luna's neck, sorry to make her have to move again after she rode all night, a whimper of pain sounds behind me. I glance over my shoulder—then dart forward. "Wren!"

She's collapsed to one knee, leaning heavily on her elbow. Her head hangs low. I brush the hair from her face and blanch at how sickly she looks, her forehead shiny with sweat.

"Wren, what's wrong?" I ask, pulse skittering, as the others come in around us.

Shifu Caen crouches beside her. "Was it the magic?"

Wren breathes heavily, swaying slightly. Then she presses her lips into a thin line and, with Caen's and my help, pushes to her feet. I feel how much she leans on me, but she holds her chin high. "It's just what we were talking about the other day," she says. "Magic is getting harder to access, so it takes more time to recover. But I'm fine."

I frown at her. The others also look wary—none of us has missed the shake in her voice.

"Hiro," Nitta says, going to the shaman boy's side. She bends, curling an arm around his shoulder. "Are you sure you can walk? You don't look well, either...."

Before Hiro can answer, Caen holds out an arm. "Take the horses," he orders Wren and Hiro. "Get whatever rest you can before we reach the village." When Wren starts to disagree, he holds up a hand. "No arguments."

We start the walk to the village across the wind-brushed grass-lands. The mood of our group is sullen, and in his usual fashion, Bo attempts to lighten the atmosphere. "Off to steal a boat!" He claps his hands and beams around at the rest of us. "You have to admit, it's kind of exciting. This'll be a new achievement for me. A shiny new entry for the resume."

None of us share his enthusiasm.

Merrin sighs. "You do realize we're talking about an actual sea-faring vessel here? I haven't spent much time at sea, but even from my limited experience I've noticed they tend to be rather...substan-tial. Quite a bit more so than your usual trade."

From where she's leading Arrow and Hiro, Nitta replies, "You sure about that, Feathers? I'd say secrets are some of the heaviest things in the world." Her voice darkens. "As well as the most dangerous."

It takes us just under an hour to reach the forest that climbs up the Shomu coast in a spine of green. The smell of wet earth fills my lungs as we step under the dense canopy woven by mossy cedars and pines. Light dapples the loamy floor. For a while, all we hear is the crunching of our boots and the nickers and snorts of the horses. Then—waves.

Excitement thrums through the group. We pick up the pace, the rush of waves growing louder, and the unmistakable scent of salt unfurls in the air. We approach the town, using the forest for cover. Beyond the trees, the ground slopes down to the sea, rows of wooden houses painted in pastel colors: coral, rose, pale teal. Despite their pretty colors, the buildings look tired and sad, hunched low as though hunkering down against the strong coastal wind.

There are no signs of activity, at least from our vantage point. In the distance, a door slams. There's a child's shrill yell.

Nitta frowns, stepping to the village border. "Where is everyone?"

Before any of us can answer, there's a flash of movement.

Merrin slots himself awkwardly behind a cluster of thick-trunked trees, his arms tucked in, as the rest of us duck. We wait, listening to the footsteps as they disappear around the corner of one of the houses closest to the forest. We emerge only once it's been quiet for a while.

"We stick to the original plan," Caen instructs, cautious to keep his voice low. "Merrin will wait off the coast with Hiro while the rest of us make our way to the harbor. Remember, we only defend ourselves if necessary."

Everyone nods. Nerves trickle down my neck as we edge closer to the perimeter of the forest. Instinctively, my hand moves to the hilt of my dagger where it's tucked into my belt. Magic thrums to life under my fingertips, and for a second it's almost as if the knife is urging me to draw it free.

I snatch my hand back.

"Everyone ready?" Wren asks, giving my arm a squeeze.

"Honey," Bo says, "I was *born* ready."

Caen gives him a withering look. "If you get injured, we're leaving you behind."

As Nitta helps Hiro onto Merrin's back, the owl demon watches Wren. "I have room for one more."

Her jaw ticks. "I'll be fine," she replies stiffly.

Merrin's eyes click to me. "Lei?"

I shake my head. "Shifu Caen hasn't been training me for nothing." I don't add that I'm also staying because I'm worried about Wren, and would rather be close to keep an eye on her.

Merrin nods. "Well, lovelies. See you all soon." His eyes sweep over us. They hang on Bo for a fraction longer, and then he turns, heading farther up the coast for a less exposed take-off point, one arm crooked back to help Hiro where the shaman boy is hunched over his back.

I give Luna's snout a final kiss good-bye. The others pat her and Arrow's flanks appreciatively before we slip out from the trees one by one.

Tiers of flat roofs stretch to a glittering sea. We move low, trailing between the houses in single file, Caen leading the way while Wren and I bring up the back of the group.

The village seems strangely deserted. The rhythmic hum of the waves hides our footsteps as we tread lightly across the cobblestones and stubby grass. I glance left and right as we move down the narrow winding pathways, heart thudding in my ears, fully expecting someone to jump out at any moment. But no one does, and we make quick headway.

"Looks like we got lucky," Bo says from just in front of me. "Must have been an intense party last night if everyone's still sleeping in. What a shame we missed it."

I ignore him. "I don't like this," I murmur over my shoulder to Wren. Her face is pale. "Me, neither."

After less than a minute, we reach the houses facing the sea, huddled along the top of the low cliff-edge like overgrown limpets. Sparkling indigo water stretches to the horizon. Low clouds scud across the surface. I spot Merrin out over the sea, circling a safe distance away as he and Hiro wait for us to get the boat, the two of them just a dark silhouette against the gray.

"There." Caen points farther down the village, where a colorful collection of boats bob on the water. More springtime-colored buildings front the harbor, opening up in the middle into what looks like a market square partially obscured by the houses.

We jog along the cliff, waves crashing noisily against the bluffs. Tangled lines of fishing nets hang between the houses and trays of salted fish have been left out to dry in the sun. The quietness unnerves me. There should be people about: fishermen getting ready to leave for a day at sea, children playing catch in the square, dogs barking for scraps.

As we pass the only house with its shutters open, I glance inside—and stifle a yell.

A pair of eyes blink out at me. Human eyes.

"Wren!" I hiss, flinging an arm out to stop her, when a scream sounds in the distance.

In an instant, the face behind the shutters disappears. Caen throws out a hand, ordering us to a stop, and we slip closer to the house, huddling under its porch.

"What's going *on* here?" Nitta whispers, lacing her arm through her brother's.

I flinch as there's a second scream. It cuts off abruptly, and the silence afterward is somehow even more violent, threatening in its emptiness.

"It's coming from the square," Wren says. Peeling off from the rest of us, she eases forward and peers past the corner of the house. Her shoulders stiffen. When I go to join her, she holds me back. "We need to get out of here. *Now.*"

"Wren," I say, my voice shaky, "what's going on?"

Ignoring me, she turns her attention to the boats bobbing on the water. "Which one?" she asks Shifu Caen.

He points to one of the larger boats, an old-looking junk boat with a faded red hull. Its fin-shaped sails are lowered. "Nitta will help me free the ship from its moorings," he says. "Bo and Lei, you're in charge of the sails. Wren, get us moving. Let's put those summers at Lake Nsukka to good use."

The others nod. Caen is about to move when I hiss, "Wait!"

Wren shakes her head. "Lei—"

"People are *screaming* out there. We need to help." Wren tries to hold me back, but I elbow her out of my way. Peering around the side of the house, I have a clear view to the square to the left of the harbor.

The scene hits me so forcefully I almost gag.

Wooden gallows have been erected in the square. Five humans hang from the beam, dangling by their wrists, their arms overhead. Three men, one woman, one child. All are naked. The wind carries their smell—sharp and metallic, tainted with the acidic tang of rotting fruit. Crimson lashes stripe their bodies. From the limp way they hang, it's clear they are dead.

Flying triumphantly from the top of each post is the Demon King's banner.

Horror lashes to life in my chest. These people have somehow stepped out of line, broken some laws, or just provoked demon soldiers in some way, and are being strung up here as a reminder of what happens to Papers who disobey the King.

Or maybe they didn't even do anything at all. Maybe the soldiers are simply here on one of their raids to remind Papers of their place.

Just then, two demons enter the square. They're clad in soldier's uniforms, their baju sets bloodstained. Both are Steel caste: a tiger-man with a rippling orange-black ruff of fur and a dog-form demon almost entirely human-looking save for furred legs and a tail. They carry another beaten corpse between them. As they start up the stairs to string the body up, I lurch forward, reaching for my dagger.

Wren shoves me back against the wall. "Lei, stop! We can't let them know we're here."

"They need our help!" I shriek. "You can't just leave them there!"

"They're dead, Lei," Nitta breathes, tears in her pale green eyes. "They're beyond our help."

"Then—then we can at least get their bodies down. It's inhumane to leave them like this."

But Shifu Caen only glares at me. "We stick to the plan. We wait for the demons to leave, and then we head to the boat. Whatever you see in the square, do *not* interfere."

Before I can argue, he edges out from the eaves, stalking as carefully as a wildcat to peer past the corner of the house. There's a bark of low laughter from the square. A gruff demon voice says something. More laughter bursts to life, then the sound of footsteps moving away. After a few moments, Caen gestures that it's safe.

He heads off first, sword bobbing on his back as he jogs down the slope to the harbor. With an apologetic look in my direction, Nitta follows, Bo close behind.

Wren releases me. "You can't do things like that, Lei," she growls, the ocean wind whipping her hair. "We have to think of the mission."

I cross my arms. "I thought the mission was to right injustices against Papers," I reply coldly.

"You know what I mean."

"We should at least cut them down."

"Their families will do it once the soldiers are gone. Lei, there's nothing more we can do for them—"

Something flashes past my head.

Wren reels back, clutching her forehead. Blood spurts through her fingers. A rock the size of a fist thuds to the ground.

I'm moving to help her when someone seizes me from behind.

I fall to my knees. A hand grapples at my belt, tugging my dagger free. I scramble around to see a tall Paper woman standing over me. A patterned scarf wraps around her head, holding back frizzy black hair. She wears a marigold kebaya, the wide hems fluttering in the wind. She is beautiful and terrifying, with the pewter sky shining behind her, and she stares down at me with hatred etched across her face.

"Leave me and my son alone!" she cries.

Behind her, a small boy peeks out the front door. His are the dark eyes that watched us through the slats earlier.

"We don't want to hurt you!" I say, my voice pitching. "We just—"

She slashes out with my dagger.

I spring to the side, the blade grazing my ear. I feel a hot trickle of blood down my neck.

"We don't want to hurt you!" I repeat, but the woman either doesn't hear me or doesn't believe me. Perhaps she doesn't care.

She aims another swipe at me. This time, I skip back. Taking the defensive stance Caen taught me, I'm ready when she comes at me a third time. I root my weight down through my legs and thrust my hand out to block her attack.

She grunts, my dagger dropping from her fingers. I snatch it up and scoot back.

The woman's dark eyes are a blaze of fury. She opens her mouth and spits a single word at me.

"*Dzarja.*"

Traitor.

It rocks me more than any blow could, because I know this word. I am overly familiar with its label. I have worn it for more than half a year now, and it has seared itself into my skin, lurking there, an invisible poison. Though she means it for other reasons—because I am fighting her, because she's caught us stealing a boat from her people when, judging by the state of their village, they can't stand to spare one, and because she has seen me be friendly with demons, when demons are the ones who have attacked and killed six of her fellow villagers—it strikes me with everything the word means to me. Everything I have blamed myself for all these months.

I want to tell her I understand her pain. To explain what our group is trying to do. But there's no time, so instead all I say is, "I'm sorry."

Then I flip my dagger and lunge forward to shove the blunt hilt into the woman's sternum.

She groans, doubling over, winded.

Her son runs out with a scream. "Mama!"

Wren yanks me around. Blood soaks her face and neck from the cut across her brow, but she swipes it away with her sleeve and leads me down the slope to the port.

We run fast and low. Gusts of salt-thick air hit our faces. Our boots skid on the grass. The world spins, a mixture of cloud-glazed sunshine and the turning lapis of the ocean to our right. The others have already made it to the boat. Its wide, fin-shaped wings are opening, Bo and Caen tugging on the pulleys. From the prow, Nitta gestures at us to hurry. Water splashes our boots as we clatter across the wooden boards of the waterside platforms.

We're almost at the ship when I remember the gallows.

I try to look back but Wren tugs me along so willfully it's all I can do to keep up with her. The red junk ship grows bigger as we approach. We turn down the tiny wooden gangway to the boat, and her grip loosens just enough for me to rip my hand free.

I swirl around. My heart thrums as I take in the awful scene of the gallows once more. Six bodies turn lifelessly from their ropes. A gust of wind hits me, full of the stench of blood and dead flesh.

"The soldiers are here!" Wren hisses, fingers clamping around my arm. "We have to go!"

At first I don't understand. There's no sign of the two demons earlier. Then I hear it: the stampede of hooves and heavy footfall. Distant, but growing. My eyes move to where the main road into the village winds along the forested coast, and I see a stream of red and black.

My heart flies into my mouth. Royal soldiers, heading right toward us.

Naja must have lived—alerted the nearest battalion to our location. The soldiers march in a tight formation, pennants stamped with the King's crest snapping in the wind.

"Lei!" Wren pleads again, tugging on my arm.

I'm about to go with her when one of the men strung from the gallows—the one I saw the demons carrying earlier—lifts his head.

Chills shoot down my spine. He's *alive*.

Without thinking, I wrench myself from Wren's grip.

I sprint as fast as I can across the harbor and toward the square, ignoring her shouts. I jump the steps up to the gallows two at a time. From the nearest post, the man who is still alive gapes at me, his skin ashen, cheekbones bruised. Ribbons of blood paint his body. The other bodies turn in the wind, ropes creaking. The stench of death assaults me like a physical thing. Clenching my jaw against it, I grab the post and haul myself up it. I get to the top and cling on, reach around, hack my dagger into the cords binding the man's wrists.

The rope is thick. At first my efforts do nothing. I switch from stabbing at it to sawing from side to side. Thick fibers spring loose. Frantic, I slice harder, faster.

Nitta appears at the bottom of the post. "They're here!" she yells.

Just as my blade cuts the final strand of cord.

The man drops, landing heavily. For a moment he lies still, crumpled in half. Then he stretches out an arm. His fingers dig into the floor as he hauls himself shakily to his knees.

Relief charges through me. At least if he dies now, it will be on his feet, looking his enemy in the eyes. At least it will be quick.

Something soft caresses my face. I look up. It's the King's banner, pinned to the top of the post. Scarlet and obsidian, the same colors as the soldiers coming around the corner with their hooves and hatred. The bovine skull at the center of the flag grins down at me.

Loathing like nothing I've ever felt before sears down my veins, so fierce it takes my breath away. "We are coming for you," I snarl in a low, feral growl, and I grab the banner and wrench it from the post.

It flutters to the ground just as Nitta clutches my ankle.

She drags me down, bracing me to stop me from falling over the edge of the gallows. And then we're running, speeding across the square and down to the harbor, boots clattering along the wooden gangplanks as arrows fly at us and the roars of demons and thundering steps pound in my ears, my vision narrowing to the red hull of our boat as it pulls away from the port, Wren, Bo, and Caen screaming from the deck, reaching out, urging us on—

We reach the end of the gantry, and leap.

For one heart-stopping second, I'm flying. Air rushes around me. Waves churn beneath my feet. My fingers stretch, inches from Wren where she's leaning over the railing.

Our hands clasp.

I slam into the side of the boat with so much force the wind is knocked from my lungs. Gulping airlessly, I cling on as Wren, Bo, and Caen drag me up. We topple onto the deck. She untangles to look at me, hands pushing my hair from my face. She plants a hard kiss on my lips.

"Sis!"

We wrench apart at Bo's anguished cry. The leopard-boy has clambered over the side of the railing, looking as though he'd dive into the water were it not for Shifu Caen holding him back.

My stomach lurches. Nitta must have fallen in.

"You can't swim!" Caen shouts.

Bo struggles. "Neither—can—*she!*"

Before we can do anything, a rush of air comes from behind us. I spin to see Merrin zooming toward us, Hiro on his back.

Wren and I jump up to catch the shaman boy as he leaps to the deck. The three of us crash back to the floor, my tailbone smashing into the wood. Pain claps through me. I release Hiro and roll over and clasp my lower back, groaning. Eyes watering, I drag myself to my knees. Wren and I are busy checking over Hiro when Merrin slams into the deck.

He skids across the boards before coming to a stop in a gray-white heap. His feathers are drenched in water. Big drops splatter to the floor as he flops back with a grunt, releasing the figure he'd been wrapped around.

"Sis!" Bo cries, running to Nitta.

He helps her up as she doubles over, retching. Her fur and clothes are sodden. She's tangled in her coat, which has come half off, and he drags it off her. Rubbing her back, he looks over her with teary eyes.

Nitta lifts her head. "Th-thought it was a nice day for a dip," she says with a shaky smile, before coughing some more.

Merrin's sharp gaze locks on Bo. "That's...your life twice," he pants, his chest heaving as he catches his breath, "and...your sister's... once. Time to manage a little more enthusiasm now, don't you think?"

Bo looks up. He stares at Merrin, something uncharacteristically hard in his expression. He seems almost angry as he gets up and strides toward the owl demon, green eyes blazing. It looks as though he's about to punch him.

Instead, he throws his arms around Merrin's neck. "Thank you, Feathers," he whispers. "Thank you."

At first, Merrin looks utterly bemused. Then he lifts an arm and wraps it around Bo's back, his eyes fluttering shut.

NINETEEN

M Y HEARTBEAT IS STILL RACING HOURS later. Even once
we've sailed straight through the day and safely into the
wide, moonlit expanse of open sea. The world is tender
and quiet, the only sound the hushed break of the water as the prow
of the boat slices cleanly through the surf. The others have gone to
sleep in the cabin at the back of the boat. The sails are set to scoop
the wind; the rudder has been set to keep us on course. And I am left
alone on deck as lookout with nothing but the bracing ocean wind
and my thoughts as company.

Perhaps that last part is *why* my heart is still racing.

Dzarja.

I start, pulse jumping as the wind carries the words into the whorl
of my ears, two hard syllables as ice-cold and unforgiving as a slab
of frozen rock. Breathing hard, I whip my head to the left. Right.
Behind me.

Nothing's there.

Of course nothing's there, Lei, I scold myself. *You're imagining things.*

Only I'm not. I turn back to the foam-topped waves rippling in
the ship's wake and blow out air. I can still picture the face of the

servant woman who called me by the same name more than half a
year ago. Like the village woman today, her face had been twisted
with fury, too. The same disgust soured her voice as she spat the
word from her lips. None of that is imagined. It's all too real.

Propping my elbows on the railing that runs around the deck, I
bunch the fur shawl tighter around my neck and huddle deeper into
my coat. The ship rocks beneath my feet. My belly shifts with it,
but unlike the last time I was on a boat, I'm able to keep a handle on
my nausea. Without the help of magic, we don't seem to be sailing
nearly as fast, and the water here is smooth.

"Three weeks to Kitori, if the weather is favorable to us," Caen
said when he finally got tired of yelling at me for my stunt back
at the fishing village and we were a safe enough distance from the
Shomu coast to relax. His voice was gruff and tired. There was no
sense in it of the celebration we should have been having for success-
fully stealing a boat and escaping the royal soldiers. "Nitta and Bo,
check for supplies. If you're not too tired, Merrin, I'd like you to get
high and make sure no boats are following us. Wren, Hiro, you two
need to rest. We'll see what we can find for bedding in the cabin."

"I can help," I said. My arm was around Wren's waist. She was
doing her best to seem strong, but a tremble ran through her body
that only I could feel, and her skin was gray. After such a frantic
escape from the port, the exhaustion of all her magic use during
Naja's blaze had come rushing back, hitting her like a wave. It's why
back in the village, Nitta had been the one to fetch me instead of
Wren. Apparently Wren had tried to come after me, only to stumble, and Nitta had jumped down from the boat and started running
before Wren could stop her.

Opposite us, the leopard-girl was crouched protectively by the
shaman boy, her arm around his small shoulders. Like Wren, he
looked faint, swaying where he stood.

Caen only glared at me. "*You've* done enough. You can take first shift as lookout."

"Caen," Nitta said, "give her a break. She was acting out of kindness—"

"Something that has little place in a war! In fact, it's one of the qualities that can most easily get you killed." He held up a hand. "I won't hear any more of it. Get on with your tasks. Lei, keep watch until one of us comes to relieve you."

"Great," I lied. "I'm not tired anyway."

Now, still in the same spot as I've been standing at for hours, I rub my smarting eyes. All around, the black depths of the ocean and sky sing with starlight. Clouds scud overhead. I release a long exhale, my breath a furl of white before the salt-dense ocean wind snatches it away.

We have to prioritize the mission.

You put us all in danger.

What in the gods were you thinking?

Shifu Caen's admonishments echo in my ears.

I bunch my hands into fists. "I was *thinking*," I snarl now into the night, "I couldn't bear to leave him there to die like that. That I had to do *something*."

"Who are you talking to?"

I whip around. It takes me a moment to make out Hiro hovering in the shadows around the cabin. He crosses the deck to join me, and I turn back to the sea, a flush crawling across my cheeks.

"I'm practicing my comebacks," I grumble. "You know, in case they invent a time machine, so I can go back and give better sass." I shoot him a sideways look. "If you've come to lecture me on being reckless, you're a bit late."

"You did a good thing, Lei."

I fall quiet, blinking in surprise.

In the dark, Hiro's face is a ghostly mask. Starlight shines off his bald head, paints a cluster of dots in each slate-gray iris. Yet the shadows beneath his eyes are deep pools, blacker than the water stretching out all around us. He looks as though he's been hollowed from the inside out, but his voice is clear. "The man was in suffering. We should help those in suffering."

"Is that why you're a shaman?" I ask gently.

He stares at the sea. "I was born into a clan of shamans," he answers after a beat. "I had no choice in the matter. But once my clan was destroyed, then I had a choice. Whether to continue their work."

"What made you decide to carry on?"

"My Birth-blessing pendant." Wind ruffles Hiro's black robes. "The character inside is a reminder of my family and clan. Of what their work means, and how I must honor it by continuing. When I feel lost, it keeps me anchored."

"But you're not eighteen yet. How do you know...?"

"For most shaman clans, our pendants are open from the day we're born. It's up to us to decide when to look at what's inside." Hiro's eyes cloud over for a moment, and his thin fingers wind around the railing, gripping tight. "I opened mine the morning after I lost my clan."

I resist the urge to ask him what the word is. Already, he's shared more with me about the contents of his Birth-blessing pendant than most Ikharans would dare. My left hand moves to my neck, where my own pendant hangs.

Flight. A word that once filled me with so much hope and certainty. Now it feels like it's all I've been doing for the last few weeks: running. Fleeing. Battling my way through turbulent air and trying to resist the plummet down.

"I'm scared, Hiro." My admission comes out in a whisper.

The shaman boy doesn't answer for a long time. When I'm turning to check that he hasn't fallen asleep on his feet, or perhaps gone into one of his meditative trances, he replies softly, "Fear is good. It means you care. And caring is its own kind of magic. One just as powerful as any dao I can weave."

My throat tightens. Before I can thank him, he slips back across the dark deck and disappears inside the cabin.

Nitta comes to relieve me from lookout duty just after sunrise. She hands me a flask of water and a piece of stale roti, looking apologetic. "Here. You must be starving. I should warn you, though, it tastes of fish."

I take a bite and grimace at the salty tang. "Ugh." I take a swig of water to wash it down. "You weren't lying."

She sniffs. "Not even a day yet, and I'm ready to get off this ship." With a big yawn, she stretches, popping her joints. "Sorry about Caen. He's rather grumpy, isn't he?"

"He was right," I reply with a shrug. "I put us all in danger."

Nitta eyes me for a moment. Then she twirls a wrist. "Personally, I like a little danger in my day. Gives it some excitement." After a pause, she adds, her voice lowered, "It's not right, what some demons do to your kind. I'm sorry."

"You haven't done anything."

"Maybe not personally. But I still feel guilt on behalf of my kin."

"Is that why you and Bo agreed to help Ketai Hanno?"

Nitta stiffens, a shadow drawing down over her sweet round face. "Partly," she replies, serious. But after a few seconds, her green eyes are sparkling once more, and she gives me a wink and spreads her arms wide. "And how could we resist all of this?"

I hold the stale roti aloft. "Oh yes. It's all so glamorous."

She gives me a kiss on the cheek. "Caen says to get some rest. Try not to disturb Wren and Hiro, they're still sleeping."

Stuffing the rest of the roti in my mouth, I head over to the cabin. The smell of fish is even stronger inside. Merrin, Bo, and Shifu Caen are moving about quietly. The cabin is surprisingly spacious, a boxy room lined with narrow windows around its upper edges. Its simple wooden furniture has been pushed against the walls to make room for makeshift beds, which are not much more than a collection of all the fabrics the others could get their hands on: ripped sails, moth-eaten blankets, an old coat. Among this mismatched material, Wren and Hiro sleep on their sides, the curl of their bodies making brackets around the empty space between them.

Merrin finishes adjusting the collar of his hanfu in place as he picks his way over to me with Caen. "The last few days has knocked them out," he remarks, casting a fond look over them. Then he cocks his head, his keen orange owl's eyes the same color as the light filtering in through the shuttered windows. "Looks like they've taken their toll on you, too, lovely."

"Thanks for the compliment," I grumble. But he's right. Now I'm finally in a place where I can feel somewhat relaxed, it's a struggle to stay upright. Since leaving the Cloud Palace, we've been traveling nonstop, and the only sleep I've had has been in disturbed snatches.

Shifu Caen's expression remains stony. "We'll resume your training tomorrow morning. After your actions back in the village, it's important you learn how to control yourself. You have too much yang in your system. This time at sea might do you good."

They leave, Merrin brushing me affectionately on the arm as he goes.

On the other side of the cabin, Bo waves me over to where he's crouched down near the wall. "I was going to tend to Wren's cut while she's out," he says as I join him, gesturing at the objects he's rooting through, which I see now are medical supplies. "But maybe you'd prefer to do it?"

"Thanks. I would."

He watches me for a moment, his feline green eyes—the same hue as his sister's—uncharacteristically serious. He bumps his shoulder into mine. "What you did back there was—"

"Stupid. Dangerous. I know."

"I was going to say *brave*," he corrects kindly, and touches a hand to my back before leaving me alone with the sleeping Wren and Hiro.

I shake off my coat and boots. Then I take the supplies and kneel next to Wren. Raven-colored spills of hair cover her face, and I move them carefully away. The gash across her forehead is crusted with blood, more of which has run in now-dried rivulets down her face. Using a bucket and sponge, I wipe her skin clean before wrapping a bandage around her head. Though she stirs, she doesn't wake. I'm relieved to find the cut looks worse than it is. It's big, though, and fairly deep, a jagged slash close to her hairline midway across her brow from her left temple. It's definitely going to scar. But as I scan Wren's face all I can see is how beautiful she is. The way her long lashes splay across the high apples of her cheeks makes my heart beam with love. The arch of her Cupid's bow at the center of her peach-brown lips is so sweet it brings tears to my eyes.

I wonder what worlds she's exploring behind her twitching eyelids; whether she's finding any relief from our journey. From her peaceful expression, I'm hopeful she is.

Easing down next to her, I snuggle close, pulling the moth-shredded blanket to my chin. Though I'm hopeful for a calm sleep, too, I'm not so lucky. My dreams are dark and agitated, crowded with screams and arrow-fire and banners stamped with the King's insignia, and a sky full of cruel gods laughing down at us as they place bets on which of us will die first.

None of them bet on me, and somehow that feels worse.

TWENTY

LIFE ON THE BOAT FALLS INTO a steady rhythm, as sure as the rocking of the waves beneath us and the endless stretch of the glittering sea—glittering in daylight under spells of sun or muffled light filtering through the clouds, glittering at night beneath a ceiling of iridescent stars.

I throw myself back into training with renewed energy. With nothing but time, we train almost all day every day. A few hours in the morning for meditative practice and the subtle arts of qi control and breathing techniques, before we break for lunch. In the afternoon, Caen puts me through my paces, drilling me in sword techniques and ways to surprise enemies in unarmed combat, building my stamina and strength through rigorous exercise that leaves me sweat-glossed and panting, especially as the wind grows warmer the farther south we travel. The others keep to the raised borders of the deck to give us space to train while they check our bearings and make sure the sails are set properly, or play mahjong with an old set we find in the cabin. To everyone's frustration, Bo wins every time. Each lunch and dinner, Nitta and Hiro, who's shown an increasing interest and talent for cooking since our journey began, prepare our

*   *   *

On our last day of the third week on the boat, Nitta calls us for dinner on deck. She's lit a few lanterns on upturned crates, and we gather around them, chatting easily. The mood of the group is light. Three weeks of peace has relaxed us all. It's been easy to forget about everything happening back on land when we're so far away from it all, our only concerns who will take the best blanket in bed that night or whether Bo will beat us at mahjong again.

It's a cloudy evening, the air strangely still. Our boat scuds slowly across the sea. It rained earlier, and the warm air is scented with the musk of wet wood. The temperature has been rising for days now that we're close to the southern coast, where even in winter it's hot, earning the provinces of Kitori and Jana their nickname the Summer States.

Wren gives me a kiss as she kneels beside me on the decking, her face gilded in the lantern light. Hiro passes out cups of purplish seaweed tea. I take mine, smiling a thanks at him. As they have for Wren, the peaceful weeks on the ship seem to have healed him; the bruises under his eyes are barely visible, and there's color in his cheeks now, their hollows less deep.

"What are we feasting on tonight?" Bo asks as he flops down at Merrin's side, his gangly legs stretching out. "I know today's catch was a delicacy. You were so excited when you got back you had to have a little lie-down to... cool off." His voice slinks to a purr, his grin smug. "Even needed my help with that, didn't you?"

I stifle a snort in my tea. Nitta doesn't try to hide her groan while Caen looks as though he's furiously trying to raze the images Bo's words conjure from his mind.

Merrin tips his beak, looking down at Bo haughtily, though his eyes are sparkling. "Not sure you're much help with anything, sweet boy," he teases. Then he adds, "But Bo's right. Seeing as it's our last full day at sea, I took the time to find something special."

"Tuna!" the leopard-boy guesses excitedly. "No wait—shark!"

Nitta sighs. "Why would you be excited about that? Don't you remember that banquet at the Gensharu Clan's palace? You claimed the stewed shark was the most disgusting thing you'd ever eaten."

"Hang on," I say as Bo opens his mouth to retort. I look at Merrin. "Did you say...?"

He smiles. "I paired my fishing trip earlier with a little reconnaissance. We're on course to reach the Mersing Archipelago right around sunset tomorrow evening."

Excited murmurs run through the group. I wet my lips as my stomach gives an anxious kick. Our time on the ship has been such a respite that I sometimes imagined if we could just keep sailing on into the never-ending blue then we would always be this comfortable, this happy, this safe.

Then I would remember Naja's threat. What happened at the fishing village. Everything we're fighting for. And the fire would blaze through me once more.

"Tomorrow!" Bo punches a fist into the air with a whoop, which makes Merrin laugh and smother him in kisses.

"This means that the most dangerous part of our mission is about to begin," Caen points out, serious. But his warning falls on deaf ears.

"Bring it!" Nitta sings. She leaps lightly to her feet. "It's been far too boring around here recently—we haven't had a near-death experience in weeks. We're losing our touch."

She dances off into the cabin, emerging a moment later with a big plate in her hands piled with thick fish steaks. Their sweet fragrance instantly makes my mouth water.

"Grilled swordfish!" she announces proudly, setting the steaming platter down on a crate. Bo hops up to proffer his plate. She slides two pieces onto it with her chopsticks—then prods the end of the chopsticks in his cheeks. "Get back, you'll salivate all over them."

He takes his plate with a sniff. "You could have saved the sword at least."

"Don't worry, Little Bro. I cleaned it off. You can play with it later."

Wren and I laugh at the joy this clearly brings him.

Merrin arches a brow. "Just how old *are* you?"

"Don't worry, Feathers. No one's going to arrest you for what we did earlier." Bo smirks, tickling Merrin on the cheek, and though the owl demon looks annoyed, he also seems rather self-satisfied.

"I suppose you have no need of Lord Hidei's remedy, then," Hiro says seriously, speaking for the first time that evening.

For a moment, I can't think of what he's talking about. Then I groan. "Oh, gods. The ground bison penis."

"Ground bison *what*?" Wren asks, as Nitta, Bo, and I explode into gales of laughter, the others looking confused.

I wave a hand at her, trying to catch my breath. "Trust me, my love. You *don't* want to know."

The mood the rest of the night is celebratory. We've spent enough time discussing our next courses of action over the last few weeks, so even though it's the night before our expected arrival at the Czos' palace, no one brings it up. Instead, we swap jokes and stories of home, debate frivolous things with no consequence. After dinner, Shifu Caen magically reveals two bottles of some dark liquor he discovered the first night while scouting the boat for supplies that he stashed away from the rest of us, which makes Nitta and Bo erupt with indignance.

After a less-than-furtive look in my direction, Caen twists the cork off one of the bottles. "I was saving them for tonight."

"Now let me save them from *you*," Bo retorts with a glower, snatching the bottle. He takes a long swig, only giving it up when his sister grapples it from him. She smacks her lips appreciatively after her fill, then holds it out to me.

Caen takes it from her before I can. "Lei has training tomorrow morning," he says gruffly. "It's important she keeps a clear head."

I glare at him as a ripple of tension goes through the group.

"Caen," Merrin warns, low.

"No," I say, holding up a hand. I face the shifu. "You're right. I need to keep a clear head, which is exactly what having a drink or two helps me with."

"The only thing it should help you with is feeling warm. Anything more, and there's a problem."

Wren lays a hand on my arm. "Lei…" she murmurs.

I shake my head. Though my voice pitches in anger, at the same time tears shimmer in my eyes, and I feel ridiculous all of a sudden, ashamed for being upset, and not quite sure why I even *am* so upset in the first place. "Well, I like the way it calms me, all right?" I snap. "Is that so wrong? Is it so bad to like how it makes everything go away, all those thoughts and awful memories—"

I cut off abruptly, my cheeks flaming at how much I've said. The others are all watching me with the same sad look. Water sloshes weakly against the sides of the boat. The lanterns crackle into the quiet.

"We understand, Lei," Nitta says gently. "No one is judging you."

Wren squeezes my arm. "Come on, my love." Planting a kiss to the swirl of my ear, she helps me to my feet and leads me around the cabin to the back of the ship. The voices of the others rise behind us, a wordless hum. Away from the lantern light, the sea stretches out in a dark carpet of lustrous cobalt black. Everything is oddly still: the water, the air, even the clouds seemingly suspended mid-flight. Without starlight, the ocean surface appears hard and flat, like a thick glass sheet you could skate over.

Wren draws me under the eaves of the cabin. She waits a while before breaking the silence. "What you said back there…"

I nod, avoiding her eyes.

"They haunt me, too," she admits. "All those times. With him." She releases a long breath. "But we have to find healthier ways to deal with them."

I slide a hand behind her head, my fingers tangling in her thick hair. "I can think of some," I say. And when I see her velvet-brown eyes soften with a welcome understanding, I lean forward and brush my lips against hers.

Wren and I dissolve into each other's arms, melting into the shadows beneath the eaves, and, slowly, all other thoughts disappear. Not just thoughts; thought *itself*. Memory and fear. Every haunted moment of our pasts. We kiss and touch and breathe in unison, and I become a purely sensory thing, inhabiting every inch of my body. I am pleasure and love. I am desire and need. I am Lei and Wren is Wren, the two of us neither Paper Girls nor warriors caught in the last peaceful moments before war, but simply two girls in love and lust.

We are skin and fire. We are quickening heartbeats and liquid pleasure.

And, for a while at least, we are free.

Afterward, we sit side by side, our backs to the cabin wall. We gaze out at the velvet darkness. Like that first night on the boat, my pulse is racing, but this time it's for a good reason— the best reason—and I revel in it. After all this time, making love to Wren still feels like healing, like being made anew.

A sudden flash of memory jerks me from my comfort.

The King. That night with him, the very opposite of making love, of being remade. It was like having love *stolen*. Ripped straight from my soul.

It was like being made undone.

I close my eyes and push out a long exhale, imagining the memory leaving with my breath. *Light in, darkness out.*

When I open my eyes again, Wren's lifted a hand to her forehead. She traces the jagged line of the scar winding across it, almost hidden by her hairline.

"How's it feeling?" I ask.

"Tight. A bit sensitive. Like I stayed out too long in the sun." She drops her hand. "I've never had a scar."

"How *is* that? Five weeks of training and I'm covered in them."

Wren shoots me a sideways glance. "Magic."

"You use magic to heal your scars?"

Her mouth slants. "When you say it like that, it sounds so vain."

"I mean, I understand." I nuzzle the crook of her neck. "If I looked like you, I'd never want to change."

"It's not because of that," Wren replies stiffly.

I draw back, waiting for her to go on.

"Back at the palace," she begins, "I couldn't raise anyone's suspicion as to who I was or what I was capable of. But I suppose I've also always been aware of having to look invincible. That I can't show any flaws. Scars are a physical representation of our vulnerability. When you've been trained from birth to become the kingdom's deadliest assassin, how can you reveal to everyone that you're just like them? That *you* can be hurt, too?"

"Wren," I say carefully, "being vulnerable isn't a flaw. It's the most beautiful thing in the world. If you were invincible, being brave would be easy. It's the fact that it *isn't* easy, that we have to constantly work and work at it, make ourselves believe in our own strength even when it feels like we're worth nothing, have nothing, can do nothing... *that's* power. That's resilience." I squeeze her arm. "There is nothing stronger than people who endure the worst hardships in the world, and still raise their fists at the start of a new day to fight all over again."

Wren tilts her head to me. She smiles. "You do realize you've just described why I love *you*?"

Tears spring to my eyes. I press my face into her shoulder, and she wraps an arm around me, holding me to her as we rock in silence to the soothing sway of the boat. The raised voices of the others reach us as if through a veil. Because right now, just for these few, sweet moments, it feels as though there is nothing in the world that can touch us. Even if the rest of the world collapsed around us, here Wren and I would remain, protected by our love and our hope and our sheer determination to survive whatever the universe might throw at us.

TWENTY-ONE

KENZO

THEY CAME FOR HIM IN DARKNESS. Every day, the same routine. Heavy footsteps, a snicker of metal, the grating slide of the door. Then lantern light, with its warm, liquid glow. The smell of winter carried in with his visitors from outside, and something else, something acrid and spiced and biting that he knew was an odor his mind had conjured, uncurling smoke-like not from anything physically present but from the horrors living in his mind, the maze of pain that had become his life now.

Today—or tonight, who knew which was which down in this underground realm—was no different. Kenzo stirred, his wolf ears sharpening. The footsteps on the stone outside were uneven, both claw-tipped and light, a dragging noise alongside them blurring the usual details he could use to detect who would be his visitor this day. A flutter of anxiousness passed through him before he pushed it away.

So today would be different. He was adaptable. He was strong. Whatever new hell this visitor was bringing him, he could handle it—just as he'd done each time before.

He *had* to handle it. Others were counting on him.

By the time the metal door to his cell was unlocked, Kenzo was already kneeling, which was the best he could do against the weight of the enchanted shackles encircling his arms and legs.

"Wolf."

Naja's voice cut through the thick air of the cell like a knife. Golden light spilled from a lantern held by a small figure next to her. After hours of darkness, the light blinded Kenzo. He blinked, waiting for the fierce glow of the lantern to recede. Once it did, he was surprised by what faced him.

The white fox looked like hell. Naja's usually sleek hair was matted and dull. The hollows of her cheeks and eyes sunk deeper than usual, and there was a sickly pallor to her complexion. Though she wore a heavy coat, the snowflakes dusted across it just beginning to melt, he could tell she'd lost weight. Her already thin frame seemed shrunken beneath all those winter layers. She was slumped, propping herself up with the help of the reptilian Moon girl next to her—whom Kenzo recognized as Naja's maid—and looking every bit as furious about this as he would expect.

What in the gods had happened to her?

Kenzo wrested his face into a composed expression. "General Naja. Should I be wishing you a good morning or a good night?" He waved a wrist, then winced at the fresh hurt shooting through him. His arms fell back to his sides, swinging with the weighted bands. "You'll forgive me for not knowing. It's…a little difficult to tell down here."

Despite her appearance, Naja's snarl had lost none of its viciousness. "Shut up, keeda-lover. I'm not in the mood for small talk. The past few weeks have been—" She cut off with a grimace. One of her arms was crooked inside her coat. She shifted it uncomfortably before her fury refocused on Kenzo, somehow even sharper than before. "We've been at this long enough. It's time to talk."

Though the air was frigidly cold, sweat pricked Kenzo's brow with the effort of keeping the pain from showing on his face. "What would you like to discuss?" he replied serenely.

With a snarl, Naja jerked forward as though to hit him. But she stopped short, wincing again, twisting her body toward her maid as she doubled over, panting. The arm within her coat shifted again. It seemed she couldn't let go of the girl nor use her other arm properly.

Relief poured over Kenzo in a dizzying wave. She couldn't hurt him. At least, not today.

"What happened to you, Naja?" he asked.

Fury etched her features. "*I* ask the questions, not you. Kiroku!" she ordered. "The bag!"

The lizard-girl set the lantern down. Carefully, she moved Naja to the wall of the cell, where she could lean on her own, before swinging a pack off her shoulder and kneeling in front of Kenzo.

"Show him the pin," Naja commanded.

Kenzo waited, watching. Though his head swam with light-headedness and he was panting at the effort of staying upright against the bands and the pain that sparked and buzzed throughout his body, there was curiosity now, too.

Kiroku rummaged inside the bag, her russet scales glinting in the lantern light. She withdrew an object and held it out for Kenzo to see.

It was a small silver brooch, the kind that southerners liked to pin to their saris and sarongs. He'd seen many delegates from Kitori and Jana wearing them, and knew the designs were unique to each clan. This pin was shaped into a dandelion, with barbed tendrils winding their way around its stem.

Kenzo's heart thudded hard. But he kept his face impassive as he looked up.

"Well?" Naja prompted. "Do you recognize it? Who does it belong to?"

Kenzo's gaze dropped back to the brooch. He'd seen this design before, though not as a pin but as a print on a piece of fabric. Often, that's how he communicated with the Hannos and their allies: through messages wrapped in cloth, so it was easy to tuck into robes and pass from hand to hand without noticing, and could be promptly burned once read. This design had come from a message from the Cat Clan about the disruptions to trade routes serving the palace that they were organizing. The dandelion was their unofficial symbol—the hardy desert flower that could survive in even the harshest of sands.

He pretended to inspect the brooch closely before lying, "I've never seen it before."

Naja's lip curled. "The map," she said after a beat.

Returning the pin to the pack, Kiroku brought out a scroll. It was worn, the paper rumpled and torn in places. She rolled it open.

There was just enough light from the lantern to make out what was on it. Kenzo's eyes roamed over the paper. The map was faded and badly burned in places, but he could see a cluster of what seemed at first to be abstract hills and settlements amid thicker brushstrokes. Ridges? A mountainscape of some kind? Then it hit him. These were islands.

The Czos' archipelago in northwestern Kitori.

Nothing was marked, but he recognized the shape of the Czos' island at the heart of the cluster. And besides, there wasn't another archipelago like it along the whole of the Ikharan coast. He went very still, conscious not to indicate his increasing curiosity—and worry—as to where the bag's items had come from.

"The Mersing Archipelago," Kenzo said. No point in denying it. He was sure Naja had also realized what the map depicted. "Planning a trip to the Czo?"

The white fox stared. "Someone is."

Kenzo's ears pricked. Was that a tremble he detected in her voice? His eyes took in Naja's weakened form again, more probing now. Why was she holding her arm that way, and why did it make such a strange shape beneath the coat?

But like him, Naja was doing her best not to let her discomfort show. She jutted her chin and went on, "We intercepted them at the Shomu coast, stealing a boat. We know they're heading south. Our spies along the coast have confirmed as much, and this map makes it clear where their destination is. A battleship is already on their tail, so I doubt they'll ever make it there, but just in case, we thought we'd ask you to explain it to us. What do Hanno and his supporters want with the Czo Clan?"

The calmness on Kenzo's face felt plastered there, a suffocating mask. "I have no idea. As I've told you before, Ketai Hanno never shared his plans with me beyond the King's assassination—"

"Liar!"

Naja moved instinctively, her anger overpowering whatever her new limitations were. As she lashed out, her heavy coat slipped halfway off. Stumbling, she snatched the coat back up, Kiroku jumping up to stop her from falling as she twisted into the wall. Naja panted heavily as she righted herself with Kiroku's help, and her anger and pain were accompanied with a twist of something else, something far worse: shame.

All of this happened very quickly. But Kenzo had seen what the white fox had been hiding—her right arm. Or rather, her lack of it.

Now it was nothing more than a stump, cut off halfway below her shoulder and wadded in bandages. More bandages held it in place against her chest, but they'd come loose when Naja had lashed out.

Bundled back in her heavy coat, Naja was seething, looking as if she wished she could open his throat with her claws right there. While she'd already snuffed out her look of disgrace at her new-found weakness, pity continued to course through Kenzo.

He was no fan of the white fox. Yet he also didn't enjoy seeing her affected in this way. Hurt was not something he wished on anyone, even those who deserved it. But more than that, he knew this injury would only increase the anger and hatred that Naja drew in with each breath, as vital to her as oxygen. This was what he truly pitied. Not to have lost an arm. He knew plenty of demons and humans with disabilities who were capable and happy and strong. But to be driven by such cannibalistic emotions, emotions that were poisonous to all who touched them...most of all herself.

It was no way to live.

"I'll give you one more chance to answer," Naja said through clenched teeth. "What do the Hannos want with the Czo?"

"I don't know," Kenzo repeated.

She glared at him with her cutting silver eyes. "Fine. We'll be finding out shortly, anyway. That is, if your precious keeda and their friends make it to the island in the first place." A vein pulsed in her furred temple. "Kiroku. Give the Wolf his last present so we can get going. I forgot how much this place stinks."

Of all the items, this one was the hardest for Kenzo to fake indifference to.

The piece of fabric was just a scrap, thin and frayed where it had been torn from the dress it once belonged to. Lantern light made its golden threads glitter. It was marked with stains: dark splotches across more than half the material. The shred of fabric could have been anything, but Kenzo's memory was eidetic, and this memory in particular—the image of the last time he'd seen the girl who'd been wearing the dress this cloth came from—was particularly strong.

Lei had looked so small next to Wren, the two of them facing off against Naja in the gardens around the Floating Hall. The King's discarded body lay close to the lily pond at the edge of the clearing, his blood already staining the grass and even spreading in curling tendrils across the water. But despite Lei's size, Kenzo had been struck most by the fierce determination blazing off of the girl. It had been electric, charging the air like the moment before a lightning strike.

She was a Paper Girl set on fire. He'd never been prouder of her.

Now, his eyes took in the torn scrap of her Moon Ball slip as though if he studied it long enough its secrets would reveal themselves. How did Naja get this? Were those stains from wounds Lei received the night of the ball, or another time?

"You'd better not have hurt her," he growled, before he could stop himself.

"What makes you think she's still even alive?"

This time, it was Kenzo who reared forward instinctively. Pain rocketed through him with ear-splitting force at the movement, and the dao-infused shackles held him back. He strained against them, face twisting. "You'd better not have hurt either of those girls!" he roared.

Naja smiled. "There he is. We were waiting for you to return, keeda-lover." She jerked her head. "Kiroku! Get the bag. I'll see you again soon, Wolf."

The lizard-girl let the golden scrap of Lei's dress flutter to the floor. Then she gathered up the pack and picked up the lantern. She hooked her arm around Naja's waist and, with that odd lopsided gait he'd heard in the corridor, the two of them made their way out of the cell.

Kenzo's heart drummed as the metal door slid shut. The sound of keys turning; darkness swallowed him back up. He collapsed to the floor, exhaustion finally overpowering him, and listened to Naja's and Kiroku's footsteps fading to nothing.

The Lunar Lake prison had been built deep underground for extra security. There was only one way in, which was guarded by both guards and shamans, and then there was the lake itself, more than four hundred yards in diameter and one hundred deep. There were signs in Kenzo's cell of the immense body of water that sat only a few feet overhead: the moss and mold that crawled over the stone, the steady drip-drip that punctured the silence, the wet taste of the frigid air. But there were certain times more than others when Kenzo could really *feel* the crushing weight of the lake. Now was one of them. As he sat slumped over, palms to the rough stone, it was as though the ceiling had finally buckled under all those years of pressure and had come down upon his shoulders.

He dragged in painful breaths. The way the lantern light had made the golden scrap of Lei's dress glitter played over and over in his head.

So. Naja had caught up with them. The group had made it past her, though, and onto a ship.

If it had taken her all this time to return to the palace and be healed well enough to visit him, even in the state she was in, then they must still be on the ocean right now. They were probably only a few days out from the Mersing Archipelago. Lei and Naja must have had some sort of fight if the white fox had managed to get a scrap of her clothing—though he didn't understand why she'd still be wearing that bloodstained dress—and either that fight or one with another of the group had left Naja maimed.

It was a relief to have news of the group. But the relief was tainted with Naja's smugness. Her hints that they might be intercepted again soon.

Slowly, gingerly, weighed down by everything—pain and worry and the shackles and the lake, looming, looming above—Kenzo lowered to the floor. He stretched out a hand, searching for the scrap of Lei's dress they had left with him, wanting its comfort. After a few moments, his furred fingers brushed the worn fabric— along with something small and hard Kiroku had hidden beneath it.

The item buzzed, warm to the touch. He plucked it up, hardly daring to believe it. Though he couldn't make out much in the darkness, it was clear from touch alone what it was.

A blade.

Thin, small, with a pointed edge. A pointed edge, perfect for working into locks—like those of shackles, for example, or a metal prison door. Its electric hum came from magic.

An enchanted knife, then, for picking enchanted locks.

Just then, a whisper uncurled from the blade. It must have been hidden with magic, his touch triggering its release. The soft words were spoken directly into his ears.

It was one of the most glorious whispers Kenzo had ever heard. A whisper that instantly buoyed the crushing weight on his shoulders, as though the hands of a giant god had come down and lifted the prison roof away. He drew in a deep breath for what felt like the first time in years.

Help is coming soon, the enchanted voice said. *You will know when.*
Be ready.

TWENTY-TWO

FASTER! HARDER! ATTACK WITH CONVICTION!"
Shifu Caen's shouts ring out with each of my strikes. He moves almost lazily, easily flowing with my assault, blocking each of my blows with his sword, its blade safe within its lacquered sheath. My own weapon is nothing more than a piece of the ship's railing we broke off for me to train with, a makeshift staff. The cherry-red paint is cracked, slithers littering the deck around us like scraps of dried blood. At my waist, my dagger seems to vibrate, calling me to wrap my fingers around its hilt and pull it free. But Caen forbid me to use it at practice today.

"What if it gets lost," he'd said before we started, "or someone takes it from you? What if Hiro and Wren aren't around to redo the enchantment?"

"I hope they'll be around," I countered. "And not just because of my blade."

"The one thing we can never be certain of in life is the lives of others. Especially the ones we want to protect the most." And he handed me the staff with a look on his face that said our discussion was over.

Now I clench my jaw and put all my weight behind a thrust at his gut.

Caen deflects it with a sword flick. "Lazy!" he complains. "You have to strike as though you mean it! We may be practicing, but this is real, Lei. You must treat each battle as though it could cost you your life so that when faced with ones that can, you are prepared. Weak again!" he barks, employing a sharp jab with his left hand to break my latest strike, as though the effort of using his sword would be a waste.

Sweat drips from my forehead. "I'm *trying*," I snarl through gritted teeth.

"Try harder!"

I force a steady breath and reset my attacking stance. The humid ocean air provides no relief from my sweat-soaked shirt and trousers, which cling to my wet skin. Caen and I have been fighting for more than half an hour. Before this, we practiced qi-gong sequences and drilled strikes and countermovements for two hours. Every muscle in my body is trembling, but I refuse to stop.

"Go on, Lei!" Nitta yells.

"Yeah!" Bo shakes his fists. "Stick it to old Grumpy Face for us!"

The whole group has gathered to see the results of my training. They watch from the railing as Caen and I circle each other slowly. My legs scream with tiredness, my shoulders aching. I steady myself, flexing my hands on the staff.

"You've got this, Lei."

Her voice is husky, low. I lift my eyes past Caen to meet Wren's gaze. Her eyes blaze with pride. The corners of her mouth lift—

Caen's sword crashes through the air.

I raise my staff at the last second. The smack of our weapons makes my teeth ring. Until now, Shifu Caen has played a defensive strategy, only countering my strikes.

"Never allow yourself to be distracted!" he chides.

He ducks, swooping his sword at my ankles. I jump just in time. Dodge another blow, this time aimed at my middle, then leap forward to make my own.

The last of the paint on my makeshift staff flakes off as our weapons collide. We parry furiously for a further ten minutes. I'm panting so hard it's all I can do to keep the staff level in my hands, but I don't back down. Caen and I dance across the deck. My ponytail flies behind me; his long hair sticks to his neck and chin with sweat, his bearded jaw clenched. The shouts of the others whirl around us, goading me on.

Caen advances in a strong sequence of attacks that pin me against the cabin wall. I rally my energy and drive him back, moving low and fast, not afraid to get close to him where his sword has less range and I can take advantage of my small stature to target his lower body. Without the magic of my dagger, my attacks are less powerful, but my precision has improved even without it and the determination to prove myself imbues me with more strength than I thought myself capable of.

Another five minutes pass. Ten. Fifteen. At least, it feels like it. I'm flagging now, dragging in ragged breaths, my lungs burning. Still, the pain hones my focus. Centers my concentration on the shifu, narrowing the world to a pinpoint on his body and the fierce hacks of his sheathed sword. Then I see it. We draw apart from a particularly close call, where Shifu Caen's sword almost struck my right hand where I'm holding the staff, which could have easily crushed my fingers. Caen shifts his back leg.

He's readying for an overhead strike. When he does this, he lets open a space to his right.

The knowledge comes to me so clearly it's as though the shifu himself had told me his own weakness. Which in a way he did, through weeks of training, hours of revealing his fighting habits to my subconscious.

"Thanks, subconscious," I mutter, as Caen lifts his sword in both hands.

I step to the left. Spin the staff upright, and strike.

My staff meets his side with a thwack.

Caen lets out a grunt, his sword arm faltering. Panting heavily, he steps back, watching me with his dark, amethyst-flecked eyes. His serious expression doesn't betray anything at first. Then he cracks a small smile. "Well done, Lei."

Cheers and yells ring out. I drop my staff, buckling to my knees, as Nitta and Bo run forward, bundling into me with so much force that I'm knocked to the floor. I laugh, letting them smother me. A moment later, Merrin's prickly feathers wrap around us all.

"Brilliant work, dear girl," he praises.

When they move back, I share a look with Wren, who's smiling, too, watching me from a distance, her face shining proudly. Then I meet Shifu Caen's gaze. I swipe a sleeve across my wet forehead. "That's all you have to say? After all these weeks, that's it? 'Well done'?"

He lifts a shoulder. "It was one hit."

"Against one of Ikhara's most skilled warriors."

Bo raises a hand. "Um, where is this list and can someone please verify that my name is indeed on there? With my lightning reflexes and unparalleled skills with a staff, I really should be number one."

Merrin cuffs him lightly on the back of the head.

"Hey!" Bo complains.

The owl demon smirks. "Not *quite* lightning reflexes, then. However, I for one can certainly verify your skills with a staff."

Nitta and I snort while Caen and Hiro look as though they're seriously considering jumping overboard just to get away from the rest of us.

With a slink in his gait, Bo sidles forward, flashing his snaggle-toothed grin at Caen. "Oh, Shifu," he taunts, "is that a *blush* I see—"

He breaks off with a strange gurgle. Something sharp and angular protrudes from his chest. It takes me a second to realize what it is.

An arrowhead.

It glints in the overcast light, slick with blood. More red spreads across Bo's wrap shirt, quickly, violently, like an ugly rose unfurling its petals.

The leopard-boy blinks. Then his eyes roll back in his head.

Nitta screams.

Merrin grabs Bo and pulls him down, spreading his wing-arms to cover both of them, as more arrows whistle through the air to stud the deck of the boat. One lands inches from my feet.

From the opposite side of the boat, Wren bounds forward. "Lei!" she yells. "Get down!"

Maybe I'm still in fight mode from training. Maybe I'm just tired of hiding. Instead of following her orders, I spin around and leap up from the deck onto the rail. Caen has the same idea. The two of us reach the starboard side of the boat at the same time.

Shock shudders through me. Looming upon us, cleaving through the water with a reinforced steel prow headed with a figurehead molded into the form of a charging bull, is an enormous battleship. The ship is at least six times the size of our boat. Its black wood hull slices powerfully through the water. Scarlet sails stamped with the King's bull insignia billow from towering masts. Below the web of rigging, lining the deck from prow to stern—rows of royal soldiers.

They stand in rigid formation, legs braced against the thundering speed of their ship, brandishing weapons of all kinds. Every sort of Moon and Steel demon is present: wolf, boar, jackal, fox, lion, elk, ape. There are too many to take in.

"Shamans," Hiro breathes, materializing at my side.

Heart pounding, I scan the deck and spot them standing under the sails, their obsidian robes billowing in the magical wind whipping from their outstretched hands, skin crawling with tattoos.

That's how the boat is moving so swiftly while ours flounders in the still air. Perhaps it's why the air *is* so still in the first place.

As the ship draws closer, our own starts to rock, buffeted by the battleship's waves. The heated electric ripples of magic hit me as the powerful gales of the enchanted wind reach us, flapping our clothes. We're close enough this time to hear the barked order of a deep-voiced General.

"Fire!"

We duck. I press up against the gunwale as arrows pepper the deck.

Wren looks around the group, addressing us over the slap and churn of waves beating the hull. "They're not using their cannons, which means they've had orders not to kill us. Or at least, some of us. We just have to outrun them! Merrin, do you think you can get close enough to tear their sails?"

He doesn't seem to have heard. The owl demon stares down at his lap where Bo is splayed, nestled in the crook of his winged arm. Bo's blood runs down Merrin's feathers, vivid red against the white.

The leopard-boy isn't moving.

"It's all right, sweetheart," Merrin whispers, clutching at him. "You're fine. I've got you. I'm here."

"Merrin," Caen says gently, "we need your help."

He doesn't look up.

Nitta reaches forward. "Let me take him." After a beat, Merrin helps shift Bo into her arms. She presses a hand to her brother's chest, bracing the area around the tip of the arrow to stem some of the blood. Her face is streaked with tears, but her look is fierce. "I've got him!" she says. "Go!"

Merrin blinks. His orange eyes are hollow, unfocused. "H-he needs to be healed—"

Hiro moves in a crouch to Nitta's side. "I'll do it."

"Merrin, please!" Wren shouts. "The sails!"

"You have to save him," Merrin croaks, his face ashen. He looks lost without Bo's body in his arms. Crimson patches splash his feathers and usually pristine sky-blue hanfu.

"We will," Wren promises. "Now, go!"

With one last long look at Bo's limp form, Merrin spreads his wings and pushes off into the air.

Shouts rise up as the soldiers spot him. There are barked orders to shoot, and this time, the arrows are not aimed our way.

Wren is already on her feet. "Caen!" she cries, sprinting to one of our boat's three sails.

He leaps up, understanding at once.

As he heads to move the rudder while Wren tugs on the ropes to fully open the sails, Wren calls over her shoulder, "Hiro! We need wind!"

The shaman boy had just laid his hands over Bo's chest. He hesitates, looking up.

"He's working on Bo!" I yell back.

Wren twists to face us, her face blazing, already working on the next sail. "If we don't get moving now, we'll all be dead!"

"I'm sorry," Hiro whispers to Nitta.

Her face slackens. *"Please—"*

But he has already moved away. He hops down to the deck. Taking a wide stance to brace himself against the rock of the boat, Hiro lifts his arms. His lips weave the beginnings of a dao as Wren finishes with the sails and comes to his side. She takes a similar stance, hands outstretched. I catch a glimpse of her eyes—glazed, arctic white—before her hair is whipped free of its ribbon, lashing around her face in dark tangles as a strong wind bursts to life.

Our ship jerks forward. Nitta braces herself, curving protectively around Bo. As we pick up pace, skating across the water in the enchanted wind, I risk a look over the railing.

The royal ship is almost upon us.

Even though we're sailing faster now, it's had a huge run up, not to mention its own magical wind power is that of not two but at least *twenty* black-robed shamans. Clouds roil overhead as the ship rears closer. Near enough to make out the individual faces of the demon soldiers, the blur of arrows as Merrin swoops in tight circles around its masts.

The second there's an opening, he dives at one of the black sails, talons outstretched. A soldier in the lookout post leaps at him, sword slashing through the air.

Merrin cants his wing at the last moment. The soldier plummets to the deck with a shout as Merrin tears a long rip through one of the sails.

"Wren!"

I swivel at Caen's cry. He's running across the deck to where Wren has collapsed to her knees.

I'm on my feet at once. Hiro's magical wind buffets us as he works harder to make up for Wren stopping, his face a grim, determined mask.

Caen seizes Wren, pushing back her hair as I run to join them. Her eyes are brown again. Usually it's a relief to see this, but not now. Not when we so desperately need her power.

I tuck my hand around her cheek. "Love? What's wrong?"

Her face is pale. She sucks in a shallow breath. "Blood," she breathes.

I frown, scanning her body. "I don't see any—"

With an angry growl, she pushes Shifu Caen and me away. Though we keep our arms out in case she falls, she looks steady enough as she gets to her feet.

"Wren," Caen warns, "you're still not healthy enough."

"Hiro's been making his blood payments for the last week," she shoots back. "That's why he's strong enough. We need this, Caen."

Without another word of explanation, she grabs at my belt and draws my dagger from its sheath with her right hand—

—and closes her left around its blade.

I don't have time to react. Blood is running down her arm in seconds, painting red rivers against her tanned skin. Wren's eyes roll back. Frost crawls across her irises. As she shifts back to face the sails, her hair and clothes starting to whip around her, she drops my dagger and raises her hands, the left drenched in blood.

Words spurt from her mouth, that strange Ikharan language only shamans understand. She speaks deep and fast. Undulating shivers of magic begin to flow. The wind that had faded with only Hiro to conjure it picks up with sudden vengeance, stronger this time, so cold it tears icily across my skin. At once, our boat jumps forward, crashing with a roar through the waves.

Thunder booms overhead. What had been smooth white clouds are now churning into a roiling mass of dark storm clouds. Fat beads of rain hit my upturned face, just a few at first. Then the skies release.

Water sloughs the deck, soaking me in seconds. I look wildly to Shifu Caen, hardly able to see him through the downpour. His expression is as sober as ever, though through his impassioned mask, something has loosened: fear.

My words come out in a hiss. "What the *gods* was that."

A high-pitched cry splits the air before he can answer. *Nitta.*

We whirl around. Through the rain and wind, I spot the shadowy figures of Nitta and two—no, three—soldiers fighting, Bo's body left exposed on the deck behind her.

The soldiers must have jumped over when our boats drew level, or perhaps shot a hook and rope across to climb aboard.

In the time it takes me to realize this, Caen has already drawn his sword. Shoving back the wet hair from my face, I snatch up my dagger by Wren's feet, cringing at the blood—*her* blood—that has already been half washed away by the rain. I give her one last look: whirling raven hair; open palms, one white, one red; frozen, unseeing eyes. Then I'm skidding across the wet deck to where the metallic clash of swords rings out, dark figures moving on the gunwale.

Nitta grapples with one of the soldiers. Caen fences sword to sword with the other two. Their blades flash through the driving sheets of rain, the sing of metal making my teeth ring.

I push myself into the fight. One of the two soldiers that had been attacking Caen shifts his attention to me. The demon is heavy, all bulk. He towers over me. Sparkling maroon eyes glint out from his snouted, dark-furred face. A bear-form.

Blood roars in my ears. Everything screams at me to run away. But I don't move, *won't* move.

The demon lifts his ji. The twin crescent blades at the top of the staff glint through the sheets of rain.

My mind stills. Back at the palace, Zelle taught me once that sex is a simple case of action and reaction. Touch and response. At its core, I've learned that fighting is the same. As if moving in a dream, I take the defensive stance Caen taught me when fighting an opponent of this size, brandish my dagger.

And growl.

With a roar, the bear-soldier drives the spiked end of his ji at me—just as I anticipated. I dance to the right as the pole comes crashing down. Wooden decking splinters with a crash under the weight of the blow. As he grunts, prizing it free, I spring off my back foot and fling myself forward, aiming my weapon for the weak spot beneath his left armpit.

The blade sinks into his flesh.

Shifu Caen showed me how the right angle here allows a dagger of this length to reach the heart. But just before my attack landed, the bear demon shifted. It throws off my angle by mere degrees. Though he snarls in pain, he recovers quickly. Rain drips from his dark clothes and fur. He clutches a fistful of my shirt and lifts me into the air. Flashes of lightning reflect off the crescent blades of his ji.

Move! I scream at myself. *Do something!*

But the position is too familiar, and I'm paralyzed by memories. Memories of a moonlit garden, and the King. The crack of my skull against a tree.

This is what each crack of thunder sounds like: the world breaking apart around my ears.

I watch in helpless horror as the bear demon brandishes his weapon. But just as he's about to slash it straight through me, there's a yell from one of the other soldiers.

"Iyano, stop! That's her! That's the girl!"

The bear demon falters. He lowers me a fraction, peering through narrowed eyes through the rain to see what he missed before: *my* eyes. As golden as the lightning flashing around us.

The instant recognition sparks in his gaze, I wrench my body around and clash out with my dagger.

Blood spurts from the soldier's forearm. He drops me with a grunt. As soon as I land, I throw myself forward and drive my blade deep into his gut.

The demon gasps. I wrench my weapon back. His hands go to his belly, clutching at his wound with an incredulous look on his face. Blood gushes around his fingers, slicking over his dark fur. He drops to his knees, still gaping down in surprise.

Over his head, the soldier fighting with Caen sees what's happened. He roars, a tiger's deep-bellied snarl, and leaps toward me.

Silver arcs through the air.

Caen's sword cuts the tiger-soldier down. He crumples, falling in a heap over his comrade.

I stagger back, gulping for air. Rain coats every inch of me. It thunders onto the deck, so loud it takes me a while to notice the clash of blades has stopped. I look around blearily. Nitta is hunched over Bo, murmuring low and fast, words lost to the storm. Beyond the mound of the bear demon's and tiger demon's bodies, another royal soldier sprawls prone across the railing, Caen standing over him. The shifu wipes his sword down, returning it to the sheath at his back. Then he crouches by the bodies of the soldiers, head low, and makes the sky gods salute.

A throaty cry makes us both look up.

Merrin tumbles across the decking in a messy landing, just missing knocking over Wren and Hiro where they're still casting their magic. As Caen rushes to help him, I cross to the railing, clutching it against the ship's violent bucking.

The sea is completely transformed. Gone are the relaxed waves of the past couple of days, of just ten minutes ago even. This new ocean is a living thing. It thrashes and surges, a dark mass of roiling waves and coal-black storm clouds. Day has become night. A flash of lightning illuminates the view, and through the sheets of rain I spot the hulking mass of the royal battleship.

It's far, almost too far to make out. With the next burst of lightning, it's fallen entirely out of view.

Letting out a puff of relief, I stow away my dagger—right in time to grab the rail as the prow of the boat pitches high into the air.

Seconds later, it crashes down. Water sluices over me. My arms scream as they're almost pulled out of their sockets, but I cling on, shaking, as we hit another wave. We rear high before smashing back down. The hull of the boat groans, an almost human sound. There's the sound of wood splintering—the mast.

As if in slow motion, its red, fin-shaped sail billows as the mast topples, its top smashing down into the deck with a crash.

Right by where Wren and Hiro were standing.

I move instinctively. One moment I'm at the gunwale. The next I've leaped down to the deck and dived under the heavy, soaked-through fabric of the sail, where Wren and Hiro are *still* standing, magic billowing from their outstretched arms. The mast missed them by less than a yard.

Again, relief is only momentary. The ship gives another dangerous lurch. Water splashes across the deck. I struggle to Wren's side, my boots skidding on the wet floorboards. I seize her, but she's frozen in place, her body unnaturally stiff. The prickling vibration of magic reels off her in waves.

"Please, Wren!" I sob. "You've got to stop! The storm's too powerful, it's going to drown us!"

She doesn't hear me, lost deep in the dao. Blood is still flowing down her left arm from where she cut herself. I flinch at how red it is. But it gives me an idea.

I grab her injured hand. "I'm sorry," I say—then squeeze as tight as I can.

Wren gasps, a sudden breath that ripples throughout her entire body. And then magic floods out from her, fiercer and brighter and more powerful than before.

I'm thrown back. My head smacks against the fallen mast. Lightning crawls across the sky, neon white and cyan, scrawling angry messages from the gods.

Pain, I realize dully. It makes her magic stronger. I'd wanted to startle Wren from her dao by hurting her. Instead, I drove her deeper, gave her even greater power.

Before I can think anything more, the ship gives an almighty jolt. The world erupts in a scream of noise and rush and panic and water. The last thing I feel is an arm wrapping around my waist before the world flips upside down and darkness barrels into me.

TWENTY-THREE

*L*EI.
  Lei.
  Lei!

A voice reaches me through the blackness.

It stirs my conscience slowly, nudging it awake. One by one, as though flicked on like matches being struck, come my senses. Smell: salt and dampness, something woody. Taste: metallic and more salt. Sound: steady rain-patter, the dreamlike rhythm of waves, wind combing through leaves. Touch: hands, cool and strong, on my face, and the freshness of an ocean breeze on my skin. And aching, aching *everywhere*.

Sight comes last. At first it's just the flicker of movement beyond my eyelids. When I gather the energy to crack them open, I find Wren's lovely face hanging over me, and beyond, a dark sky full of clouds.

"Oh, thank *gods*," Wren gasps. She clutches me to her, her wet hair spilling over my face.

"Ouch?" I mumble.

She pulls back, her brown eyes wide and concerned.

"What happened?" I tilt my head, wincing at the pain even this small motion calls. To our left, waves lap the coastline. A forest stretches out to our right. It is dense with tangled vegetation, leaves glistening under the rain.

"We crashed," Wren answers, muted. "Our magic was more powerful than we expected. We traveled so fast we reached the Mersing Archipelago within minutes. Caen tried to steer us, but that sort of speed amid the reefs and underwater islands made it impossible."

"We're at the Czos' palace already?" My hands sink into the wet sand as I push myself up to sitting, pain tearing through me at the effort.

"We don't know yet. We're on one of the islands in the archipelago at least. There's no sign that the battleship has followed us here, but we should still be on guard. Are you hurt?"

I press a salty kiss to her lips. "I'm all right."

For a few moments, we sit quietly, listening to the rain. The wind here is balmy, even though it's night, but my soaked skin feels like ice. I hug my arms across my chest. Noticing, Wren rubs my arms. Over her shoulder, I see debris from our wrecked ship scattered across the beach.

"How are the others?" I ask. "How's—" My breath hitches as I remember. "Bo was hit...shouldn't you be helping heal him? He needs your magic, Wren."

But she only watches me sadly, raindrops trailing down her face like tears.

"Wren?" I repeat, whispering this time.

Her wet lashes flick down. When she lifts them again, the look in them pierces me. It is powerful and angry and sad and ashamed and horrified and fearful all at once, as though the hard glass shell her emotions are usually stored in was shattered in the crash, and they have all come spilling out like marbles, dark and ugly. And among them: the truth.

I scramble to my feet, stumbling in the wet sand as my bruised muscles scream in protest. "But—what about—oh, gods, *Nitta*," I gasp, throwing my hands over my mouth.

Wren jumps up and I fall against her with a sob. Tears spill over my cheeks, hot and furious. I burrow my face into her chest. Image after image flickers across my vision.

Bo, on nights at camp, heating his furred toes by the fire.

Bo, in the northern mountains, gazing in awe at the snow leopard, his animal kin.

Bo, winking at Merrin as some lewd joke spills from his lips.

Bo, tripping over a rock on the mountain path and kicking it in anger, only hurting himself more.

Bo, flinging his arms around his sister as they collude in some joke, heads thrown back in mirth.

Bo, complaining.

Eating.

Talking.

Walking.

Flirting.

And laughing. Laughing, and laughing, and laughing. The thought of never hearing that deep-bellied, raucous roar of a sound again breaks something deep inside me. It doesn't seem right for it not to exist anymore. How can we go on without it around us? How could the *world* survive without it? No matter how bad things got, no matter how hopeless or terrible, Bo's laughter was there to protect us. To shield us from the darkness, even if just for a moment.

That's what his laughter was—a weapon.

His own particular form of magic.

A last image comes to me of Bo on the ship, his mouth falling open in surprise, an arrowhead glinting from his chest as the first blooms of blood spread across his shirt.

"Do you want to see him?" Wren asks.

I take a shaky breath before nodding.

We find the rest of the group farther along the beach, within a hooked tip of land that has created a sheltered bay. It's nestled by mangroves and palms. The sea is calmer here; waves drift serenely across the surface. Night is falling, and in the darkening light the others are just figures hunched under the shadowy arms of vine-wrapped branches, rain pattering on the leaves.

None of them say anything as we approach. Shifu Caen and Hiro sit slightly apart from the others. At the back of the group, Merrin stands so still he could melt into the darkness of the forest, becoming yet another island tree, his feathers leaves that would one day scatter to the ground to join the ones that my heels crush as I walk across the wet beach to where Nitta kneels over Bo.

She cradles her brother in her lap, just like on the boat. Her forehead is pressed to his. She's rocking, the same way you'd soothe a baby to sleep. But this is no lullaby. There are no words of comfort to offer, because Bo is not sleeping.

He is dead.

His left arm drapes off her thighs and lies limp on the ground, tufty fur peppered with sand. His palm is open to the sky. I want to hold it, slide my fingers between his. Instead, Wren takes my hand. The two of us lower to our knees. Just as we did once before during an execution at the Hidden Palace, we make the sky gods salute together with our free hands, though this time, my fingers tremble not with anger but with grief.

"I—I'm so sorry, Nitta." My voice is hoarse, my throat scoured by salt and sorrow.

She doesn't make any indication that she's heard. Her face obscures Bo's, but my eyes track his sweet round leopard's ears and the way raindrops cling from the silver hoops and studs looping them. Nitta's spotted tail curls out in a half-circle on the sand behind her, its tip curved to hold Bo's tail.

My tears come out in heavy sobs then.

Nitta lifts her head at the sound. Her face is blank, a strange, flat mask, as if her features were merely tacked on. Blood has crusted along a cut to her right brow. A bruised lump pillows her cheek-bone. She looks over Wren and me, then turns to take in the rest of us like she's only realizing now we're all here, and it's clear some-thing has been torn out from within her. Her usually shining eyes are empty pools of green, shimmering only with tears.

Bo's own eyes are closed. Nitta cradles the back of his head in both of her hands with utmost care, thumbs stroking his cheeks.

"We need banana leaves," she says weakly. She sniffs, breaking off to look down at her brother. Her lips slant; her shoulders sag. "Something blue, to link his soul to our ling-ye. Flowers, a piece of clothing, anything will do. And a stone to mark the spot. And the site should be dry, but not too covered that you can't see the sky. I—I hurt my shoulder. I'll need help with the digging."

A grave. She's talking about Bo's grave.

"Of course," Wren says.

Caen steps forward. "Anything you need."

"There are sacred places in the desert where the Amala bury their members," Nitta goes on. It's the first time I've heard her say her ex-clan's name without derision. "There's sand here, but it's not the right kind. Too close to water. Somewhere in the forest would be better."

"We'll find the perfect place," I say. I clasp her shoulder. My fingers trail down her arm, pausing for a moment when I reach her hand where she's holding Bo, his fur tickling my wrist. I snatch my hand back, battling tears.

As Wren and I get to our feet, I glance over at Merrin where he's standing nearby, half hidden by the shadows of the forest. His face is aghast in silent horror, locked on Bo's body. He looks splayed open, his beaked mouth twisted in pain, tears coursing down his feathered cheeks.

Shifu Caen approaches us. "I'll find the materials she needs. You two find an appropriate site. Hiro should stay here, he needs to rest. He spent the past hour healing Merrin's broken arm as best he could, but after all that magic on the boat, he's completely drained."

My eyes shift to the shaman boy. He's propped against the trunk of a palm, head tipped back, eyes shut. Wet black robes cling to his small frame.

"Speaking of which," Caen adds, "how are *you* feeling, Wren?"

"A bit tired, but that's it." I hear the lie in the tremble of her voice, see it in the hollowed-out look of her cheeks. "Anyway, Hiro and I aren't the priority right now."

We're turning away when Caen says, "Be careful. From what I can tell, this island is in the southwest of the archipelago. The Czos' island should be nearby. Watch out for guards."

Before we leave, I break away to go to Merrin. Raindrops from the leaves overhead drip down his feathers, clinging to their pewter tips. He cradles his injured arm in the crook of his other. His eyes flick to me as I approach, then drop back down. Something in the rawness, the wildness of his expression scares me. There is not only sorrow there but *rage*.

I start to reach for him, then think better of it. "I'm so sorry, Merrin. I know how much you cared for Bo."

His silence ripples out in cold waves.

"We *all* cared for him," I add quietly.

I'm walking away when he replies, a low rasp that sends shivers up my arms, "Are you sure about that?"

It's still raining when Wren and I take the others back to the grove we found for Bo's grave. We make the walk together to the south-western part of the island, none of us speaking. Though my muscles are heavy, every inch of me aching from being thrown about when the ship crashed, and my soaked clothes cling heavily to my limbs, a part of me feels untethered from my body, as though my soul is somewhere just outside of myself, floating.

I watch with dull eyes as we dig a shallow grave. Bo's body waits nearby. It is already stiffening, already turning into a thing rather than a him. None of it seems real. How can someone so alive be rendered so *un*-alive in just a few hours? I think of Zelle. Like Bo, she was vibrant, bursting with life. A snap of her neck stole all that away.

My thoughts stray to Lill, Aoki, the other Paper Girls, my father and Tien, and all the people I care for, all those I left behind when I escaped the palace the night of the New Year. It's been a con-stant battle to not think of them every minute of every day, to keep focused instead on the here and the now, the things within my immediate control. Because if I let myself dwell on them, this is what I would imagine: the ease at which their lives could be taken away. And if I think too much about that, my already fragile composure would shatter.

Nitta conducts the preparation of Bo's body for burial in rain-silvered silence. First, she pulls the loop of his Birth-blessing pen-dant from his neck to hang around her own. Next, she brings one of his hands to his chest and places in his palm the tiny blue night orchid Caen found, so it looks almost as though he's plucked the flower himself, a gift for a lover or a friend. Finally, she folds the large leaves of a banana tree around his body until he's fully wrapped before finally lifting him—with no sign how much this might be hurting her injured shoulder, and not allowing any of us to help—and climbing down into the patch of dug earth.

She sets him in the center. Her outline flickers in the firelight of the makeshift torch Caen holds down for her to see as she kneels by his body. She blows out a shaky breath. "From now on," she tells Bo, so low I almost miss it, "I will only ever be half of myself."

Her words spear my heart. I grasp Wren's hand tighter.

Nitta is about to climb out of the grave when Merrin speaks. "Wait." He comes forward, holding something out. "I—I was hoping to leave this with him, too. It's...blue."

She looks at whatever is in his hands. Then she takes it and leans down, tucking it into the folds of banana leaf sheathing Bo's body. As she pulls away, I see what it is: a scrap of Merrin's favorite hanfu. Pale, cornflower blue.

A lump comes to my throat.

Hiro recites a prayer, offering a good luck dao reserved only for the dead. The glowing characters of his enchantment fall over Bo's grave like tiny stars, golden sparkles in the rain. Then we work together in silence to move the wet soil onto Bo's body. All this time Nitta has kept her composure. But as she finishes the ceremony by placing the beautiful fist-sized agate Caen found atop the head of the grave, she crumples.

Falls to her knees, fingers sinking into the wet earth, and screams. Wren and I dash forward. Her shuddering breaths and jagged cries are so violent they shake us, but we hold her tightly, as if we could somehow keep her together through willpower alone.

"Get away from her."

The voice is unexpected and harsh, slicing through the silence.

Wren and I peel away, our arms still around Nitta, knees in the muddy soil.

Merrin is standing over us. He cradles his injured arm to his chest. The talons of his other are curled into a fist. Firelight dances in the wet globes of his eyes.

Wren starts to her feet. "Merrin? What's wr—"

Crack. The sound of the impact echoes through the grove.

It takes me a second to realize that he hit Wren. Not even a slap; a full-on fist to the face.

"Wren!" I jump up. She's twisted around, one hand to her face, more in surprise than in pain.

"How dare you!" Shifu Caen roars. He storms at Merrin, his face a blaze of fury.

An almost relieved expression crosses Merrin's face as he turns to meet him. "Just what I was going to say to *you*," he replies with eerie serenity, before throwing a second punch, this time aimed at Caen.

Hiro leaps at him at the same time as Wren and me. The three of us wrestle Caen and Merrin apart.

"You could have saved him!" Merrin screeches, a crazed pitch to his voice I've never heard. All sense of composure has fallen away, as swiftly and final as a curtain pulled across a stage. Spit flies from his beaked mouth. His feathers are ruffled in his rage. "Wren and Hiro were right there! She promised Hiro would save him! Instead, you left him for dead!"

"What choice did we have?" Caen retaliates. "The royal ship was almost upon us. If we didn't use magic to escape, *all* of us would be dead!"

"They didn't need to both work the wind! Hiro's specialty is healing and protection—why didn't he do that? All of you promised to take care of him!"

"Bo was already dead."

Hiro's voice is quiet, but his words ripple through the grove with a deep, cool power.

Merrin falls still, blinking.

"He was already dead," the shaman boy repeats. "Magic cannot bring life back to an empty shell. Once the soul has been untethered, there is no way of reconnecting it."

"I—I don't believe you," Merrin stammers. "He wasn't dead. I saw him. I *held* him. He was still breathing." The venom returns to his voice. "He was alive, and you *let him die.*"

Tears are coursing down my cheeks now, merging with the rain. "Look at who you're accusing!" I cry, digging my fingers into his arm. "We all cared for Bo. Don't you think Wren and Hiro would have done everything they could to save him?"

But even as I say it, there's a flutter of doubt. Because Wren *had* commanded Hiro to leave Bo. Had she known he was already lost?

You can't do things like that. We have to think of the mission.

That's what she told me when I'd wanted to help the Papers back in the fishing village. It's what I've been afraid of ever since meeting Ketai and seeing that same fevered glow in his eyes as the King.

The mission over everything else. At the *cost* of everything else.

Merrin wrenches free. "All I know," he croaks, leveling an accusatory talon at me, "is that after *you* were injured at the Moon Ball, Hiro worked to heal you every day. Even though it was draining him. Though he was still casting protection daos each night. You all found a way then to spread magic to two things that needed it. There was a way this time, too. You just didn't care enough to try." He backs away, chest heaving. "Tell me," he says, addressing Wren now. "If it had been Lei who was hurt, you would have done everything you could to save her."

She stares him down. "It wasn't possible, Merrin."

"Tell me!" he roars. When she still doesn't answer, he laughs. The sound is horrid, a broken, rasping thing, completely devoid of humor and warmth, of the Merrin I'd come to know and care for over the past couple of months. He looks between Wren and Shifu Caen. "She won't say it, but we know the truth. The rest of us are disposable to you. Ketai Hanno doesn't care about anyone but his precious princesses and his lover."

At first, I think I've misheard. His lover?

Then I follow Merrin's gaze.

Caen has fallen still. Something dark lashes behind his eyes. He seems to grow in his silent anger, his flame-lit shadow looming larger.

All of us are staring at him now. Rain beats down, and I blink the drops away, hardly breathing.

"We all know, Caen," Merrin says. "How long have I worked for you and Ketai? I've seen the way you look at each other. The way you touch each other when you think no one's looking."

At my side, Wren is as still as a block of ice.

A frustrated sound rips from my throat. "Oh, who cares! None of this has anything to do with Bo's death. It was an accident. A horrible, horrible accident, and I wish it hadn't happened, but it did. We all knew coming into this that death was a possibility. We knew how dangerous this mission would be!"

"More dangerous for some of us than others!" Merrin shoots back.

"Enough."

Nitta's voice is low and cool. She hasn't moved from Bo's grave. Firelight glints off the beads of rain coursing down her matted fur. One of her hands rests against the earth. The other is pressed to her chest. It's an echo of the position she put Bo in before burying him, and my heart wrenches again, something tearing through my insides with the speed and force of a swinging sword.

"Enough," she repeats. "I just—just buried my brother. Please let me mourn him in peace."

Merrin's shoulders sag. "I loved him, too," he says, hoarse. His eyes shoot back to us, hardening. "That's why I will never forgive any of you for letting him die."

He swoops around, stumbling off into the forest.

"Merrin!" I shout after him. But he doesn't turn.

After a pause, Nitta says, "If the rest of you cared about him, too, then you know what we have to do."

"We have to go on," Wren answers.

"No more wasting time," Nitta agrees. "We secure the Czos' allegiance, then find the Cat Clan. That's why Ketai hired Bo and me after all. At least one of us can finish the job. Lei's right. We knew we might lose our lives in the process. But it was worth the risk to us. We have to respect Bo's wishes."

"Nitta," Caen begins, "if you need to leave us here, we'd understand."

"Bo wouldn't." Her hand goes to the hollow of her neck, where her brother's Birth-blessing pendant hangs alongside her own. "You know what he'd say if he could see us all now?" Her voice adopts Bo's mocking tone. *"Look at them moping around over my grave in the rain like some scene from one of the operas sad old aunties love so much. What a bunch of losers."*

A bark of laughter bursts from my lips. "He'd tell us to get a move on. That there's no way his soul can make it to the Heavenly Kingdom with all of us crowding him like this."

"And he wants to get there soon, because there's an all-you-can-eat dessert buffet calling his name." Nitta's face falls. She lets out a half-gasp, half-sob.

This time it's Hiro who goes to her side. The shaman boy holds her elbow, a strangely affectionate gesture given his usual aversion to physical touch. "Let me heal your shoulder," he says. "The sooner a wound is treated, the better it will heal."

Nitta blinks down at him. "A-all right."

"You two stay here," Shifu Caen tells them, readjusting the sword at his back. "I'll go with Wren and Lei to get a view of our surroundings." He gestures to where the middle of the island rises in a series of peaked hills. "We should be able to spot the Czos' island from there—"

Boom!

The thunderous sound cuts him off.

"What was that?" I gasp.

Wren and Caen have already drawn their swords. Nitta flinches, hunkering lower over Bo's grave, as though he is still in need of her protection.

A second explosion echoes through the night. Then a third, fourth, fifth. I pull my dagger free as we look in all directions, half expecting royal soldiers or the Czos' guard to come running from the undergrowth at any second.

"It's coming from over there!" Wren shouts, and starts up the mountainside in a run.

I chase after her, feet skidding in the mud.

As Caen goes to follow us, Wren turns to him, throwing out an arm. "Stay here with Hiro and Nitta!"

The two of us run up through the steep jungle. Wren hacks away the rope-like loops of hanging roots and tangled vegetation with easy swipes of her swords. The booms grow louder, studded now with little sparking sounds that make me think of arrow fire, of magical explosions. The mountainside we're climbing grows narrower and rockier, and all of a sudden we skid to a stop as the trees break, the jungle falling away to reveal a dizzying view of the Mersing Archipelago.

Silvery darkness drapes over a vast sea that sweeps out in all directions. Islands of varying shapes and sizes lie scattered across it, like the humped backs of sea monsters. In the distance, the shadowy line of the Kitori coast is just visible.

For a few moments, everything is dark. Then the night erupts with color.

Gold and emeralds and flaming rubies burst into the sky. They hang in the air, a kaleidoscopic starburst against the dark clouds, before raining down in a shower of glittering shards.

"Firecrackers!" I exclaim.

Wren lowers her swords. She's staring, too, her eyes wide as colors burst in her eyes.

Each glittering pop lights the night sky, their reflections sparkling in the water below. I barely notice the rain drenching my skin, the heaviness of my limbs. As the firecrackers shatter the darkness, I watch in awe, a sad, aching joy spouting up from deep within me to dance twirling formations with my grief.

We wait in silence after the last dazzling starbursts fade to nothing.

Wren stows her swords. She turns to me, her eyes blazing. "Do you think he saw?" she asks.

She means Bo.

I smile, linking my fingers with hers. "I do."

After a moment, she points to an island a few miles away. It's small and flat, almost perfectly circular, sitting high above the water on a rocky base. Dimmed by the rain, clusters of lights shine amid the dark forms of buildings and trees. More lights twinkle off the rugged coastline. Boats.

"The Czos' palace," she says.

I squint to make out more details. "What do you think the firecrackers were for? I can't think of any festivals around now, though maybe they have different ones in Kitori."

"Whatever it is, they're having a party of some kind." Abruptly, Wren turns, heading back the way we came. "This could be the perfect cover for us to get in and speak directly to Lord Mvula!" she calls over her shoulder. "But we have to be quick. We don't know how long the party will go on."

I hurry after her. "Perhaps you haven't quite noticed," I say, my breath catching as we descend the steep mountainside, "but we're not exactly dressed for a ball. A masked ball, maybe. I guess we could pass as pirates who almost died in a shipwreck after getting chased across half the sea by royal soldiers. But we might look a *bit* suspicious if everyone else is in hanfu and gowns."

"So we'll borrow clothes from a couple of guests."

"Right. Because it'll be easy to find two people who are happy to spend the rest of the party in their undergarments."

"Have you not learned by now, Lei?" Wren answers without turning, something more than impatience weighing her words. "Sometimes you have to take things by force. Sometimes it's the only way to get what you need."

The memory of her slicing her hand open on the boat flashes into my mind. Hiro must have healed the wound for her after our ship crashed, or perhaps she did it herself. But I can't vanish away the image of her blood as it tracked rivers down her forearm. How the vivid red softened to pink as it mixed with the rain.

Wren needed magic, so she took it by force—*from herself.*

Even with my rudimentary knowledge of magic, I can tell this isn't the usual shaman's tithe, the small gifts they offer to the earth in exchange for use of qi.

A slow horror unravels in my gut. I recall all the times Wren and Hiro have used magic. How they've both begun to look a little more drained each time they draw their power. How bigger incantations almost wreck them. Though none of us understand exactly why, we know it's been getting more and more difficult for shamans to draw qi because of the Sickness. Is this what Wren and Hiro have been doing all this time? Instead of taking qi from the earth, have they been forced to start taking it from *themselves*?

Could that be what the marks I saw on Hiro's arms are? The blood payments Wren mentioned on the boat when telling Shifu Caen that's why his magic was still strong?

A shiver skims up my spine. Because I've seen what happens when you take more than the earth wants to give. When you don't respect the balance of the universe. And that was frivolous magic; silly, vain daos with little consequence.

Wren's words spin in my head. I want to tell her that she's wrong. That if the cost of winning something is too high, it wasn't meant to be yours in the first place. Especially if what you're paying with is your blood. Because blood—like qi, and magic, and almost everything in life—is not infinite.

But there is one thing that *is* infinite: greed. The ability of humans and demons to want. To desire. To hunger after things that don't belong to them.

Sometimes you have to take things by force. Sometimes it's the only way to get what you need.

Wren's words hit me afresh. Because I've heard something similar before—from the Demon King. To hear them now, from the lips of the person I love most, is all wrong. I've experienced firsthand how desire can twist and corrupt a person. What happens when it lives untamed.

Like fire, it destroys everything in its path.

Like fire, it burns, until there is nothing left.

TWENTY-FOUR

W E DECIDE IT'LL BE EASIEST TO infiltrate the party if we
send only two of us. As her father's representative,
Wren will be in charge of convincing Lord Mvula to
ally with the Hannos, but Shifu Caen thinks he should be the one
to accompany her. "As proud as I am of Lei's progress over the past
few weeks, she won't be able to handle a full onslaught from the Czo
guards if things turn ugly."

Eventually, Nitta points out wearily that it won't matter who goes
if the party is over by the time we decide.

In the end, Caen concedes to Wren when she reminds him how
my being the Moonchosen plays to the Czos' superstitious nature.
"My father was adamant on this, Shifu. And I know you respect
his opinions." He tries to interject, but she goes on firmly, "And
no, I don't care that you are lovers. You and my father brought me
up almost single-handedly. If anyone is a part of my family"—at
this, her hand brushes mine—"it's you. But I wish you hadn't gone
behind my mother's back to do it." She rounds her shoulders. "Anyway, we have more important things to focus on. How will we get
to the island?"

Before we leave, I check on Nitta. She's still sitting by the head of Bo's grave. Hiro moves away to give us a moment of privacy.

"I know you'll do great," she says, attempting a smile as I crouch beside her.

I wrap an arm around her shoulders. "Thanks."

Her smile wobbles. "He was so looking forward to this one, you know? The Czos have so much fancy stuff. He was sure he'd beat me this time."

Their game. I'd completely forgotten.

"Do you want me to try?" I ask. "I've never really tried to steal anything, but I could probably manage something small…"

Nitta shakes her head. When her gaze snaps up, her expression is hard. "Just get what we came for. That's the only game we need to win now."

We leave Nitta and Hiro and make our way down to one of the north-facing beaches, where by a stroke of luck someone left a small rowing boat pushed up on the sand. Caen came across it earlier while looking for Merrin. We move it out to sea. The water is dark and choppy. We cross it, veiled by the rain and the darkness. Caen rows while I'm squashed at the front of the boat, Wren hugging me from behind, her head propped on my shoulder. We pitch with the boat, a tense silence between the three of us.

Twenty minutes later, the lights of the Czos' island appear through the rain. The noise of the party lifts into the air: spinning music, the thrum of voices and movement blending into one. It grows louder as we near the craggy coastline. The Czos' island sits high out of the ocean, waves breaking against its rocky bluffs. Knotted roots of banyans and towering meranti spill over the cliff, and from high up in the canopy birds squawk noisily, competing with the squabbling of monkeys swinging through the leaves.

Wren points to a spot along the shoreline where there's a deep overhang. Caen maneuvers the boat, the water growing choppier the closer we get. I throw out my arms as we pitch dangerously. After we narrowly miss a jagged head of rock poking up between the waves, a violent surge pushes us forward. We brace against the side of the boat as the cliff looms overhead. Then we are under, the sound of the rain and waves diminishing as the sea calms almost immediately.

We glide through darkness until our boat hits the shore.

Shifu Caen holds the boat steady as Wren and I hop into the shallows, water splashing into our boots.

"I'll wait here," he says. "Good luck. Remember—"

Wren stalks away without waiting for him to finish.

"See you soon," I reply awkwardly, before hurrying after her.

Toward the back of the cave, the small pebbles of the shore shift to larger rocks stacked high on top of one another. We scale them in silence. A light patter of rain kisses my cheeks as I turn my face up to the opening overhead.

"From the plans I've studied of the Czos' island," Wren says, keeping her voice low, "the main palace complex is on the west side, not too far from here. That's where the firecrackers were coming from."

She crouches to give me a knee up. I reach my hands out through the opening, rain on my upturned face. Finding the thick root of a tree, I use it to haul myself up. The sounds of the party drift through the dark jungle, louder here out of the echoing chamber of the sea cave.

I'm turning to check on Wren when there's a shout.

The guard is upon me in seconds, lunging from the shadows where he must have been keeping watch. A blade whirs through the air in a flash of silver. I dodge aside just in time. The sword hits the wet ground with a muffled whack. I whip out my dagger, the blade glowing bronze.

The guard falters, surprised.

Magic tingles down my arm. Sensing the sureness of the blade's dao guiding my aim, I jump and drive the knife into the exposed side of the guard's neck.

He spasms as my blade pierces his leathery reptilian skin. It sinks wetly through muscle and sinewy cartilage. Blood gushes out, glossy black. With a low hiss, the guard falls forward, twitching on the grass until his face goes slack.

I'm making the sky gods salute with trembling hands when Wren grabs me and pulls me into a run. We dash through the under-growth, leaping over roots and rocks, our footfall muffled by the carpet of waterlogged leaves. As the noise of the party grows, lights appear through the trees. We slow. Wren pulls one sword free, a metallic *shing* that sets my teeth on edge.

I look down at my own weapon, the blade wet with blood.

That's two demons I've killed now.

Dully, I wonder why it hasn't hit me yet. Because of me, two lives, two sets of thoughts and fears and loves and dreams and secrets and hopes were snuffed out in mere seconds. Just as I can't comprehend that Zelle and Bo could be taken from us so easily, others will be wondering the same about these two demons.

"Lei."

I start at Wren's whisper, hastily joining her where she's crouch-ing to peer out through a gap in the leaves.

Just yards away, the palace grounds unfold in a staggering sweep of color and noise and movement. The lights hit me first: deep pools of gold from lanterns spotting the lawn, as tall and wide as adult humans, hanging globes of flickering magenta and sapphire as rare fireflies dance within, like trapped stars. Everything is awash in color. Between the polished teak frames of thatched-roof pavilions, waxy canopies have been strung to keep the guests dry and winding walkways crisscross the lawn. Demons of every kind move across them. There are lean jackal-forms in black baju sets; the enormous hulk of bristling gorilla demons. On the balcony of a house, a group of gray wolf-women flirt with a trio of handsome lion-forms. A stout pair of male Steel ram demons walk arm in arm, swaying slightly from drink, their forms human save the colorfully painted horns curling from their heads. There's a flash of white feathers swathed in ivory silks—a member of the White Wing. Like the Demon King's Moon Ball, clan representatives from across Ikhara must have been invited to the party.

Then there are the lizard-like Czo themselves. There are hundreds of them, both Steels and Moons, wrapped in luxurious tunics and sampin of emerald-green and cobalt and deep, rich corals, all intricately embroidered. Many of the women wear veils over their faces, the delicate fabric thin as brushstrokes. Their scales and leathery skin, every shade of ochre, from light brown to dark moss, sparkle with decorative jewels.

Wren stares out. "I don't like this," she murmurs.

"The party?"

"We're a kingdom on the brink of war. A strange time for throwing parties."

"They're probably trying to win allies," I point out.

"Which means our mission just got a thousand times more dangerous. We'd better hurry."

Keeping low, she leads me along the perimeter of the jungle to a quieter part of the grounds. Pools of shadow stretch between the lights. What look like two small bathhouses sit at a distance from each other, simple one-story huts ringed by a covered veranda. Guests trickle in from the rest of the grounds, disappearing inside the buildings for a handful of minutes before returning to the party. A guard stands between the two huts, his back to us. A long lizard tail pokes out from his trousers.

"Here," Wren says.

We move into position opposite the female bathhouse. I'm not exactly sure what we're waiting for until minutes later, when a trio of giggling reptile-women round the back of the bathhouse. Two Moons, both wearing veils, and one Steel. The Steel demon stumbles. The women clutch at one another, screeching and giggling as they try not to spill the liquid in their glasses.

"Now!" Wren commands.

We sprint out from the trees. Wren reaches the veranda first and jumps up easily. The lizard-women have little time to react before she loops her arm around the two Moons, draws one of her swords, and presses its blade against their throats.

"Not a word," she hisses.

I stuff a hand across the mouth of the Steel woman just as she's about to scream. She's taller than I, but her bony frame is the weak body of someone who's lived a sheltered life, and as a Steel the only part of her that appears to be lizard is the scatter of indigo scales over her cheeks and down her neck, like an embroidered scarf. Overpowering her easily, I drag her off the veranda. Her brass anklets clink as I haul her toward the jungle. Wren is already halfway across the lawn with the other two demons.

I don't stop until the wet flick of palm leaves brush my face. Hidden safely in the shadows of the jungle, I let out a sigh of relief that the guard didn't hear us—only to jolt as I see Wren already laying down the slumped bodies of the two Moon lizard-women.

The demon I'm carrying sobs against my hand as she sees her friends. She sobs even harder as Wren turns to us, her sword lifted.

I splutter the words out. "Did you—are they...?"

She shakes her head. "Just unconscious."

My hand is wet with the reptile woman's tears. She struggles, panic bubbling in her throat as Wren closes the distance toward us. In one practiced movement, Wren lifts her sword, the blade turned back, and strikes the reptile-woman on the top of her head with the butt of its hilt.

In an instant, the woman wilts in my arms.

I lower her to the grass, trembling. For a moment, I'd been sure the silver of the blade was arcing toward my own head.

Wren stands over me. "Strip these two," she says, pointing. "I'm going to find something for ties." Without waiting for a reply, she moves off toward a tree choked by climbing vines and swiftly begins cutting down the leafy tangles.

I look down at the unconscious lizard-women. "I'm sorry," I whisper, before undressing the ones Wren had indicated to me as quickly as possible. By the time she comes back, the two demons are naked except for their undergarments.

Wren crouches, skillfully wrapping the vines she collected around the arms and legs of all three women. I help her tear two strips from the sari we're not using to create makeshift gags. It makes me feel horrible, seeing the demon women like that. Even if they're strangers, they are still women, and they hadn't done anything to us. But I swallow down my nausea and help Wren finish the job.

She stands once we're done. "Usually it takes a couple of hours for the pressure point effects to wear off," she explains. "And these ties should buy us a little more time."

"They'll be all right, though, won't they? They'll be able to get free once they wake up?"

Wren nods. "I made the ties purposefully easy to get off." She starts to undo the sash at her waist. "Do you know how to wrap a sari?" she asks, already slipping off her trousers.

"No. You?"

She answers distractedly. "Someone showed me once."

Once undressed, we use the rest of the spare sari to clean our skin as best we can of blood from the battle on the ship and mud from our journey through the jungle. Then Wren wraps the Steel demon's sari around my body, sheathing me tightly in its beautiful rose and magenta silk. She drapes a gold-and-peacock-blue sari around herself. To finish, we pin the veils from the two Moon women into our hair. I make sure my dagger is well hidden in the folds of my sari while Wren straps her swords across her back. Her eyes drain of color behind the delicate fabric, a crackle lifting into the air as she chants a dao. Light limns the swords and their harness. They glimmer for a few moments more before disappearing from view.

Wren's eyes slip back to normal. She pants for a moment, as though the magic tired her, but recovers quickly. "How do I look?" she asks me.

"Not like yourself," I reply, muted.

"Good."

She reaches for my hand and we edge back to the perimeter of the jungle. I cast a final glance over my shoulder at the poor demon women, tied up and slumped together on the muddy ground. Then we slip from the shadows and into the Czos' palace grounds, where the party still whirls on in a spiral of color and noise and shining lights sparkling in the downpour, its guests and guards oblivious to what just happened.

TWENTY-FIVE

I KEEP MY CHIN LIFTED AS we move through the party, a calm expression plastered across my face. Inside, panic clatters through me. It takes all my effort not to jump at every roar of demon laughter. My anxious breaths stir my stolen veil where it covers my face. Like Wren's, it's thin, the barest disguise. Still, as long as no one looks too closely at us, we should pass for Steels. I try to take comfort in this, but the press of demons is everywhere, and my nerves are making me light-headed and dizzy, as though like the rest of the guests I, too, have been sipping on sweet wine all night.

We weave through the crowd. The air is heavy and humid, the kind we only get in Xienzo during monsoon season. It smells like perspiration and rain, like sandalwood incense and smoke from the mosquito-repellent coils that spin from the pavilion eaves. I'm sweating within my tightly wrapped sari. The smallest of the lizard-women was still a head taller than me, and I walk with the fabric of her skirt balled in my fists. None of their sandals fit me, so I'm barefoot, moving carefully to avoid large demon feet stepping on my exposed toes.

"Hello there, beautiful."

A tall lizard demon stops me, his large scaled hand landing on my arm. We're under the sloping roofs of one of the pavilions. A dance swirls around us, garlands of colorful flowers dangling from the exposed beams over the heads of twirling demons.

Wren stops just ahead of me.

"How have we never met before?" The man is a Moon reptile demon. Scales of deep umber sheathe his body like armor. A tongue—pink and forked—flicks out as he leans in, his smile growing fatter. "You're from one of the mining families, am I right? The Zouar?" His breath reeks of alcohol. His fingers brush over the delicate embroidery of my sari, where rose-colored flowers wind across magenta silk. It must be a pattern particular to the family he's mistaken me as a member of. "I work over at Baraghi myself. We got your shipment of Paper slaves through two days ago. The ones to replace those we lost in the eastern mine collapse. More than three hundred, the largest shipment yet. You must let me find a way to thank you."

I snatch my arm back. "I think you are mistaken, sir," I mutter.

His scaled brow furrows. His gaze locks on my eyes; their golden, demon-like hue. "But—"

I duck my head and push past him to rejoin Wren. She links her arm through mine as soon as I'm at her side. We hurry from the pavilion and across a raised walkway, melting into the crowd.

"Did you hear?" I murmur.

"About the slaves? It's becoming common practice. Slavery of any kind is illegal, of course, but with the royal soldiers and representatives focused on rebel activity and curtailing disagreements between clans over land due to the Sickness, they've started to turn a blind eye."

Anger burns through me. "And it's not like the King and his soldiers set a good example."

Wren throws me a sideways glance. "That, too."

"Well," I say roughly, "if these are the kind of demons the Czo invites to its parties, I doubt they're going to be open to what we have to say. I'm not so sure I even *want* them on our side."

Wren is about to reply when she freezes.

Falling still, I follow her gaze—and spot him immediately.

Not even thirty feet away, General Ndeze stands by a pillar at the edge of the pavilion facing us.

The building is magnificent, three stories glittering with lights and packed with demons chatting in clusters amid tables of delicious-smelling food or reclining on the four-poster divans, the shadows of couples entwined behind gauzy curtains. But the whirl of the party fades into the background as my vision narrows in on the General.

He is dressed in royal crimson and black. Light slides over his leathery, moss-colored skin. With his hulking crocodile-humanoid form, he is the biggest demon here by far—still the biggest demon I have ever seen—and his muscles are barely contained beneath his elegant silk hanfu. His neck cranes down to talk with a fat-bellied lizard-man in tangerine-colored robes. The glass the General is holding looks ridiculous in his huge fist, tiny as a toy. I suppress a mad bark of laughter. Then all traces of humor dissipate.

General Ndeze, one of the King's personal guards and closest advisers. *Here.*

Less than ten yards from us.

"We've found him," Wren says, her eyes shining darkly.

It takes me a moment to realize she means Lord Mvula, Clan Lord of the Czo and whom we came to the party to find. That must be the fat-bellied demon the General is talking with.

"Wren," I say slowly, "I think we should go. This doesn't feel right."

She stares ahead, jaw tense. "Once they find the body of the guard, and the three lizard-women tell them what we did, the Czo will increase security at least for the next few weeks. It'll be impossible to access Lord Mvula, even if we directly ask for a meeting."

"So we leave it. Come on, do you really believe the Czo are going to listen to what we have to say? You heard what the lizard-man said! These aren't the kind of demons who are sympathetic to Papers. And if General Ndeze is here, that means the relationship between the King and the Czo is still strong. What if Lord Mvula hands us straight over to General Ndeze? If he wants the King's favor, there'd be no better way to earn it."

But Wren's look is decisive. "We have to try. Cutting off the King's access to the Czo mines could reduce the royal army's power eight-fold, not to mention the Czo have strategic alliances of their own across the Summer States we'd benefit from. I promised my father we'd do everything we could," she adds, almost to herself, and without waiting for a reply, she starts toward General Ndeze and Lord Mvula.

With a growl of frustration, I follow.

Even in disguise, I feel exposed as we approach the pavilion. The wide veranda is packed. Steel lizard-form servers weave through the crowd, carrying silver platters piled high with toasted peanuts and candied guava cubes, syrupy coils of jalebi and coconut slices drenched in melted molasses. A server narrowly avoids stepping on my toes as he moves past with a glistening pyramid of gulab jamun showered in pistachio pieces, and it takes all my self-control not to snatch a fistful, my mouth instantly salivating.

Of *course* we would arrive during the dessert portion of the night.

We get as near to General Ndeze and Lord Mvula as we dare. Wren leans nonchalantly against the wooden pillar they're right behind while I stand close, knotting my hands. Half of the General's hulking outline looms past the pillar. His sheer size sends a thrum of fear through me. I never had much interaction with him in the Hidden Palace, but he was always an intimidating presence, with his size and dark-scaled body and slit crocodile eyes.

"—and we cannot permit just anyone these days, you understand." General Ndeze's voice is thick and low, the words churned up from deep in his throat. Though I can't see his face, I imagine the gloating curve of his dark lips.

The last time I saw him, he was flirting with a group of Night House courtesans at the Moon Ball, Zelle included. It's not an image that ingratiates him with me.

"I understand, I understand." Lord Mvula's voice is high and reedy in comparison. "The Hidden Palace is still on lockdown, hmm? It's been a while now, General. Some of us—not me, you understand, but some others—are growing worried. Why, I was just speaking with Lord Dakah of the Shugur. A convoy along their usually protected trade route to the Black Port was attacked by robbers. They lost more than two hundred tons of prime cane sugar. You can imagine he and his clan were rather upset about this."

"And *you*, Mvula, can understand that the King is rather preoccupied at the present moment."

"Yes, yes, indeed. But...business must go on."

The General's reply is curt. "War is a business of its own."

"Exactly my point, General. That's why I'm so delighted you accepted my invitation tonight. Have you had a chance to consider what I proposed earlier? I hope we've been able to show you that the Summer States are not just the rebel holdings others make us out to be. Jana's long been a lost cause, yes, and with what happened with the Hannos, Ang-Khen is not far behind. But here in Kitori, we have always stood strong with the court. Imagine it, General. The south under one united rule—"

"You would do well to remember that *all of Ikhara* is under one united rule," General Ndeze cuts in, his voice dangerously low.

"Ah, yes, I didn't mean to suggest otherwise. Eight hundred apologies, General. What I'm talking about is a united rule *beneath* the court's jurisdiction, of course. I would merely be the King's humble servant." His tone grows silky. "I don't suppose to know anything of the court's plans, but it would seem an attack on the Hannos could not be more than a few weeks away. Let me offer our help. Soldiers, weapons, whatever you need. How about an increase in steel and copper shipments? The mines have just had an influx of Paper slaves. Our net production has never been better."

Before General Ndeze can reply, a lizard-form demon in a green tunic and sampin comes to Lord Mvula's side. He leans in, whispering something.

Lord Mvula's smile tightens. "Excuse me, General. I have some business to take care of. Please, enjoy the rest of the party. I hope to continue our conversation later tonight."

General Ndeze inclines his head. He turns, lifting his glass for a sip.

And meets my stare.

Blood rushes to my cheeks. Despite the veil, I'm sure he recognizes me. That my golden eyes are as much a beacon in the thronging crowd as his imposing form is to me. But he only swats at a mosquito buzzing by his ear and stomps off into the party without a backward glance.

I loosen a breath I didn't know I was holding.

Wren's hand closes around mine. "Come on."

We trail Lord Mvula through the crowds, careful to always keep a few guests between us. After overhearing his and General Ndeze's conversation, my earlier apprehension has evolved into a gut-level dread, an instinctive gnaw that tells me we should never have come here.

"Wren, you heard Mvula!" I hiss. "The Czo are loyal to the King. He's not going to help us."

But she keeps on as though not hearing me. Every few minutes, more of the Czos' guards arrive. They whisper into the Clan Lord's ear and he replies curtly before they hurry away.

Something is happening. Something the Czo didn't plan on.

After fifteen minutes or so, we've crossed most of the party grounds. The Czo Clan's home is made up of interlinked pavilions and raised platforms, reminding me of the Women's Court back in the Hidden Palace, though instead of manicured gardens and courtyards, here the buildings are almost swallowed up in the thick tangles of jungle. The humidity gives the air a weight. Sweat spills down my back and forehead, my breathing smothered by the veil.

Soon the stretches of walkways between the pavilions grow longer, the grounds darker as more of the jungle swallows them up. Under the rain and the calls of birds and monkeys, there's the sound of waves; we must be close to the coast.

Wren and I fall back as Lord Mvula and his guard turn a corner ahead. There are no party guests here now, only the occasional member of the Czo passing swiftly by. A young couple kiss in the shadows of the walkway. Rain drips across its open sides in a shimmering curtain. Eyeing the couple to make sure they aren't watching us, Wren draws me to the edge of the walkway.

We jump through the curtain of rain down to the grassy jungle floor. My bare soles sink gratefully into the mud, a respite from hard wooden floorboards. The raised walkway comes up to just past our shoulders. We tear off our veils and pull the fabric of our saris through our legs to create pant legs before following the raised path at its base, moving even more cautiously now.

After the bend, the walkway opens to a complex of one-story pavilions set on a covered circular platform. We crouch in the shadows. At first, there's nothing but the drip-drip-drip of raindrops on palm leaves, stormy darkness and electric heat. Then a door slams.

A group of lantern-lit figures exit the closest pavilion, voices drifting down.

"Where did you—"

"So there could still be more—"

"They might be in the party—"

"Make them talk—"

Rain muffles their words. Even so, dread rolls through me, icier and more certain than before.

Keeping low, we move closer to the platform. A lantern hangs from the corners of each of the pavilions within. The view is blurry through the veil of rain, amber light revealing the muzzy outlines of moving figures.

There's the creak of the floorboards, the click of clawed feet on teak. The serpentine curl of a reptile demon's voice sounds from just a few feet away. "My Lord, should we alert the guests? We can have the party cleared in less than half an hour."

"No, no. They mustn't know what is happening. We do not want to cause panic, or give any of them an opportunity to claim the captives as their own. This is a chance sent from the gods themselves. We must use it wisely."

"Yes, my Lord."

"Keep the captives here. The two girls will not be far. Scour the grounds for them. We must get to them before any of the guests notice."

"Yes, my Lord."

Heavy footsteps—guards heading back to the party. Only a few figures remain on the veranda.

I send Wren a panicked look. *The captives*, I mouth.

I know.

We have to do something!

Not yet.

Still, she reaches behind her back where her swords are still hidden thanks to her dao. As she draws one free, it shimmers, its silver blade visible once more. She lifts her free hand to the edge of the walkway.

I pull out my own weapon, the magic imbued within the dagger sending a tingling burr down my arm.

"Yes, this is indeed a gift from the gods," Lord Mvula muses into the rain-steeped quiet. "They've seen our work. Our patience. And they mean to reward us." His voice has taken on a heavier tone, as though caramelized with greed. "They know that we above all other clans deserve this. The King will not be able to refuse my offer once he finds out we have the Moonchosen and her associates. He will gladly appoint me as General and give me charge over the Summer States. Once we have them under our control, the Czo will be the most powerful clan in Ikhara."

"And soon we will have the King's throne in our sights."

"Exactly. Our plans are falling into place."

There's the click of hurried claws. "Lord Mvula," pants a guard, his breathing labored, "our shackles are not big enough to fit the bird demon. It's taking four of our men just to keep him down.

We've bound him with rope but it won't last long. Permission to cut off his wings?"

Lord Mvula doesn't hesitate. "Permission granted."

I grasp Wren's shoulder. Her eyes flash in agreement. Looping her arm around my waist, she tightens her grip on the platform edge and launches me up onto it.

I burst through the dripping curtain of rain, landing with a grunt, knees bent, an open palm hitting the floorboards. There are three demons on the platform—Lord Mvula and two guards. Their faces swivel to me in shock as I spring to my feet.

Wren swings herself up beside me. She lands gracefully, stunning in her dark, soaked sari, her face pale and fierce, her eyes already shifting white. A thrum of electric coolness rolls off her as she draws her second sword free.

Lord Mvula lets out a shrill scream. He staggers back as his two guards jump in front of him, brandishing their own weapons.

Action. Reaction.

Fire in. Fear out.

I clutch my dagger. The blade glows copper. A cry builds in my throat as, in perfect unison, Wren and I dive at the guards.

The air bursts with the squeal of clashing steel. There are cries, anguished yelps as weapons meet their mark. More guards emerge from the pavilion. I barely have time to register it all. Moments narrow to split-second flashes, timed to the slam of my heart and the gasp of my breath.

A reptile guard lifting his sword.

Me, ducking, spotting a gap in his sword range.

Waiting for him to strike again, then powering a forward thrust at the center of his belly.

The now-familiar wet, hard-soft sink of blade into flesh.

The guard falls, and more are upon me.

I grit my teeth against a barrage of swords and pikes. Wren dances at my side. She moves unnaturally fast, almost flying, a blur of whipping hair and flapping robes. There's a shriek. Something hot splatters across my face. More blood splashes over me as I slice my dagger across the exposed throat of a tall Steel guard, moving aside before he collapses to the floor.

From the walkway leading back to the party comes the sound of shouting and claw-tipped footfalls. More guards.

"I've got this, Lei!" Wren cries. "Go!"

As the weapons of two guards collide over my head with an ear-ringing clash, I duck from under them and run to the pavilion that we saw Lord Mvula and the guards leaving from earlier. I jump the short flight of steps to the veranda. The building is a single-story hut of paneled teak. I brush through the cotton curtains hanging across the entrance and into the shadowy interior—

And stumble to a halt.

Time freezes as I take in the scene. A high domed ceiling. Wooden beams crisscrossing the rafters. Hanging from them: four bodies.

It's too dark to make out their faces, but I would know them anywhere.

Nitta, Merrin, Hiro, and Shifu Caen.

TWENTY-SIX

ALL FOUR OF MY FRIENDS ARE struggling, hands and feet bound by rope. Gags stifle their ragged screams—but they *are* screaming, and moving, which means they're alive.

Relief crashes through me. "Gods," I breathe, half-sigh, half-sob.

I run to Merrin first. His long feathered arms are twisted behind him, thick cords of rope lashed around his body from shoulder to hip to keep his wings pinned. Pinned, but not cut. As I start to hack at the rope, he shakes his head frantically, his orange eyes piercing in the dark.

"What?" I snarl, delirious with panic. "Worried I'm going to spoil your precious robes?" I cut harder, frenzied, the last few fibers pinging free. I move to the next binding. "Well, deal with it. You know what, I'm not really sure blue's your color anyway—"

Breath whooshes from my lungs as something heavy crashes onto me.

I'm slammed to the ground. My face smashes into the floor. There's a snap, loud and precise. Pain fissures through my nose with a blinding flash. Hot blood gushes over my hands, splattering the teak as I push myself up, only for an arm to wrap around my neck.

It's scaled and muscled. A Czo guard.

The arm tightens. Spots pop in front of my eyes. I gulp for breath. My left hand scrabbles at the guard's arm. I fumble on the floor for my dagger with the other. Its bronze blade glints in the low light, tantalizingly close.

Gurgling breaths build in my throat, trapped under the squeezing crook of the lizard demon's arm. The metallic stench of my own blood fills my nose and mouth.

I lift my gaze, vision fuzzy. Before me, like reluctant gods come to watch my execution, my four friends hang from the ceiling beam, straining against their binds. Their screams are muffled. Merrin is suspended right above my head. He moves differently than the others' frantic jerking, instead shrugging his shoulders in an odd, rhythmic way. At first I get the mad idea he's doing some sort of bird demon death ritual to bestow good luck on my soul when I die. Then it hits me.

He's trying to free his wings.

His determination reignites my own. With a last, teeth-gritting push, my face flaming from the strain, I crawl my fingers a tiny bit farther—

And tap the hilt of my dagger.

I nudge it closer. The second I'm able, I wrap my fingers around it. The blade hums in response, and with a flush of power I drive it behind me—straight into the belly of the demon guard.

He releases me with a moan.

I fall to my hands, gasping, as there's a rustle of wings above me.

Merrin drops to the floor. He leans over me. There's a sickening snap as he breaks the guard's neck clean in two. Then he holds out his hands and lifts me to my feet. "Lei—"

"Help the others," I croak, waving him away. "Wren's alone out there."

Plugging my sleeve against my nose to catch some of the blood gushing from my nostrils, I stagger forward. The room sways, but I drag ragged breaths into my lungs. As Merrin frees Nitta and Caen, I go to Hiro, slicing the rope around his body before lifting him down.

The instant I pick the wad of fabric from his mouth, he closes his eyes, a chant drifting from his lips. The warm prickle of magic ripples as he lifts a hand to my broken nose.

"No," I say, pushing his arm down. "Save your energy."

After the briefest of greetings to check everyone is all right, Nitta, Caen, and Merrin get their weapons from where they were tossed in the corner of the room and together we run out from the pavilion into a flurry of clashing swords.

Wren shines at the center of it all. She moves with an uncanny smoothness, a supernatural glide to the way she ducks and springs and dives and slices, her loosed hair floating as though she were moving through water. Coldness ripples through the air around her. Attacks rain down, and she counters them with the grace of a dancer, spilling blood like the scarlet silks of a performer's ribbons.

Across the platform, bodies litter the floor. The wooden panels are stained red.

While I'm momentarily stunned, Caen and Nitta leap into the fray without any hesitation. Nitta doesn't even use her bow, fighting instead like Naja when she battled Wren at the Hidden Palace, all slashing claws and feral ferocity. I stumble over the body of a guard on my way to join the fight. Fresh pain jars through my nose. I spit out a wad of blood and pick myself up when Merrin grabs me, dragging me back.

"We have to go," he says, as more guards thunder down the walkway.

"I'll get Wren."

Shoving him away, I push into the heart of the battle. The air whirs with weapons. Metallic clashes ring all around me. I duck, squeezing through the teeming bodies.

"Wren!" I shout. "Wren, it's me!"

Something silver glints overhead. I spin around just in time to knock aside the slashing arm of a snarling reptile-man. Before he can recover, I hack my blade across his wrist. Dark red sluices out, coating both of us in warm, glossy waves. He drops his weapon, already crumpling to his knees by the time I pivot back around.

"Wren!" I yell again.

She doesn't hear me. The air crackles around her; her eyes are the iced white of freshly laid snow. She kills so easily, an arc of her swords here, a neck-snapping kick there.

Awe is a common feeling for me when it comes to Wren. Any time I touch her, her beauty renders me speechless. The way her body curves and rolls beneath my fingertips astonishes me anew every time. When I see her leading the group or making difficult decisions, or simply being there for me, day in, day out, coaxing out fresh reserves of strength when I think I have none left. Wren has always impressed me, but this time, the wonder thrumming down my spine is different. As on the boat, when she weaved a magical storm so strong I thought it was going to kill us, my awe is laced with fear.

Fear *of* her—and *for* her.

Bodies pile on the floor around her. I have no choice but to step on them to get to her. She finishes a kick aimed at a lizard guard's jaw.

I grab her wrist, wincing at the pain the impact shoots through my broken nose. "Wren."

My voice is almost a whisper, too quiet for her to hear. But something within her seems to hear me, some instinctive part of her that would sense me just breathing her name even if there were miles between us, mountains and valleys and whole oceans.

She stills. Her eyes meet mine, white upon gold.

Then she slips out of her Xia trance.

Her hand snaps around mine, and without a word, we're spinning around, sprinting to the edge of the platform through the skirr of blades and lashing claws.

The others follow. Together, we vault off the raised platform into the jungle. Fat drops of rain pummel us as we dash across the dark grounds. Some of the guards come after us, but Nitta brings them down with rapid strikes of her bow, aiming over her shoulder with lightning reflexes. At first, Wren and I lead the group. But within minutes she's lagging, her face turning pale.

I catch her just as her legs buckle. "Merrin!" I shout.

He understands immediately, running back and slinging her over his shoulder. With strong beats of his wings, he takes to the air, flying low to stay close to the rest of us.

The ground is sloping now. The crash of waves rises over our noisy progress through the jungle, the barking orders of the guards as they chase us. Moments later, the silvery flicker of moonlight on water appears through a gap in the jungle. It's still raining, but the storm is easing, the clouds parted ahead. The glowing arc of a crescent moon peeks out through the break.

Near the sea the ground becomes more uneven. My bare soles are already cut up from stones and spiked leaves, and my eyes water as the earth shifts from wet soil to jagged rock, each thud of my feet making my nose throb harder.

Merrin reaches the cliff bluffs first. He flies out, scanning the coast, before looping back. Wren slides off his back, her face ashen.

The rest of us skid to a halt.

"No convenient boat to steal?" I pant, doubled over to clutch at a stitch in my side.

Merrin's expression is answer enough.

"We can jump," Shifu Caen suggests.

"Too many rocks."

"So we find a way down to the water."

Nitta runs a hand over her furred brow. "I don't do the best with water, if any of you remember the fishing village incident."

"It doesn't matter," Merrin replies. "The nearest island is more than ten miles away, and the currents of the archipelago are strong. Even experienced swimmers would have trouble."

"Can't you fly us all to the nearest island?" I suggest.

He shakes his head. "We'd just be stranded somewhere else, and the Czo would soon mobilize their boats."

Nitta worries her lower lip. "And the mainland...?"

"Too far."

As the others continue debating, I step to the cliff edge, looking out across the dark sea. The other islands in the archipelago loom in the distance, dark huddles spotting the ocean. Moonlight creates a path of silver along the water, so solid-looking it's as though we could step down and walk across it. As if that's all it would take to escape capture at the hands of the Czo.

A lump comes to my throat.

We were so close.

"Will you keep these for me, Lei?"

I jump, startled by Hiro's silent approach. His wide gray eyes shine. One hand is outstretched, palm open. Starlight silvers the object he's holding, but even without light I'd have known what it was the second my fingers wrapped around it, the instant I felt that familiar weight in my palm, the smooth casing.

"I—I can't take that," I say.

Behind us, the raised voices of the others are interrupted by the sound of Nitta's arrows being loosened. From the jungle comes shouting, the sound of bodies crashing through vegetation.

"Now would be a good time to decide what to do!" Nitta yells. She picks off the first guards one by one as they emerge from the jungle.

Hiro's expression doesn't change. "Please. Give this to Wren when she's recovered. She knows what to do with it. The other item is for you."

I stare at him. "What do you mean, when she's recovered?"

Without an answer, he pushes his Birth-blessing pendant into my hand, along with what it was sitting on, the little lacquered box I've noticed him carry. He closes my fingers around them. Then turns back to the others and steps up to Wren.

"Use me," he says, his voice clear and steady.

She blinks at him. Her face hardens with understanding. "Hiro, *no.*"

"You don't have enough energy to do it without me."

"We don't even know if it will work!"

"Yes." The shaman boy's pale face glows in the dark. "We do."

Nitta's voice rings out behind us. "A little help, please!"

We spin to see a wave of guards emerging through the wall of rain-glossed leaves. More follow close behind.

Merrin swears. With a flap of his wings, he charges forward, lifting off the ground just high enough to slash at the guards with his outstretched talons.

There are cries. Some of the lizard demons double over, clutching their bleeding heads.

Caen draws his sword as Merrin dives again. "Remember what your father told us," he growls at Wren. "Do what you have to do!" He runs to join the attack.

I stow Hiro's Birth-blessing pendant into the small box before tucking it into the folds of my sari with shaking fingers. I unsheathe my dagger, but I hang back, not wanting to leave them.

"You know what to do," Hiro tells Wren softly.

Her face is pale, her eyes sad. She glances at the approaching guards, then at me, and when she turns back to face Hiro, her expression is one of determination tinged with something painful.

Something like regret.

"Get back, Lei," she orders.

I do as she says.

Sword-clash and battle cries cut through the night. Despite Nitta, Caen, and Merrin's skill, they are heavily outnumbered, and the guards advance mercilessly, pushing forward in a slowly tightening semicircle around us. Soon, we'll be forced onto the jagged rocks of the shallows below—or into the weapons of the Czo.

Wren's eyes drain of color. An icy ripple flows from her body, plucking goose bumps down my arms. Her hair lifts, caught in an unseen wind.

"*Hiro,*" she says, and her words echo eerily.

The shaman boy gives me the tiniest smile. "Good luck, Lei. And thank you."

"Wait—" I start.

He's already at Wren's side. He fiddles at the sash at his waist and pulls free a slim blade I've never seen. I hardly have time to be surprised before he slashes a long gash up his right forearm, all the way from the heel of his hand to the crease of his elbow.

Blood bursts forth in a thick gush.

He falls to his knees.

"Hiro!" I yell, lurching toward him.

But his face is serene as he holds up his bloodied arm. Wren reaches down. Her fingers curl around his wrist.

The effect is instant. The roar of wind that bursts from Wren is so strong it knocks me off my feet. Arctic gusts billow across the cliffs, whipping aside the rain. There are cries and yells. The clash of blades halt, everyone taken by surprise. I move a shaky hand across my face to push away the hair that's sticking to the blood from my nose, and my touch stings, the air crackling with static.

Struggling against the powerful waves of Wren's magic, I stagger to my feet, nose throbbing. Wren and Hiro are silhouetted against the dark. Wren's voice rings out as she chants. The golden characters of the dao glitter as they rise into the air, spinning around her and Hiro in an amber storm.

Dimly, I'm aware that the clash of blades has picked back up, but I'm paralyzed, staring through horrified eyes at the scene in front of me. Wren's fingers are coated in Hiro's blood. Though his arm is lifted, his blood flows not down his arm but instead *up*, scarlet rivers crawling up Wren's own arm, weaving around her skin like ruby bracelets, thick and glistening.

Heavy footsteps pound behind me.

I don't have time to draw my dagger. I pitch forward to bring my right leg up and around. The heel of my foot meets the lizard guard's side as I spin. He grunts, thrown off balance. Grabbing the staff he's holding, I wrench it around, smacking him across his chin with his own weapon. He staggers before regaining composure.

But I've already drawn my dagger. Heart knocking, my vision flashing with red, I leap at him and drive the glowing blade into his chest.

He lets out a stunned puff of air. We drop to our knees together. Then I pull my blade free, rolling aside as he falls face-first against the rock.

Gasping, I push myself up. The guards are all around us now. Merrin cuts through them with whirling dives, scattering them into Caen and Nitta's waiting attacks, but they're being pushed back toward us. A whorl of sparking gold dances around Wren and Hiro, the air crackling. The two of them are dark silhouettes in the center of the circle of magic: Wren stands tall and terrifying; Hiro is slumped at her side, wrist dangling limply from her grip.

I drag my eyes back to the oncoming demons. They're almost upon us. Whatever magic Wren and Hiro are building, it's still not ready.

My breath hitches. We won't make it. We're going to die here, the blood of my friends spilled across the rocks only to be washed away by the rain—

Boom!

Something arcs overhead with a flash, and this time it's not firecrackers. The reverberation of the blast forces me to the ground. The breath is shocked from my lungs. I lie on my back, gaping at the sky like a stranded fish. Raindrops pelt my face, mixed now with flakes of gray and strange scraps of fluttering material that I realize are clothes.

Clothes, and skin.

My ears ring loudly. The air tastes of ash. My broken nose throbs so forcefully my vision pulses with white. Gritting against the pain, I flip to my stomach and push myself to my knees.

There's another thud, close this time, and far softer. No explosion follows. As I get shakily to my feet, I notice a harpoon sticking up through a crack in the rocks, inches from my toes. A thick rope is attached to its end. It trails down past the cliffs and over the rocks, out to a ship bobbing on the water.

Yellow sails stamped with claw-tipped paw prints fly from its twin masts. On the deck, two figures are moving about, steering the boat around. Standing on the bow, one leg propped on the low rail, is what looks like a large lion-form girl. The wide hems of her trousers and wrap shirt whip in the wind. A marigold scarf trails from her neck. She has what looks like some kind of cannon balanced on her shoulder.

She spots me, and grins.

Tossing the cannon to the floor, the lion-girl leaps onto the rope as it pulls taut between her boat and the harpoon embedded in the cliff. With incredible nimbleness given the impossibly dangerous careen of the cord, she starts up the rope in a run.

A powerful wave shocks the boat. The rope slackens, shifts. The demon-girl wobbles, but she keeps her composure, only unbalanced for a few seconds before she makes the last few yards in an easy sprint. She leaps up onto the cliff top and lands with a heavy thud.

She tosses back her blond hair as she straightens, flashing me a wide, sharp-toothed smile that crinkles her sandy-colored furred cheeks. Feline eyes glitter, framed with thick lashes and darkened with kohl.

"I know," she purrs, her voice deep and assured. "That *was* impressive. But save your adulation for later. As much as I'd love to bask in it, we've got a dramatic escape to execute."

She tosses me a bunch of curved steel objects, rope handles looped at their ends.

I gape at her. "Uh…"

"For the rope," she says, gesturing behind her.

I still don't move. "Sorry, who *are* you exactly?"

Now she looks outright offended. "Hasn't Wren told you about me?" She shoots a glance at where Wren is still weaving magic. Her thick hair ripples in the gust of the enchanted wind. "My sweet girl.

She was no doubt trying to be considerate." The lion-girl beams at me. "I'm General Lova, Wren's first love. You must be Lei—her second. Such a delight to meet you."

While I'm still goggling at her, she draws a huge curved blade from her back.

"Caen!" she shouts. "Get everyone to the boat!"

And then she dives into battle, her cutlass whirling.

Shifu Caen's surprise at the lion-girl's appearance lasts only a second. He finishes off the reptile demon he was fighting with a slice to the side of the neck, then falls back, running to where I'm still standing, holding the strange objects Lova gave me.

"Nitta!" he shouts over his shoulder. "Time to go!"

Nitta has long since run out of arrows. She's been using her bow as a staff and her claws as blades. She waits for Merrin to cover her with a diving swoop before she jogs over, panting heavily.

"The Amala are here," Caen says. He grabs two of the metal pieces from me.

Nitta wheels around. Spotting Lova, she turns back, eyes narrowed. "And we trust them?"

He tosses her one of the metal objects. "We have no choice."

"Wait," I say. "We can't leave Wren and Hiro—"

"We won't. Now, Nitta—you first."

The leopard-girl moves to the harpoon. She fits the curving steel hook over the top of the rope and kicks off. We watch as she speeds over the water, her long body dangling beneath the cord, all the way to the boat.

The instant she leaps off onto the deck, Caen pushes me forward. "Your turn."

I look to Wren and Hiro. An empty circle rings them, the force of their magic still protecting them. Lova stands between them and the wall of advancing guards. She fights with astonishing speed and power, her huge cutlass flashing silver as it arcs through the rain-pelted air, while Merrin continues to attack from above.

The lion-girl spares us a glance over her shoulder. "Go!" she yells.

With a frustrated growl, I stumble to the edge of the cliffs. My hair lashes around my face as I hook the metal piece over the rope.

There's a stomach-swooping drop as I jump. Then my arms lock above my head. My shoulders jerk, shooting fresh pain into my nose. Teeth gritted, eyes searing from the rush of salt-rich air, I cling to the handles as the bar slides down the rope. The sea yawns beneath my bare feet, foam bubbling around the slabs of seaweed-choked rocks that would smash my head clean open if I fell.

The waves rear higher; ocean spray wets my skin. The boat looms ahead. The second I'm at it, I let go of the handles. I tumble across the deck, sky and floor spinning around me, the breath shooting from my lungs.

When I come to a stop, I lie in a shaking huddle. It's a few seconds before I can open my fingers from their tight clench. I shove myself up onto my elbows with a moan.

"Slowly." Nitta's come to my side. She tucks an arm around my waist to help me up.

Whirring metal sounds from behind us. We move out of Caen's way as he comes in to land, leaping to the deck with barely a wobble. A few moments later, another figure comes speeding down the rope.

Lova jumps to the deck with impossible grace. Without missing a beat, she pulls her cutlass from its sheath and slices through the rope.

"What are you doing!" I cry. "Wren and Hiro are still there!"

"The Bird is bringing them," she responds curtly. She stows her weapon, striding past me to bark orders to the two cat demons working the sails and rudder.

I stumble to the gunwale.

The Czos' island looks impossibly far. The water is dark, the silvery glow of moonlight tracing a path across the waves. Heavy clouds scud across the horizon. Water stings my cheeks as waves break against the hull. Even from here, the air crackles faintly with magic. And then the air—

It *explodes* with magic.

A thundering, sparkling, iridescent golden wave erupts from the Czos' island. It billows into the ship, knocking me off my feet. The back of my head smacks against the decking. Night turns momentarily to day as gilded characters spark and fizz in the air. I watch them rain down, gulping like a stranded fish, hearing only the beating of my heart and the rush of blood in my ears.

I get up slowly, tasting blood. Gold sparks are still falling all around, a shower of tiny stars. Across the deck, the others are also picking themselves up.

Ahead, the Czos' island burns. The whole island is aflame, orange tongues lashing high into the sky. Ash rains down, filling the air with the now-familiar scent of smoke and devastation and endings.

Backlit by the flames, a figure flies toward us, winged arms spread wide.

Merrin lands heavily. We run over as Wren slides off his back, slumping against his side, her legs sprawled across the deck. My hearing is still muffled, and everything seems strangely silent as I throw myself around her. I bury my face in her hair. We rock with the pitch of the boat. Her breaths come shallow and labored.

When I peel back, Wren's face is drawn, dark circles looping her eyes like eclipsed moons. I smooth my hand over her brow. She's still so beautiful, of course she is. She would be beautiful even if she were one hundred and fifty-one years old. But it's as though she's aged ten years in the blink of an eye. She's trembling from head to toe. Her cheeks are sunken, her lips cracked, her skin drained of color. The scar across her forehead appears deeper now, pink and raw-looking.

"Gods, Wren," I sob. I lean in, but she jerks her head to the side before I can kiss her.

"Don't," she croaks.

Her voice is broken. Hoarse and scared, and…something else. A common thread I've noticed running under her words more and more over the past few weeks.

I recognize it now for what it is.

Guilt.

An alarm goes off inside me. "Wren, where's Hiro?"

She shakes her head, refusing to meet my eyes.

Understanding slots into place with a neat, horrid click. Tears well up. They spill past my cheeks in a warm gush. "That's the secret, isn't it?" I whisper thickly. "The secret to your magic. Pain. Blood."

She doesn't answer.

Dimly, I grow aware of the others' presence.

"Lei." Caen's voice is gentle but firm. He eases me away by my shoulders, and Wren doesn't stop him. "Give her space. That was powerful magic." There's awe in his voice, too—awe *and* horror.

Silence stretches out. The air is soft with the lap of the waves, the patter of raindrops on the decking. My whole face throbs with pain, but the way Wren is avoiding my eyes is a hundred times worse.

"We should pick up the pace," Nitta says eventually. "It won't take long for the Czo to catch up to us."

"Oh, little cub. You really think we're their priority right now?"

General Lova stands tall, one hand on her hip, her feline eyes flashing. With a pang, I notice her eyes are amber—almost the same shade as mine, though hers are darker, thickened by a hint of brown.

"The Czo will be focused on evacuating their guests to the surrounding islands." She wipes her blade on her robes, leaving streaks of red. "Lord Mvula invited them to the party tonight to secure their support if war breaks out. If any of them are hurt, it'll be difficult for him to retain their clan's allegiance." She stows her cutlass. "We'll sail to a spot on the Kitori coast a little more south from here. This ship is made for both sand and water. We can take it across the dunes to the desert. We should be at Jana by nightfall tomorrow."

The lion-girl comes toward us, her generous hips shifting from side to side. She lowers to her knees and takes Wren's face in both of her palms. "Don't worry, sweetheart," she purrs, tracing her thumbs along Wren's cheekbones. "I'm here now."

And in full view of the rest of us, she plants a kiss on Wren's lips.

TWENTY-SEVEN

"M Y SPIES HAVE BEEN TELLING ME all sorts of fascinating tales about your escapades these past few weeks," General Lova says as we sit around the deck, our hands cupping mugs of steaming chai. "All very brave, if slightly chaotic. Honestly, though, I'm rather hurt you didn't come to us first. The White Wing?" She shoots a look at Merrin. "Those birds can never commit to anything. You'll see. They'll lose interest in this war after ten minutes and will go back to hiding in their precious cloud kingdom, leaving the rest of us to keep Ikhara safe for them." She tosses her head back and adds smoothly, "Isolationism is only a political strategy for the privileged."

Merrin crosses his arms. He's sitting back, slightly apart from the group. "You're lucky we birds are taught to respect other clan leaders," he replies coldly. "Otherwise I'd have a few choice words for you, *Lady* Lova."

"What a shame," the lion-girl sighs. "I do love a little disrespect. Gives me so many more opportunities to practice witty comebacks." Her amber eyes gleam, her voice a throaty purr. "As well as my sword skills." Taking a sip of tea, she catches my gaze over the rim of her cup and winks.

After making it to the Kitorian coast last night, Lova and the two other cat demons deftly made the adjustments to transition the ship from sailing ocean waves to sand dunes. They unfurled new sails that span out over the sides of the boat to snag the low winds of the desert and changed the rudder in a gravity-defying move that had Lova dangling over the stern of the ship, her toes hooked over the rail.

Now, hours later, the sun is beginning to rise. The boat rocks gently as it skates across the dunes, warm wind rippling our hair. All around, the sands stretch out, golden slopes gilded in pinks and amber. We're huddled around the center of the bow. From the masts to the gunwale, a fabric sheet stretches overhead to protect us from the sting of flying sand and the heat of the desert sun. Being too shallow for any below-deck quarters, the Amalas' ship has only one cabin, small and low-ceilinged to keep the ship's speed high. Wren has been in there all night, being tended to by one of the General's crew who has nursing experience.

"How long have you been following us?" Shifu Caen asks General Lova.

"From the minute our spies in the Hidden Palace reported what happened at the Moon Ball. Earlier, actually—when Bhali Hanno was killed. That was when we knew a war was inevitable. Ketai would never let the King get away with that. Then our scouts alerted us that you had arrived at the Cloud Palace, and from there it was pretty clear what Ketai's next steps would be. I had lookouts placed along the whole of the southern coast just in case, but I was fairly sure you'd be paying the Czo a visit, so I made sure to stay close. Lucky I did, huh?" She grins, but none of us return it.

"So you're going to help us?" I ask bluntly. "Is that what you're saying?"

Lova twirls her scarf around one finger, the corner of her mouth curving. "Is that what I'm saying?"

Nitta glares. "None of us are in the mood for games, Lova." Sitting next to me, she hugs her knees, her pretty face still splattered with blood from the battle with the Czo. Though she's as tall as Lova, she looks withered now, as though some of her own presence has been drained away by her brother's death.

"Just Lova now, is it?" Lova returns, sounding almost amused.

"You're not my Clan Lord anymore." Though Nitta's words are defiant, there's hesitancy in her tone. "I don't owe you a title."

Something hardens in Lova's expression. "I suppose you're right. Good to see you, anyway, little cub. It's been a while. Where's that annoying brother of yours? According to my scouts, he was with you when you boarded the boat in Shomu."

Nitta's lashes flick up. "Bo's dead," she says, almost violently.

Lova doesn't react—or at least, she doesn't let any reaction show. Her right ear flicks at a fly hovering too close. After a beat, she says, "I'm sorry to hear that. He was a good cat."

"He was more than that," Nitta whispers.

Knowing she wants to be left alone, I get Lova's attention. "Since you've been following us all this time, you know we've not always had the most welcoming reception from the other clans. Could you just make it clear whether you're going to help us?"

"Of *course* I'm going to help you, Lei," she responds, smiling warmly. "There's no need to worry. I might not care for Ketai Hanno, but I do believe in his cause. And I believe in his daughter. She's the reason we're all here, after all, isn't she, Moonchosen? She is the future of Ikhara."

I wither slightly under her intense look. It's impossible not to be intimidated by Lova. The rising light sets off the gold tint of her fur and glimmers in her high-set, curving eyes. Sharp cheekbones lead down to a strong jaw, half-human, half-lion. But it's her body that draws the most attention, the way her generous curves seem to be practically pouring out of her clothes. A loosely tied cotton wrap shirt only just manages to contain her impressive cleavage. Her wide-legged trousers cling at the hips, which she sways so lavishly when she moves it's impossible not to notice.

There's an ache in my chest. General Lova is so beautiful it hurts. And not in the way Wren's beauty does, but because whenever I look at her I can't help but think of Wren enjoying *Lova's* beauty. Images of their bodies pressed together crowd my mind, turning my stomach.

The lion-girl's smile relaxes. "But you're right, Lei. It never hurts to spell it out. I don't want any misunderstandings." She faces Shifu Caen, fully serious now. "The Amala are prepared to give the Hannos our allegiance. But we do so on our own terms."

"Which are?" Caen asks.

"No faffing around." It's one of the other Cat Clan members who speaks—Nor, an old scarred-face tiger demon. Her rust-colored fur is faded and wizened, but she holds herself with the same easy confidence as her much-younger General.

"We all know what Ketai is like," Lova agrees. "Speeches and councils and painstaking planning for everything. I bet that man even schedules when he'll go to the toilet." Caen's jaw tightens at this, but she waves a hand, continuing sharply, "Now is not the time for airs and graces. My spies have confirmed that the King's attack on the Hannos' palace is imminent. We're talking three and a half weeks, a month at the most."

The words hit me like a blow. I'd been hoping what Naja told me back at the Fukho Grasslands—that the palace would be marching on the Hannos' palace any moment now—was only to scare me, to frighten me into submission.

Nitta lays a hand on my shoulder. "We'll get there first," she assures me quietly.

"We will if we do exactly as I suggest," Lova amends. She sets down her empty cup and twirls it absently with a furred finger as she talks. "My cats and I know the desert like the back of our paws. We should continue southeast from here to reach Jana. After what happened at the Czos', all of Kitori will be crawling with royal soldiers, and there's a big outpost just northeast of here I'm keen to avoid. It'll take six days' travel to reach the closest of our camps. We can rest a little there, spread word to all three camps to mobilize our fighters. In staggered groups, we'll then head north across the desert to Demon's Ridge. There's a secret pass through the mountains to get into Ang-Khen that avoids the checkpoints along the Thousand Mile Road. Once in Ang-Khen, we can reach the Hannos' palace in three days on horseback." She leans back, rubbing the back of her head. "It'll be tight, but we can make it."

Nor gives her a wry smile. "We've made harder."

"Ooh," Lova replies gleefully, "remember that time in the Kuroz Valley when we accidentally demolished the Yuri Clan's sacred ritual cave? They were *not* happy."

I raise my brows. "How do you accidentally demolish a *cave*?"

"I've been known on occasion to get a little…trigger happy with my cannon."

"Not just your cannon," Nor reminds her. "Also flaming arrows, sulfur bombs, smoke shells, fire lances…"

The lion-girl grins wickedly. "What can I say? Explosions make me happy."

Shifu Caen clears his throat. "I think we've gotten somewhat sidetracked."

As the group falls back into discussions over the plans for the next few weeks, I get up and head over to the small cabin at the back of the deck. I wince as each step makes my nose throb with fresh pain, but I push past it. A broken nose is nothing compared to what Wren's been through.

The sleek-furred face of a Moon panther demon pops around the door at my knock. He eyes my bloody face. "Need me to take a look at that?"

"Oh. No, actually I'm here to see how she is."

The demon's serious, pale yellow-green eyes glitter out from obsidian fur, the tips of which are beginning to tinge gray in places. "The girl is drained," he replies, in a voice deep and cool and crinkled, like the dry brush of a cotton sheet on a winter's night. "But she'll live."

I try to look past the door. "I'd love to see her."

"She's sleeping. It's not the best time to disturb her."

I move back as he slides out and shuts the door behind him. "Thank you for looking after her, um…"

"Osa." Arms crossed, he leans against the wall of the cabin, rocking with the boat. "She shouldn't be," he says abruptly.

"What do you mean?"

"She shouldn't be *alive*." The panther demon pushes off the wall, moving toward the rest of the group in a sloping gait, his tail slinking behind him. He lifts his voice to address them. "I don't know how that girl is still living. We all saw it. The magic she wielded. Even the most skilled shaman wouldn't be able to create such a dao alone."

"She wasn't alone."

Merrin's voice is bitter. The others look around where he's standing off to the side of the boat, kneading at his injured arm.

Vivid images come to me of the crimson skeins of blood tracking up from Hiro's wound. How they'd wrapped around Wren's forearm like a gauntlet. His limp body slumped at her side.

Use me.

It's what he said seconds before taking a dagger to himself. Hiro offered himself to Wren as a sacrifice. His life, in exchange for power so strong it could take hundreds more.

"What do you mean?" Lova asks Merrin sharply.

"She used Hiro. He gave up his life so she could cast that dao. Even after what happened with Bo, she used him. Just as she's used us all this time."

Lova springs to her feet at the same time I take a step toward him.

"You know that's not fair!" I retort, my hands balling into fists.

"And what would a bird know of loyalty?" Lova challenges.

Merrin laughs, a harsh sound that pulls goose bumps across my skin. His face is wild, his voice shockingly cold. "Bo told me, Cat. He told me why you exiled Nitta and him from your clan. Don't pretend you understand loyalty."

"Hiro offered himself," I say before the conversation can devolve into yet another stupid bird-versus-cat debate I have no interest in witnessing right now. "He told Wren to use him. I heard him. She didn't want to, but he insisted, and we were under attack. There wasn't another choice. She did what she had to do to save us."

Merrin turns his penetrating stare to me. "You really believe that, sweetheart?"

"Yes."

Something sad crosses his features for a second; a lost, sorrowful look. Then he snuffs it out. "What would Wren have done if Hiro hadn't been there?" he asks me.

"She—she couldn't have created such a powerful dao without him—"

"Yes, she could." Merrin's eyes flick to Caen. "You know what I'm talking about, don't you, Shifu?"

Caen wears a deep frown. He doesn't say anything.

With another harsh laugh, Merrin jolts into motion, pacing the deck with sudden impatience, his neck cocked at an unnatural angle. "There are stories throughout history of shamans creating daos everyone thought impossible. Daos not even the strongest, most skilled shamans could execute in ordinary circumstances. The Xia clan is the most well known of these legends. But what is magic if not the exchange of qi? The exchange of life force between a shaman and his land? And what is the ultimate gift you can offer the earth? The ultimate sacrifice?"

The answer comes to me, a hoarse whisper on the sand-flecked wind. Death.

"Hiro may have offered his life," Merrin goes on into the uneasy silence, "but Wren chose to take it over giving up her own. Sacrificing others' lives in pursuit of their own goals." His voice is scathing. "Like father, like daughter."

Lova launches herself across the deck at Merrin, pressing the point of her cutlass to his throat. "I may not care for Ketai Hanno, either," she growls, "but that human girl means the world to me, and I have been lucky to know both her heart and her mind. Just because she isn't scared to do what it takes to win a war doesn't mean she lacks integrity. She cares more deeply about others than you could ever imagine, Bird. And if you dare speak one more word against her, I'll throw you off this ship myself—after I've sliced open your throat."

Merrin blinks down at Lova, again the briefest flash of sadness— and even *relief*—passing over him. He backs away. "No need," he says sourly. "I can't bear to stay here a moment longer."

"Merrin!" Nitta cries, lurching forward.

I run with her. My hands snap around the railing, a sharp pain tearing through my chest as we watch him lift higher and higher into the light-washed sky. So many times throughout my life I've wished to have wings. To be able to take off into the sky and fly away, either toward something I wanted or away from something I was trapped by. And then my Birth-blessing pendant opened, and the word inside—*flight*—seemed to finally confirm that I had the ability to do just that, even without physical wings.

Now, though, it feels as though any wings I might possess have been broken. Merrin soars farther away each second, and all I can do is cling to the railing and watch him go.

A terse hush rings out, broken only by the flap of the sails and the whispering rush of the boat's hull over the sands.

Eventually, there's the sound of a sword being sheathed. "Because of Wren," Lova says, her voice low and threatening, "many of the leaders of our biggest adversaries in this war have been killed. What she did has saved many of our own side's lives being lost. If you have a problem with that, perhaps you need to refamiliarize yourself with what being at war entails. People of all castes will be killed. If we want to win, then we'd better be the side to kill the most." There's a pause, then she orders, "Nor, we're running too far north. Head us farther south."

Claws tap against floorboards as the old tiger demon gets to her feet. "Yes, General."

Lova turns. "Osa, come help me with breakfast."

While the cat demons busy themselves, I stare out over the dunes. Morning sunlight glitters on the undulating landscape, the golden slopes muzzy from sand skimming over their tops. In the distance, the rising sun sits just above the horizon. Silhouetted against it, a winged figure flies away.

"You know what?" Nitta says thickly at my side, tears streaming down her furred cheeks. "I'm glad Bo wasn't here to see that. He would have been so disappointed." She sighs. "I can't blame Merrin, though. Caen was right. Grief does strange things to a person."

I touch my shoulder to hers. "Nitta, you've been really amazing."

"Aren't I always?" She gives me a wobbly smile. Then she gazes out, her wet eyes filled with the orange of the rising sun. "I'm trying to be strong for Bo. But honestly, Lei…" Her voice hitches. "Most of the time, it's a struggle even to breathe."

I move my hand to hers and take her fingers in mine.

When Nitta speaks again, her voice has hardened. "Merrin was wrong about a lot of things, Lei, but he was right about Ketai. There's nothing he won't do to bring down the King. And for Wren, that's all she's grown up knowing. His obsession. His hatred." She spares me a sideways look. "You're not the same. I see you, the way you fight. The way you are toward others. You're soft where they are hard. You have love when they only have hate." She squeezes my hand. "Hold on to that as tightly as you can, Lei. Because war will do everything it can to take that goodness from you. I think sometimes people forget there *will* be a time after all of this—for the lucky ones, at least. And when that time comes, we'll all have to live with what we have done." She stares out at the horizon, where Merrin's silhouette has already disappeared. "And what we have left of ourselves."

TWENTY-EIGHT

MISTRESS AZAMI

"HURRY UP, GIRLS! WE'RE LATE!"
Mistress Azami's rough voice barked through the Night Houses. Most of her girls were already outside, heading down the shortcut that led to City Court, where their carriages were waiting. But there were always a few stragglers. Her padded dog feet marched briskly down the corridors as she prowled through the three buildings that housed the palace concubines, throwing open sliding doors to scan each room with a trained eye before moving to the next.

When she checked on Darya's room, she found its occupant in plain sight on the bed, not even trying to hide. Lying on her front and propped up on her elbows, the statuesque Moon panther demon was serenely painting her long nails with gold lacquer. Dust motes danced through the air. She hummed as she worked, twirling her ankles behind her.

Mistress Azami stood in the doorway, a hand on her hip. She waited until Darya eventually looked up.

The young panther-woman smiled. "Yes, Miss A?" she purred

in her deep voice, her heavy-lashed yellow eyes glinting. "May I help you?"

"Time to go, Darya."

She cocked her head. "Wherever to?"

"Don't play with me," Mistress Azami snapped. "I'm not in the mood for it today."

"Luckily you're not one of my clients, then."

Mistress Azami shifted her hips, her eyes narrowing. "If you think I'm going to enjoy this any more than you are, then you are mistaken. But attendance is mandatory. Unless you fancy spending the rest of your days locked up beneath Lunar Lake, where certainly *no one* will care about the state of your nails—least of all you—you'll get up right this minute."

With a sigh, Darya swung her long legs off the bed. "They'll get spoiled, now," she complained, blowing on her curving feline nails.

Mistress Azami's expression remained unchanged. "However will you cope." She waited in the doorway even after Darya was past her. "You, too, Lill," she ordered at the empty room.

There was no answer.

"I know you're there."

From behind her, Darya leaned in and said, serious now, "Let the girl stay here, Miss A. She won't be noticed."

"I'm not taking any chances." Mistress Azami raised her voice, a rough canine bite entering it. "If you don't come out in three seconds, I'm going to drag you to Ceremony Court by your ear. We'll see whether it's still attached to your head by the time we get there, shall we? Three...two...one!"

A pair of furred doe ears popped up from behind the bed. The next moment, the small girl they belonged to darted out, the messy knot her hair was piled up into bobbing as she ran. She dropped to the floor at Mistress Azami's feet, hands splayed across the bamboo matting. "I'm so sorry, Mistress!" she cried.

"How many times have I told you to stop with all of that?" Mistress Azami pulled the girl to her feet. She was rough, just as she was with all her girls. But no more than necessary, and something tender touched her face as she looked down at the little Steel child, just a slip of a thing, her features human save for her delicate doe ears, which were quivering with fear. Mistress Azami softened her voice. "We'll be in and out as quickly as possible. Stay by my side. I'll look after you."

"Th-thank you, Mistress." The girl almost went to bow again, stopping at the glare the dog-woman gave her.

"Come." She tucked her hand around the back of Lill's head to nudge her down the corridor. "The others will already be at the carriages."

Darya leaned down to take Lill's hand. "Once we're back," she said kindly, "how about we paint *your* nails, too?"

The young girl's voice pitched with excitement. "Really?"

Darya nodded. "They'll look so pretty in gold."

"That's my favorite color!"

"Your mistress had beautiful gold eyes, didn't she?"

Lill's voice shone with pride. "The most beautiful in the whole palace."

As she followed the two of them down the hallway, Mistress Azami couldn't help the hot rush of anger that furrowed through her. She wasn't a young demon anymore. Far from it. She'd been around long enough, and had run the Night Houses for enough years now that hardly anything surprised her. Especially when it came to the cruelty of men. But even she had been shocked when, the morning after the Moon Ball, guards had turned up and had thrown—literally *thrown*—Lill at her.

"She can take the dead one's place," one of them had sneered.

The dead one's place.

The words had cleaved her. Yet Mistress Azami had simply hugged the little girl, whose face was ruddy from the tears leaking down her cheeks, and took her in without question. Of course, she'd never allow a client within twenty feet of Lill. If any tried, she'd gladly slice off their genitals herself. But Mistress Azami knew the child would at least be somewhat safe here under her attention. The other girls were delighted to have such a sweet thing to coo and preen over; she'd have no shortage of love here. And, more important, none at the court seemed to suspect Mistress Azami's involvement with what had happened the night of the New Year.

At least, not yet.

Her fingers strayed to the sash of her plain ash-gray cotton hanfu, where she'd tucked the important item she was to deliver to one of their allies at the King's announcement. She made sure it was well hidden before picking up pace, her rough voice barking at Darya and Lill, "What is this, some ahma's smoking club? Hurry up, or it'll be over by the time we get there."

Darya's reply dripped with sarcasm. "Yes, and wouldn't that be a shame?"

Ceremony Court was packed. The last time Mistress Azami had seen it like this was during the executions last year of the three failed assassins. Demons of all kinds poured into the enormous square, turning it into a heaving sea of bustling bodies and voices pitched in both excitement and concern. Posts had been erected throughout, displaying red and ebony banners stamped with the King's crest. They snapped in the icy wind.

The crowd was too thick for the carriages, so Mistress Azami and her girls abandoned them at the entrance and made their way on foot.

"Ow!" one of the girls whined, as the elbow of an ox-form demon caught her on the ear. She huffed. "Why can't we watch from here?"

"It's not like there's anything to see," another grumbled. "The King's going to stand around and talk, we'll all cheer and pretend to be happy, and then we'll go home and try to forget this ever happened."

"Aren't you curious to see if any of the rumors about the King are true?" the girl at her side asked. "My bet is on the lost-eye story. I wonder if he'll be wearing a patch…"

A curvy fox-girl behind her snorted. "Can you imagine? They'll be calling him the Pirate King, next."

"Didn't Darya get called to service him the other night?"

"That was Ki. She wouldn't tell us a thing, though, apart from that he wasn't in the best of moods."

"That Paper Girl definitely cut off *something*, then."

A girl sniggered. "Bet she kept it as a souvenir."

"Maybe she ate it. Bull penis is a delicacy in some places, you know."

"Hope it tastes better cooked than it does raw."

Mistress Azami shot them all a fierce look as they dissolved into laughter. "Remember where you are," she commanded, "and who you are talking about."

She spared a look down to check on Lill. The little doe-girl walked close, flanked on her other side by Darya. Her lips were pinched, her hands gripping fistfuls of her robes. She hadn't said a word since they'd left the Night Houses. Bundled up in a winter coat and among the press of much taller bodies, most of them Steels and Moons, she looked even smaller than usual. She walked with her head down, her hands balled into fists at her sides.

Mistress Azami's eyes slid up to where Darya was glaring at her over Lill's head. Then they lifted even farther, drawn to something hanging from the nearest flag post.

It was a dead body.

The lion-form man swung from his wrists, which had been tied over his head. His yellow robes were bloodied. Though his head hung down, long golden hair obscuring his face, Mistress Azami recognized him at once.

It was part of her job to know every member of the court. For her official role as Mistress of the Night Houses, but more important, for her work with helping Ketai Hanno and his allies plot against the King. Since Ketai had recruited her many years ago, Mistress Azami had become one of his most vital contacts in the palace, largely due to the incredible exposure and trust her role in the Night Houses gave her to so many high-ranking court officials—as well as their darkest desires. *Secrets between friends create enemies, but secrets between enemies create friends,* or so the old saying went. The demon hanging from the flag post just a few feet away, however, had never set foot in the Night Houses. Mistress Azami had only met him in passing at palace banquets and balls. He'd stood out with his generous, deep-bellied laugh and the way he'd always gaze at the handsome lion-form man by his side—his husband, a court musician—with love-drunk eyes.

Now, Adviser Chun's body hung lifeless. She averted her eyes from him, scanning the vast square. More bodies hung from the posts closer to the stage at the center of the court. Some were too far to make out, but she recognized the ones nearby: Adviser Umi, General Khotaku, Madam My. That large panda-form there was Commander Sun. And, beyond him, the slim body dangling by delicate wrists and draped in delicate robes—

Mistress Azami's stomach gave a dull kick.

It wasn't that she was surprised to see this particular court member. After what had happened at the Moon Ball, her execution had been a certainty. But it was particularly unpleasant to see her dead body handled in this way, something that had once been inhabited with such care and grace so carelessly discarded.

Mistress Azami had never exactly been fond of the Paper Girls' instructor, Mistress Eira. She thought her softness with her girls ill prepared them for the emotional and physical strain they would face as the King's concubines. But she'd never wished ill of her. The woman had cared, in her own way. As Mistress Azami did with her own girls, the woman had looked after her Paper Girls as best she knew how.

With a low sigh, she turned away from Mistress Eira's body.

Darya was still glaring at her. "Fun day out for all the family, hmm?" she murmured, deadpan.

Luckily, Lill was still staring at the floor; she hadn't noticed the court's gruesome decorations yet. Shifting course slightly to avoid passing directly below Mistress Eira's lifeless body, the dog-woman continued leading her girls through the crowd.

Meet by General Yu. Bring the item.

That was the message she'd received last night. She'd had her suspicions what "by General Yu" might mean at the time, but now it was clear.

More than a hundred arrests had been made within the court in the feverish panic following the Moon Ball. And with the King's edict that charges of treason need not be put through trial, Mistress Azami suspected many were taking advantage of this to fulfill old grudges, as well as for the benefit of future political strategizing. Some of those who'd been arrested, however, such as Mistress Eira and General Yu, were simply being punished for their connections with Lei and Wren.

As she did many times a day, Mistress Azami spared a hopeful thought for the two escaped girls. Had they managed to reach Ketai Hanno and his allies safely? Where were they now? And, as always, her heart stung at the thought of the girl who should have escaped with them.

Zelle.

She inhaled sharply to push the pain away.

It took another five minutes of elbowing and jostling to reach the post where General Yu's body hung. It was closer to the main stage than Mistress Azami would have liked to be, but at least their attendance would be noticed by those who mattered. A quick sweep of the immediate area showed no sign of one of Ketai Hanno's allies, so she picked a spot to wait that was close enough to the bull demon's body that they could hear the creak of the ropes looped around his wrists, yet not too near to be standing directly beneath him. The tight pack of the crowd filled the air with the ripe scent of demon and human bodies, and smoke from the braziers topping each of the flag posts. Still, underneath it all Mistress Azami could make out the distinct odor of rotting flesh.

"Which rumor are *you* betting on, Miss A?" Darya murmured to her as they stood with Lill between them, their eyes on the stage.

It couldn't be long now. Ceremony Court was full to the brim. Only the huge golden throne that sat upon the stage was empty. It glittered in the gray afternoon light.

Mistress Azami gave Darya a tired look. "Enjoying annoying me today, aren't you?"

She lifted a shoulder. "Without Zelle around, someone's got to do it."

Darya's voice was light, affectionate even, but Mistress Azami received her words like a slap. The knowledge that Zelle was dead still burned her with a fresh fierceness each time she was reminded of it.

Heavy drumbeats burst to life, thundering throughout the square. At once, the electric energy of the crowd skipped even higher. Claps and stamping and excited shouts joined the pounding drums.

Lill grabbed Mistress Azami's legs. The poor girl was trembling.

Darya leaned down to her level. "What color are we painting your nails when we get back?" she asked, raising her voice over the noise.

Lill looked confused. "G-gold?"

Darya smiled. "The color of your mistress's eyes. And what was she like, Mistress Lei?"

"B-beautiful." Lill's voice strengthened. "And kind, and funny, and brave."

"Brave, exactly. Which is what you are, Lill. It's what we all have to be right now." Darya took the young girl's hand. "Can you be brave for me, Lill? Like Mistress Lei?"

The doe-girl's fluted ears were vibrating, her eyes wide. But she nodded, and held her head a little higher.

They were being jostled now, shifted with the excitement of the crowd. A large path had been kept clear by guards, cutting right through the center of the square, and from over the heads of the tallest demons, Mistress Azami spotted the King's palanquin arriving. It was an elaborate carriage, carried on the back of eight oryx demons.

They set the palanquin down at the foot of the stage, and the King stepped out, gilded horns catching the light. The muscles of his lean bovine body flexed beneath a layered black hanfu trimmed in gold as he crossed to the throne. Guards flanked him;

more surrounded the stage. The crowd surged, craning their necks
for a better look. Even those high up in the court hadn't seen the
King since the Moon Ball. Only shamans and his two personal
guards, Naja and Ndeze—both conspicuously absent from his side
today—had been allowed into his private chambers, and Mistress
Azami knew from the complaints some of the court members had
made during visits to her girls that these two generals had divulged
practically no information on the King's condition. They'd been
merely relaying his orders with little embellishment.

Below the drumbeats and noise of the crowd, whispers began to
slink amongst the jostling bodies. Whispers about the King.

From the back, he looked normal; so the rumors about him missing limbs weren't true. Then he turned, standing rather than taking
his throne, and many of Mistress Azami's girls gasped.

Mistress Azami herself only stilled. Cold ripples of anger and
grim, prideful satisfaction flowed down her veins.

Lei, Wren, and Zelle had done well.

"His eye!"

"I know!"

"It's kind of disappointing, isn't it?"

"Not for me—that's two weeks of cleaning duty you owe me,
Prim."

"Really, Hasfah? You're calling in your reward *now*?"

The girls fell silent as Mistress Azami shot them a stony glare.
She checked on Lill. The doe-girl was still clinging to her legs,
trembling despite the defiant tilt of her jaw.

Darya crouched down again. "Well," she said, draping an arm
around her. "The view is *much* better from down here."

This made Lill crack a nervous smile—which disappeared in a
flash as the drumbeats stopped.

An expectant hush fell. For a few moments, there was only the rustling of clothes and muted murmurs, punctuated by the snap of flags in the wind. Then the King's magnified voice boomed out across the square.

"Members of the court. My fellow demons and humans."

Shocked whispers threaded through the crowd. Mistress Azami frowned, peering through the rows of robe-clad demons that obscured her view of the King. She could see the hole where his right eye should have been; though smoothed over by shaman magic, the wound was still conspicuous. But otherwise there was no indication why his voice should sound…like *that*. It was rough and grating, hoarse and deep, as though the voice had been shattered and reassembled haphazardly, a broken mess of sharp edges that wouldn't fit back together again.

The layered robes of the King's hanfu folded around his neck, but they came up higher than usual. Were they hiding something?

Mistress Azami felt another thrill of pride. The girls had fought valiantly if they'd managed to damage his vocal cords this badly.

"I come before you all today to share an important announcement," the King went on in that awful, scraping voice, the jaggedness of it amplified through the magical enchantment that made his voice bellow throughout Ceremony Court. "It pertains to news I know many of you have been waiting anxiously to hear."

While other members of the audience were looking around, speculating with those around them, Mistress Azami's focus honed in on the King. Everything else blurred away, leaving only her fast, steady heartbeat and the arctic-blue stare of the King's remaining eye as he surveyed the crowd.

"First, let me clarify the rumors." He paused. "Yes, I was attacked the night of the Moon Ball."

The noise of the crowd grew, bodies surging. There were angry shouts, shocked outcries.

The King waited for quiet. "The details are unimportant. All you need to know is that the attack was orchestrated by the Hannos." The audience exploded at this, and he went on over them, throwing up his hands, "As such, Ketai Hanno and any found allied to him are now considered traitors to the court, and will be arrested and punished for the highest levels of treason. Look around you!" He flung his arms wide. "You can see some of those we have already discovered to be enemies to the throne—*this* is the fate awaiting all who dare conspire against the might of the court! The might of the *King!*"

His words were whipping the crowd into hysteria. By Mistress Azami's legs, Lill shrank even further into Darya's protective embrace as all around them the onlookers stomped and yelled, their faces lit in a feverish glow.

"To any of those who still plot against us, I have just one message." The King's mouth curved. "Prepare to join your friends."

Frenzied clapping, cheers, and shouts. There was the sound of wood snapping. Mistress Azami whipped her head around to see the post where Mistress Eira's body was tied tipping over, a group of demons at its base pushing it down to excited yells.

She looked away, feeling sick.

The King's gaze roamed over the crowd, as cold as the winter wind blowing through the square. "To the rest of you, my loyal subjects, I bring you today's announcement with the knowledge it will have your full support. This is not a decision I have made lightly. But when those closest to you betray your trust and plot to undermine you, to take away not only your life but your life's *work*, the kingdom you have spent all your years serving with tireless loyalty, it's the only response that fits the severity of the attack. Ketai Hanno and his allies have given us no choice! They brought this upon themselves when they took a shot at the very heart of our kingdom, when they made a mockery of all we stand for here in our gods-blessed realm! We demonstrated it before, and we will demonstrate it again—ours is not a power that can be broken! Our eight great provinces stand united, and we will do what we must to keep it that way!"

The King's fingers curled into fists, his face a twisted mask of anger. He lowered his hands, his voice barely audible over the frenzied roar of the crowd as he finished, simply, devastatingly, "We are at war with the Hannos!"

The crowd erupted. Darya gathered Lill to her chest as they were shoved and shunted in the surge of packed bodies.

Drumbeats picked back up. Mistress Azami noticed onlookers turning to the front of the square, pointing, mouths open in shouts the uproar drowned out. In a wave of jet black and fiery crimson, a procession of royal soldiers was making their way up the path down the center of the court. Something struck her as odd about the soldiers, though it took her a few moments more to realize why.

The demons in red were soldiers—but the figures in black were shamans. They wore only robes, no leather armor and harnesses for weapons, like the soldiers, and each of them marched beside a soldier, creating precise lines of color. Red, black, red, black. The court's colors.

"Behold, the finest division of our army!" the King bellowed. "The Shadow Sect!"

As the rest of the crowd cheered and clapped, Mistress Azami stilled.

Over the years, she'd heard snatches of what the King might be doing with his army. Whispers of an evil darkness in the heart of the palace, of magic that had no place being used. But the rumors had been fractured, their impact weakened with age. Most of the time they came via her girls, throwaway sentences their clients whispered or boasted to them, thinking the courtesans too dumb or careless to notice. There was much information that came to her that way, much of it far more pressing and condemning, and Mistress Azami couldn't believe everything lust-drunk men said when they were trying to impress. What gave weight to these rumors however was that Kenzo himself had reported noticing the suspicious use of shaman power at the palace. He'd expressed concerns that perhaps it was one of the things driving the Sickness.

This had been a year ago. Up until now, Mistress Azami hadn't known what to make of it. But seeing the procession of the soldiers, things slotted into place.

Each of the shamans was paired with a soldier.

A division of the army, up until now completely hidden, known as the Shadow Sect.

And the Sickness: land across Ikhara dying due to what most feared as some kind of corruption of magic on a grand scale.

"Miss A!"

Darya's shout broke Mistress Azami's concentration. She looked over her shoulder to see Darya and Lill a few feet away, shunted by the crowd.

"We'll meet at the carriages!" she called. "Protect the girl!"

She herself was struggling to hold her place in the tumult, members of the crowd all trying to get a better look at the King's new soldiers. The note had said to meet by General Yu. She couldn't move too far. As she scanned the crowd once more for a sign of the ally she was to meet, a hand seized hers in the crush.

The hand was cool and scaled. Mistress Azami whipped around to see a sharp-boned reptile-girl blinking up at her, her face pinched. Kiroku, Naja's maid. She was one of their newest recruits, but had already proven herself one of their most vital allies within the palace.

"The small bird flies," Kiroku hissed under the noise of the crowd, her striped reptilian eyes fierce.

"On the wings of the golden-eyed girl," Mistress Azami returned.

The lizard-girl didn't say anything more, simply waited as Mistress Azami slipped the small package from the sash at her waist and pressed it into her hands.

Kiroku tucked it swiftly away. "We go for him ten days from now," she said. "Be ready to hide him."

Mistress Azami's eyes widened. "You're bringing him *back* to the palace?"

"It's the only way to get him out of there without being seen. Can you do it?"

There was only one answer. "Of course. I'll figure something out."

"Good." Kiroku nodded, already turning to go. "Gods blessings."

"Gods blessings," Mistress Azami replied, though her voice was lost under the roar and pounding feet and hoof-fall all around. She began fighting her way back to Darya, Lill, and the rest of her girls, her mind whirring.

The King, as expected, was waging war on the Hannos.

In ten days' time, they would be breaking Kenzo out of the Lunar Lake prison—and it was Mistress Azami's responsibility to hide him within the Night Houses.

And, somewhere out there in the kingdom, Lei and Wren were racing against the clock to secure the help Ketai and their allies desperately needed if they were to face the might of the royal army, now with the added power of the King's dangerous new division she was only just starting to understand the implications of.

Kiroku's parting words echoed in her head. *Gods blessings.*

Mistress Azami was not a spiritual demon. Nor had she been raised as one. Now, for the first time in her life, she found herself sending a prayer to whichever gods might be listening to bestow a little luck upon them in the coming weeks.

She had a feeling it was the very least they needed if they were to survive the storm that was no doubt headed their way.

TWENTY-NINE

THE ATMOSPHERE ON THE AMALAS' SHIP is still tense the morning following Merrin's departure, as well as the next. The three Cat Clan members go about the running of the ship, chatting easily and swapping jokes, but even their laughter doesn't do much to break the subdued mood permeating our group. Nitta and I act as though Shifu Caen isn't here. Though he tries to talk to me a couple of times, Nor and Lova save me with requests for help I'm sure they didn't really need. To take my mind off the dark thoughts Merrin's parting words invited, I spend the days keeping Nitta company as she mends our tattered clothes, or squashed in the cabin with Osa, doing what I can to help him as he tends to Wren, the two of us dripping sweat in the stifled air of the confined space, its wooden walls baking under the fierce desert sun.

Since she collapsed after our escape from the Czos' island, Wren still hasn't woken.

"I've seen shamans drained from less," Osa tells me when I express my concerns to him during another of our nursing sessions. He's pressing a cool wet towel to her forehead while I do the same to the tops of her feet. "She'll wake eventually. But only when she's ready."

I don't admit that part of me is relieved she's still not conscious. Though of course I want Wren to be all right—I'll *always* want her to be all right, whatever has happened between us—I'm aware of the heavy conversation that awaits us, and something tells me *I'm* the one who won't be fine once it's over.

"How about you?" Osa adds, his feline eyes lingering on my bruised face. "Healing well?"

I touch my nose gingerly. "I think so." While it's not yet stopped throbbing, the pain and swelling have definitely lessened, and Nitta assures me it's still the same shape as before.

When she said this, I couldn't help but think of Bo. How he'd have smirked and added something along the lines of it being a shame my nose *hasn't* changed.

Later that day, after a dinner of vegetable tagine so delicious it has Nitta pressing Osa for his recipe, Nor fetches something from the below-deck compartment where the Amala keep some of their supplies. "I just remembered," she says, holding up a small lacquered box. "I found this on deck after we rescued you from the Czos. Does it belong to any of you?"

Caen squints. "I'm sure I've seen that before."

I almost choke on my chai. "Oh, that's mine!" I say, setting down my mug and scrambling up. "Thank you for finding it, Nor."

"Lovely craftsmanship," she says as she hands it over. "I was going to use it for my scorpions if it wasn't any of yours."

"Your...scorpions?"

"I always like to have one or two nearby. You'd be amazed how often they come in handy." Her wizened face creases with a smile. "Would you like to see?"

"Um, I'm all right. Maybe another time."

I angle away from the others to open Hiro's box without them seeing. I'd completely forgotten about it in the chaotic aftermath of the fight with the Czo guards; it must have fallen from my sari when I landed on the Amalas' ship.

A light floral fragrance unfurls as I lift the lid. The golden egg of his Birth-blessing pendant is still safely nestled inside, its chain slinking over strange folds of textured...paper? I pick the necklace up and stow it in my lap. Then, carefully, I lift out one of the origami-like pieces. The violet paper is dry and crinkled, shaped into a perfect flower. In the low light of the lanterns swinging from the masts, it takes me a few moments to realize that's exactly what it is.

A flower.

I inspect some of the others. There are little pink plum blossoms and multi-petaled camellias, the symmetric starburst-shape of white lotus and delicate lavender pearls, half of them still clinging to their stem.

A souvenir?

I like flowers.

A lump rises in my throat. Many of the pressed flowers have been damaged, but their beauty is undeniable, and I think of the meticulous care with which Hiro must have collected and looked after them.

Anger flares down my veins with a sudden rush.

I click the box shut. Snapping my fingers around the Birth-blessing pendant, I put Hiro's box away with the rest of our things where they're strapped down in boxes to the deck so they won't fall off or get blown away in the wind, then go to the cabin.

Inside, it's dark and warm, the heat less intense at this time of the evening. The shadows shift. "Lei?" Wren whispers. There's the rustle of clothes as she sits.

"You're awake," I say.

Her voice is small. "Just."

I crouch down to sit next to her. Dim light filters in through the cracks of the door. Her face is pale, her eyes two flashes of white enclosing dark irises.

I resist the urge to touch her. "How do you feel?"

She clears her throat. "I . . . I feel like I've died, and only just about managed to come back to life."

"Do you remember what happened? At the island?"

A pause. "Yes."

My fingers tighten around Hiro's pendant.

"I'm so sorry," Wren whispers.

"We all are," I reply, my voice rough. I exhale, hard. "Merrin left," I say abruptly. I sense Wren stiffen. "He argued with Lova—who is lovely, by the way. Beautiful. Fierce. Totally intimidating. She's just like you."

Wren reaches across my lap. "Lei—"

I tug my hand away. "She, however, is not afraid to speak her mind. I'm so tired, Wren. So tired of you hiding things from me."

Tears well, and I blink them furiously away. Even though it's dark, I don't want her to see my pain. If she sees how much this is hurting me, she'll want to comfort me, and there's nothing more I want right now than to have Wren's arms around me, to melt into her embrace and forget any of this ever happened.

It's also the last thing I can bear.

"Pain strengthens magic to a certain extent," I state in a flat voice. "But *your* magic—the Xias' magic, the technique your clan guarded all their lives . . . Hiro offered his life to you to use, and you said you weren't even sure it would work. But you think that's what it is, don't you? That not only pain, but *death* is what gave the Xia their superior force."

She's become so still it's as though she's not even here. "Yes."

My heart twists at her whispered answer. "Hiro offering himself was important, right? He had to do it voluntarily."

"Taking a life isn't in keeping with the balance of the earth," Wren replies, muted. "If anything, it drains it. Certainly some gods appreciate blood spilled in their honor, but our lives come from the earth, have taken qi to create, and so to recklessly disregard those lives and that effort of creation goes against a shaman's code of keeping the earth in balance. But if one were to offer their life to another, *knowingly* sacrifice themselves—"

"It would count as a fair exchange of qi for more magic," I finish.

"That was our theory."

"And now you've proven it."

"We still don't know exactly how it works. There could be more to it. But...yes. It seems so."

I close my eyes, letting out a long breath. Then a half-forgotten memory comes back to me. My lashes spring back open. "Is that what your father told you and Shifu Caen the night before we left the temple? What he reminded you about when we left? That you should use Hiro if necessary?" My stomach kicks. "Is that why Hiro was with us in the first place?"

"Of course not! And no, it wasn't what he told us."

"What *did* he tell you, then?"

Wren averts her gaze. "That we were to do whatever is necessary to ensure the mission is successful. Even if it meant losing some of the others."

A cold silence unspools at her words.

"So Ketai doesn't know about your power yet," I say.

"No."

"Are you planning on telling him?" When she doesn't reply,

I go on, "You know what he'll do with this information, Wren. He'll find others to pledge themselves to your power. Other broken boys like Hiro who have every reason to hate the King and don't value their own lives enough. You'll have a whole army of willing sacrifices."

Carefully, her sad, sorry stare fixed on mine, Wren reaches for my hand, and this time I let her, wanting so much to go back to a time before, when her holding my hand would have been simple. When I wouldn't have felt secrets and pain trapped between our palms.

Merrin's words ring in my head.

It wasn't just Wren. You killed them, too. All of you.

Shaking, I untwine my fingers from hers. I press Hiro's Birth-blessing pendant into her palm.

She freezes, understanding immediately.

"Hiro gave it to me before he died," I say. "He told me you'd know what to do with it."

Wren swallows. "There's a small ceremony. Will you do it with me?"

"Now?"

"In a few days? It needs magic, and I'm still too drained right now."

"Whenever you're up to it," I reply stiffly.

Wren shifts closer, the darkness thick and coiling, the stuffy warmth pricking sweat across my brow. "Will you lie with me, Lei? Just for a while, please—"

"I promised Nitta I'd help her with something," I interrupt, jerking to my feet. Guilt spears through me at the lie, but I shove it away. "Later, maybe. You should get back to sleep."

As I'm about to open the door, Wren whispers, "Do you know how hard you're making this for me?"

In an instant, all the months and miles between now and the

last time she spoke those words to me fold away, until it is just the two of us as we were back then, alone together in a darkened room crowded with unspoken feelings. How easy it would be for me to go to her. For us to forget all that has happened and fold ourselves into each other and the blissful comfort of the memory of that moment, when I'd felt so keenly the delicious potential of my future. How my world was pivoting on the precipice of something new, something beautiful.

Instead, I open the door. "Don't do that," I say coldly, something barbed pricking my chest. "We're not those people anymore, Wren. I love you, but it's not that easy."

Then I step out and close the door behind me, feeling something else shutting between Wren and me.

Something we might never be able to open again.

THIRTY

THE FOLLOWING DAY, WREN HAS JUST enough strength to
emerge from the cabin. Osa and I walk her around the
shifting deck. She's a little unsteady on her feet at first, but
Lova puts it down to her having not yet developed her "sand legs."
The next day, she has a bit more energy, even making a few laps of
the ship without wobbling. The day after, she seems fast on her way
back to full strength, helping out with chores around the ship and
eating full meals for the first time since we left the Czos' island.

Wren joins us on deck for dinner that evening. It's the last night
before we reach the Amalas' camp, and the mood is a strange mix
of celebratory on the Cat Clan's side and somber among our group.
Though Wren sits next to me, we're a little farther apart than we'd
normally be. We spend most of the meal in silence, listening to
Lova, Nor, and Osa swap stories of their clan wreaking havoc across
Ikhara as we eat a delicious dried salad of bulgur wheat and nuts,
plump raisins nestling in the mix like gemstones.

At the end of dinner, Lova whips out a bottle of some dark, glossy
liquid. "To our girl's recovery!" she toasts. "And sleeping in actual
beds in one night's time!"

Everyone takes a swig before passing the bottle on. I'm last, and I hold it for a moment, feeling everyone's eyes on me. I know they're remembering the last time I had alcohol. I get an impulse to throw the bottle across the deck, watch it smash and spill its contents across the wooden floorboards. Instead, I take a sip before passing it on.

There's the near-instantaneous flush of relief as the alcohol warms my belly. I hadn't realized how much I missed it, but I resist the urge to grab the bottle and drink some more.

Though Caen watches me, he doesn't say anything. I almost wish he would. There are so many words I could throw back at him. So many dark secrets that have been spilled to wield as weapons.

After dinner, Wren and I head away from the others to perform Hiro's Birth-blessing pendant ceremony.

"Are you sure you've recovered enough?" I ask as she leads me to the back of the boat.

"For this, yes."

We kneel at the stern. It tips down slightly, the railing lower here, giving the sensation of skating almost directly on the dunes. Sand flies in liquid-like streams where the boat cleaves through it. The loud rush wraps around us, creating a barrier between the two of us and the rest of the group that feels appropriate given what we're about to do. Overhead, the new moon is round and full. Waves of opalescent light spill across the desert. Stars dance across the sky in kaleidoscopic constellations.

Wren takes Hiro's Birth-blessing pendant from her pocket. She holds it carefully, as though cradling a baby bird. "I never told you the word inside my pendant, did I?"

The night air has a chill, and I clutch the collar of my robes closed, my hair lashing my cheeks. "Wren, you don't have to—"

"My father always told me it was bad luck. I know most Ikharans feel that way. And maybe it is. After all, Hiro told me his and now he's dead." The word is hard and ugly in her mouth. She swallows, as though trying to get rid of it. Starlight fills her eyes as she looks earnestly at me. "What you said yesterday, about being tired of me keeping things from you...I don't want that. I want you to know all of me, Lei, because my heart, it's all yours."

She palms the Birth-blessing pendant in one hand, bringing the other to my lap. Our fingers twine together easily, instinctively, as familiar as the way my lungs draw in breath. For now, the pain of the conversation we shared yesterday is muted.

With a sigh, I soften into her, pressing my nose into the scoop of her neck.

She kisses my hair. Then she lowers her face, turning her cheek to mine. "Have you ever heard of kinyu?" she asks.

"Kinyu?"

"Sometimes two people have the same word in their pendants. It's not so uncommon. There are only so many characters in our language, and far more people to share them between. But it's rare to actually *meet* someone with the same word as you, especially since we don't usually reveal our Birth-blessing characters."

"Why are you telling me this?"

Wren draws back. She strokes her thumb across Hiro's pendant, the golden casing catching the moonlight. "We had the same word. Hiro and I were kinyu."

A shiver licks the back of my neck.

She stares down, her chest moving with slow, deep breaths.

"What is it?" I whisper. "Your word?"

There's a beat before she answers flatly, "Sacrifice."

The word lands in the air with a weight. Another shiver ripples through me, colder this time. "Wren," I say, "that doesn't mean you'll share the same fate as Hiro…"

Her gaze snaps to me, her eyes blazing. "Isn't that *exactly* what it means?"

Before I can answer, she flicks her wrist to toss Hiro's pendant into the air. She chants a short dao. A rustle of enchanted wind blows from her, lifting her hair and skating a shiver across my skin.

There's a flash. A whirl of golden characters spin out, circling the pendant where it hangs in the air, suspended. A flutter of magic ripples through the atmosphere, then the pendant disappears with a flash.

Golden sparks rain down before fading away.

Wren's face is blank, as cold and hard as the day I met her.

"There are many forms of sacrifice," I say, trying to keep the pain from my voice.

She doesn't make any sign she's heard me. After a long while, she says, "Are there?"

Something twists in my chest.

"When my pendant opened on my eighteenth birthday," she goes on, "I cried. Not because I was sad, or scared. Because I was *relieved*. All this time, dedicating my life to this cause. Giving up everything I could have had, all the lives I might have lived instead, to fulfill my father's goal. When I saw that word, I knew I was right. This is my sacrifice. My life, for the King's."

My heart kicks. "Don't give him that, Wren. He doesn't deserve it. Your life is *yours*. Fighting against him is just a part of it. You don't have to sacrifice everything to defeat him. If you do, you'll just end up defeating yourself, too."

She closes her eyes. "When we found out he was still alive, a part of me was relieved. Can you believe that? Relief, again, because it meant that my life still had purpose. That I had another chance to prove myself."

"Wren, you don't have to prove yourself to anyone! Not to your father. Not to the King. Not to me."

She turns to me, her face glowing in the moonlight. "That's one of the things I love about you, Lei. You always see the best in everyone."

I grab her cheeks, tears springing to my eyes. "That's because there's so much good to see. You're incredible, Wren."

When she replies, her words are just a whisper, a ragged flutter that the wind steals away. "Incredible is not the same as good."

That night, for the first time in what feels like months, Wren and I make love. Though the last time was just under two weeks ago, that night on the boat crossing the ocean to Kitori, it seems like lifetimes ago. As though the people we were then are strangers to us now. Wren's touch has always made me feel renewed, her tenderness and desire drawing out fresh reserves of energy within me, revealing new reservoirs of love and strength I didn't know I had. But tonight, her touch empties me. We move against each other, melt our mouths and bodies into one, and when we come apart I feel less than whole. Less, even, than half. I feel cleaved, scoured, carved apart.

Our love usually feels like a beginning.

Tonight, it feels like an ending.

Like a good-bye.

Afterward, my tears come quickly and with surprising force.

"Lei?" Wren whispers, sounding concerned.

"I-I'm s-sorry." I pull away from her in the dark warmth of the cramped cabin, linen sheets sliding over my bare skin. "I don't kn-know what's wr-wrong."

Sitting up, Wren draws me to her. I collapse against her chest with heavy, gasping sobs. The weight of everything I've been carrying these past few months has been suddenly released, and it crashes down on me, so heavy it crushes my lungs.

Aoki's family.

Naja's attack.

The hanging stocks at the fishing village.

Losing Bo.

Losing Hiro.

Losing Merrin, to his grief and anger.

That same grief and anger twisting within me.

The Czos' island, decimated by the beautiful girl in my arms.

And the King, the demon who started all of this. Who took my life, and the lives of everyone I love, and tore them apart. Back from the dead.

I cry so hard it sears my throat. My tears soak Wren's shirt, but she either doesn't notice or doesn't care, her hands holding me tight. "Oh, my love," she breathes. She pours kisses into my hair, whispers my name over and over, like a prayer, a call to bring me back to myself.

But I am gone. Untethered.

That door I felt shut between us a few days ago refuses to open. Even though our bodies are pressed together, skin to skin, heartbeat to heartbeat, our souls remain on either side of the door, close but not able to touch.

Minutes slide by, and gradually, my tears calm.

We lie back down. I'm tucked in the crook of Wren's arm, my cheek to her shoulder, left arm over her belly. She braids her fingers along my spine. A hush swallows us back up. Outside, the wind throws sand across the deck, the ship creaks. But we are worlds away.

"Lei." Wren's breath stirs my hair. She talks slowly, clipped, a nervousness I've never heard before chopping her words. "I love you. You know that, don't you? You still know that?"

"I know."

"Because I couldn't live with myself if you thought otherwise."

"Do you know how much I love *you*?"

"I...think so."

"I love you so much, Wren. So much that sometimes, it hurts."

She pulls me closer. "I don't want to hurt you," she says. "But there's something I need to tell you."

I go still.

"I wanted to tell you this whole time," she carries on, quick and breathy now, "but my father promised me to keep it to myself. It's not that he doesn't trust you, but he didn't think you were ready to know such things. The rest of us have been trained for the realities of war. We know that sometimes, you have to do ugly things in order to win. Things you aren't proud of, but that in the end—"

"Just tell me." I can hardly breathe now, the thump of my heart like a fist in my throat.

"The raid we saw on our way here. In Shomu. That wasn't..." Wren swallows. "That wasn't the King."

Coldness pours over me. The hairs on my arms lift.

"Most of the raids *are* ordered by the King. But for the past few years, my father has been...creating some of our own. Only when we felt it essential. We do extensive research for each one to target the right areas, key clans and villages that would bring about the right kind of response. None of this is ever done lightly. You have to understand that, Lei. It's all to further the distrust of the King and his court, and to recruit allies to our cause. We would never, *ever* do anything if it wasn't necessary."

I don't say anything.

Can't say anything.

The silence in the cabin is terrible, hard, and smothering, like a hand clamped over my mouth.

Wren wets her lips. "I knew my father wanted to target certain areas in Shomu to help convince the White Wing they can't evade the King's cruelty forever. The clan is prideful about its province, and the grasslands and paddy fields are key to Ikharan food trade because of their perfect weather conditions, so it's a highly important region. In the end, we were able to get the White Wing on our side without any of that—and a lot of that was because of you, Lei. But my father had already given the orders. And it didn't hurt to keep them and the other local clans angry. To keep up dissidence against the King's rule. These weeks are essential as we build up to war—"

I shove her away and scramble to my feet, clutching a sheet against my body. My tongue is like a slab of concrete. It takes three tries to get the words out.

"Aoki's family died in that raid."

Wren's eyes shimmer. "I—I know—"

"*AOKI'S FAMILY!*"

She starts to her feet, but I thrust out a shaking hand. "Don't you dare! I don't want to hear one more word. I can't even—I can't even *look* at you right now. First Eolah, then Bo and Hiro—"

"You know about Eolah?" Her face falls. "Lei—"

"Now you're telling me *hundreds* of other innocent people have lost their lives under your father's orders?" My voice vibrates with disgust. "How many more murders will you commit in the name of justice until you realize you're as bad as those we're meant to be fighting against?"

Tears fill Wren's eyes, but they don't fall. "I'm not proud of any of it," she replies sharply. "But if it helps us take down the King, if it helps stop the terrorization of Papers across the kingdom and make Ikhara safe again for us, for everyone, then it was all worth it."

I stare at her, my chest heaving, my pulse wild. I think of Nitta's words to me the other day. "Nothing is worth losing yourself."

The atmosphere in the cabin hardens.

"I am still myself, Lei," Wren replies after a few beats. "This is who I've always been. This is what I was trying to tell you about my Birth-blessing word."

"Sacrifice doesn't mean being heartless!" Tears stinging my eyes, I drag on my clothes with shaking hands. "You know, all this time I thought the King was our only enemy. Now I realize there's been another one all this time—your father. The Hannos. *You.*"

Then I shove the door open and run out, my heart shattering into a million pieces in my chest, a silent explosion no one but me can hear.

THIRTY-ONE

I AVOID WREN THE NEXT MORNING, throwing myself into a training session with Shifu Caen. He seems surprised but pleased when I ask him. At first he's impressed by my strength, praising my sudden renewal of energy, the passionate determination with which I fight. But as I drive attack after attack, not pausing for breath, not stopping to take even a sip of water after almost an hour in the baking heat, he looks increasingly concerned.

"It's time to stop," he orders, countering my aggressive strikes with his sword. He gave up forming his own attacks half an hour ago, and stands in a deep-kneed defensive stance, back to the masts.

I keep fighting. Sweat flies from my brow. Blood pounds in my ears, drowning out almost everything else. I'm dimly aware of my cracked lips, of sand sticking to my skin and the taste of blood in my mouth. I must have bitten down on my tongue.

I spit out a wad of bloody saliva and push on.

We've drawn a crowd on the deck that forms our arena, but I ignore them, my focus narrowed on Caen. I move mechanically, driven by fury and guilt so strong it hardly feels any different. *This is what you wanted all this time, isn't it?* I want to growl at him. *What you've been trying to teach me? To merge body, mind, and soul?* That's what I've become: just a body, moving; a mind, homed in on Caen; and a soul, a shattered, ragged thing, broken and raging.

A soldier's soul.

This is what you were training me to become, isn't it?

What you made Wren? The perfect warrior.

Because they did—Caen and Ketai, they broke her. They're to blame for what she's become.

Wren was right last night. Being incredible is not the same as being good.

Aoki's sweet face flashes in my mind, burned away the next second by images of her family, the charred bodies huddled together in the ruins of their home. A snarl tears from my throat, as feral as the growl of the snow leopard Nitta, Bo, and I faced in the Goa-Zhen mountains all those months ago.

"Lei, it's time to stop!" Caen barks again, louder now.

I reply with a high kick. He shifts back, pushing my thigh away. I recover quickly; leap forward with a yell.

My timing is lucky. As the ship pitches over the top of a dune, I gain more air. I slam into him. The two of us crash back against the mast, pressed chest to chest, like lovers, like enemies.

Clinging to his shoulder with one hand, I lift my sheathed dagger to his neck, releasing a bark of triumph.

Caen butts my weapon away and shoves me off him. I stumble for a second to catch my balance. Then I launch myself at him anew, throwing a balled fist toward his jaw.

He elbows my hand aside. "I said *stop!*"

I'm aiming another punch when arms scoop my waist. "Please, Lei!" Nitta cries. "You're going to hurt yourself!"

"We're practicing!" I shout as she wrestles me back.

"That was *not* practicing." Panting, Caen pushes back the wet strands of hair from his brow. "We are honorable warriors, not common shisha den brawlers. We fight with respect and control. Have I taught you nothing?"

My lip furls. "Oh, you've taught me *plenty*. Merrin was right. You and Ketai, you'll do anything to serve your own purposes. No matter whom it hurts."

"That is what war is, Lei. You have to fight with conviction."

"Don't you think that's exactly how the Demon King justifies what *he* does?"

Caen glowers. "*He* fights with no honor. He seeks only destruction."

"What does it matter in the end?" I shake Nitta off me, though she hovers at my side, ready to jump in again if needed. "All fighting comes down to is who gets the killing blow in first." My eyes shift to where Wren watches from the back of the deck, her face half-hidden by long locks of her hair blowing in the wind. "And how many times you can do it."

Claw-tipped footsteps pad across the deck.

"She's absolutely right, you know," General Lova says, one hand on her hip. She holds out a leather flask with the other. "Here, little warrior. You should hydrate."

I take it from her with a scowl, draining it in one go.

She regards me warmly. "That was some impressive fighting. Your stamina and speed could rival some of my top warriors. You didn't have *any* experience before Caen's training?"

"I...had a few lessons back in the palace." I avoid looking at Wren.

"They're teaching concubines to fight now?" Though Lova's tone is light, there's hardness in her eyes, a tough set to her smile. "About godsdamn time." She's about to say more when her face jerks up— and instantly sours. "What's *he* doing back?"

We all turn to follow her gaze. The glare of the midday sun is so fierce it's hard to see anything at first. Sand and sky melt into one, a glaze of fiery white. Then my eyes adjust.

Silhouetted against the hazy clouds, a winged figure is speeding toward us.

With a gasp, Nitta sprints to the railing. She lifts to her tiptoes, leaning over to peer out across the golden hills. "It's him!" she cries. "It's Merrin!"

His familiar outline draws closer, lowering now, long wing-arms gilded in the sunlight where they're spread at his sides. Just when he's near enough for me to make out his narrowed owl eyes and the graphite tips of his feathers, there's a bone-shaking *boom*.

Something hurls toward him through the air.

Merrin swerves. The ball of gunpowder explodes in a shower of sparks and curling smoke where he'd been flying only seconds before.

I spin around. More smoke plumes around Lova where she's shouldering her cannon.

"Lova!" Wren shouts.

"What are you doing?" Nitta yells.

"Easy, General," Nor adds calmly from where she's leaning against the cabin next to Osa, her arms crossed. "Let's not waste gunpowder, now."

Lova ignores them all, her face a fierce mask as she stalks forward. "Bird!" she shouts, her deep voice booming over the noise of the boat. She doesn't lower her cannon. "The last time I saw you, you insulted one of my favorite people in the world. What makes you think I'd welcome you back to my ship with open arms?"

Merrin keeps his distance. "I don't expect any forgiveness for what I said!" he calls back, flying alongside the ship. "But I promised Ketai I'd follow this mission through to the end, and that is what I intend to do."

"Oh, really? Is *that* why a few days ago you flew off in a huff?"

"Please, General." Merrin's eyes sweep the deck, pausing where they meet mine. There's a strange look on his face I can't quite place—something like guilt, but sadder. "It was childish of me. I just needed some space. It won't happen again."

Shifu Caen steps forward, his sun-browned forehead crinkled. "Merrin has worked for us for many years, General. He can be counted on."

The lion-girl raises her brows. "Two 'generals,' huh? You lot really *are* trying to get on my good side." The amused cock of her mouth disappears. She adjusts her grip on her cannon, though she still doesn't lower it. "I've made it a habit not to trust deserters. Fail me once, lose my trust for life." Her gaze flicks to Nitta as she says this. "Now leave, Bird, or—"

"Lo."

Wren has moved to Lova's side, standing a few fractions closer than I'm comfortable with. They talk in low voices so the rest of us can't hear, heads bowed. Standing side by side like this, the hot desert wind whipping their clothes and hair, they look like a pair of goddesses, poured in gold from the Heavenly Kingdom, and it makes my gut twist at how right they look together.

After less than a minute, Lova lowers her cannon and turns back to Merrin. "I hope you know how lucky you are to have a friend like Wren on your side, Bird. But make no mistake. If you step just *one* talon out of line, I have no problem blowing you out of here in a thousand pieces." As Merrin takes a loop around the yellow sails to come in to land, Lova adds with a shrug, almost to herself, "Maybe I'll use my sword instead. It'll be far less messy." She looks over at Nor and Osa. "Remember the last time I blasted a demon apart with this baby?"

Nor smirks. "We found bits of him on the boat for days."

"Came in handy for desert-dog bait, though," Osa says smugly.

When Merrin lands, Nitta, Wren, Caen, and I are the only ones to go to him. The Amala busy themselves with ship work, steadfastly ignoring him.

Nitta throws her arms around his neck. "I'm so glad you came back!" she sobs, burying her face into his wind-ruffled feathers.

Merrin blinks, looking almost angry, and pushes her roughly away. His feathers ripple as he fluffs them before folding them down to lay against his body, his arms reducing to half the bulk. "I made a mistake in leaving," he says gruffly. "I was...reacting to recent events. Recent losses. But as I told Lova, I made a commitment to Ketai. I do not believe in breaking promises." His eyes move over us, something dark turning within them as they latch on Caen and Wren. His expression is softer when he looks at Nitta and me. "I hope you can forgive me."

Nitta lays a hand on his arm. "Of course, Merrin."

I give him a smile. "Already done."

"Thank you for returning, Merrin," Shifu Caen says.

Wren shakes her head. "I'm so sorry for not being able to protect Bo and Hiro. You were right. I failed you." Her voice catches. "All of you."

Merrin clears his throat. "Thank you, Wren," he replies stiffly.

There's a shout from the other side of the deck. "Lunch is ready!"

We gather under the canvas. As Lova passes me with a bowl of lentils drizzled with honey and cashews, she dips her head to my ear, her voice a silky purr. "Such a shame whole-roasted bird isn't on the menu. Nor has a recipe with a sweet chili sauce that's just exquisite." She smacks her lips; her eyes glint mischievously. "It's *almost* the best thing to have ever graced my tongue." As a blush heats my cheeks, she looks up, raising her voice to address the group. "The

Bird has good timing. We're just two hours' travel out of camp. So don't eat too much—we'll be feasting tonight in true Amala style, and you'll want to have room to properly gorge."

"Never thought I'd see one of the infamous Cat Clan's secret hideouts," Merrin says wryly.

"Never thought I'd be *back*," Nitta murmurs.

"Actually," Lova says, "I think it best if you two stay outside the camp, given everything. I'm sure you understand. I'll have food, clothes, and bedding sent over to the ship, along with bathing tubs. You'll have everything you need."

To my surprise, Merrin seems relieved at this news, while Nitta nods. "Good idea," she says curtly. "Thank you."

"Wait," I say. "That's not fair. Nitta and Merrin have fought at our side every step of the way. They deserve just as much of a warm welcome as the rest of us."

"Exactly," Lova agrees. "And I'm afraid my cats won't be able to give it to them. We have a long-standing distrust of bird demons, and Nitta is an exiled clan member." She scoops lentils into her mouth with her fingers. "It'll be far more comfortable for everyone involved this way."

"It's fine, Lei," Nitta whispers to me. "It's not like I'm in need of more friends, anyway. I have some pretty great ones right here."

We bump shoulders, smiling. On her other side, Merrin turns away.

With a stab of sadness, I realize Nitta's words must have made him think of Bo.

After lunch, Lova, Osa, and Nor prepare for our arrival at camp, the rest of us helping where we can. The Amala are a nomadic clan. They travel the desert in five groups in case of ambush, never stopping in any one place longer than two months. As I help her strap our supplies securely down to the deck, Nor tells me how each camp is named after one of the gods the Cat Clan worship.

"Which one are we going to?" I ask.

"Camp Samsi. It's the smallest, but it's by far the rowdiest—as to be expected when their namesake is the God of Tricks and Trouble." She winks. "I hope you're in a festive mood."

"It doesn't exactly feel like the *best* time for a party," I reply dryly.

The old tiger-woman turns serious. "Sometimes, Lei, a party is *exactly* what's needed at times like this. Things are about to get very dark, for a very long while. It'll do all of us good to have a little fun while we can." She looks up at Lova's whistle. "I'd advise you to get to the gunwale and hold on tight. We've been away from camp for weeks. The General is going to want to make her favorite kind of entrance."

I sigh. "Let me guess—a dramatic one."

As we all make our way over to the railing, I cross paths with Nitta. She looks nervous.

"How long has it been?" I nod in the direction of the camp.

She runs a hand through her sandy hair and puffs out a breath. "Too long. And not long enough at all."

"What exactly happened between you all?" I ask, lowering my voice. "I can't imagine you and Bo doing anything to upset anyone." When she arches a brow, I add, "All right, maybe Bo. But still, not anything serious enough to warrant being exiled over."

Nitta's pale green eyes are sad. "Remember when I told Merrin secrets are some of the most dangerous things in the world?" She glances over her shoulder in Lova's direction. "Even worse is when those you're sharing secrets with don't trust you to keep them."

Before she can explain more, there's another whistle from Lova, and we hurry to the rail. Lova perches alone at the prow of the boat like a figurehead brought to life, her muscled lion haunches flexed, her luscious blond hair billowing in the wind. Sunlight picks out the gold threads in her peach-colored wrap shirt and flared cotton trousers. A length of rope stretches from the sails to her wrist. The boat moves fast, skimming lightly across the top of the sands like a dragonfly.

The high sun glitters down on the camp's dense settlement of patchwork tents and yurts, all in multicolored fabrics. Braided ribbons strung between them are beaded with lanterns and good luck charms. The camp sits beside an oasis. The tents cluster close to its bank, its water sparkling. Date and fig trees dapple the sand with shade. A number of horses are tied to their trunks, necks down to sip at the water.

As we skate closer, a horn-blow erupts from a lookout tower at the center of the camp. Some of the Amala run out, cheering and clapping their hands.

Lova whoops in excitement.

"Felines," Merrin grumbles at my side. "Always so *noisy*—"

He jumps as Nor returns the call by blowing on her own ivory horn, right in his ear.

"Here we go!" Lova shouts from the prow.

She leaps backward.

My fingers clamp around the rail just in time. Lova sails back, gliding through the air. The rope around her wrist catches. With a gleeful yell, she loops around the central mast, rolling the sails around. The ship careens to the side. We fall against the gunwale as the opposite side of the boat pitches high. Sand flies into my eyes. I cough and splutter, hanging on as the hot wind sears my skin and snaps at my clothes, the sand-boat making a sharp turn. Lova's laughter sings through the air as she springs again, swinging the sails in the opposite direction to take us around Camp Samsi in a wide circle.

When we finally come to a stop, raucous whoops and cheers greet us. Hands batter the sides of the boat. Nor, Osa, and Lova are grinning, already hopping down to join the welcome crowds.

I pick myself up from where I've curled into a ball at the railing.

Wren comes over, offering a hand. "She's ... a little extravagant," she admits.

I puff the hair from my eyes. "You think?"

Merrin ruffles his feathers to shake loose the sand, while Nitta clings to the rail, looking queasy. Still, both of them look relieved not to be joining us, and I give them a brief good-bye before I make my way off the boat with Caen and Wren. Lova, Nor, and Osa are already far ahead, having been swallowed up by their fellow clan members the second they touched the ground. We hurry after them, crossing the sands.

After spending the past week traveling the empty expanse of the dunes, the noise and busyness of the camp make me feel jumpy—not to mention the sheer number of demons. From all around come the flash of feline teeth and the glitter of sharp eyes watching us pass. The desert air is choked with the smells of fur and sweat and cooking food. Incense smoke curls from big outdoor burners, laying a hazy film over everything. We jostle our way through the winding tangles of passageways between tents, clan members bartering for wares and swapping gossip and jokes. Most of them stick to the shade of the fabric coverings that have been unfurled across the streets. A few choose to bake in the sun: children lying stretched out on the sturdy roofs of yurts, boots kicked off and hands behind their heads, and old wizened felines sunning themselves in the golden pools of sunlight that make their way between gaps in the covers, spitting out duku and papaya seeds onto the dusty floor.

Even with all the noise, it's impossible to miss the whispers that trail us through the camp.

"—Ketai Hanno's daughter—"

"—wasn't she sleeping with the General—"

"—no doubt they're here for our help—"

"—Moonchosen, just a little Paper slip of a thing, can you believe it—"

Finally, we arrive at a large round tent standing several feet higher than the others. Ribbons strung with amulets spin out from the domed roof, and pennants with the Amala insignia—three obsidian claw-tipped paw-prints stamped on yellow—dance in the wind. Two hooded guards in white shirts and sarongs stand outside the entranceway. Drawing the fabric aside, they nod in welcome, clearly recognizing Wren and Caen.

As soon as the tent flap shuts behind us, the noise of the camp muffles. It's stiflingly hot inside, the shadowed interior lit by oil lamps, flies buzzing around their flames. Rugs lie haphazardly across the dusty floor. Lova, Nor, and Osa are gathered at the far table with a few other Cat Clan members.

Their conversation stops when they notice us.

Beaming, Lova pushes back from the table. "Clan committee!" she announces. "You remember Shifu Caen, Lord Hanno's aide, and Lady Wren, his brilliant daughter." She throws an arm around my shoulders. "Meet Lei. Some of you might know her by her nickname—the Moonchosen."

Furred faces break into smiles. There are cheers and applause, and Lova pushes me forward, laughing throatily as I'm showered in compliments and back-claps. The older members pinch my cheeks in what must be a sign of respect among cat demons for those younger than they.

"Alamak! A tiny thing like you took on the King?"

"Look at those eyes! You *must* be part demon."

"My bet's on lion."

"I say tiger!"

"It's got to be serval. She's as skinny as one, too."

Lova waves them quiet. "All right, give the girl some space. She's had quite the journey. All of our guests have." She clicks her fingers at a Steel girl kneeling patiently by the doorway. A furred tail peeks out from her sarong. "Fetch two more pitchers of aloe juice. And tell the cooks to get started on preparations for tonight's banquet."

The girl bows. As she runs out of the tent, Lova gets the attention of another young servant. He's also Steel, his bare skin conspicuously plain save for feline haunches wrapped in spotted white fur. I'm reminded how even among demons there is a hierarchy of power.

"Plio, I need two guest tents prepared. They'll also need a change of clothes. Ask old Madam Chokri, she'll know what to do."

"Two tents?" Caen asks as the boy scurries from the tent.

"I'm assuming our lovebirds want to share one," Lova says, her gaze sweeping over Wren and me with the barest hint of jealousy.

Though Wren and I stiffen, we don't say anything. The committee welcomes us around the table and soon the conversation is deep into Ikharan politics, the demons updating us on news from elsewhere across the kingdom: clan conflicts, more displacement and unrest due to the Sickness, exposed rebel hidings. Their information is important, and I try to focus on the discussion, even as my mind keeps replaying the words of my argument with Wren last night, like a rotten, half-loosened tooth your tongue can't stop worrying.

THIRTY-TWO

BEING CONSTANTLY ON THE MOVE, THE Amala must be used to working quickly. In the hours between our arrival and night-fall, a vast wooden platform has been constructed over the sands by the oasis, jutting out on one side over the water. Strings of lights weave a glittering canopy overhead, the real stars beyond only pale twinklings in comparison. Grand tables stacked with food run down the center of the platform, delicious fragrances lifting into the warm night air. There are towering piles of couscous showered in coriander and chili, and steaming bowls of laksa, a curried noo-dle soup Tien has always been particularly fond of. Banana fritters speared on sticks sit by half-moons of lime for squeezing and irides-cent bowls of sugar have been laid out to sprinkle over milk buns fresh out of the oven. Rose lassi and spiced rhum swill in earthen-ware goblets tall as my shoulders.

Earlier, Wren and Caen went ahead with Lova on clan business, so I walk with Nor and Osa through the party. The Amala shower them in claps and shoulder-slaps, some of which also rain down on me. If the presence of so many demons unsettled me earlier, here the whole *clan* is gathered. The crowd heaves with hundreds of feline bodies. Some stand, heaping their banana-leaf plates with food, while others lounge on cushions and rugs. Steel servers weave through the party, refilling mugs and cleaning up spills. A jostling line of young demons sit at the end of the platform, legs dangled over the water. There's a splash as one of them falls in. Laughter and good-natured jeers rise up, along with more splashes as some of their friends dive in.

A few feet away, Wren, Lova, and Caen are deep in conversation with a pair of old-looking felines. My stomach lurches. Wren is stunning, her dark hair—clean for the first time in more than a week—spilling in luscious waves down her back. An indigo sari with intricate gold threading wraps around her muscular frame and long legs. The smooth skin of her shoulders, darkened from the desert sun, glows under the lights.

A thrum of love and desire hums through me, only to be chased away by nauseating memories.

The burnt huddle of Aoki's family.

Smoke and searing heat stinging my eyes.

The Bull King's flag fluttering overhead, even more of a mimicry now because I know who actually placed it there.

Wren shifts to open up a space next to her as we join their group and, not wanting to make a scene, I take it.

"You look beautiful, Lei," she says, so tenderly it brings a lump to my throat.

I swallow it down. "So do you."

Osa passes me a glass of rhum and I drain it gratefully, face scrunching at the burn. Caen shoots me a disapproving look, and a flash of concern passes across Wren's face. But Osa doesn't seem to notice as she leans over to refill my cup.

Lova looks over me appreciatively. "I'm so glad the clothes fit.

Yellow really is your color, Lei." Her kohl-rimmed eyes glitter. "We'll make an Amala out of you yet."

I smooth a hand over the cotton kebaya wrap shirt and trousers a maid brought me earlier this evening. They fit perfectly, but their plainness stands out in comparison to the luxurious saris both Wren and Lova are wearing. Could Lova be trying to tell me something by dressing me so differently than everyone else?

If so, her smile is friendly, faultless. She sips her own drink and stretches her fur-wrapped body with a sigh, the jade bangles at her wrists and ankles clinking. "It's so good to be back." Limned in lantern light, the young General is beautiful, full and curved in every way I am not. Marigold silk flows over her golden fur. She leans forward, gold amulets tickling the deep shadow of her cleavage. "Remember that weekend you and Ketai came to visit, Wren? We ate so much dadar gulung our teeth hurt from all the sugar. And afterward, when we stayed up all night stargazing? I'd never seen the desert skies look so beautiful. But maybe that was all the rhum we drank—or a side effect of being in love."

My hand tightens on my cup.

Nor laughs. Her voice is a husky scratch, as jagged as the puckered scars running across her face. "I remember that. You were both supposed to be at a council meeting the next morning, and when neither of you showed up we found you in Lova's rooms, still sound asleep."

"Not to mention, naked," Osa adds with a sly smile.

Caen coughs. "I'm...not sure this is appropriate dinner conversation."

The Amala laugh heartily.

"Oh, Shifu," Lova teases. "What sad, boring dinners you must have over at the Hannos'. Come, have more rhum. Let's see if we can loosen that stiff little behind of yours. We'll have you dancing on the tables by the end of the night."

As the others snort at this, I turn to Wren. Though we're only inches apart, the gap between us seems to widen, spiraling open with a physical weight. "You never told me you came to visit her," I say, hating how childish I sound but unable to stop. Heat pricks my eyes. "You said you only met one time, when she was at your father's palace for a meeting."

Wren looks at me under long lashes. "Lei…"

She speaks my name like an apology.

Or an excuse.

I shake my head. Willing my tears away, I pour myself more rhum. The spiced liquid sears my throat.

"I know what you're doing," I tell Lova with a scowl. "But it won't work."

Wren's face flashes with alarm. "Lei—"

I hold up a hand. "I want to hear it from her. You want Wren back, don't you, *General*?"

Lova watches me serenely, her golden fur shining under the lights. She sets her cup down. "Yes," she answers matter-of-factly. "I do."

My eyes widen.

"I wouldn't have said anything in front of you, Lei," she continues, "but you asked for the truth, so here it is." Her kohl-rimmed eyes flick to Wren. "We were in love not that long ago. And I haven't stopped thinking about you ever since. All the girls I've been with since haven't been able to change that, because my heart is still yours."

Wren stares back, deathly still.

A strangled sound traps in my throat.

"I'm sorry," Lova says, sounding genuine as she addresses me.

"You don't deserve to be hurt like this. From what I've seen these past days, I can understand why Wren fell in love with you. But Wren and I, we belong together." She faces Wren, her face alight with a fierce excitement. "Imagine it. Two of the most powerful clans in Ikhara united. A Paper and a Moon. We can show Ikharans everywhere the future kingdom we dream of—a place of equality. Of unity." Her voice lowers to a silky purr. Her expression softens. "But more than anything, we would be happy together, honey. You know that. You remember those beautiful days we spent together. Those nights."

I don't even realize I'm doing it until the cup has left my hand. It flies through the air, hitting the lion-girl squarely in her temple before bouncing off to smash on the decking.

Lova rubs her head. "Really? A *cup*?"

"You're lucky I didn't have something bigger handy!" I clutch a fistful of the hem of my wrap shirt, my face hot. "Is that what this is? Keep me looking the part of my common, non-clan-bred self so I remember I'm not in the same league as the two of you?"

To my surprise, Lova looks hurt. "Actually, I thought perhaps you'd like to wear the clothes of your own region. That it might make you feel more comfortable. And after what Wren told me about your time at the palace, I didn't want to remind you of what you were there for by dressing you up in silks and skirts."

There's an uncomfortable silence. Everyone's eyes moving uneasily between Wren, Lova, and me.

My mouth slants. "Thank you," I force out. "That was kind of you." Cheeks burning, I lurch to my feet. "I should go."

Wren starts after me. "Lei—"

Her hand brushes my shoulder, but I shrug her off, tears smarting my eyes. "Please. Not now. I just need some space."

She hesitates. "We'll talk later, then."

I shake my head. "I'm going to stay with Nitta and Merrin tonight. I think it's for the best. I'll—I'll see you tomorrow."

I stumble away before I can change my mind.

When I've left the noise and merriment of the party behind, I cross the now-empty streets of the Amalas' camp, passing half-hidden cat-form couples entwined together in the shadows. Beyond the camp, the desert is cold and vast. Where the sun turns the dunes golden during the day, the moon silvers them, transforming the landscape into a spectral ocean of smooth glowing hills. My boots slip in the sand as I make my way to the ship where it's nestled among the moonlit sandbanks. Above, the sky is alight with stars. A gentle wind sifts the sand, filling the air with whispering, as though spirits live here in the shifting slopes. It's easy to imagine them; the desert feels old, like gods' bones.

Without the rush of the boat skimming across the dunes, it's unnervingly quiet. But as I approach, voices sound from the lantern-lit deck.

"I don't think that's such a good idea. Why does it have to be now, anyway?"

"I'll explain later."

"You're being weird, Merrin. What's going on?"

I climb up over the railing to find Merrin pacing the deck. His arms hang slightly open, as though ready to spread wide into wings any second. Nitta watches him, hands on her hips.

Relief flushes her face when she spots me. "Lei! Perfect timing." She runs over, throwing an arm around my shoulders. "Feathers here is adamant about going to the party. Says he needs everyone here for an important talk."

"On...the boat?" I ask with a frown.

The leopard-girl pivots, gesturing at Merrin. "See? I'm not the only one who thinks it's odd."

He opens his mouth, then shuts it. Then his eyes shift from us, focusing on something behind our heads. His expression hardens.

Nitta and I follow his gaze back to camp. Five figures are striding toward us. In the shadowy slopes of the dunes, it's impossible to make out their faces, but Lova's hips-shifting slink and Shifu Caen's smart stride are unmistakable, and I would recognize Wren's long-legged gait anywhere. Her hair swirls around her in the dry wind. As they draw closer, I see Nor and Osa bringing up the back of the group.

Nitta throws up a hand. "Well, you got what you wanted."

Merrin doesn't seem happy at the news.

Nitta and I jump down from the boat to meet the others, Merrin following a few moments later.

"What's going on?" I ask.

The atmosphere is tense. Wren stands a little off from the rest of them, her face so blank that if it weren't for knowing her I'd think she couldn't care less to see me. Instead, I recognize this: her mask, the wall she builds between herself and the world. Our eyes meet, and a warm tremor runs down my veins.

"We thought it important to come back together as a group," Caen says. "We've journeyed this far together, and especially now, right before things are about to get even more dangerous, it isn't good to leave the group fractured in this way."

Lova shrugs. "I'm only here because Shifu here insisted."

The others glower at her. Even Nor leans in to whisper, "General…"

She sighs. "Fine. It's not just because of that." She throws Caen a scowl. "Though he *was* insistent. Wouldn't even let me finish the curry puff I was eating." With a little toss of her head, her long blond hair rippling, the lion-girl steps forward. Bronzed eyes meet mine, a crescent of moonlight caught in each one. "I owe you an apology, Lei," she admits, her features softening. "After everything you've been through, all the brave things you've done to help us, I shouldn't have acted like that. It was childish and petty and disrespectful. Caen is right. Now is not the time to be divided." She reaches out a claw-tipped hand. "Truce?"

I don't move. "You mean you'll stop trying to flirt with Wren every few minutes?"

"How about I take it down to every few hours?"

"Once an hour, max."

"Deal."

Our hands clasp briefly. Then Lova releases hers to comb her fingers through her luscious fur, batting her eyelashes at the others. "Now can we *please* return to the party? It's quite rude for the guest of honor to leave her own welcome-home party."

"Well, she'll have to endure it a bit longer," Nitta says, and jabs her thumb to her right. "Merrin has something he wants to discuss with everyone?"

Lova's smile disappears. "Can't it wait until tomorrow?"

"When we're all hungover?" Nor replies.

"Good point. What is it, Bird?"

Merrin hesitates. His orange eyes meet mine, and he looks almost apologetic. He's about to say something when he looks jerkily to the left. His body goes tight, like a coil of wire.

My heart thuds. "Merrin? What's going on?"

But it's Wren who speaks. "Look."

She's staring in the same direction as Merrin where, beyond the boat, the desert spills out, an unbroken landscape of moonlit dunes.

A cool wind stirs my hair, and I hug my arms around my chest; now that the alcohol is wearing off, the coldness is rushing back in.

At first I don't see anything. Then—

There. A strange blur in the distance.

I still. Hone my focus. There's a patch of wavering light along the horizon, standing out from its surroundings. It reminds me of when we were at sea traveling to the Mersing Archipelago. Sometimes there would be waves larger than the others, and this is how they began, as a far-off shifting shimmer breaking the horizon.

It takes a few more minutes for *this* wave to reveal itself—and when it does, the dread that was gnawing at me explodes into a starburst of panic.

"It—it shouldn't be," Merrin breathes.

Nitta's voice is small. "Is that…?"

"Soldiers!" Lova growls.

Soldiers. One word, simple enough. But ever since the Night War, that word has carried others within it, words that instill fear in a heartbeat, words *built* from fear itself: suffering, destruction, blood, death.

Understanding crashes into me with such force it leaves me breathless.

I've found you.

The King's army is heading straight for us.

THIRTY-THREE

CAEN, NOR, AND OSA BURST INTO action, sprinting up the nearest dune to get a better look at the approaching soldiers. Lova and Wren immediately set about tying back their hair and tucking the fabric of their saris through their legs and into the folds at their waists to create trousers, all the while firing questions and statistics about the camp's resources and the surrounding terrain back and forth at breakneck speed. Their urgent exchange washes over me. My feet seem to have sunk into the ground, as though it were mud instead of sand. Nitta wraps an arm around me, rubbing my shoulders, while Merrin stares with glassy eyes at the horizon, where distant flames flicker.

Less than a minute later, the others return.

"How many?" Lova asks.

"At least five hundred," Nor answers, wind stirring her graying fur. "One mile out, max."

My legs go weak. Five hundred. The number is incomprehensible. Even if most of the Cat Clan weren't drunk, we're at least two hundred people down.

Lova nods, maddeningly composed. "And you're sure they're royal soldiers?"

"They're carrying the Demon King's flag," Osa confirms.

"They're more likely a collection of local militia who've been mobilized in response to an alert on our location," Caen says, "rather than soldiers from the palace. We didn't see any cannons or battle animals, and they're on foot."

"Must have been a hasty roundup," Nor agrees. "But their numbers are still…"

Impressive. Overwhelming.

Damning.

We all finish her sentence in our heads.

As we watch, the braziers carried by the soldiers suddenly flicker out. A chill runs through me; they're planning to ambush us, take us in the dark.

Nausea rises in my throat. I imagine the army raging toward us over the slopes like a tsunami of dark, furious water, ready to swallow us whole. Capped not by foam but the points of swords and claws and glinting demon teeth.

"No battle is won before it is fought," Wren says firmly. "Remember who we are. Have confidence in our strength."

Lova nods, her amber eyes fierce. "Our priority is to stop them before they reach the camp. We need to stall them while we round up more numbers. Merrin!" She throws out an arm. "Take Nor or Osa back to camp!"

Osa stalks forward. "I'll go!"

"Get Hond and Clio to organize everyone!" Lova commands as Osa shouts at Merrin to let him onto his back, the owl demon hesitating before seeming to realize what's being expected of him. "Cut all the lights—and find hiding places for all the cubs and those who can't fight!"

With a great rush of wings, Merrin takes off toward the camp. From his back, Osa lifts a hand to show he's understood.

"We can ambush them here," Nitta suggests, breathless, looking between those of us left. "The ship is right in their path. They'll see our lights, head this way first to check it out, just to be safe."

Lova's eyes flash. "That's it!" Without any explanation, she grabs the side of the ship and launches over the railing. Padded footsteps run across the deck. Barely ten seconds later, she returns, landing heavily in the sand. Her cannon is propped on one shoulder; a match pokes from her mouth.

"How long, do you think?" she asks through clenched teeth, peering in the direction of the approaching army, just a dark wave now against the moonlit dunes. "Ten minutes?"

"Fifteen if we're lucky," Caen says.

Lova's grin sharpens. "I do like a challenge." She takes the match and twirls it in her fingers, pointing it at us. "I have enough gun-powder for four shots. Nor and I will hold them here as best we can. The rest of you, get to camp. Osa, Hond, and Clio will organize our fighters. Follow their orders."

"But...you'll die if you stay here alone," I say.

She shrugs. "Better two bodies than a hundred."

"No." Wren's voice is low but fierce. "We're not leaving you behind. There's a way to stop the soldiers before they even reach camp, every one of them, and we all know it."

Silence rolls over us.

I gape at Wren. A sudden wave of rage wells within me. It foun-tains up, a hot channel coursing down my veins and into my throat, and I grit my teeth, dig my fingernails into my palms to stop from screaming my next words. "Don't you dare." My voice shakes. "Don't you godsdamned *dare*."

"Couldn't have said it better myself," Lova agrees coolly.

When Wren begins to retort, Nor lifts a hand. "Wait." The

tiger-woman's face is intent, her ears pricked. "General, you said there's enough gunpowder for four more uses?"

"Would have been six had I not wasted one on Feathers yesterday."

"So what if we combine them?"

Lova shakes her head. "The measurements have to be just right. A fraction too strong, and the cannon itself will explode—and me with it."

"I don't mean the cannon."

Lova stares for a moment. Then she smiles. "Oh, you brilliant tiger, you."

Nor grins, her scars twisting. "Use the boat. Sand would stifle the flames."

"And the brightness of the fire will half-blind them," the General adds excitedly. "We can attack while they're stunned."

"And if we break some of the decking, some of them will fall through. We can trap more of them that way."

"Someone will need to set it all off, though—"

"Not if we have a fuse—"

"Rope! From the masts!"

"Yes!"

And then the two of them clamber back onto the ship without another word.

I blink. "What the gods was that all about?"

Nitta's smile is sharp. "We're going to create a bonfire of royal soldiers."

"Everyone on deck!" Caen orders, moving to the hull.

The four of us climb up over the railing. Nitta goes to help Nor collect rope from the masts and under-deck stocks. Caen begins to break the wooden floorboards in strategic parts. Taking care to avoid these spots, Wren and I cross the deck. She heads to the cabin while I bend down beside Lova, who's crouching at the base of the masts.

She pushes a heavy metal orb into my hands. A cannonball. "Empty the gunpowder," she orders.

I do as she says, following her lead. Wren emerges from the cabin less than a minute later, arms full of weapons. By some stroke of luck, we hadn't yet taken them off the ship. She moves around, passing them out.

"What happens after?" I ask Lova as she slings her heavy cutlass over her shoulder before finishing up with the pile of gunpowder from the emptied cannonballs. "This isn't going to stop all of them."

Lova doesn't look up. "We fight, of course."

"But—"

"We *fight*, Lei," she repeats, meeting my eyes this time. "It's all we can do."

That's when we hear it. Even at a distance, the metallic clink of weapons is unmistakable. A swishing, rising noise accompanies it, the sound of hundreds of bodies moving.

"Catch!" Nor calls from over our heads.

The heavy end of a rope whips down. Lova snatches it and buries it into the pile of gunpowder. Nor shimmies back down the mast. With powerful bites of her tiger's teeth, she cuts the other end of the rope where it's fixed to one of the metal rungs attaching the sail to the mast. Nitta's been at work knotting other sections of cord together. She comes forward, taking the end of the sail-rope from Nor and looping it with the long trailing length she's already made.

Lova is busy dousing the thick coils of rope with bottles of liquor from the under-deck stash when Wren jumps down from where she was keeping watch at the railing.

"They're coming!"

My heart flies into my mouth. At once, we run across the deck, minding the broken boards, and leap from the ship. The rope flies with us. It trails from Lova's hands, thick and white, like a desert viper. The sand shifts under our feet, making us slip and slide as we lurch downhill. My feet sink deep into a drift and I tumble face-first. Momentum rolls me, pulls me down until I stop at the bottom of the dune, grains in my eyes and mouth and ears and up the arms and legs of my clothes.

Someone hauls me to my feet—Nor. We keep running. The next slope is lower, just a ridge of sand. We come to a stop on its top just as the sound of wings makes us look around.

His wide wings spread, Merrin soars toward us, low over the moonlit sand. Osa clings to his back. The two of them cut a dark shadow against the lights of the camp—then everything goes black. Now the only light comes from the lanterns we left burning on the boat deck.

Instead of sounding relieved, Lova curses. "What's he *doing*?"

Our eyes track Merrin. Where he should have stopped to join us, he's flying on toward the ship.

"Damn Bird!" Lova growls.

Nor lays a hand on her shoulder. "General…"

Lova stills; her eyes widen with understanding. *"Damn Bird!"* she repeats, grinning now. "Nor, go help them!"

At once, the tiger-woman runs off, tail swishing behind her.

Lova turns her attention to the rest of us. Before I can ask what exactly she thinks Merrin is up to, she launches into a speech, talking fast. "After the explosion, we'll have two minutes, maybe three, before the soldiers understand what's happening. The ship will be unstable. Don't go up there. Wait for the survivors to jump off. We'll surround it from this side and pick them off one by one. The rest of the soldiers will hold off approaching the boat at first, but it won't be long until they realize what's happening. That's when they'll come around the ship. We need to be careful not to be cornered. If we're surrounded against the burning ship, we're done for. As soon as they start to come around, we pull back to this ridge. It's better we have the advantage of height. We'll spread out and fight in pairs. Caen, Nitta—you two take the far right. Wren—take the far left with Lei. I'll stay in the center with Nor and Osa." Her eyes flick up, and we look around to see Merrin, Osa, and Nor returning from the ship.

Merrin flies low to the sand, while the cat demons walk bowed over. All of them are carrying planks of wood. They must have removed them from the hull of the ship. It takes me a moment to realize why: Merrin means to drop them on the soldiers.

We dash over to help them.

"Hond and Clio are gathering every available warrior," Osa updates Lova, the two of them heaving a heavy board down on the sand. "They'll be here in twenty minutes. We should have at least one hundred and fifty more."

One hundred and fifty? *It's not enough!* I want to scream. *The King's army is at least five hundred!*

But Lova nods. "Excellent. They'll be just in time for the second wave." She turns to Merrin. "Fantastic idea with the planks, Bird. Wait until after the soldiers have come around the ship and we're engaged in hand-to-hand combat. We want to keep the element of surprise."

"They're here!" Wren announces.

We drop down behind the ridge. My pulse trips in an irregular beat, my breathing fast and shallow. Beside me, Lova clasps the rope in one hand, the match in the other.

We wait, backs against the cool sand, looking out away from the ship over the moonlit dunes. From behind us comes the distant shout of orders, weapons clanking.

The soldiers have found the boat.

Scrrrch.

The tiny flare of the match blooms in the darkness.

"Climb on up, you dirty demons," Lova hisses under her breath.

For a few moments, nothing happens. Then: heavy thuds of boots against wood. Shouts ring out.

Lova brings the lit match to the rope.

The rope crackles. She drops it as smoke curls, stirred by the wind. Then, catching the alcohol, the flames burst brighter. We crane our necks, looking out over the ridge to watch them lick down the length of the rope, a thick orange tongue moving faster and faster.

"Get down!" Lova orders.

We throw ourselves onto our bellies, hands over our heads, faces buried in the sand. Someone dives over me. I have only a second to recognize her cool, ocean scent, the weight of her body on top of mine, before the sky splits apart.

The explosion is so immense it rocks the ground.

A weighted ripple bursts through the night, sucking the air away. Silence whams into us.

Seconds later, sand rains down, sprayed with the power of a monsoon.

High-pitched ringing fills my ears, the buzz of hundreds of mosquitos in my eardrums. Hands grab at me, pulling me to my feet. I stagger up, finding myself in a strange new world, Wren's hand slipping into mine as she leads me down the side of the dune, the two of us pelted by the sand still raining down, sounds rushing back now, awful sounds, nightmarish and all too familiar. Screams and shouts of pain, and the fierce crackle of flames.

Ahead, the ship burns.

Wren releases my hand to draw her second sword. Coldness ripples from her as she engages her magic. Her eyes slide to white. Flames reflect in them, golden tongues reaching high from the ship against the midnight sky, like slashes in the very fabric of the night.

There are thuds all around as flame-wreathed bodies drop over the sides of the boat. Some lie still. Others writhe, groaning in the sand.

Others pat themselves down. Roll out their flames and scramble to their feet, drawing sabers, spears, pikes, axes.

I pull my dagger free, its magic humming darkly to life, just as the first of the soldiers reach us.

THIRTY-FOUR

AT FIRST, IT'S ALMOST EASY.

The soldiers from the boat are injured or dazed. Some are even still on fire, their clothes and fur gleaming with flames. Smoke chokes the air. Our group sees off each soldier with a single slash or after a short parry, bearing down on them with grim determination. I don't feel any of the kills. It's mechanical, the simple translation from my desire to live to the drive of my dagger. My sword arm is like a foreign body, detached somehow, just an extension of my blood-slicked blade.

More blood sprays across my clothes, my face.

Claws slash grooves in my forearms as some of the soldiers fight back; sword tips nick my skin.

I hardly feel any of it. Every moment is simple and focused.

Action, reaction.

Fire in, fear out.

Teeth gritted, I drive my blade into throats and guts. Slide it between ribs and shoulder blades. Sink it deep into eye sockets and the tender napes of necks, watching the flash of bronze wink out as it is swallowed by soft, parting flesh. Magic strengthens my attacks, but it's more than that—it's *my* skill, now, too, my own blood lust.

Grunts and groans and the occasional ragged cries fill the air, an ugly chorus of pain. It is less a fight than an execution. A slaughter.

Then, all of a sudden, it's over.

Wren and I pant, facing the flaming ground-ship with our swords lifted. My hands quiver, making my dagger shake, while Wren could be a statue were it not for her wind-stirred hair and the fan of her sari fabric around her ankles.

An unnerving stillness ripples out. The sand around the boat is piled with bodies. Firelight slides over blood-wet faces and dark, gaping mouths. The only sounds are the roaring burr of the flames and our own heavy breathing. For a few stunned moments, all I can do is stand and shake and stare, the horror of it all—of what I was just a part of, what I *did*—present in the metallic stink of opened bodies and the drip of red from my dagger.

"Get back," Wren orders.

We retreat to the top of the ridge with the others.

"Everyone in one piece?" Lova asks, wiping her cutlass on her trousers.

"Nothing like a bit of murder for dessert," Nor replies, though her voice is humorless, her smile grim.

Osa comes to my side. He examines my arms where my pale skin is slashed with red. Ripping strips from his shirt, he bands them around my forearms.

"Are you all right?" Wren asks me, inspecting his work.

"It—it doesn't even hurt," I say.

"That's not the same as being all right," Osa replies.

Lova's voice sounds out before I can respond. "Into position!"

We fan out along the rise of the dune, Caen and Nitta on the right, the Amala in the center, and Wren and I to their left. Behind us, Merrin picks up the first of the beams prized from the hull of the ship.

Lova throws a hand out. "Not yet."

Noises rise as, like a living nightmare, soldiers spill around the sides of the boat. They charge toward us in the churning wave I'd imagined earlier. Roaring, snarling, spitting. Weapons held high or aimed forward, the flames of the burning ship reflected in the metal blades of pikes and jian and swinging battle-axes.

The sand shifts beneath our feet with the force of the oncoming army. Digging my feet against the moving currents, I cling to my dagger with trembling fingers and stare down at the approaching onslaught with as much strength as I can muster.

The soldiers reach the bottom of the dune and start up ours. They move in a buzzing, gnashing swarm. Swathed in crimson and black, pennants with the King's insignia trailing the horde, there are all kinds of demons: jackal, lizard, wolf, bear, leopard, bison, bull. Horns and claws and scythe-like incisors glint in the flame-red glow.

My tongue feels like a pad of cotton in my mouth. I blow out a hard breath, shift my stance.

"Stay close," Wren commands me. "I won't let them touch you." She plants a kiss on my forehead. I get a last glimpse of her velvet-brown irises before a flood of chilled air ripples from her as she shifts into her Xia warrior mode, her eyes crawling over with white.

To my right, Lova lifts her arm. "Now!" she yells at Merrin.

He launches into the air, sand lifting with the beat of his wings. He flies out over the teeming horde of soldiers before banking tightly to circle around. Shouts rise up. A few arrows stutter into the air, but Merrin evades them, speeding toward the front line of the army.

The beam slams down with a sickening crunch.

The front section of soldiers crumple. There are screams as the demons behind them trample over them. Others scatter. A hole forms in the center of the wave.

With a feral roar, Lova charges from the ridge, cutlass held high, her honeycomb hair glowing in the firelight as she leads us into battle.

And then more noise erupts—this time from behind us. As I skid down the dune, I'm aware of demons swarming around us, seemingly appearing from over the ridge at our backs. For a few sickening seconds, I'm sure it's a surprise ambush; that these are more of the King's army. Then I realize *these* roars and shouts and battle cries belong to the Amala. Cat demons—roaring like their fearless General—are joining our attack, swelling our ranks by at least a hundred.

Merrin soars overhead, a second beam in his talons.

The arrival of the Amala warriors fills me with so much hope that for a moment it's razed my fear to dust. But it explodes back as we reach the first line of soldiers.

There's a beat of silence—

Then the night bursts with the clash of metal.

Our two sides collide with force and fury, the air heavy with the thuds of bodies slamming together.

Time takes on a staccato effect. I lurch from one second to another, everything happening in jerky fragments: the shuddering impact of my sword meeting another, spit-flecked lips peeled back in battle cries, blades digging into hard muscle, the snap of tendons and the weight of my blood-drenched arm as I drag my dagger back over and over, plunging then prying it from opened flesh.

The scream of metal upon metal rings in my ears.

The air is a flurry of flashing blades.

Hot sprays of blood splash my face.

Wren and I fight back to back, falling into an instinctive rhythm, as though we've worked together like this a thousand times. She faces the onslaught of soldiers while I fight one-on-one with those that make it past her. It's impossible to see the rest of our group amid the confusing rush of bodies and blades. Every shriek of pain could be one of them, every fresh thud a body falling to the ground.

As I withdraw my weapon from the chest of a short but muscled boar-form man, a wiry lynx demon descends upon me. His tufted ears are pulled back. Incisors flash, two sets of sharp, razor-like points.

"Die, keeda!" he snarls, and brings his saber down over my head.

I throw my blade up with both hands. Metal squeals as our swords clash. The sound makes my teeth ring. My feet slide back in the sand, my heels burrowing deep. Veins pop in the lynx's furred temples as he grinds his saber down.

A growl loosens from my throat. I grip my dagger with shaking hands, battling to hold off the soldier's blade. Even with the help of my own weapon's enchantment, I feel my arms weakening.

Merrin's flame-lit silhouette passes overhead. Another sickening thud sounds not far from us; more pained cries loosen into the air.

The lynx demon has forced my hands all the way back to my chest. The thick end of his saber touches my left shoulder, first with the gentleness of a kiss, then biting, a kiss with *teeth*.

Slowly, slowly, the blade sinks in. My muscles scream with effort as I try to hold it back. But the demon is too strong and his saber burrows deeper.

There is no pain yet, only an intense pressure.

And then the pressure bounces back.

The lynx-soldier pulls away with a gurgle. Blood spurts from the side of his neck as his head peels slowly away where Wren's blade carved a deep, bloody gash.

His head topples first; his body, a second later.

I stare, panting, his hot blood splattered across my face.

Already, Wren has spun back around, her twin swords whirling in a furious metal cyclone around her body. Magical static crackles off her. Though soldier after soldier falls around her, more keep coming to replace them.

I have just enough time to press a hand to my shoulder, almost surprised to see it come away wet and red, when I sense the skirr of air overhead.

I dodge to the side. The blade slices down so close it shears off a flutter of my hair. With a snarl, I whisk around, slashing out. My dagger catches the soldier—a tall, broad-shouldered dog-form—across his upper left arm, ripping open the sleeve of his black soldier's baju.

He retaliates with a flurry of hasty jabs. Metal clashes as we paint a song with our parries, the heavy pant of our breathing the ugly percussion.

The dog soldier is relentless. Though I try and get in killing blows—Caen always taught me to strike accurately and quickly to save energy—it's impossible. He laughs, his blade dancing through the air, driving me back.

My foot lands on a body in the sand behind me.

The lumpy mass throws me off. I feel my weight tip back past the point of recovery, watch my arms pinwheel as I tumble backward and land in a sprawl.

With an ugly grin, the dog-soldier leaps into the air—

Aims the point of his sword down—

A vivid arc of blood spurts from his middle before he can drive it through me.

The soldier's body slides cleanly in two.

His legs and hips crumple to the floor. For one long, surreal moment, his top half seems to hover over me, suspended in midair, the demon's brown-furred face leering down at me in triumph.

I elbow away his sword just before his severed torso lands on me. My crotch and legs turn warm. At first I think I've wet myself. Then I realize it's the soldier's blood.

I heave his body off me, retching.

When I stagger to my feet, sinking into the blood-soaked sand, a hulking demon stands before me.

"You had orders not to kill the girl," General Ndeze growls.

He kicks the cleaved halves of the dog soldier away. Blood drips from the curving claws of his crescent moon blades.

My veins turn to ice. I try a hasty spin, circling out with a high kick. But General Ndeze bats my leg away from him as easily as swatting a fly.

The crocodile-man towers at more than three times my height, an immense figure wrought from straining muscle and dark leathery skin. Firelight makes his reptilian eyes glow, frames his silhouette in flickering gold. His jet-black robes are almost perfectly intact, hems folded back at the sleeves with ridiculous asymmetry, the thick knot around his waist keeping the wrap shirt closed as tight as a fist. He leers down at me, mouth twisted with disgust. Blood drips from his claw-like butterfly blades.

He smiles. "Lei-zhi," he greets me.

Before lunging.

THIRTY-FIVE

I RUN.

The sloping dunes are a graveyard, littered with bodies. As I press through, I grow dimly aware our side has achieved Lova's plan to break the mass of soldiers into smaller, more manageable clumps. The battle rages on around me in a roar of flame-burr and sword-clash. I clamber over fallen bodies. Sink in blood-drenched sand. I don't turn to check how close General Ndeze is. My vision funnels to one, maybe two yards ahead. Every movement I make is instinctive.

A mound of bodies caught under one of Merrin's dropped boards?

Don't climb. Go around them.

A screaming soldier careening toward me?

Duck to the side.

Action, reaction. As simple a formula as pushing out a breath to draw a new one. It seems what I've learned for fighting works for fleeing, too. I pant, zigzagging through the writhing mass of clashing bodies. My shoulder screams with pain, but terror burns the tears away. I focus only on staying alive, on the pound of one boot in front of the other. At one point I catch the flare of golden hair, a lion-girl's beautiful, ferocious face, but it's swallowed up by the writhing bodies too quickly for me to be sure.

The next time I see a familiar face, there's no mistaking it.

A break in the battle opens up ahead around Shifu Caen. He leaps and spins, his sword flashing through the air. He faces five soldiers at once, fighting them with skilled precision. I shift course, springing past, relief charging through me at seeing him alive and fighting well—

And smack straight into the demon who's run into my path.

I fall back, the wind blown from my lungs. A head appears over me: green eyes, round ears peppered with hoops and studs, beige fur spotted with pale brown swirls the shape of unfurling rose petals.

"Lei!" Nitta gasps. She pulls me up. "Are you hurt—"

She cuts off with a grunt. She sways, face slackening, then collapses to her knees.

I grab her, looking up at a heavy bull-form soldier looming over us. He lifts the thick wooden club he hit her with. His expression is blank. Focused.

I squeeze Nitta to my chest and throw us to the side as he slams the club down. By chance, it embeds itself in a dropped sword lying in the sand—that by mere chance I only just missed being injured with when I fell back. As he struggles to free it, doubling over with the now-clumsy weight of the two weapons, I slash at his wrist.

Blade sinks through to bone.

The bull demon yells—just in time for a dagger to fly into his open mouth.

He cuts off, choking, hands flapping uselessly at his face and throat before he keels over, twitching.

Out of nowhere, Nor is running over. She yanks the blade free and stows it at her waist. She gives me a nod. Then she disappears back into the fray.

Shakily, I return my attention to Nitta, who's lying beneath me in the sand. She's pale, a scarlet trail trickling from the side of her lips.

She gives me a smile. More blood coats her teeth.

"L-Lei," she croaks.

"Shh," I say, smoothing a trembling hand across her furred brow. I look over her body. No visible wounds. But the bull demon's club hit her in the back; is her spine broken? And the blood in her mouth—did she just bite down on her tongue, or is she damaged internally?

"Lei," she repeats, firmer this time. She's looking behind me.

I have less than a second to launch to my feet, dagger pushed out.

General Ndeze releases an angry hiss as my knife scores a deep gash in his forearm. His face is twisted, thin lips pulled back to reveal two rows of small, sharp teeth. "Stop fighting, girl," he snarls. "If you come with me, I can call all of this off. All this bloodshed is because of *you*. Come quietly, and they can all live."

Come quietly. Keep them safe.

I've heard words like that before about my father and Tien. A lifetime ago now, but as clear to me as if it were yesterday—which, in a way, it always will be. Because that was the moment that marked the end of my past, of my childhood, of the safe, spherical world of my simple village life in Xienzo.

The life I lost.

Every day before I was brought to the palace is yesterday, forever gone.

General Yu promised me then exactly what General Ndeze offers me now: safety for those I love, if only I offer myself up.

Except they weren't safe. The King had my father and Tien brought to the palace to watch me die. And even if he hadn't, the war would have found its way to them sooner or later.

Papers are never safe, and never will be. Not under the Demon King's rule.

I take an uneven breath, blood pounding in my ears. Magic sparks under my fingertips as I squeeze my hand on the bloody hilt of my dagger.

"I will keep them safe *myself*," I spit at General Ndeze, before throwing my body at him, blade lifted high.

My attack takes him by surprise. He steps back a fraction too late. I bring my knee to his groin at the same time my sword finds his cheek.

It digs in. Easily at first, slicing through thin flesh. Then jamming as it hits bone. Jaw or teeth.

He howls and shoves me away.

I drop to the ground. He hits out. The back of his hand knocks across my chin, snapping my head back. Lights explode across my vision. I slash out blindly. My dagger collides with something: his arm? Torso? But right when my vision begins to sharpen, it bursts apart.

A scream tears from my throat.

The General digs his fingers deeper into the wound the dog demon opened in my shoulder. The pain is incredible, less a physical thing than a sound, a color, white and keening and rendering me momentarily blind.

All of a sudden, his fingers withdraw.

There's a thud. A shriek.

I drop to my knees, drawing in ragged breaths, as Merrin flaps back into the air before diving once more.

This time, General Ndeze steps aside. He seizes hold of one of Merrin's taloned feet. Wings flapping frantically, Merrin draws the spear from the belt slung across his chest. He strikes—only for the crocodile demon to hook the spear with one of his deer-horn knives and toss the weapon aside.

The General readies a slash of his own, aiming for Merrin's legs—

Just as I jump up and sink my blade into his gut.

The General moans.

With a triumphant shout, Merrin lashes out with his free leg. His foot smashes into the General's face. As the demon staggers, I yank my blade free from his body and drive it across his upturned chin.

Blood sprays across my face, warm and thick.

A horrible gurgle escapes General Ndeze's lips. Then he crashes onto his back. Blood bubbles from his throat, leaking in glossy rivers over his leathery reptilian skin.

He tries to say something, but only a choke comes out. He twitches. Moments later, he falls still.

"Merrin!" I yell, not wasting a second. "Nitta's injured!"

The owl demon lands beside us as I crouch back over her.

Nitta is sprawled on her back. She doesn't move at first, but then her lashes flutter open as I cup her cheek with one hand.

"Can you get up?" I ask.

She lifts her head feebly, only to drop it back down with a grimace. "I—I can't."

As carefully as he can, Merrin reaches a hand under her. His face drains. "I think it's her back. Something doesn't feel right in her spine."

Around us, the battle rages on, a chaotic roar of sword-slash and pained cries cutting the smoke-thick air. A shrill scream pierces my ears. I look up, my blood running cold.

Wren? Lova?

"It wasn't meant to be like this."

I whip back around to find Merrin staring down at Nitta. Her eyes are closed now, her breathing shallow and pain-clenched.

"What?" I snap distractedly.

His face is blank. "It wasn't meant to be like this," he repeats flatly.

"You have to take her somewhere safe," I urge him. "She'll be killed if she stays here."

Merrin doesn't make any indication he's heard me. Then he mutters, "Somewhere safe. Yes. That's it." With a flutter of wings, he sweeps Nitta up onto his back. Then before I can react, before I can even try and struggle—

He seizes *me*.

I skid across his feathers, throwing my arms out to grab them, to steady Nitta and myself, as he lifts off from the ground, his feathers ruffling, sand and flecks of ash circling around us with the powerful gusts of his wings.

"Merrin!" I yell, clinging on, my arm strapping Nitta down. "What the gods are you doing?"

"Saving you!" he shouts back. "Fixing my mistake!"

"*What* mistake?"

Without a reply, he lifts higher. My head hangs over his shoulder, so I get a perfect view of the scene below as it opens up beneath us.

The desert has become a writhing battlefield. Dark lumps of blood and bodies bloom across the sand like ugly flowers. The husk of the ground-ship still burns. Flames leap from it, reaching after us as we rise up into the sky. The battle is so dense, it's impossible to tell one moving figure from another. Only one person is unmistakable amid it all.

Surrounded by a crawling horde of soldiers, Wren fights with unrelenting fury, icy waves of frozen air rippling from her as she moves in a brutal dance, her swords catching the firelight so she is almost like a sun, throwing out gold and orange rays, whirling beams of liquid light.

Just like the sun, she is just as she's always been: almost too bright to look directly at, but far too beautiful not to try.

My heart cries out.

I clutch Merrin's feathers so fiercely my fingers drain white, pinning myself low over Nitta so she doesn't slide off. Merrin flies jerkily, listing to the right. Blood stains the feathers of his right arm close to the shoulder; he must have been injured in the fight.

"Take us back down," I croak. My eyes well. I repeat it, a scream this time. "Take us back down! They need help!"

But he flies lopsidedly on. The flaming ship recedes into the distance, the noise of the battle growing faint.

"I'll kill you!" I yell, yanking at his feathers in shaking handfuls. "I have a knife! I'll slit your throat unless you take us back *right now!*"

"So, kill me," Merrin replies, his voice so cold and unfamiliar it could belong to a stranger. "I'll crash, and we'll all die."

I cry out, long and loud and pitiful, shaking with the fury and helplessness of it all. Because he's right. If I kill him, it'll kill all of us. And he knows I wouldn't do anything to hurt Nitta.

We're too high up now to hear much from the battle. There's only the distant clink of sword-fighting and the weak crackle of fire. Blinking my tears away, I twist my neck to look back.

Moonlit dunes spread out below like some ghostly sea. Far behind us, the Amalas' ship burns orange, as tiny now as the flare of the match between Lova's fingers earlier, a single, lonely firefly in an ocean of darkness.

I bury my face in Merrin's prickly feathers and sob.

The spot of light of the flaming boat stays for a moment, dancing behind my closed eyelids. Then it, too, fades.

We fly on until the air grows eerily still. Until, save for the wind combing our clothes and the tears pouring tirelessly down my cheeks, nothing stirs.

THIRTY-SIX

ERRIN BRINGS US DOWN ABOUT TWENTY minutes later,
when his flying has grown dangerously erratic, his
injured arm making him weave drunkenly through the
sky. It must be hurting him, and carrying Nitta and me all this way
can't have been easy. But instead of pity, my rage makes me relish his
pain.

Let it hurt him. It's the least he deserves.

We land heavily, half-crashing into a ridge of sand.

I get off Merrin's back as carefully as I can, trying not to shift
Nitta. Once I'm off, he holds his left arm steady as I use it to slide
her off onto the ground. We're somewhere in the desert still, the air
arid and cold. Wind whispers through the sand.

Nitta stirs. Moonlight glows in the whites of her eyes as she looks
up at me. "Where are we?" she asks faintly.

I smooth my fingers over her fur. "Still in the desert. But…we're
not with the others anymore. You're injured, Nitta. You couldn't
fight anymore. Merrin has taken us somewhere safe."

Safe. The word is a blade, slicing my tongue when I speak it.

There should be no safe for me. Safe was meant for Merrin and

Nitta, while I was meant to be back at the burning ship alongside Wren and the others. Unsafe, but fighting. Unsafe, but doing what was right.

Unsafe, but *trying to make things safe*.

Nitta trembles under my touch, though whether from pain or the cool wind, I can't tell. I wish I had a coat to give her. Instead I hiss venomously at Merrin, "Come here! Keep her warm."

He sits down at an angle and opens his uninjured wing-arm over Nitta, laying it across her like a blanket. He ruffles his feathers full to make it as warm as possible.

"There were so many of them," Nitta croaks. Her eyes shut, then open again. "They'll die without us."

Sickness surges through me so fiercely I almost gag.

"No," I force out. "No, they're strong. They'll be all right."

She mumbles something unintelligible.

"There's...there's a river to the east," Merrin murmurs. "I saw it when we were flying. It's not far."

"What?" I snap.

"We'll need water," he continues as if to himself, "to drink and clean our wounds before we move on. I can't fly, and we're not safe staying out here like this with no shelter, no food. We should follow the river. It'll lead us to a settlement. Maybe they'll have a sandship or horses for us to borrow. If we keep north, we'll make it to Demon's Ridge. My arm should be better by then. I can fly us over the mountains to the crossing point into Ang-Khen we arranged with Ketai before we left."

I gape at him, disbelieving. "I'm not going anywhere with you!"

Merrin doesn't lift his eyes. "I understand your anger," he replies weakly.

"You left them there to die!" I snarl. "And now you're talking about returning to the Hannos as though there's no point in even *trying* to go back and save them!"

A light snore sounds into Merrin's silence; Nitta's asleep.

I move carefully back and get to my feet. Merrin stays where he is, one arm still spread across her body, his downy white-gray feathers a thick quilt.

When he finally looks up, his eyes are dull and empty, his face slack. "There's more." He takes a shaky breath, then carries on in a small, defeated voice, "It was me. I'm the one who told them. That's how they found us. How they knew where we were."

My pulse roars in my ears. I cross my arms, clutching at myself shakily, my nails digging at the bloodstained fabric of my kebaya top.

"But it wasn't meant to happen like this!" His eyes grow wide, panicked and pleading. "Qanna promised me! She said she only wanted to capture you and Wren and Lova to keep the Hannos and the Cat Clan from joining forces. She told me she'd send soldiers of her own, and they'd take you with as little force as possible. She— she promised me..." He trails off, withering under my glare.

"Qanna?" I choke out. "Lady Dunya's daughter?"

Merrin looks desolate. "After what happened to her sister, she launched a coup with the help of Commander Teoh and the rest of the guards and took over her mother's reign. She had her mother and father locked away. Seized control of the Cloud Palace. There was a White Wing representative at Lord Mvula's party, and Lady Qanna ordered her to follow us to find a way to approach me with her offer—"

"*What* offer?"

"To make me a member of the White Wing."

Horror vibrates through my body. "When you left us, after the argument on the boat. That's when she found you."

"You have to know, Lei," Merrin pleads, "I didn't do it for that!

I don't care about that! The only clan I ever felt a part of was the Hannos, but after what they did…" His voice sours. "Ketai Hanno is not the right person to lead this war. You know that, Lei. I know you do. You distrusted him from the moment you met him. I saw that. But it wasn't until Bo——"

He cuts off, looking away. "They let him die, Wren and Caen. And then they used Hiro, as if he were nothing to them, as if his life was just more collateral damage in their quest for power. When I realized it was Wren who killed Eolah at the Cloud Palace, that was the last straw. I knew I couldn't support a leader who has such little disregard for the lives of others. We have a King like that already. We don't need another."

The worst thing is, Merrin is right. And that makes me angrier than ever. I have to remind myself to breathe; I dig my nails in deeper.

Merrin's expression is anguished. "I had no idea she would give the royal army the camp's location!" he cries. "She promised me it would only be a select guard from the White Wing, just enough to overpower the group without excessive force. That's why I had everyone come back to the boat. So no one else would be hurt. You were to be brought to the White Wings' palace and held with Lady Dunya and Lord Hidei, both of whom are being treated well by the clan. Lady Qanna promised me none of you would be hurt," he repeats, as though speaking it can make it true.

Even though, *as* we speak, it's being made untrue.

Right now, across miles of empty, moonlit desert, Wren, Caen, Lova, Osa, Nor, and the other Cat Clan warriors are facing an army of hundreds of demons on their own.

I lurch to the side to vomit.

"Lei——" Merrin starts.

"Stay away!" I swallow, trying to calm the hammer of my heart and the pounding of blood in my ears. I swipe the back of my hand across my mouth, then announce, "I'm going back."

"W-what?"

Ignoring him, I smooth my clothes and check my wounds with trembling fingers. Osa's bandages on my forearms have held well, but my left shoulder is raw and open where the dog demon's sword pierced my flesh. Pain throbs within, a rising ache I know will only grow with time. I shift the fabric of my shirt as best I can to keep sand from getting in.

"Stay with Nitta," I order Merrin. "Make sure she gets to the Hannos safely."

"You can't walk all the way back!" he calls as I start to trudge away, my feet slipping in the sand. "We're miles away!"

I pivot, my eyes flashing. "Don't tell me what I can't do! You have no *idea* what I'm capable of!"

He doesn't reply, and I spin back around, hands balled, and trudge on. The desert ripples before me. Hills of starlit sand roll out to a shimmering horizon where the first signs of a new day are gathering, the palest pink touching the sky, the color of a single drop of blood in water.

As I walk on, I recall the last time Wren and I spoke properly, that horrible night in the cabin, when it had felt as though the world was ending.

Something *was ending, anyway.*

How many more murders will you commit in the name of justice until you realize you're as bad as those we're meant to be fighting against?

I'm not proud of any of it. But if it helps us take down the King, if it helps stop the terrorization of Papers across the kingdom and make Ikhara safe again for us, for everyone, then it was all worth it.

Nothing is worth losing yourself.

I am still myself, Lei. This is who I've always been. This is what I was trying to tell you about my Birth-blessing word.

Sacrifice doesn't mean being heartless! You know, all this time I thought the King was our only enemy. Now I realize there's been another one all this time—your father. The Hannos. You.

How could I have told her that? Wren, who has only ever loved and protected me. Who fights for what she believes in. Who would burn down the whole world to keep me safe.

She thinks I hate her.

She is going to die thinking I hate her.

My feet skid in the sand as I crest a dune. I fall. Pain sears through my left shoulder. With a low, guttural growl, I push myself back up, only to stumble again.

Pain, dehydration, and exhaustion reel through me in competing waves, each one trying to make me more miserable than the others. My legs buckle. I hit the sand face-first. I clutch helplessly at the cool grains filtering between my fingers, as evasive as the energy I'm trying to summon.

Get up! I scream at myself.

Out loud, sand filling my mouth. "Get up!"

But my body doesn't cooperate. My head swims. Blackness creeps at the edges of my vision.

"Wren," I whisper, before the darkness draws itself over me fully, like a blanket laid over a child, or a dead body.

When I wake, it's light. It can't be long past sunrise, the horizon glowing with that same ruddy pink I saw earlier. Pale light washes over the desert, not yet hot.

My mouth is dry, my throat scraped raw.

I pick myself up slowly. My shoulder shrieks with pain when I use my left arm for support. Blood and sand crust the wound. I shift, and the wound opens, raw flesh peeking through. Grimacing, and more careful this time, I get to my feet. Though I wobble, I stay upright.

In all directions, the dunes stretch out in endless golden waves. There's no sign of Merrin and Nitta.

Relief floods through me, though it's soured with fear.

"Fire in," I whisper through cracked lips, and, steeling myself, I walk on into the endless slopes of the dunes.

I don't know how long I go on. My focus narrows to the trudging of my feet, the effort of dragging one in front of the other. The sun beats down, higher and higher, a burning spotlight on the back of my neck. My head throbs. Everything swirls around me, a glazed, honeyed haze. Sometimes I stumble. Wait for a while on my hands and knees, allowing myself a moment, just one moment, to breathe. Then I drag myself back up.

Wren.

Her name, that simple, perfect single syllable, becomes a mantra. A prayer. It falls in time with the rhythm of my pulse, the pull and push of my lungs.

Day drags on in a blaze of searing heat before slipping slowly into twilight.

I've barely stopped walking all this time. The drop in heat and light stuns me for a moment, and I lift my head, noticing it properly for the first time. The desert lays out before me, exactly the same as it was when I started walking this morning, a sea of rolling sand, almost entirely featureless. Overhead, the sky is a deep magenta, touched by the first blush of stars.

It's so beautiful I tip my head back, almost gasping as I drink it in.

My head spins. I throw out my hands, almost falling.

Wren: her name again, calling me back to myself. To her. Exhaling feebly, the dry air like knives in my throat, I force myself on.

Just as my eyes are drifting back down to my feet, I stop. Raise my head.

There, a few dunes away, directly ahead, stands a figure.

Wren.

Her name pounds faster, louder, following my pulse.

Wren, Wren, Wren!

The figure moves toward me. She is tall against the darkening horizon, a slinking gait that lifts hope in my heart like the sudden swell of a tide.

Wren!

I stagger into a run.

The figure continues to walk steadily closer.

My movements are sloppy. It feels as though the ground is shifting under me, trying to hold me back from reaching her. But I won't let it. Sobs rack through me as I drive my body on, forcing it to my will. Blood whooshes in my ears. My vision pulses. But I'm almost there, and so is the figure, the woman who I can now see *is* Wren, it's her, it's her, my love, my wings, walking calmly, not a scar on her, smiling like a dream.

Her arms open, calling to me.

I've found you, I think as I fall into her embrace.

She grips me tight. My eyes blur with tears. I blink them away, not wanting to miss a second of this moment. And, slowly, as my sight clears—I notice the straight line of footsteps stretching out behind her.

Footsteps.

Not in the shape of boots, or even human feet.

Instead: paw prints. Padded feet, long and slim, tipped with claws.
"Wren," I croak.

I try to draw back, but the white furred arm hooked across my back clasps me tight, tighter, until I'm struggling to breathe and I start to fight her grip, a flare of panic alighting in me, though it's all too late.

"Don't struggle," Naja purrs in her high, silky voice, as gentle as a lullaby. "Don't struggle, Lei-zhi. It's time to take you back to the Hidden Palace. You're going home. Don't struggle," she repeats, a little sharper now.

But I do.

I buck and fight and shake and yell, until more demons emerge from nowhere, slipping out of the hazy dunes like honey sliding off a spoon. Demons garbed in royal black and red. They lay heavy hands on me. Pry me back.

With a snarl, I head-butt Naja. She hisses, grasping my chin. Her finger and thumb pop my mouth open.

An antlered elk demon comes up beside her. He shoves something between my teeth before I can close them.

It's bitter. Earthy.

A mixture of poppy and valerian root. My herb shop knowledge brings the realization that I've been given a sedative too late, my body already becoming weaker, lighter, a feather of a thing. As my eyes flutter shut, I hear the voice again, the one that had been whispering in my ear all this time. Words that only moments ago had finally morphed into something beautiful, now once again mocking and cold.

I've found you.

After all this time, it finally came true.

And then the black pull grows too much and I let myself fall, swallowed up by the wide, starlit arms of the twilight sky and the silky brush of white fur.

AUTHOR'S NOTE

WHEN I WROTE *Girls of Paper and Fire*, my goal was to create a book that felt totally authentic to me. A story, world and characters richly informed by my own experiences. I did this purely for myself, because it was what *I* needed. But then something amazing happened. The book was published, and readers—readers who looked like me, who shared the same cultural background, who were also survivors of sexual assault—started telling me this was the book *they* needed, too. Reading Lei's and the Paper Girls' stories made them feel just as seen as I did writing them. I've since learned that there is a special kind of magic in knowing you are not alone in your experiences. It is an intimate magic, but so very powerful.

While *Girls of Paper and Fire* deals more with the direct aftermath of abuse, *Girls of Storm and Shadow* looks at its longer-term impacts. There is a line in the book where Lei, contemplating her and Wren's future, thinks, *Before, it seemed as though the only thing between our happiness was the King and the palace itself. That once we left, we would be free.* Through my personal experience with trauma, I've found that true freedom is rarely so easy to achieve. Even once we have distance from the immediate danger, it can continue to live within us, a poison with no simple antidote.

Trauma recovery takes many forms. It is intensely personal. In this book, I've drawn from my own experience to write Lei's, Wren's, and the other girls' journeys, but it is by no means a comprehensive or definitive account. If there is anything I've learned through my own recovery and speaking to other survivors, it is that there is no one path to follow. No path more right or wrong than another. We simply do the best we can, even if sometimes that doesn't feel like much.

To readers on your own journeys of recovery, my hope is that you treat yourself with compassion, gentleness, and patience. Please know you are stronger and braver than you may think. Healing from that poison is an imprecise, imperfect journey, but the important thing is to be *on* the journey. To never give up on yourself.

If you are the victim of sexual, emotional, or physical abuse, or struggling with addiction, please consider speaking to a trusted adult, or contacting one of the following resources if you need to seek help anonymously.

Rape Crisis
Call: 0808 802 9999
Info: rasasc.org.uk

National Domestic Violence Helpline (UK)
Call: 0808 2000 247
Info: nationaldomesticviolencehelpline.org.uk

Galop National LGBT+ Abuse Helpline
Call: 0800 999 5428
Info: galop.org.uk

Childline
Call: 0800 IIII
Info and chat: childline.org.uk
9781473698536

ACKNOWLEDGMENTS

IT TURNS OUT ALL THOSE WRITERS weren't kidding—the middle books of trilogies really *are* hard. This was definitely the toughest process of a novel for me yet, so I feel a deep gratitude to those who helped along the way. At times it seemed impossible I'd ever have a finished book in my hands, but here we are. A heartfelt thank-you to all those who had a part in making this happen:

To my friends in Paris, in particular Celine, Cheryl, Farah, Jay, and Paul, for everything from serious conversations to apéros and picnics. Thank you for filling my days with laughter and love. A special shout-out to Jay for helping me fix a plot hole—hope you've got your plaster and cement ready for book three!

To new author friends—well, not so new now—who have been with me on this journey and shared in both the triumphs and the lows: Sarah Farizan, Aliette de Bodard, Kristina Perez, Victoria Lee, Rebecca Kuang, Maura Milan, Kerri Maniscalco, Laura Sebastian, Tasha Suri, Samantha Shannon, Julian Winters, Patrice Caldwell, Rebecca Hanover, and so many more. You amaze (and intimidate!) me with your talent and kindness. May we scream and gossip and commiserate and vent about this crazy life forever more.

To my Hodder dream-team, Sam Bradbury and Kate Keehan, for not only working so hard to make *Girls* a success in my home country but also making work so much fun!

And, of course, to everyone in book one's acknowledgments: thank you again, so much. Especially the amazing people at Jimmy Patterson and Hachette, for going above and beyond. I couldn't have done it without you all.

Finally, an enormous thank you to everyone who supported book one: bloggers, reviewers, librarians, journalists, teachers, festival organizers, podcasters, book subscription box companies (looking at you, Anissa!), booksellers, and readers. You are the reason I'm able to be here writing these words. Your passion and support and commitment to books means the world, not just to me but to so, so many people. Thank you for everything you do.